The IRISH WINE TRILOGY

The IRISH WINE TRILOGY

DICK WIMMER

Soft Skull Press
Brooklyn

Library of Congress Cataloging-in-Publication Data is available upon request.

ISBN 10: 1-59376-222-4
ISBN 13: 978-1-59376-222-3

Cover design by Brian McMullen

Interior design by Maria E. Mendez, Neuwirth & Associates, Inc.
Printed in the United States of America

Soft Skull Press
An Imprint of Counterpoint LLC
2117 Fourth Street
Suite D
Berkeley, CA 94710

www.softskull.com
www.counterpointpress.com

Distributed by Publishers Group West

10 9 8 7 6 5 4 3 2 1

CONTENTS

The IRISH WINE TRILOGY

Irish Wine

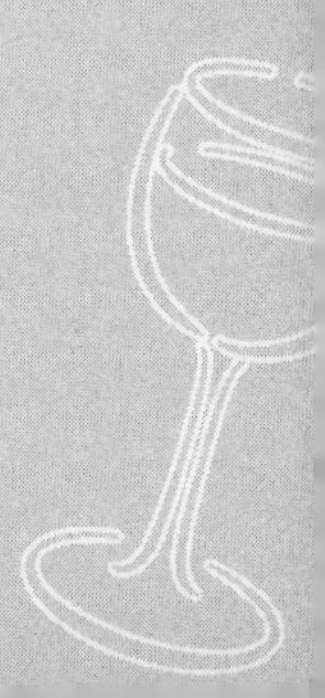

September 1967

Boyne

"*CRAZY*! Good God, this is *CRAZY*—absolutely *CRAZY*—finally having my life come down to me parked across these railroad tracks by a stormy, surging Irish Sea, lightning bolts streaking the sky, in the green Jaguar sedan with the canoe still atop it—Bach's 'Sleepers Awake' booming out over my tapedeck (E. Power Biggs on the organ)—gargling down this last bottle of Irish wine, drunk blissfully out of my mind, and waiting for the train from Kilcoole to come roaring round the bend and end it all with a bang!

"I mean just *LOOK* at me, Billy, seven bloody years after conquering the whole of London's art world, 'the most promising painter of his generation,' I'm broke, bereft, and totally *forgotten,* three pounds six in my pocket, my patron Sligo (so dismayed by my upcoming show?) blowing his brains out a month ago today, and now they're taking my *daughter* away (stealing her from me, I should say!), so what the hell's *LEFT* to live for?"—a cascading cloudburst wildly lashing the glass, more flashes of jagged lightning across Erin's green and fragrant shore—"Though soon we'll be together at last, you, the greatest painter of the nineteenth century, Joseph Mallord 'Billy' Turner, and I, the greatest painter of the twentieth, Seamus Eamon Boyne! 'Cause they were ALWAYS out to get me, never giving us our due, having killed off Van Gogh, Cézanne, Gauguin, and Modigliani or calling me 'a sheer pornographer'! All those agonizing struggles to seize my blazing visions and pin 'em down, wasted, gone astray—But Christ, what the hell's it matter anyway? Might as well ascend with this torrential shower thundering in my ears and these long tapering fingers (that still hold as much talent as you) trilling my grizzled beard!

"For Good *God*, just *LOOK* at that patrician's face, of regal grace, and that glazed yet piercing royal blue gaze staring back from my rearview mirror! Thirty-eight-year-old comfortably rumpled Boyne in his red hooded sweatshirt, slightly frayed, and the cant of his dashing beret!—time fading, my wine draining, Billy—and this gray rain still insanely splashing across my Jaguar sedan and canoe strapped to the silver roof rack—seven years driving around Ireland this way while those yahoos jeered 'the eccentric painter' out to play, Boyne the blusterer, the artist manqué!

"Though what'd those whorish critics once say: 'A remarkably gifted original,' 'Far ahead of his time'? Compared initially to you, Billy, then ignoring me in my prime—as only *Hagar*, dearest friend of mine (just wiring him that farewell note: 'By the time you read this I'll be dead'), truly understood! Starting me painting again right after Laura'd left when I produced the finest works of my life: those early 'pornographic nudes' aswhirl in a fluttering vortex of light! Show after disastrous show and the one tomorrow night that the critics'll surely pan—*O Jaysus,* those bastards driving me MAD!!" tears suddenly streaming out of my eyes, flinging this wine behind me, "Sons of *bitches,* bloodsucking *queers*—and now *NOTHING* left to live for: no daughter, wife, friends, or life, and the public couldn't care *less* as I've grown 'distinctly out of favor,' yahoos Warhol and Bacon still the rage, reaching the end of my tether! Laura in Baltimore with her wealthy Jewish lawyer and Tory, my girl, whom she's trying to deny me from *ever* seeing!

"God*damn* you, Laura, you avenging *BITCH*, you just had to twist the knife, last straw, that pushed me over the edge—" **"Zounds, lad, no NEED to kill yourself now!"** Turner's gruff London basso sounding in my ears. **"For I've seen your work and it's no doubt the finest since my own nearly a hundred and twenty years ago! So never you mind—they called my *Snow Storm* 'a mass of soapsuds and whitewash,'**

brought tears to my very eyes—but NONE of 'em are going to beat you again!! A final laugh, lad, you'll have your revenge!" "Yes, but how do I *achieve* it now, an artist's lasting fame, recognized as the genius I've always been—?" **"Precisely! and hang forever in the Tate beside me! There's a marvelous spot on the wall nearby, be just right for you!"** "O Mother of Christ, what if it could be? Sligo a trustee! Just get *one* of my paintings hung and my struggles would all be *worth* it—"

WHEEEEEEE!

GOOD GOD! and here comes that bloody Kilcoole train *roaring* round the bend, its whistle loudly wailing—

"*Wait, wait,* can't die *now,* have to get out of here and hang in the Tate beside you!" Starting my car—trying to start my car—*O Jaysus,* not *now,* not *NOW*! Come on, come on! Stereo running too long, Bach still booming, big bang looming—the train bearing down, shrilling its whistle again, making my beard stand on end—*CRASH!!* Mary and Joseph, the back window's shattering glass! A *shotgun* blast? Aiming at me? But why? No one even knows I'm *alive*!—The Jag *finally* turning over, and jamming my foot to the floor as I go careening forward with a screech of spinning tires, bumping and bouncing over these teeth-rattling tracks and on through this thundering rain with that monstrous train filling the rearview mirror and—*Suffering Christ*! *ANOTHER* gunshot knocking my canoe clear off—as I keep speeding along past dripping hedgerows, blurry fields of grass and hay, and that surging Irish Sea—

"O get off my *arse,* you blasted train, bloody assassin, 'cause *no one's* going to kill me NOW!!!"

Hagar

Screeching up before our Long Island City office, *Hagar Pest Control* above that blinking neon roach, and hurrying through the metal door past the tan plastic paneling, my father's picture on the wall—already haggard two years ago, a round-shouldered Ralph Bellamy with distinguished graying temples, raccoon squint, and double chin—by chemical company calendars, huge insect photos, and my mother with her new blonde perm and gold-rimmed glasses with their beaded chains—plumply seated at the front desk, tamping out her Chesterfield and talking on the phone.

"—O sure, I know it takes time to adjust, but I just hate staying alone, so I come home, I cry, I empty my stomach from nervous cramps, then I take a pill to relax—*Who's there*? O Gene! God, you scared me! See, like I told you, Mrs. Shish, perfect timing, my son *just* walked in! Yeah, so listen, Mrs.—yeah, I'll have him call you right—no, no, right back, right"—raising her eyes to the fluorescent lights and shaking her head, pushing the ashtray aside—"O no more than five minutes, tops, as soon as he gets his bearings. Sure, sure, of course, of course, bye-bye," and hanging up, "*Oi gottenyu*! Your friend Shish from your softball playing, his mother, the beauty, lives in Great Neck Estates, pays Harder five dollars a month, says she only wants to talk to the boss, so maybe you can meet Herman there at three?"

"Yeah, yeah, well we'll see," sitting down at this cluttered desk and leaning forward on the edge of my chair with my eyelid twitching away.

"And how come you're late? You feel all right?"

"I'm fine, fine, I just didn't get much sleep last night."

"You're still carrying on over that *meshuggener* from Ireland?"

"I've been trying to reach him—"

"Running around like a chicken with your head cut off, don't sleep, don't eat—"

"Ma—"

"Who in his right mind sends a telegram like that? And whatta you hear from Teri?"

"Nothing."

"Nothing! But she's still in North Dakota? O God, crazy altogether! Some *facocktah* wife—"

"Ma, just forget it, will you!" The phone ringing.

"And look at your eye! How long's your eye been twitching like that? Wait just a minute, let me get this," placing her Chesterfield in the ashtray, "Hagar Pest. What? O, hold it. Gene, do we do bats?"

Blinking and glancing over, "No"—but you're driving me bats! "Where are they?"

"Northport."

"No, it's a nuisance, let them get somebody local there." She hanging up. "Yeah, so what else is happening?"

"What else? I'm workin' like a dog, just one after another, and Nick is on vacation, Rodriquez took the whole weekend off that he wasn't entitled to, three other men are out sick, and we're getting so much business now."

Loosening my tie and arranging my calls in order beside this stack of mail, "What, termites?"

"No, the other stuff, roaches, rats, bees, fleas, everything—and I'm all alone here, getting a beautiful cold," daubing her nose with a tissue, then lighting up another Chesterfield.

"Where's the girl you hired to help you?"

"She didn't come in today, so I'm knockin' my brains out. All the work on her desk, the accountants're coming in Tuesday, and all those termite inspections to make—always at the end of the month, you know, so we'll have to date back a few days."

"Yeah, well listen, Ma, before I forget, did you hear anything else about that offer to buy the business?"

"O come on, it could take forever! They have to consult with their lawyers, their accountants, God knows who—they all want something for nothing! Your father, may he rest in peace, built up this entire business himself without a penny—" The phone ringing again.

"Hold on, I'll get it. Hagar Pest. Santoro, right, go: twenty-five for the service call and five dollars a month. Fine, 'bye," then back to my mother, "So what were you saying about that part-time girl, why isn't she working?"

"O nothing, nothing," and taking a final puff, she tamps out her cigarette in the glass ashtray, "We had a fight."

"Fight? What kind of fight?"

"Who knows! She got annoyed, said she wasn't coming in today, says she wants to talk to you."

"Talk to me?"

"Yeah," smiling as she keeps on tamping, "says she likes you, feels you understand her. So *you* talk to her, whatever good it'll do—" The phone ringing again.

"OK, OK, I'll talk to her. Hagar Pest. Yeah, White Plains, go: fifty and eight—"

"She's got a terrific deal here for herself. Where else is she gonna go home in the middle of the afternoon? But that's the kind of help you get nowadays."

"OK, OK, I said I'll *talk* to her!"

"Your father, may he rest in peace, should only know, he would've thrown her out one-two-three and that'd be that!"

"Yeah, well I'm *not* my father—" All the phones now ringing at once. "Hagar Pest. Right, Herman, that job in Roslyn, OK? You quoted her forty dollars and she'll call tomorrow. How much guarantee? Sixty days. How is it, bad? Right, anyway—Hello?—O I thought we got cut off, 'cause this place is really a madhouse now, I just walked in and I've gotta get outta here, I'm already late as it is—O and Herman, listen, I got one in Great Neck Estates, a Mrs. Shish on Deepdale. Right, 42 Deepdale, so I'll meet you there at three, fine, 'bye."

My mother lighting up another Chesterfield as she talks on her line, and turning to me, "They towed you away? How could they possibly—?"

"What's going on *now*?"

"Just a minute, hold the wire," as she cups her hand over the phone. "Roger, the colored fellow, was parked on Madison Avenue and Sixty-third Street and they towed his car away."

"What was he parked *there* for?"

"Well he was doing a job around the corner, cop told him to watch it, so they towed him away. Costs fifty dollars."

"Fantastic!" standing—all my papers scattering over the floor.

"And Mastro got mugged in the Bronx last night—"

"Wait a second, wait a second, take it easy, *Christ,* one at a time!" hearing my father's voice in mine. "Is Mastro on the line?"

"No, no, I talked to him before but he's better now. O and that one from August came through on yours, that Chock Full O'Nuts—"

"OK, OK, fine," gathering all my calls together.

"—then I took one this morning, Gene, just before you came in, out in Huntington, has carpet beetle larvae and I told her you'd take a look at it this afternoon and there's another in—"

"All right, *enough,* will you, let me get *out* of here already!"

"OK, OK, but wait just a second, Gene, before you leave, I've gotta run to the bathroom now, empty myself out again, so just stay a minute longer to answer the phones and I'll be right back," and she goes rushing up the stairs.

Riffling through this stack of mail, bills, payments, Pest Control Conference in Amherst, Mass.—as I keep rubbing my fluttering eyelid—and Boyne *can't* be dead! No way! Still madly jigging in my memory with his beard and beret, wildly swaying to that Irish reel, and into the dance I went, gathering momentum, heel and toe, do-si-do, feet flicking, kicking out, and my mind zigzagging as we spun about—a massive wave crashing in, swallowing him up, he dying, our dream dying, have to get to him in time!

Seven years gone by—Carnaween in that summer of 1960: our mad, whirlwind spree, Boyne's twelve-room house by the Irish Sea, Delgany, County Wicklow, Ireland. He who persuaded me to write and forsake my father's world on that first trip to Europe when I was twenty-four and the wash and wear I wore as I fled New York with Joyce in my teeming brain and writing somewhere, who knew, out there to find, and I found Boyne and Dublin and Ciara, my blonde poetic dream (before I was blackmailed home!): our first time alone, her hair of Scandinavian shine as she moved around that houseboat on the Seine in her purple robe—and I moved, too, tumbling her waywardly onto their bed, "—*No,* Gene, I have to wash and dress if you still want to go to the Louvre"—the firm crease of her spine as I kept widening the purple silk—"Please, leave it alone, stop playing—O all *right*!" and flipping open the robe to reveal her high breasts, hips, and fleece before shutting the sight with a silent slam, muscular dents in her calves as she swept into the bathroom and closed the door—then soon reappeared with her hair slightly damp, holding a dripping brush, "Just you keep still for a while!" serious, looking down her nose, "I cannot possibly love you yet, I hardly know you," her ripe rump shifting as she brushed out the shine, "God, still so dirty and I just washed it!" "It looks grand to me, *seraphically* filthy!" "O you and your blonde hair!" and spinning about with impish eyes, she hopped onto the bed, fanning her hair over my surprise, her robe flopping open and hastily shed from those kindling curves I just couldn't stop feeling as I buried my head between her thighs—

The phone stridently ringing!—Jesus, *now* what? Some crazy customer with a cockroach in his bed? "Hagar Pest, hello? Hello?" The sound of breathless panting. "Anybody there? *Hello*? *What* is this, an obscene phone call? Maybe you should talk to my mother?"

"Good *God,* Gene, that has to be you!"

"And who the hell's—*BOYNE*? You're *ALIVE*!! How the hell *are* you, *where* the hell are you, and what the hell's going on, sending me that *telegram*?"

"O bit of a hullabaloo, being pursued by killers and choo-choos—and somebody just took a shot at me!"

"At *you*? But who? Why?"

"Haven't got a bloody clue! *Suffering Christ,* you can't even kill yourself in peace anymore without someone trying to do it for you!"

"But where are you now, still in—?"

"Where am *I*? O I'm *all* over, Hagar, in the sea, the air, the clouds—there's no place I'm not! I'm matter, pure matter—Jaysus, I'm *what* matters in this insane zoo of a world! But how the blazes are you, tell me how you are? You have a wifey yet, that dream girl of your past, Dutch colleen?"

"No—you never met her."

"I see, but a wifey nonetheless? And what's she do, doing to you?"

"She just left me."

"Ah right, off on a spree! Well *my* wife's stealing my daughter from me!"

"Stealing your daughter?"

"O no way she'll ever succeed, just get *one* of my paintings hung in the Tate and my struggles will all be worth it!"

"Yeah, well how'd you get this number, called my home, my parents—?"

"No, no, left Da-da alone."

"My father just died, two months ago—"

"Ah, Mother of Christ! sorry to hear that now, never met him but I felt I knew him."

"And I've been calling Ireland God knows *how* many times since I got your note, trying to find you but you had no phone, weren't listed—"

"Well here I bloody well am in this Irish booth, calling the reigning King of the Cockroach World to tell him I'm having another show, my Comeback Show, the greatest show of my career, so you have to come over *now*, Hagar, *tomorrow*, only one left I can count on, the two of us *together* again in this moment of dire need—and we'll stay in Kew, Dungannon's cottage, no one suspect us there!"

"*Tomorrow*? Well hold it, you still haven't told me—wait a second, I mean, Jesus, how can I just take off?"

"You just get on a plane and go! 'Cause this is the last chance for me and a *second* chance for you to recapture the past before you're engulfed *forever* in that bug business—and I knew you'd come through, could *always* count on you—"

"Seamus, no—"

My mother mincing back down the stairs. "*Oi gottenyu,* took another pill to relax—Who's that? Who're you yelling at?"

"—or take a cab from Heathrow, fastest way, to Tattersall Wharf in Kew and—*Good God*! somebody's coming, have to go! I'll see you tomorrow, Gene, God bless!"

"Seamus—?" The clanking rattle of his phone—with my eyelid really twitching away.

"Gene, what's going on, what's the matter, *who* was that?"

"My friend in Ireland."

"Now he's alive, the *meshuggener*? I thought he was dead!"

Boyne

Slinking swiftly by my greenhouse with the rain still pummeling and slashing down and on through the vestibule—the front door locked. *LOCKED*? O Suffering *Christ*, locked it before I left, never planning to return—and Hagar'll soon be over—with me out here all day in this endless Irish shower, sopping wet grass, waiting to be picked off by some IRA marksman, crazed creditor, purblind hunter, Laura's hit man—my battered Jag safely out of sight after I came hurtling off the tracks over that low retaining wall, the canoe a splintered mass! Smash in these windows? My waterlogged reflection on the drizzled glass, while out here, gray sheets of rain bucketing over my beret and grizzled beard, I sip the streaming drops and slip deftly through these hedges, odd laurel and sodden yew, to look in at my studio—

Ah, *this* window's slightly open! Gusts fluttering the tattered drapes and up with this splattered sash, onto the ledge—and *plunk*—into the cluttered room. Guinness bottles glittering as I slosh past half-finished canvases, easels, my ancient organ by the wall, and briskly down the hall toward the kitchen, dusty motes pollinating the air, alone again in this cold house by a stormy sea—nobody here but my paints and me?—and over the cracked black tile of the kitchen.

Rummaging frantically through all these cabinets filled with empty tins of Danoxa Irish Stew, Birds Eye Minceburgers, Buitoni canelloni as I wolf down this stale pile of crumbs and slivers of moldy cheese—so ravenous after fear! Just pass it off as an errant shot or definite sinister deed? 'Cause who the hell knows I *exist* anymore, groveling for my daily bread?—"Though soon, Billy, there'll be wine, food, and wonders *galore* before we reach Jerusalem!"—then scurry wetly up the stairs, over this once-varnished floor to my unmade rumpled bed, green sheets in need of a wash—green from mold or their natural verdant color? God only knows anymore! Lived up here off the frozen food with newspapers up to my chin, my Sterno stove placed upon my chest, a pot of boiling water and popped 'em right in—no mess, no fuss, I never left the bed! Ah, and here are my sunglasses under these musty socks and towels. Cleaning 'em off and fitting 'em on—and let's see, what disguise should I wear to go meet Sligo's daughters? Something funereal? My raveling Claddagh sweater for the warmth that's in it, dashing black beret, and this yellow slicker from my seafaring days: I'll go as the Ancient Mariner—who soon'll be displayed in the Tate!

Toward this dark chilly loo, past the mirror as my eyes snap into focus, to unleash a long, arching pee—setting a new Olympic record for tapping a kidney as these last few drops come dribbling down. And what did poor Sligo say last time I saw him: *If you come visit me again, Boyne, my only requirements are that you must have bathed and are fulfilling your true potential*—and I haven't done either, not having washed in weeks, months, or God knows when, odors wearing themselves out! My water shut off yesterday: no heat, light, gas, nor water, bubbling urine lying stagnant in the bowl, can't even flush it down—so I'll pop into Dublin and sneak in a bath—before paying my respects to those two crazy daughters of Sligo-Moeran, living in their castle in Phoenix Park, where I'll turn on the charm and tell 'em my plan!

The rain still falling, a steady, splattering pour as I come trotting down the stairs and full speed out the door—an elusive, moving target—round the greenhouse with its long slanted panes, sprawled in there these last few days, my face to the sky, gray colors filtering down and black despair filling me up—and the sea out there still cresting with whitecaps and gulls floating low, their wasp legs dangling, to sit upon the rocks and be rained on as over this rickety gate I go, splashing past the garage and my battered Jag.

Along Tobercurry Road and up these metal stairs, across the railroad bridge, my suicide spot way down there around that bend, the Irish accepting such shenanigans as the routine gestures of the avant-garde—fewer suicides in Ireland than anywhere else on earth—as the sun like a peeling tangerine in this lustrous air comes slowly peeking through, all these windows turning aqua-blue (assassins lurking behind them?), and down this narrow street, worn holes in my soles, and my sodden feet soaking up the wet—

"Ah, Mr. Boyne"—nearly leaping out of my shoes!—"about yer bill, sir?"

O Mother of *Christ,* Dennehy, the bloody bartender, no shotgun in sight!

"Not Boyne—Apparition—Celtic ghost!" quickly heading the other way.

"Just that it's gotten out of hand, Mr. Boyne, been several months now—Watch *out,* man!"

GOOD GOD!—a trio of massive lorries—another attempt? Who knows!—passing between us as I dodge nimbly across the road under this dark green awning, the savor of feety cheese, wasps swarming round the peaches and pears—fat pears, ripe shamefaced peaches—and briskly through this crowded shop, pesky flies buzzing all about, stall heaped high with fruits and vegetables, comestibles, oranges, lemons, and Cavaillion melons—pressing and palping their shiny skins—and Dennehy still out there wiping the spray from his face and wondering where I went, could disappear without a trace: Houdini's alive and well and living in Ireland! And that elderly lady by the door complaining to Fanning the grocer, a bald walrus with his Turkish mustache, about the high cost of grapes nowadays as I continue fondling the peaches and pears and these ripe juicy pippins—small curves of sheen on their applegreen surface—and swiftly under my slicker (refreshing change from my Minceburgers and moldy cheese), but the question still remaining: how the hell do I get *out* of here? as I filch another pear—last few farthings in my pocket and this linty Chiclet—

"Say, what the hell're ya *doin'* up there?" My heart violently pounding! "And what've you got under yer coat?"

"Coat? No, no, just a ratty old fisherman's sweater," shuffling a few steps back, "examining these fine fruits here—" as jowly Fanning with a raging scowl comes charging by the melons.

And narrowly missing the swipe of his paw as he chases me into the chemist's next door, spinning round and round these postcard racks—peekaboo—and out once again, Dennehy now joining the hullabaloo, and down this cobblestone alley beside the Fluff 'n' Fold Laundry, skipping across a back garden, trampling cabbages as I go—God, better off *killing* myself, for Christ's sake, or *being* killed, all my creditors coming out of the woodwork!—and a fast left toward this fancy entrance, sign above: "Pavlova Dance Institute, Class now in progress," the *Nutcracker Suite*—

And a few moments later soaring out the rear with a great Baryshnikov leap in a pink tutu and crown over my beret—the *grand jeté* carrying me into the kitchen of Wong Fat's Mongolian Barbecue reeking of monosodium glutamate and past that tall black chef slicing bamboo shoots and bellowing, "Hold the rice, baby!" as I breeze by the watercolor Buddhas—the restaurant empty, owner Wong Fat probably down in the cellar carving his Szechwan ribs—to a small corner table and this bowl of dry noodles! panting as I munch 'em down and fluff out my tutu—my slicker back with Pavlova's *corps de ballet* (through shrieking, tulle, and that Tchaikovsky Suite!)—So damned famished now, my heart still pounding away! used to come here often during the winter to observe Mongolian food on display: the pale green of snow peas and succulent peppers a scarlet red, all the while wolfing down these free noodles, then pretending to order two from column A before shaking my head and leaving—till Wong Fat chased me out with a cleaver—

Slam! The doors to the kitchen crashing open and Wong Fat, looking like a ferocious little Buddha with gleaming cleaver in hand, "You-you, you clazy man," making a beeline straight for me, "now I gonna *keel* you!"

Knocking over this table in my haste and scattering dry noodles all over the place, apples and pears bounding by me as I burst out the door, sprinting through these puddles round the corner—and O Jaysus, there goes the bus to Dublin!

Signaling and frantically waving it down in my pink tutu and crown—Wong Fat, Fanning, and Dennehy now joined in hot pursuit, the *corps de ballet* behind them—a kindly ballerina tossing me my slicker as I scramble aboard, grabbing onto this door—and the bus goes roaring off up the hill, a blur of them back there fading in our wake!

"Ah, turned out to be a grand mornin', didn't it, sir?" The driver just smiling without dismay, eccentric painter out to play—"Yes, grand, grand"—taking off my crown and hooking it—"O sorry, madam, sorry"—in this woman's hair, prunish face of a Pekingese, "Here, let me just free these"—her blonde hair rising up from her scalp—Good *God,* it's a *wig*! and she's bald as a billiard ball! The woman screaming and pounding me with her umbrella. "Madam,

I'm terribly sorry—" The bus bouncing, swerving—Christ, we're going over this goddamn cliff, tumble down Bray Head into the sea! And she's still hitting me—Only one thing to do: chewing my Chiclet a couple of times, "Here, madam, this should work," and pressing it first to the wig, then onto her scalp—the woman screaming even louder now, "Mother of Jaysus, please let me *out* of here!" as she rushes off at the next screeching stop, holding her lopsided hair, and the whole bus laughing as we go bouncing away.

Down, down to Dublin on the Stillorgan Road, by the tulip blossom and thyme and Booterstown sign—Lautrec's father wearing a tutu to dinner in lieu of a kilt—and all these Irish eyes smiling at me as I take this seat in the rear between gaunt raw-boned features and decaying yellow teeth, and the whole bus, including the driver, crossing themselves en masse as we go rattling past that Gothic church down the long curving hill, old women with black shawls and hobnail boots and the girls with windy hair waiting by the queues for buses of another number, the signs for Milltown and Ranelagh—and "*Guinness,*" reads that clattering truck, "*is Good for you*"—Good *God,* I agree, could really use one now!

"'Cause you see, Billy, what I have to put up with? Every great artist *hounded* in his time and widely misunderstood! When I ventured even further into a riot of color and light, they called me mad and dismissed as disasters my subsequent shows as quickly as they'd once honored and praised the first one! Vilified and ridiculed, and labeling all my new work 'sheer pornography,' 'sinking to lurid sensuality,' insinuating I was suffering from some *mental* disease! Tears, too, in my eyes as I read those reviews—but Billy, the hell with that now 'cause *one* work's all I need to hang in the Tate beside you!"

And what a marvelous face that woman has over there, looking like an ostrich about to bury her head in the sand—no chin below her slender beak and bloated eyes—and staring straight ahead as though she hasn't seen or heard a word I've said. Love to give her a gentle pet, then do her in gay pastels! But I still haven't had my bath as yet, so I'll try some Dublin hotels—if I ever survive this morning!

On down deeper into the city toward Ballsbridge and the Royal Canal, that policeman out there with his white baton and three-quarter-length gauntlets directing traffic across those wide blocks of zebra stripe, past gold nameplates, black spoke fences, and the fanlights of clear polished glass, Merrion Square, Clare, and the back gates of Trinity, with a flock of students scurrying to class and the soft wet grass glistening in the sun as we sweep by Westland Row under the Loop Line Bridge and left toward the Abbey, Pearse, and College Street, the Trinity railings where the bus pulls to the side of the road and I hop off with an agile bound—donating my tutu and crown to the driver!

And round this madding crowd and the Dublin of today, fitting back on my slicker, sunglasses, and the black beret, toward Dawson Street and the massive Royal Hibernian where I'll have me a proper shower!

Spinning up the elegant steps of this veddy, veddy English hotel with the doorman bowing and across the high-ceilinged lobby with its pale blue draperies, a pair of wrinkled-jowled dowagers glancing over through ducal lorgnettes from their wicker chairs as I nip up the back stairs to the first-floor landing and I'll give that room a try—Rap-rap: "Yes?" "O sorry, wrong room"—and off the other way, following these stairs to the top, over the polished runners and green floral patterns, and down the end of that hall: an open door—looking in, no one about, probably just checked out—Yes or no? Never any doubt as I ease it softly shut.

Tell the char I just popped back for an urgent pee, had to tap a kidney—and Suffering *Christ,* will you just *look* at that desecration on the wall: these apples appearing as plastic fruit! Still-life print of Cézanne's, who once said, "With an apple I will astonish Paris." And prints of my own work much the same, never coming *close* to the seething heart of the color, pressing 'em out all joyless and flat like Turner seen through gauze, with little left of the coarse and lumpy, pulsing lovely gleam of the paint! And shedding this yellow slicker now and the rest of my clothes as I skip on into the shower.

Right, all the essentials here, pink bars of soap, reams of towels—and my heart still resounding with fear, keeping the demons at bay! Someone come busting through that door to expose me in the raw or drill me full of holes, bump me off, rub me out, expunge me from the face of Erin's green and fragrant shore: the finest painter of the twentieth century who'll soon be enshrined in the Tate! The shower's warm spray ricocheting off my bald dome as I keep gargling and spewing gleefully away, now crooning Bach's "Sleepers Awake"!

"Both of us, Billy, needing water and coastlines to stimulate our work: your beloved Thames and my Irish Sea or childhood's Hudson River! For I am my work, as Courbet said, even part of the composition—caressing my handprints over the canvas—however long I may live! Everyone dying around me—and still so shaken by Sligo's death (now Hagar's father), hiding out in the bogs of incognito—For, Billy, yours was a barber and devoted friend who hung your early works round his shop and mine was a short-order chef who thought he was Escoffier incarnate! Crazed with grandiose dreams by the sauces he'd invented, he strove toward immortality and went mad for never attaining it: dear Timothy Patrick Boyne, sweet father of mine, from Valhalla, New York, who died—*Jaysus!* in that private asylum—and my mother, Aideen, from Glengarriff, who dabbled in watercolors and guided me through my first museums—till driven up the wall by poor Tim, she finally deserted him when I was nine!"

And now for this pink, sweet-smelling soap, circular motions around the wool of my prime, across my middle, and down my thighs—could use a little meat on these wasted bones, must be twenty pounds underweight—and pausing to rest in soapy foam, watching the hot droplets race down the tile, one in particular as it wends its way in a serpentine rimple—now caught and destroyed in the gust of a splash (like that Kilcoole train smashing me flat, shotgun searing my brain, this shower never occurring!)—and Hagar, dear friend (exterminator's son thinking he's James Joyce), and I soon together again as I rinse fresh and clean and turn off the taps—A *voice* from the other room?

"—Ah yes, t'irty-foyve years oyve been here the Hoybernian, rabbi."

Who the hell is *THAT*?

"Well that's marvelous and thank you so very much. This is for you."

"Ah, that's grand. And if there's anythin' else you'll be wantin', sir, just give us a shout."

GOOD GOD, and there's no way *out*! Sure to come in here—So what do I do, just walk on through? Hear them puttering around outside, English rabbi and his wife, muttering and unpacking—Just frolic in nude and welcome 'em to Ireland or claim I'm an *Irish* rabbi and that it's *my* bloody room? Be in here soon, have to beat 'em to the punch, with the element of surprise!

Patting myself dry and holding on to these clothes and small paunch of underwear—and what'll I say? No idea.

Just a deep breath as I appear, grinning in my birthday suit, before their dumbfounded stares, and closing this blue door behind me.

Not a sound, exhaling as I look around and down the empty hall, my nape hair wildly splayed—

O Mother of *Christ,* forgot my beret! *Have* to have it, *can't* live without it—Only one thing to do, heart still pounding, spinning about.

Knock, knock.

"Who's there?"

"Wet man!"

The door slowly opening as I saunter in with my chin held high toward the shower and my precious beret (probably assuming it's part of some ancient Irish custom or, like Gilbert and Sullivan, I'm the checker of the loo), and back through the room with the wife shyly nodding and—Good *God,* tipping me a shilling—as I flash bare-arsed out the door once more!

And down the carpeted stairs to slip struggling into my clothes, get these over the moist toes—there! mismatched socks, shirt, pants, the raveled Irish sweater, and yellow slicker that fell on the floor—my heels scuffing over these polished runners and across the high-ceilinged lobby with its pale blue draperies, my reflection gleaming in the passing glass: grizzled beard and the dashingly canted beret, the doorman still bowing and wishing me a good day as down the front steps I go, off now to Sligo's with my jiggling paunch of underwear, up the slope of Dawson Street—

"Look *out,* sir!"

—O *JAYSUS*!

And a monstrously grinning gargoyle crashing at my feet!

Hagar

Aging Rose Shish loudly clacking through her vestibule with her tanned horsey face and brassy harridan hair, wearing a pink chenille housecoat and a pair of pom-pommed silver mules, "Well look who finally got here, took you long enough 'cause I'm nearly *hysterical* already with these water bugs!"

O Christ, this is all I need today! following behind her and paunchy Herman in his Hagar Pest jacket and baggy brown denims—

"Been calling and calling—So go 'head and take care of them, will you please, figure out what you have to do and get them the hell *out* of here!"

"We'll do our best, Mrs. Shish—"

"You know I hardly sleep anymore, have no idea what I've been going through, my nerves so frazzled—Thank God for Valium!"

"Well just relax, Mrs. Shish, I'm here now and I'll go take a look—"

"And you're the *boss* now? Do the actual work with your jacket and tie on? You and my son Harry used to play together as *kids*!"

"Right, and you know, Mrs. Shish, what we do for special customers—"

"'Cause I'm just so disgusted! I don't know what your mother told you, everything that happened, all the details?"

O *Jesus,* here it comes now! "Well only that—"

"I'd just got home from this bar mitzvah Sunday, eating like a pig—the Fingerhuts, I don't know if you know them, they live near Harry in Russell Gardens—and naturally I rushed right into that bathroom over there, the closest one I could find and—God, I don't even know if I can talk about it now, I get so nervous, palpitations! I mean ever since I was a little girl in Yonkers, the sight of a bug, even a little gnat or an ant, and here was this *enormous* black thing sitting right there on my toilet seat—"

It should've bit you in the ass! "I understand, Mrs. Shish—"

"—and I let out such a scream the neighbors must've thought someone was being murdered in here, and ran and called Harder and he sprayed, but this morning he, the bug I'm talking about now, was back again, except now there were two of them—he brought along his cousin, I suppose—"

"Mrs. Shish—?"

"—and Harder couldn't get here, some nonsense excuse, so I finally called you, spoke to your mother, this man came out—"

"Mrs. Shish, why don't I take a look—?"

"—and now I'm getting *hysterical* again!"

"Right, I know how frightening it can be," massaging my twitching eyelid—

"Last night I heard them in the attic, the cellar—"

"Well you don't have to worry anymore, Mrs. Shish, I'll take care of it—"

"—and it's worse now than it's ever been, twenty-six years I've lived here—I'm going to sell this damn house! Ever since Oscar, my late husband, passed away, I've been all alone by myself. Harry says I'm crazy living alone but what does he know, he never calls, never comes over anyway, I can't depend on him with his *goyisheh* wife, that *courveh* from the Five Towns—"

"Well I'll take a look downstairs—"

"Yeah, and listen, as long as you're here, I also saw these tiny little flying things in my closet, you know the kind, that flit around—?"

"Right, Herman'll be happy to check those out for you, Mrs. Shish."

"And you'll take care of the other 'cause I have to run to the bathroom now, I get so nervous. The one upstairs is safe, your man just sprayed again—and call me if you need me," and she goes waddling off with her clacking heels, pink housecoat—and the face of Native Dancer—as I take another deep breath and keep rubbing my fluttering eyelid!

"Herman, what'd you use?"

"Malathion, but I mixed it myself this morning! Look, Mr. Hagar, I sprayed ever damn *inch* of this house already and God knows I don't need nothin' else now with my son—"

"You told me—"

"—gettin' eighteen stitches in Youngstown, Ohio—"

"Herman, I know—"

"—him'n his cousin playin' with huntin' knives—"

"Herman?"

"—lucky he didn't take his freakin' arm off!"

"I know, Herman, I know, so why don't you take care of those things that're flitting around upstairs and I'll go have a look in the cellar, got some Diazinon in my bag."

"OK, OK, it's just, Mr. Hagar, I been under a helluva lotta pressure lately, kids'll drive ya crazy! Seems like they're always messin' themselves up when they get far away from home!"

"Yeah," and I go trotting down to the basement—Just what I need right now, Herman with his slasher son! And thank God Boyne's still alive, can't believe him calling—shot at? Wife's stealing his daughter? Comeback Show?—and how the hell can I go over, still haven't told my mother, made a reservation as my eyelid keeps twitching away—Christ, my nerves so damn *raw*! being pulled in three different directions: Boyne needing me there, my mother needing me here, and so needing Teri beside me!—flicking on these bright fluorescents: this bare cellar running the length of the house with gray cinder-block walls, a folded Ping-Pong table, and taking my flashlight and spray gun out of my bag to look behind this Sears hot water heater with these shaking, sweaty hands! Water bugs usually follow the pipes straight up, Herman probably giving them a fast spritz and missing most of that crawl space back there as I start blasting Diazinon all around—

And maybe I shouldn't go, just fly to North Dakota and try to patch up what's left of our marriage? Still feeling the press of Teri's goodbye!—ducking into this crawl space as I keep spraying side to side—but never giving up that dream of mine, and she screaming, "What it's been like *throughout* our marriage! You don't even realize for the last seven years all I've heard about is your Irish summer, Boyne and Ciara—you care more about your past or the characters you write about than real people you have to get involved with—unless they're perfect like Ciara!" "Ciara? Whatta you talking about?" "Your dream girl, perfect girl! Why don't you go back to her? You're still in love with her!" "'In love with her'? I haven't seen her in years. I can't even remember what she looks like." "O sure, that's why all I ever hear about is Ciara this and Ciara that: Why isn't my hair blonde, why aren't I as smart, as poetic, as sensitive as she was? Why don't you go back and find her? I'm sure you could steal her away!" "Teri, I never said—" "And the only time I ever see you come alive anymore is when you're talking about what I've *never* been a part of!"

And all so long ago: Ciara now married with kids of her own? Or dreaming of me in *her* turmoil? Living in the past, an eternal hazard, writing spurring it on, the lessons of Nabokov's class—"You come home from that damn office and the termites and roaches and bedbugs hating the world and screaming at the slightest thing, because suddenly the only involvement you have is with your father's business that you've always hated and were terrified of taking over!"—Teri finally leaving and filing for divorce, the first divorce in my family! And Christ, so needing her now!—feel like I'm in a pressure cooker, end of my rope, about to explode!—and Boyne's desperate pleas! Last seen in front of the Irish pub, tears running down his bearded cheeks, beret tilted, back in Carnaween, really needing *me* now—or me really needing *him*? Seven years gone by—and back to Carnaween with all I'd ever wanted, all I'd ever dreamed? Flynn first telling me about him ("Born on a boat off the coast of Ireland but raised in Valhalla, New York") on that stormy ship across and then again in Paris: a brilliantly gifted, Turner-like artist and underground legend, most promising painter of his generation—who became too controversial and far ahead of his time—and the work I saw was fantastic! Convincing me then to stay, he painting, me writing, and the hell with the exterminating business! "Christ, life is *leaping*, boy, never a lying down!"—O Jesus, I don't know! Recapture the past, a second chance to fulfill my dreams? So what the hell do I do?—backing quickly out of this crawl space with the sweat now pouring off me as I finish spraying all around, behind the water heater—and the phone shrilly ringing!—Mrs. Shish shouting from above, "Herman, would you get that, please?"

"Mr. Hagar?" Herman calling down from the cellar door. "It's for you, your mother's on the line'n I'm goin' outside, get a new spray can outta my truck."

"—OK, OK, fine," and picking up this wall phone below the stairs, "Yeah, Ma, what is it?" as my eyelid keeps twitching away!

"You're still out at the beauty's, huh, drivin' you crazy I'm sure. O just more trouble, you know, Rodriquez won't be back now till Tuesday, Mastro hadda go to the hospital, and you got calls in Bellmore, Patchogue—"

"*O dear GOD*!" Mrs. Shish shrieking upstairs. "There's one in *MY* bathroom!"

"—and another somewhere in Hartsdale—"

"Get him *OUT* of here!"

Blinking rapidly now, "Ma, how can I possibly go to Patchogue *and* Hartsdale?"

"O God, they're all *OVER* the place!!"

"Well then I would just do the ones in Bellmore and Patchogue—"

"I'm gonna have a *HEART ATTACK* right here in my *BATH-ROOM*!!"

Shouting, "Be right *up*, Mrs. Shish!" as I keep rubbing this god-damn eyelid!

"Gene, what's going on there?"

"Nobody ever *BELIEVES* me—"

"She's going banan—*CHRIST ALMIGHTY!*" and jumping a mile as a huge black water bug goes crawling over my hand—and I swat it away—dropping the phone and stomping it dead—then hurling my spray gun across the room, noisily banging off the wall!

("—Gene, Gene, are you *there*? What happened? What's going *on*? Are you *OK*?")

Snatching up the swaying receiver, "No, I'm *not* OK! I'm on the verge of a goddamn *breakdown* and if I don't get away from this business, the bugs, and these customers, someone'll have to exter-minate *me*!"

"'Away'? Whatta you talking about 'away,' not to Ireland and that *meshuggener*?"

"No, to London, Kew—"

"*London*? Whatta you saying? How can you possibly go to *London*?"

"I'll just get on a plane and go!"

"But there's the business and your wife just left—Gene, whatta you crazy?"

"Yeah, maybe I *am* crazy!"

"Will someone please get *UP* here!"

"Now you wanna kill me, too?"

"O Jesus, Ma!"

"—God, I'm gonna *DIE,* I'm gonna *DIE*!"

"It wasn't enough with Ireland seven years ago when you almost killed your father?"

"I didn't *kill* my father and he didn't get sick 'cause I was in Ireland!"

Herman looking down, "Mr. Hagar, what's she screamin' about this time?"

"(Herman, just get the hell up there!) *THIS* stroke killed him, a real cerebral stroke!"

"All right already, what does it matter now, but how can you possibly go running off to London, three thousand miles away?"

"'Cause if I don't, I'm gonna have a fucking stroke of my *OWN*!"

Boyne

Across the lush green meadows of Phoenix Park with the blood leaping along my veins, past the Zoological Gardens—*Mary and Joseph*! the squeal of seals and the roar of those yawning lions (my nerves so on edge, picturing killers behind every hedge!)—and up to Sligo's elegant vine-covered domain, looking strangely seedy now, grayish paint peeling away, as I nip by the filigreed gate, skip onto the Doric porch, and begin rapping on this large gold knocker—nervously licking my lips, seafaring slicker rippling in the breeze (feeling so exposed and alone out here!)—as the black front door swings open with a creak and hoary old Ordway, deaf as a coot in his blue butler's suit, peers out with a doddering bow.

"Ah, *Ordway, dear* Ordway!" clasping his nodding head in my hands and kissing each of his bristled cheeks, "it's *marvelous* seeing you again!"

"—Is it *you,* s-sir?"

"It is *I,* Ordway, *only* I who's finally arrived here in the flesh! But how the hell've you *been*?"

"Thin, s-sir? Yes, well I may have lost some weight."

"But still looking rather *spry,* I'd say, for an old Sinn Féiner like you!"

"Certainly, s-sir, right this way."

"And I'd just like to add how grieved I was to hear of your master's passing—trust that his daughters are to home?"

"No, you needn't have phoned. Any bags, s-sir?"

"No, no, Ordway, I shan't be staying, sorry—"

"In the car, s-sir? I'll go have a look round the car."

And sauntering past him with a grin down the long shadowed hall under these gilded portraits of Sligo's family, all dour-faced rhinos, and into this white-walled room: white carpets, white furniture (like being in a bloody asylum!)—and Good *God,* will you just *look* at that wondrous sight! One of my early works still blazing above the mantel: "Painting up a bloody *storm* then, Billy, with my worn brushes and palette knife, frenzied fingers and thumbnail gouging, scratching, and scrubbing cobalt green across a field of white—till gradually and, as if by magic, that widening gyre of color turned into lusty Laura nude in the throes of passion swathed in a Turner-like haze and seething vortex of light! O so young and supple-bellied she was in those days with her smooth buttermilk rump and breasts as plump as avocados!" **"Zounds, lad, but surely**

it was Renoir who said, 'A painter who has the feel of breasts and buttocks is truly saved'!" "Right, and now here she is stealing my *girl!*" as I keep pacing around in my growing state of agitation, circling this white-carpeted floor. "Last time I was back in Baltimore, whisking Tory away to the Museum of Art, hiding out till they were closed, then slowly emerging to see it the only way you should, by flashlight and alone! Some people spend a lifetime studying those paintings, Billy, but we needed only a night—and Laura calling the police, swore she'd kill me if I ever came near her again—and I had to flee back to Ireland once more! Such a selfish bloody *bitch* she's become, avenging *whore*—"

And the door flying open with a thunderous slam as Sligo's two spinsterish daughters come prancing in, "O Mr. Boyne, we've been so trying to *find* you!"

"Brenda, please!" older sister, Vi, brandishing a vinyl riding crop, now striding on by with those tan hairy tweeds and ballbearing eyes as the frilly, flirting Brenda flitters behind, sheathed in white organdy and ruffles of lace and twining her long feather boa.

"Find me—why?"

"O nothing, nothing at all, Mr. Boyne, Brenda was just so delighted to see you." Brenda still flirting and giggling with glee. "But please do sit down, and would you care for a drink, an apéritif or there's red wine, white wine?"

"O any wine'll do!" Brenda drifting sinuously toward the sideboard. "Though I must say when I learned of your father's passing, lost myself for a month or more in the bogs of incognito—Ah, that's very kind, could really use one now!" draining this crystal glass in a gulp—"But what in God's name happened?"

"Well we're none of us quite certain, the weight of his years, a final straw, I doubt we shall ever know."

"So it had nothing to do with my show?"

"Your show? O dear Lord no, not at all, not in the slightest, Mr. Boyne! In fact, we *have* been trying to find you—"

Brenda behind me now, "And you'll never know how consoling during this period your paintings truly were," tracing her feather boa seductively across my nape, "Found them terribly, *terribly* exciting"—over my ears—

"Brenda?" under my nose—

"—they just opened me up completely—"

"Brenda, please!"

"And you *look* so wonderful!"

Thwack! Vi's riding crop whacking her thigh as I shoot straight up out of my chair!

"Smell so wonderful—"

"Yes, well, Mr. Boyne," Vi pausing in profile before the mantel with her long-lipped rhino face as Brenda and her boa continue twining toward backpedaling me, "you must be looking forward to your show tomorrow night?"

"O far *more* than that, ladies," dodging deftly round this ottoman, "since I came to what can only be called an extraordinary decision this morning talking to Turner—"

"Turner, Mr. Boyne?"

"—concerning the Tate!" weaving between white settees—

"O I adore Turner, simply adore—"

"Brenda, please—So you've been in *contact* with the Tate?"

"No not at all—"

"O Vi and I were just there for a board—"

"Yes, yes, well what Brenda's referring to is the fact of our recently succeeding our father as trustees for life, Mr. Boyne—"

"Trustees for *life*, ha-ha!" as I feint right and zip left round the sofa, "'Cause suddenly out there on those tracks, Billy told me—"

Thwack! "Brenda, please!"

"—if I can just get one of my works hung in the Tate, my struggles will all be worth it!"

"Yes, of course, Mr. Boyne, but we still haven't received the remainder of your works for *this* show."

"O just some last-minute touching up to do, Vi, be bringing them over myself, you know."

"Ah, that's grand, because we *are* counting on you"—Vi rapidly tapping the riding crop in her hand as Brenda now comes gliding in from behind, *ha-ha*—"and as far as the Tate goes, you have my word"—*thwack!*—"we'll provide you whatever support we can."

"Ah, that's marvelous, bloody *marvelous,* Vi, you're an angel in disguise!" being forced into this corner—and Ordway comes doddering in—

". . . Still haven't found your bags yet, s-sir—" as I sidestep her once again.

"Yes, Ordway, well that'll be all."

"Of course, m-madam," and he goes bowing and doddering out as Brenda continues chasing me about—thinks she's performing a Noël Coward play—snaking that sensuous boa across my beret!

"O this is all so exciting, I can hardly *wait* for your show!" with Vi now sliding between us as I go veering toward the door.

"Yes, well we're *both* looking forward to it, Mr. Boyne, and all we ask is that you give us your word—Brenda, will you please *stop*!—that by tomorrow night everything will be complete?"

"O absolutely, ladies"—reaching the hall—"you have my fervent vow that tomorrow night in Londontown you'll see the Comeback Show of the *Century*!"

Hagar

Coming down through this late morning mist over the immense sprawled shimmer of the Irish Sea, a green, toppling sea, dots and white smears of sailboats and the sunny hill of what must be Howth, wildflowers blooming, those heathery, hedgerowed fields, Pigeon House and Poolbeg Flasher, palms sweating, my free hand sliding back and forth over the blue musty edge of my raincoat hem—another plane out there, silver glint fading in the distance—and I still can't believe I'm on my way to London, leaving that goddamn business behind, Mrs. Shish's water bugs, accountants coming in Tuesday, and my mother's final pleas, "Crazy altogether! You couldn't take a day or two out in the Hamptons, we could go together, why all of a sudden London?"

One of these sexy stewardesses passing by, the smooth-fitting green tweed of her airline suit snugly accentuating her swaying rump as she moves down the aisle, offering assorted sweets and masking the small fire of annoyance that flickers within—Last chance, said Boyne, before I'm engulfed *forever* in the bug business—he needing me—but so needing *him* now with everything in my life exploding, marriage falling apart—speeding on, my dreams of escape, flying through flung nets out of reach, heading back to the world of my past . . .

To Carnaween in that summer of 1960: our mad, whirlwind spree, Boyne's twelve-room house by the Irish Sea—and now seven years later at thirty-eight, God knows what he's like, the incredible Seamus Boyne, trying to take his life—or someone doing it for him? Should've called him before, told him my flight—maybe thinks I'm not coming, can't wait any longer, slitting his wrists, blowing his brains out—*No,* stop it, stop it, sure he's OK, *must* be OK!

And in those seven years since we met what have I become: a man enchanted with the world (Teri saying, "You were that way when we met!") or just jumping out of my skin, locked in my father's office and letting no one in? Not what I was then—thirty-one now, nose with its Roman bump and the shock of high-school hair fast receding, my father's widow's peak—accepted then as Joyce's forehead, my monumental conceit, seeking someone to back my dreams, spin illusions, and let me fly. And my father screaming the day that I left, his raccoon eyes squinting in the sun, "The biggest mistake we made was sending you to Columbia, one graduate school was enough. You've gotta settle down, start earning a living like the rest of your friends. This was your last semester, I'm not paying for any more schools, Cornell, Yale, now Columbia—*enough* already! After this trip you come into the business!"

A final fling, his summer bonus, before I settled down. And going, not knowing what to do, running I knew not where—till I ran into Ciara that first night in Paris, a dazzling blonde Swedish-looking girl with bluestone eyes and dimpled cheeks, who loved Joyce, Dylan, and Synge, spoke five languages fluently, the brightest girl I've ever met, up at the Contrescarpe to see Flynn perform (Boyne's art school pal, "Part-time Actor, Painter, Balladeer: A Superior Catholic Standing at Stud") as I just kept staring at her and finally worked up my nerve to ask, "But you're not *Irish,* are you?" "Pardon?" and she smiled as I kept on staring, her eyes roaming over my face. "I said, you're not Irish—?" "I am Irish? No, not entirely." "Then you must be Swedish." "No, I must be Dutch." "Dutch? Yes, well I think you're very pretty and I hope you understood what I just said." And Flynn still singing as she smiled again, "But *you* are not Irish, are you?" "No, just American, bewildered American." "Ah, and I was nearly thinking you were Irish. But what do you do? You are a singer also?" "No, I write." "I see. Is that your ambition, or are you already fulfilled?" "How old are you?" "You want to know how *old* I am? Nineteen, but very soon I shall be twenty." "Very soon. By the way, my name is Gene." "Gene, and I am Keer-ah." "Keer-ah?" "Yes, it is spelled with a C, C-i-a-r-a. An uncle of mine was Irish, though my family actually is from Delft." "Dutch-Irish? I never heard of that." Flynn kneeling down from the stage above, his orange curls and mustache reeling, "Never *heard* of it, Gene? Jaysus, if the Dutch had Ireland it'd be a garden and if the Irish had Holland, they'd all drown!" as her English boyfriend suddenly appeared in his deerstalker cap and pin-striped slacks and off we sped to their houseboat on the Seine, Ciara, Milo, Flynn, and I.

(And God, she's *still* so vivid to me, her ability to make it all seem possible, be anything I wanted her to be!)

Then next morning, after we'd stayed up to bring in the dawn with Flynn staggering away to Belleville and Milo to British Intelligence, Ciara and I went capering all around the Louvre and down to the Grecian rooms, she peeking in and out of those marble statues or gracefully posing with her hand upheld.

"Ciara, listen, did you ever play tag in Holland?"

"Of course, only we didn't call it that. Why, you don't want to play *here,* do you?"

"Why not? I'll bet I can catch you—and you're it!"

"But the guards?"

"Asleep in the Egyptian rooms. I'll count to ten, give you a head start, so you'd better get going. One—"

"Wait! Let me take off these then," doffing her high heels, "At least you can make it fair, with you wearing your gym, your tennis shoes, and I'll put mine here," placing her purse in a corner, "I could not run very fast, elude you, carrying them, could I now?"

"Two. No, you couldn't. Three. Better get going. Four—"

And she was off, past pediments and pedestals, Etruscan amphorae and a tulip-shaped vase, noble busts and limbless torsos to disappear giggling round a Caesar head, Octavian pose, as the tourists smiled, frowned, stepped aside, my sneakered feet darting this way, that, not far behind her hair of Scandinavian shine, harried glance over her shoulder as she dizzily turned a corner on one foot—and by God, she was gone! Passing votive sculptures, Venus, the caryatids, and back to the Greeks for a fast look in—and there she was, barefoot under a bronze Apollo, poised, panting, waiting to move, didn't see me, couldn't hear me, creep up behind—"*Eeeee!*"

"*Got* you!" whirling her round and round.

"O *God,* Gene!" collapsing back against me, "I never even heard you!" as I nuzzled her small cup of bone where the collar came away, and she kept gazing up at the statue, "And who is that?"

"Apollo."

Ciara whispering in my ear, "He has your Roman nose."

"Only the nose?"

She laughing, "Though he does have a rather small penis, doesn't he?"

"Probably just finished showering."

"But that doesn't happen to you too, all shriveled up?"

"Don't you know?"

"Not things like this. Shy little me with my Calvinistic—"

"I know, nineteen and never been kissed, ho ho!"

And following the arrows to the dark polished floors of the Grande Galerie as she shook loose her hair with a bright flashing smile (her front teeth's slight charming overlap), the blonde down shimmering on her arms and the sweat of health glimmering on her brow, lithe hips swaying in her prideful gait, the ripe swell of her breasts straining against the balance and poise of her motion, animal balance and poise and that spark of impulsive gaiety, her tight-fitting blue skirt snugly accentuating her sassy rump, firm outline of her panties, dark elliptical folds of her blouse. "Ciara, I love to see what your body does to clothes, swelling and curving them into a sensual shape! *Je t'aime, ma chérie, Liebe* also, and how do you say love in Dutch?" "*Liefde. Ik ben gek op jou als ik bij je ben.*"

And cramming all my delights, insights, and insistent need into that whirlwind week or more as Milo left for Liechtenstein and I kept galloping down to their houseboat on the Seine. And what did I really offer? Words, dreams, create the conscience of my race, pen *Ulysses* ten years after? Writer, wife, come share my hazardous life, or common-law lovers like Joyce and Nora—Milo returning, the two of us vying for her, and Ciara couldn't decide, "Gene, I don't really know if I could even live your dream, but I promise I will write if I should change my mind."

And a few days later I left for Ireland alone, hoping her letter would be waiting, posted on to Dublin and reposing under the dust. Didn't really expect it. Hoped, to be sure, though not much more.

But her letter *was* waiting at the American Express:

Dear Gene,

If Ireland is half as lovely as you told me, please write me, and I will come.

"Christ *Almighty*!!!"

Heads turning and staring at my whoop of joy, "Sorry, sorry," as I went skipping the light fantastic out the door, give me that old soft shoe, I said that old soft shoe, ah one, ah two, ah clickety-clackety boo! The Irish leaning back, wide-eyed, eschewing me—Screw!—for there was champagne in my sneakered feet, Mumm's bubbly, all my senses with their hands in their pockets as I gamboled down toward the heart of the city, raincoat tossed carelessly over my shoulder, in my wine-colored T-shirt, khakis, and white Converse All Stars—under the stained gray shade of the Bank of Ireland, pigeons balanced along the narrow ledge, and stepping suddenly into a bright patch of sunlight, my shadow flung out before me, through Bewley's Oriental aroma and down Westmoreland Street at half past the hour by the *Irish Times* with church bells ringing and my reflection in the shop windows flickering near, a wild and rowdy brown bear singed by the summer, unruly shock of hair, the girls with rosepink smears on their cheeks, and seagulls zealously flapping like torn white wrapping paper in the breeze as I followed the green double-decker buses on toward the river, the Liffey slowly flowing along with oil slicks and refuse wallowing about its shaggy banks.

O I had it *all,* Ireland, Joyce, and Ciara on her way, Boyne convincing me to stay, he painting, me writing, reading aloud to him every night or admiring his amazing talent, days of rain and grass, trees and paths, sketching in the canoe, all I'd ever wanted, all I'd ever dreamed as we jigged together in Carnaween—till that telegram from my mother arrived:

```
Dad suffered a stroke. You must come home.
```

And that last gray morning with Boyne in great agitation (and looking like a wild-eyed Augustus John) walking me down to the bus and waiting outside the pub in the blustery rain, wearing his beret, sunglasses, and that billowing green windbreaker.

"Good *God,* Gene, just why the hell're you *going*? I mean what the hell for? Listen to me, will you, and take my word—I know all about American mothers'n their ways, he's probably OK—'cause you're making the biggest mistake of your *life* leaving here!"

"Seamus, I have to go back and see how he is!"

"Just *stay* here, will you! America's mad, insane! Ireland's the *only* place to paint, to write, and do one's art—I mean you leave now and you'll *never* come back! Suffering *Christ,* end up a bug man living in Great Neck! I mean we've got it all here, Gene, everything you wanted. You *yourself* said so and you're a writer, hell of a writer, really, all the elements're there, I heard your work and the way you handle language and, Jaysus, you *have* to write, this dream girl's coming over—so Christ, you can't leave *now*!"

"Seamus, I'll be back and I wrote Ciara to wait—"

"Good *God,* boy, at least call your mother first—just to check if it's true—but you don't *leave,* there's no reason to leave, just toss it all away! God*damn* it, Gene, you *have* to stay, started painting again 'cause of you, never painted *better,* period of my greatest creativity—"

"Seamus, I give you my word—"

"Making the biggest *mistake*—" The bus splashing and swaying round the bend, "—biggest mistake of your *life*—"

"Probably be back in another week."

"—I'm telling you, you'll be *sorry—Listen* to me, Gene, I know!"

Shaking his hand, "Good-bye, Seamus," and hugging him, "be back before you know it."

"—Biggest mistake of your *life* leaving here!"

Still muttering to himself within the shelter of the doorway as I mounted the bus, a wave over my shoulder and down the aisle toward an empty seat, my luggage dropped on the floor. And turning around as we slowly pulled away, I glanced back to see him huddled in the doorway, the tears running under his sunglasses and down his bearded cheeks—

"Ladies and gentlemen, we are beginning our descent into London now. Fasten your seat belts, please."

~

Along this rainy towpath, rushes and poplar trees churning above the Thames and that rising tide of anxiety sweeping over me again—arriving too late and Boyne's already dead!—Jesus, where the hell's his *home*? Never gonna find it! This the way to go? Past a pale brick row of Edwardian cottages, jets coming in low through those storm clouds overhead, this windy drizzle flapping and slapping my blue raincoat all about me, drenching my small valise—and the leafy path sharply curving round to this secluded little cottage down by the river—must be Tattersall Wharf!—most of the lawn's been cut, flowerpots along the windowsills as I hurry on toward this flaking green door—

And a thunderous peal of organ music bellowing out, dark keening chords—*Holy Christ,* Boyne (or who knows) in there writhing over the keys, about to do himself in!

Pounding on the knocker again and again, then shouting, "*Seamus*?" The music resounding through the windy air. "Seamus, it's me, Gene, I'm *here*! I'm *here*!" banging on these latticed panes, still can't see who it is, riddled and tinselly with rain—and the organ suddenly stopping, echoes wheezing away—

"Ah, *Hagar,* ha-ha! Be with you in just a jiff!"

And the door flying open with bearded Boyne standing there stark naked—except for his beret and those green-striped socks—grinning from ear to ear, "Good *God,* boy, right in the middle of my *concerto,* ha-ha!"

"Seamus, are you *OK,* weren't about to—?"

"OK?" laughing, "Jaysus!" The whites of his eyes glazed with a fiery myopic glare.

"—I mean—What the hell're you, *drunk*?"

"*Drunk*? Why of course I'm *drunk*! Wasn't Bach drunk? Turner drunk? Fucking Brian Boru? And it's bloody *marvelous* seeing you, Gene!" shaking my hand with both of his, "But come in, come in—O Christ, I don't have any *clothes* on hea-ah! Appear to have forgotten my entire *ensemble,* ha-ha, and you in your Ivy finery thea-ah," leaning forward and looking out from side to side, "Anybody else with you?"

"No."

"You sure?"

"Yes. Why?"

"Thought I heard other footsteps."

"No, just mine."

"Fine, fine, just being careful, you know, all sorts of creatures lurking about, regularly occurring incidents—"

"Why, what else happened?"

"—I'll just whip on some togs and be down in a flash!"

And he goes loping up the stairs, his lean, rangy body, bouncing balls, and fleshy white ass streaked with a bright greenish smear as I take another deep breath in this hall before a row of dazzling Turner-like paintings of shadowy couples making love in all sorts of positions bathed in a shimmering, swirling light. *Fantastic* they are! Even better than the last ones I saw—all this work he's done over the years while I've let the years drift by!—and turn right into a room literally *filled* with Guinness bottles, hundreds of them glistening in silhouette, tumbles of books, boxes, and an old-fashioned organ (like the one in Ireland: the two of us dancing a madcap jig, laughing uncontrollably) as Boyne comes cantering down wearing a frayed red sweatshirt with the hood bouncing behind and a pair of gray seersucker shorts.

"Ah, Gene, found the Guinness Room yourself, have you, navigating round me bottles?"

"Jesus Christ, how many *are* there?"

"O three or four thousand—but they're all *over* the bloody house!—been commuting back and forth incognito, cornering the Guinness market in Delgany and now half of Kew, ha-ha!" his sinister throaty laugh exposing his whitish teeth—a thin gap along the bottom row—within his grizzled beard.

"But I thought you were into wine."

"Well I am! Just a variation of Gandhi's line: I believe in God so long as he takes the shape of a bottle, ha-ha! And Hagar, you really *got* here, didn't you?" slapping my arm and broadly grinning, "It's absolutely *marvelous* seeing you again—"

"Yeah, it's great seeing you—"

"—alive and kicking, and ready for my Comeback Show, 'Your Show of Shows'—The Comeback Show of the *Century*!" and chortling, he goes loping by the organ, raking his shaggy beard, "Though Jaysus, you caught me by surprise, so damn hectic now, working nonstop, then flying over last night—just wasn't sure when you'd arrive!" quickly lighting up a Player's from a pack in his pocket and flipping the match over his shoulder, "But tell me, Gene, how the blazes *you* are! You look the same with that mop of floppy hair, the All-American boy with his Apollonian flair! And marriage seems to've aged you, like vintage wine, *Irish* wine—Well hell, it's *been* seven years, we had a few laughs, had a few tears—and now you've fled your home, wife's left so you could roam! Well how does it *feel* off on this spree—?"

"God only knows," tripping over these bottles—

"—up to your ears in bugs—"

"—what's going on with my life!" this damn eyelid twitching again!

"—and now *King* of the Bloody Bugs! Well everybody's going buggy these days anyway, ha-ha! But Suffering Christ, how does it feel to take over the Holy Vermin Empire, become a Captain of *Pest* Control?"

"It's driving me out of my mind!" striding by the latticed windows, "No, I'm serious, Seamus, everything in my life's exploding, I just had to get away! I mean, you know, this time my father really has a stroke and dies and now here I am *running* it, my wife taking off—"

"Wait, what do you mean 'really' has a stroke? You received that telegram from your mother when you were over—"

"I know, but you were right, that was just to get me back, he was simply exhausted, needed rest, and was out of the hospital before I got home. Anyway, the point is now I am running the business, what I've hated all these years, driving me up the wall—"

"Or one day awake as a Franz Kafka cockroach waiting to be stomped on, ha-ha!"

"—never really involved—"

"Remember that marvelous line Franz said to *his* father, Gene: 'Think of me as a dream'?"

"—just drifting along and now locked in my father's office!"

"Yes, but now we're *together* again! And you can't tell me all these years all you've been doing is stomping out *roaches*? Jaysus, boy, you need training for that, lessons with José Greco to master the art of the flamenco," and clapping his hands and snapping his head, "*Olé!*" he stamps out his half-smoked Player's.

"No, but seriously, Seamus"—as I keep rubbing this fluttering eyelid—"so much's been going on in my life with my father, the business, marriage falling apart, that I really needed to *talk* to you now!"

"O I know, I know, can feel what you're going through, believe me I do, and it'll all work itself out, I promise you—But first let me tell you about my show—have you seen the *Times*?" reaching atop the organ, "the London *Times*? Ad here, half a *page* practically!" pointing to a large box in the left-hand corner:

NOW THE LONG-AWAITED COMEBACK OF THE
MOST CONTROVERSIAL PAINTER OF HIS GENERATION:
SEAMUS EAMON BOYNE
The Sligo-Moeran Gallery
62 Cadogan Square

"Isn't that bloody *marvelous*, ha-ha!" lighting up another Player's and tossing the match over his shoulder, "All part of our strategy, Gene, all part of our dreams!"

"Yeah, some dreams!" and pacing again, "For seven years all *I've* been doing is working in the shadow of my father, now he dies, my mother's driving me *crazy*—"

"Gene, later, later, we'll sort it later—"

"—then my wife takes off—"

"—never let you down before and have no intention of doing so now—"

"—my marriage suddenly over—"

"—but Good *God*, Hagar, more than anyone, I know what it's like to end a marriage, lose a daughter."

"—Yeah, well what's that all about?"

Boyne adjusting his beret and snuffing out another half-smoked Player's, "O they won't let me see her, see my only girl, burnished little girl, but I do, *still* do, they can't stop me, *never* stop me"—the whites of his eyes growing glossy—"no one is taking my *girl*!" as sniffling, he turns the other way, raking his grizzled beard, "O I'll *see* her all right! Damn right I'll see her! Be back in Baltimore, what is it, next week for the hearing and when she sees what her father's become—not what they've told her—my talent finally recognized, she'll come back to Carnaween!"

"You're going over next *week*?"

"Well, you know, just to clear this up, be in and out in a jiff—But Gene, come on with me for a minute," as he goes loping into the hall, "'Cause there's something I want you to see!"

And really feeling uneasy here, things somehow not the same—but so needing to talk to him now with my eyelid still twitching away—as I enter this wide skylighted room with its tall black walls, an easel standing in the center, his multicolored palette, cans of oily water, brushes sprouting from earthenware pots, open tubes of paint, and Boyne, like P. T. Barnum with a flourishing sweep of his hand, presenting it all to me:

"Pure, sunless light from the north, Gene, pure as light can be!"

"Yeah, well I've been married now for seven years—"

"Light *bursting* out of darkness!"

"—soon after I got home—"

And still grinning like a horse with his lips curling away from his teeth, he steps back from his canvas of a beautiful blonde-haired girl amid a radiant swirl of color seductively offering herself from the rear—

"*Holy Christ*! but that's—that's *CIARA*!" The same bright flashing smile—

"Isn't she *marvelous*?"

—slight charming overlap, tiptilted nose. "But where, how the hell'd you *meet* her?" whirling quickly around, "Is she *here*?"

"No, she's there before you on canvas, re-created from your words!"

"My *words*? But how'd you ever—?"

"When you read me your work seven years ago, it was those descriptions of her I remembered, after you'd left and I couldn't afford real models, that ignited these blazing visions—"

"But why *that* pose?"

"Soul of a bearded Celtic satyr, ha-ha!"

"But all I did was *describe* her—"

"And I took it from there!"

"How many more—?"

"O portraits galore, which've never been seen till now! But you really think I've captured her?"

"It's incredible! But come on, tell me the truth, where the hell'd you meet her?"

"Believe me, Gene, it's only your words, I swear!"

"And all these years you've been—"

"Producing the finest works of my career—though you'd never know it from my reviews and that host of disastrous shows before I started painting Ciara!" picking up his palette with his right hand and a long dark brush in his left, "'Cause making love and painting've always been one and the same to me, same expenditure of energy, same virile joy—"

"Yeah, I can see, I can see, but—"

"—and the sensate tip of my brush," Boyne leaning forward now and sideways to his right, "is like an organ of physical pleasure, an inseparable part of me"—laying on the paint with a kind of brute relish—

"Yeah, well it's still a helluva shock to me!"

"—the surface of my canvas like living skin," applying sensuous strokes of red and green, "but listen, all I'm really doing, Gene, is making public what Turner did in private—"

"—*everything* getting crazy now—"

"—those lusty sketches of naked lovers that Ruskin burned in a fit of Victorian pique!"

Jesus *Christ,* he doesn't even *HEAR* me! This whole trip becoming a nightmare—you can't repeat the past!—and that rising tide of anxiety rushing over me again, rubbing this goddamn eyelid!—as he keeps on painting, using the palm of his hand to blend all those tints together—

"Heighten these round persimmon nipples and pubic hair like wild mountain thyme! And soon, Hagar, she'll be hanging in the Tate beside Turner—"

God, I can hardly *breathe*! as I go racing blindly out of his studio, down this hall, and tripping, stumbling through the door—still drizzling, the wind scudding the falling leaves along this towpath with the Thames below tossing about—*had* to get out of there, couldn't talk to him, make it clear, feeling so out of place, sight of Ciara, offering herself from the rear—just breathe, keep on breathing—has his *own* problems here, Comeback Show, losing his daughter, and now I appear, needing to talk about *me*!

Down this lane behind the Edwardian cottages and out onto Bushwood Road toward that black cab waiting—

"Hagar, Good God!" Boyne grabbing me from behind as I hop into this taxi, "where the hell are you *going*?" and he hops in too and slams the door.

"—I-I don't know!"

"Where to, sir?"

"I looked around and suddenly felt like I did, Mother of Christ, when my daughter was *taken* from me! Just drive, keep driving!"

"But where, sir?"

"Around the fountain and take it slow!"

And off we go with a rasp of gears round that small stone fountain out there.

"But Gene, what's the matter, why on earth'd you *leave*?"

"'Cause I couldn't talk to you, felt—I don't know—Seamus, look, it's not your fault—I just thought it'd be like Ireland again, but you can't repeat the past, turn back the clock."

"Turn back the clock, no, but you sure as hell can rewind it!"

"Now where, sir?"

"Damn it, man, just keep driving till I tell you to stop!"

"But where to, sir?"

"Around the fountain!"

"*Again*, sir?"

"Yes, again and *again*! But Good *God*, Gene, you're here and that's all that matters now!" as we putter around the fountain once more. "The two of us together and back to Carnaween! 'Cause I still have the house, the castle—and I've always believed in you and your writing, unlike your father—"

"I know but—"

"—and especially now when you're being sucked down into that business you've always hated—'cause seven years ago, hell, I was where you are now with a wife just having left and you got me painting again—Driver, driver, go the *other* way now, I'm getting dizzy with just one direction!—and I know the kind of free spirit, Gene, you really are, what all of them back there probably've never *seen*! 'Cause all they know back there is Hagar the *bug man* or Hagar the *homeowner* or Hagar the *consumer*—haven't got a clue as to what's going on *inside* you!"

"Seamus—"

"No, no, *listen,* just imagine someone like Beethoven back there buying chopmeat in one of those Muzaked supermarkets while the Fifth Symphony is going off inside his head: 'One pound of ground round, please.' *Dada da Dum*! 'That'll be sixty-nine cents a pound, sir.' *Da-da da DUM*! O Suffering *Christ,* what a scene! All those suburban matrons fighting behind him, trying to bump him out of line, the bloody Muzak going—and all they know is that little old deaf man who buys chopmeat and reads lips! Enough, driver, our circular journey's over, we're getting out right hea-ah! What's our fare?"

"One pound, sir, should cover it."

"Right, and keep the change. Most refreshing spin, must do this again some time!" and back along the leafy towpath with his arm around my shoulder, "And now you know *why* you're coming, Gene, not like before, running from your father, vaguely seeking Joyce," under these shimmering willows, "know bloody well where you *are*!"

"Yeah, on the verge of a nervous—"

"'Cause the art is *always* worth it and you *need* an immediate change, the freedom and distance to do your work!" Speedboats bouncing over the gray and choppy Thames. "And as for females, we've an *abundance* of 'em, one of our Irish beauties, exquisitely slim colleens—O the country is just full of 'em waiting to serve, concubines galore! And now your wife has opened the door, so as soon as I succeed, of course we'll leave and you'll come back to Carnaween!" side by side up the flagstone path with his arm still round my shoulder.

"Yeah, well God knows, Seamus, if I'm ready for Ireland now, 'cause lately everything's driving me crazy!"

"Ah, then you'd better come out back now, shoot some baskets and restore your sanity!"

"Baskets?" following him through the door, "But it's still raining—"

"No, no, those are just windswept clouds, sun'll soon be blazing!" and back into the Guinness Room as he kicks some bottles aside, "Come on, boy, once you restore your sanity and put things in perspective, none of them can ever *touch* you, 'cause you do seem a little tense."

"Me, *tense*? How could you possibly tell? And since when are you playing basketball?"

"Ah, well see, Dungannon put it up, became a rather fanatic Celtics fan—but let me just find the ball," and he goes searching through the room in his beret, red-hooded sweatshirt, and seersucker shorts, kicking aside the drapes—"Ah, here we *are*!" holding up a dusty Spalding and wiping it off, "Knew it was around here somewhere, picked it up at Harrods where they've everything, elephant tusks and Assam tea—but listen, Gene, you know you could take off that raincoat now 'cause it hardly ever rains in here—*and* your jacket and tie, and I'll go get some sneakers, an extra pair in my room," and loping rapidly up the stairs, he goes rummaging around up there, the sound of clinking bottles, then comes cantering down again, "Adidas blue and whites—those all right?"

"Fine, just what I need right now," shaking my head and lacing them up, "a game of basketball!"

"But you *played* basketball, didn't you, within those hallowed Ivy walls of Cornell and Yale? Good God, an Ivy League *Jew*—Amazing! The Irish'd have you running for Lord Mayor if they only knew! You could win in a *breeze*—Or no, it was soccer that you played, now I remember. Though actually you do look like a soccer player, thick neck, brawny. What position?"

"Fullback."

"Fullback, yes, blocking them off from the goal. Well I used to run track myself, a sprint man, real quick, ha-ha!" and back out the front door he goes with the wind still blustery and shafts of sunlight suddenly slanting between the clouds, "See, just look at the *weather* you brought! Absolutely *marvelous,* Hagar!" his loping stride and his red hood flapping behind, "O this weather is *unbelievable,* makes me feel like Ireland for once! Really, this is the first time it's felt like Ireland since I arrived—except there are no people there, just pigs, cattle, and an odd assortment of elves—Well hell, like when *you* were there—on the ground, in the green, near a glade!" around the side to a damp blacktopped drive and a white fan-shaped backboard, rusty orange rim, nailed over the garage, a window above it, "But here, let me try, see if I can make a quick ten in a row! Actually the first time I've been out, Gene, haven't done this in *years*!" flipping the ball left-handed toward the hoop with an excessive amount of spin—he finally banks one in, "Ah, think I've found the range . . . No"—as the next shot rims the basket and rolls off—"not quite yet. Here, Gene, you try for a while," tossing the wet ball toward me with a casual flick of his wrist—that misses me by a yard—"Sorry there, I can get it—"

"No, no, I've got it," bouncing it off the damp ground and up with a soft fadeaway jump—swish. Putting in several short jumpers in a row, then a long floating hook.

"Christ, you don't *miss,* Hagar!"

"Yeah, well I've been practicing," another fadeaway jumper from the corner, "Have my own basket at home—"

"O you do, do you, out there every night, eh?"

"—Just about."

"How many in a row is that?"

"I don't know—six, seven."

"Right, well here, let me show you my Helen Keller shot, Gene, high percentage shot, never fails, usually do it with a blindfold," dribbling back, two fast bounces, then eyes closed, he steps forward and heaves the ball—*crashing* through the upstairs window! "O Good *God*!" shattered glass tinkling down, "Bit off course there"—as I burst out laughing, can't *stop* laughing—now both of us laughing—as he bumps into me, doubled up and roaring uncontrollably like we used to long ago, his arm around my shoulder—"And—O Suffering *Christ*!—to think, Gene"—Boyne adjusting his beret as he gains a giggling breath—"I once led the Art School League in scoring! Though that's not saying very much—with all those fruitcakes prancing about, you were more likely to get fondled rather than fouled, ha-ha!"

"—Yeah," and still smiling and drying my eyes with the back of my hand, "I think we'd better clean this up."

"O right y'are, whiskbroom's just here in the garage, have the glaziers pop out tomorrow," and sweeping the glass into my dustpan, "But listen, that's enough sport for today," dumping it into a trashbin, "'cause you'll never convince *me* you flew three thousand miles, left your wife, just to play basketball here in Kew!" and back around the house once more with our arms about each other, "For there's wine and women and wonders *galore* before we reach Jerusalem—and a party at my show besides!"

"What party's this?"

"Behind the gallery in Cadogan Square," passing these uncut hedges, "though we won't get there till late anyway, keep 'em *panting* for my arrival—then off to Ireland where there's still poetry and the dance! The dance, you see, is what's gone out of America, the old romance—and now, Gene, we'll be bringing it *back* to Ireland!"

"Organ and all?"

"O of course, 'cause I do know three notes: fee, fi, and fo."

"No fum?"

"Never had time for fum, ha-ha!" and through the flaking green door, "Come on, I'll play you the dance right now!"

"But what time's your show?"

"O I don't know, eight, eight-fifteen? *Irish* time—no such thing as eight precisely—give or take a millennium or two!" his loping stride, beret, and a thick curl of hair at his neck, swinging back into the Guinness Room—with seemingly even more bottles than before, bottles all over the place: on tables, chairs, in corners, throughout the dusty bookshelves, on top of the organ, within a grate, on settees, love seats, and this worn floral rug as he kicks some clinking out of the way, pulling up a swivel stool, and adjusting his black beret in a mirror on the wall, "Now a bit of the trill to begin!" pumping the pedals, a loud diapason welling out, "Touch of the E. Powers Biggs—Ah Gene, what a marvelous hour for music, feeling at one with the few remaining *four*-footed creatures out there! Well Good *God,* I finally knew that here in this garden of Kew I, too, was one of nature's endangered species, along with the pig-footed bandicoot, the West African manatee, and the Block Island meadow vole, ha-ha!" Boyne grinning and rearing back and forth over the deep, wheezing chords as he keeps on warming up, "But hea-ah, a little Bach for Squire Hagar now from Great Neck! Though actually this is a Prelude and Fugue fusing with a Toccata and Passacaglia—O Christ, what a cadenza, pedal trill—'cause Bach lost nine sons himself, went blind—his eyesight returning ten days before his death—but *still* drove on till the very end," a tender smile upon his lips, swaying from side to side, "and proved it was all worth it!" as he abruptly breaks it off,

"Ah, but *enough* of that now, far too sad—How about an Irish reel or 'The Wild Rover'?" glancing up, the whites of his eyes gleaming with delight, grinning teeth, gap-tooth and all, beard and beret as he writhes over the keyboard, gay with the lilt of this Irish reel, leaning back, left foot pounding to keep up the rhythm and the music pealing madly away, "It *gets* you, doesn't it, boy? Come on, Gene, *into* it now! Show me some steps, a bit of the jig like we used to do—*fling* yourself into it! To Hagar's cutting the cord, an *Umbilical* Reel, it's time for a *CELEBRATION*!"

The lively beat thundering on and into it I go, heel and toe, slowly at first, dancing in place—God, haven't done this since Ireland! as he quickens the pace—hands on hips and crossing over, feet flicking, kicking out, "Ah, *Jaysus,* that's it! Clog dance, boy, goat dance, *Bumpa, bumpa, bumpa*!" mind zigzagging as I whirl about, gathering momentum, heels flung out—and Boyne leaving a long lingering note as I begin to slow, "Wait, don't fade now, we'll give 'em a show!" and head high lifted, knees well lifted, hands down, stiff at his sides, and singing, "*Bumpa, bumpa, bumpa!*" off he goes, do-si-do, linking arms and whirling right, linking arms and whirling left, my thighs aching, his red hood flapping, "*Bumpa-bumpa-bumpa*!" to sashay forward and sashay back—faster and faster and round once more, panting, kicking, my feet still flicking, mind a blur, a whirling daze—till we spin to a dizzying stop and topple backward into these chairs!

"—O *Christ,* that's enough leaping for a *lifetime,* Gene—my heart's in my fucking teeth—and I can hear the sea blood within me!"

My own heart thumping, thighs swollen tight—as I lie sprawled, exhausted in my shirt and pants and the sweat keeps pouring off me—

"A Guinness, Gene?"

"—No, no—let me just rest."

"You sure you're all right?"

Nodding, "—You?"

"Fine, fine, just letting the organs find their proper place—a little coronary trip—Good *God,* but that was it! Bloody marvelous, Hagar! Gardens of Kew're probably *still* dancing! O *they* know who it is, all right—bringing back the dance, the old romance—and now the two of us *together* again! *Two* of us, Gene, to contend with! But you're really *sweating,* aren't you?"

"Yeah, I think I could use a bath pretty soon."

"You want to take it now or later?"

"No, now," standing and swaying, "better take it now."

Boyne getting up too, "Right, and I'll help you carry the water."

"Carry the *water*? You mean there's no hot water in the tub?"

"Never was, you get it from the tank downstairs, then carry it up."

"In what?"

"O anything that's handy, pots, pans, sometimes we've even used hot water bottles!" down the long front hall lined with his old erotic paintings, none of Ciara.

"And how many trips does this usually take?"

"To fill the tub? O no more than nine, maybe ten—twenty-five gallons I guess they hold."

"And the water isn't cold by the time you've brought up the tenth pan?"

"No, not really, you only use steaming water. It makes for a nice blend, piping hot on top and lukewarm down below."

"When's the last time you used the tub?"

"O well as you know I don't usually bathe very often, but it's perfectly reliable—an Irish tub. Here, let's find the proper pans," into the kitchen, across a blue tile floor littered with more Guinness bottles, a china cabinet, and a red-checkered tablecloth as Boyne eels round the corner into a scullery, "Ah Christ, what a bloody mess this place is and I just swept it out this morning! Let's see: copper pots, pewter pots, tin pots, cups, saucers—Ah, *here* we are!" as he hauls out a couple of large and dented dishpans, "Still seem in fairly good shape."

"And ten trips should do it?"

"O absolutely, of course! These things hold a hell of a lot of water, just don't tip 'em over on the way up, burn those sneakers right *off*, ha-ha!"

"All right, then you go first."

"A little case of the jitters, eh, boy? Well it's you that wanted the bath. See, fill it just to here, not quite to the brim—that's enough, get a good grip—now up we go." Both my hands holding this pan of scalding water with the steam rising. "Easy does it, watch you don't slip on the floorboards." And carefully up the dark, narrow stairs. "Should've turned the lights on first, I guess—steady now, one last step—then on round this corner. Still there, Hagar?"

"Yeah, don't stop!" edging precariously into the bathroom toward that wide green tub on lion's paws.

"Right, dump it—and off we go again! Have to keep up a constant rate of speed if you don't want the heat to fade."

Quickly down the stairs and back to the scullery—he's filled his pan and is out of the room before mine is halfway to the brim—passing each other on the stairs, I'm going up, he's coming down, leaning sideways to let me by—as I start down, he's on his way up again.

"Jesus, you'd think we were building the Great Wall of China!"

"Coolie labor, ha-ha!"

The water slowly rising, steam clouding the air.

"You better get in soon, Gene."

"But we've only brought up seven pans!"

"Better get in now!"

"What about the blend?"

"*Hell* with the bloody blend, I'll bring the rest up myself!"

Unlacing these sneakers and shrugging out of my clothes, a soft pile on the cold floor, this bar of Lifebuoy cupped in my hand as I slip a bare toe over the—*YOW*! *Christ,* is that hot! Scalding the skin, singeing the foot. Gotta do it, though. Must. Letting it soak for a while, you masochist, biting my lip—*Ooo! Aahh! Eeee!!* And slowly lowering into it—God Almighty, I'm being *boiled* in an Irish tub! My exposed chest shivering and the gooseflesh running up my chin as Boyne comes teetering back through the door.

"Watch your feet, lift your feet—and I'll ease it in down here!—is it hot enough?"

"You *kidding*? I feel like a fucking lobster!"

"Right, well stir it around a bit. The problem, you see, is the tank's too small and may give out at any moment."

"Seamus, will you please tell me what I'm *doing* here?"

"Having a bath in Kew!"

Out and down again he goes.

And back in a few minutes, "This one's cooler, tank's starting to fade—watch it, lift your feet again!" the water splashing in, "Still hot enough for you?"

"Hell yes, it'll be this way for hours!"

"Well let me just close this window or you'll catch your death of cold. Anything else you need, m'lord?"

"No, I'm fine," settling low in the bath.

"Something to drink, squire, while you're floating?"

"No, just a towel."

"A towel? Right y'are, bring you one of mine, sir, me own floral pattern, I'll drape it over the knob," and he closes the door behind him.

Smiling and soaking in this hot, steaming tub with my knees bent as I lather up with the Lifebuoy rub-a-dub-dub—and now back to Carnaween with all I'd ever wanted, all I'd ever dreamed, Boyne's high energy, creative support—and this last chance to recapture the past! "Biggest mistake of your *life* leaving here!" as he wheezes out another lively reel on the organ down there. "Never let you down before and have no intention of doing so now!" Limp, red-tipped phallus coming up for occasional nosings of air, water over the ears, echoes from the sea. And Ciara—Jesus! Still can't believe—He in love with her, too? Erotic paintings of my dazzling Dutch colleen—Teri screaming she's a fantasy. So little sex during the last few months, ever since my father died. Gone, those early fun-filled days when we re-created Paris to some degree, the fun wearing off as I kept working in the business and Teri became more demanding, wanting me to break from my parents, and finally couldn't live with me—But could *anyone* live with me? Primed now for flight—wanting commitment, but freedom, too—and the fear always returning, my dreams of escape—"Thank God we didn't have kids!"—She wanting two before she's thirty, now twenty-six, but still looking nineteen as on the day I met her: jogging one morning through Central Park not long after returning from Ireland, I was gazing up past Fifth Avenue's tall wall of buildings at a drab, blank sky, dreaming again of rain and grass, trees and paths, when crashing into me around a leafy curve came a green-eyed girl on a gray Arab mare—off she fell and down I went—and as she rose smiling like Sabrina Fair and I helped her to her feet, there was this whinnying collision behind us of horses and saddles, riders and bridles, and squealing fifth-grade girls—"Gene, the point is the marriage has been over for some time now!"—And the next night meeting down in the Village at the White Horse Tavern for cheeseburgers and porter as we huddled together in a backroom booth and Teri, slender blend of lash, gleemouth, and glow, told me all about her nineteen-year-old life: growing up in Fargo, North Dakota, dirt poor with a drunken father and a brother who really raised her, three semesters at nearby Moorhead State before running off and getting married to the first boy who asked her—"Just to get to Minneapolis, and that lasted a year (he turned out to be a Peeping Tom), and when I eventually got over that, I packed up my one suitcase and nine pairs of jeans and took a Greyhound bus to New York to study art or really, as I said to myself at the time, find fame and fortune as a model, but you had to be five-eight and skinny as a rail, so I wound up teaching riding in Central Park and then ran into you, the first writer I've ever met, who it turns out lives just around the corner from the Parke-Bernet!" And a few weeks later driving up to the University of Massachusetts for a Pest Control Conference as my father's representative and sneaking Teri along (my mother already worrying about my "dating a *shiksa* so much," and Teri increasingly torn between returning to North Dakota and wanting to stay with me). In our heated needs and the early days of fall as up the Merritt Parkway we drove at dusk, our conversation florid and warm as we sped past leafy Greenwich with its lack of squalor, snuggles and teasing laughter, and, filled with the desire to escape the car, I went veering off on the embankment, to doff my sneakers, her loafers, and race hand-in-hand across a dark field of grass, tumbling and sinking down, kissing and clinging and fumbling over her breasts and rising thighs, her hips revolving as she kept sighing and moaning—and her voice suddenly shattering the air: "Gene, let's go back to the car, someone might see us." And never really accepting her all these years, so wishing she were another free-spirited Ciara, and now she's filed for divorce—

BOOM!!!

Christ, what the hell was *that*?

Boyne lurching headlong through the door, "*Hagar, Hagar,* let's go, we have to get out of here *now*!"

"What *happened*?"

"Water heater blew sky high—bomb was meant for me!"

"What bomb?"

"In the heater, water heater—probably plastic explosive in the boiler—anyway we'll go to my show by boat!"

"Boat? *What* boat? You have a boat here, too?"

"Of course, picked one up in the rushes, be in Chelsea in an hour, the grand entrance, the two of us together again cruising down the Thames, singing the whole way in—Ready?"

"Ready, ready!" as I swing dripping out of this bath to towel off with his floral pattern and, quickly dressing, zipping up my pants, come bounding down the stairs, the smell of the explosion filling the air—and Boyne tossing me a matching Irish sweater, "Jesus, we're going to look like twins, Seamus!" that I pull blinking over my head.

"Through the bloody looking-glass!—O Good *God*, nearly forgot my paintings!" dashing into his studio and back in a flash with an artist's portfolio under his arm, "We're off!"

Outside the wind still blustery and that gray sky gusting along as we go galloping down the narrow towpath, gulls wheeling and shrieking over the trees, and Boyne knifing through the poplars past this damp sloping shrubbery, "See, there's our Donegal trawler and the pier, wharf, or whatever the hell it's called!" to a small white dock with an old bobbing fishing boat some twenty feet long as we broad jump aboard, the deck loudly creaking—a bewildered-looking dragon with its foot in its mouth painted above the wheel, and the Thames seething and receding.

"That the name of the boat?"

"—What? O right, right," *The Good Ship Wino* stenciled on a life buoy, "and the dragon's my trademark, after the Book of Kells—be worth a bloody fortune someday!"

A couple of dinghies gliding by the glowing seaside cottages with Boyne crouching low. "And you can really handle this?"

"Of course, I'm a superb navigator, Gene! Clear seas, stiff breeze, zip all about, another Vasco da Gama—do a good twelve, fifteen knots, perfect for escape!"

"But why're they trying to kill you? Will anyone gain by your death?"

"Nobody, I'm not worth a farthing, a bloody sou!"

"But who?"

"*Who, who, who*? You sound like a fucking owl! O Laura, I suppose, get Tory free and clear, creditors, old lovers' husbands, IRA or the Prods—"

"IRA?"

"O I made some statements once to the press, 'A plague on both your houses,' wouldn't contribute to their cause—But I'd better get my garb on here—always pays to have on the proper garb!" Boyne fitting a sou'wester over his beret and slipping into a yellow slicker, his grizzled beard ruffling in the breeze, before giving the engine a swift kick as it shudders into life.

"And you really know what you're doing?"

"O *absolutely,* smoothest ride you'll ever have, I'm most adept at nautical things, boats and the like—Well hell, it's in my blood, God bless—I was *named* for an ancient river!" and slamming the throttle forward, we go speeding away with the *Wino* slapping roughly through the waves, "Now where?"

"'Now *where*'?"

"Ha-ha! just testing you, Gene, see if you're paying attention! That's Strand-on-the-Green 'cross there with her bay-windowed houses—no one behind us, so I'll just nip round these barriers, buoys, various flotsam and jetsam—never remember if it's right or left, port or starboard, who the bloody hell knows, probably end up at Wimbledon serving for the match! And time to break out the wine!" Boyne reaching under the wheel and holding up a green slope-shouldered bottle labeled with that bewildered-looking dragon with its foot in its mouth.

"This isn't the same stuff we got drunk on seven years ago?"

"Essentially, yes, Flynn and Dungannon's ancient blend, now revived! Threw in half of my savings or Sligo's quids before mice invaded the chateau, our enterprise went defunct—though they still want to buy out my share!"

"I never knew there were vineyards in Ireland."

"O, of course, Glengarriff, my mother's home, down the southern coast where palm trees rub branches with bamboo. But Good God, they were drinking wine when the King of Ireland in the sixth century, Murktagh mac Erca, a relative of mine, had his palace set afire by an avenging woman, dove into a malmsey butt to avoid the blaze, and was drowned to close out a dynasty! But here, Gene, use my opener, my phallic corkscrew—there, right!"

Quick spin, the cork popping free, and I fill his glass and mine to the brim.

"In other words it's the sort of wine given to you in times of stress or under duress by a bearded Celtic satyr! Ready?"

"Ready."

"First swirl it round to bring up the bouquet, plunge in your nose to breathe the aroma, then a brief sip before swilling it down."

". . . *Wow*!"

"Well?"

"*Jesus*!" still smiling and licking my lips. "This stuff is *nectar*!"

"Didn't I tell you, Hagar? Here," Boyne draining his glass in a gulp, "Ah, that's the taste, frisky, coltish—just a hint of nymphomania—O *great* gulping wine!"

"Yeah, and we'll probably be blind by the time we get in."

"Absolutely! the two of us *together* again—but now, Gene, see if you can come up with a weather report on the BBC, radio's in that compartment."

> ". . . *The inshore forecast from Sheerness to Dover, including sea area Thames and the outer estuary: Fresh to strong northwesterly winds, force five to six, good visibility, becoming moderate to poor in showers. Gale warnings have been posted—*"

"O Christ, the seas're whitecap and the winds're twenty knots, toss of the roaring main! Though, of course, boy, what it really means is we're probably in for a bloody monsoon! 'Cause you never believe what these people say, they're always off by a couple of days, like Stonehenge, rattling the bones! Here, let's shut this off—you ready for another swirl?"

"Not right now."

"Yea-ah, well nothing like this wine when the game is afoot, adventure brewing—Come on, just a final toast to lubricate the larynx!"

"All right, last one."

And refilling our glasses as we breeze into clear water, cleaving the waves, and under this concrete bridge, waves rocking the stern with the river sharply curving now—and Boyne suddenly singing, "*Gentlemen songsters off on a spree, doomed from hea-ah to eternity*!" the trawler tossing, riding the fierce, churning tide with me bracing one hand against the side—

"*SEAMUS, LOOK* OUT!!!" A giant prow heading straight for us.

"—What? O Good *GOD*!!" and he swerves furiously out of the way, narrowly missing a rusty unmarked tanker, "—*Sons of bitches*, they nearly ran us *down*!" the towering black stern sliding past, spreading a foamy fan in its wake, "—You all right, boy?"

Mutely nodding with gulls shrieking low through the blustery air and my heart still hammering away.

"Ah, but no need to fear, Hagar, with me at the helm—hell, even da Gama ran aground off the coast of Mombasa!" by warehouse walls and power station chimneys, Boyne taking another long belt of his wine under the shadow of Battersea Bridge—"And that's Cheyne Walk up there where Turner climbed upon his roof posing as 'Admiral Booth' and sketched the dawn from his railing! Had himself lashed to a bloody spar—but of course you know that story: four hours in the teeth of a gale on the deck of the steamboat *Ariel* so he could get the desired effect? Even tried it myself once during a thunderstorm, tied myself to the greenhouse, got waterlogged and nearly drowned! But *now*, Hagar! *Now's* the time to do it! Here, boy, take the wheel—" The boat careening left.

"What the hell are you *doing*? We've got to get to your show!"

"Kick danger right in the arse, only way to respond, never give 'em the satisfaction of showing fear, stiff upper lip and splendid erections!" and Boyne goes climbing, clambering atop the cabin in his sou'wester and yellow slicker, "Make the grand entrance and we'll *really* give 'em a show!" with the boat wildly pitching to and fro.

"Seamus, will you get *down*!" as he staggers and hangs on to the flagpole, "You're going to *fall off*!" trying to slow the motors, steady the wheel, and not jar him loose!

"*Nonsense,* boy!" his chin high, beard rustling, and the whites of his eyes gleaming with that fiery myopic glare, "—Here, you *bastards,* take your best bloody shot—with Runty Billy up there, *Hannibal Crossing the Alps, Burning of Parliament*—and now *The RETURN of Seamus Boyne*!!"

His chin still high under the billowing sou'wester, gripping the slender pole behind him as I keep struggling with this wheel against the buffeting slap of the waves, spray slicing across my face, "Seamus, get down, will you, before you *kill* yourself, we've gotta get going!"

"—*Going*! Going *where*?"

"To your *show,* goddamn it!" desperately trying to steer her straight rather than go listing crazily about like a toy boat in a bathtub!

"O Jaysus, Gene—*absurd, absolutely* absurd my going! We're staying hea-ah, right hea-ah for the evening—take the *Wino* down the Thames past Greenwich and Gravesend and round to Carnaween—Erin's green and fragrant shore!"

"Yeah, OK, OK, but first just get the hell *down*!" The *Wino* angling in toward those houseboats—then back out into the rapidly shifting current, cruisers veering widely out of our way.

"—Who *cares* what those whorish critics say? Never giving us our due, nor appreciating Turner in his lifetime'n killing off Van Gogh, Cézanne, Gauguin, and Amedeo Modigliani—"

"Christ, we're really going to *crash* this time! I don't know how to steer this fucking boat!" easing the throttle back with one hand and still fighting the wheel with the other.

"Such bloodsucking queers they are! Who in the hell *needs 'em*?"

"—But everybody's *waiting* for you!"

"Yea-ah, all my fans and hangers-on, Hagar!" Boyne reaching up now with both hands to adjust his sou'wester—and nearly falling off—blindly clutching the flagpole behind him as the boat keeps thrashing vainly about, "—Ah, the high-wire balance's still thea-ah, boy, like one of those Flying *Wallendas*!" his beard gray-flecked like foam in the eerie river light, that manic, ear-to-ear grin, his chin raised high again, and the current sweeping us back toward those jutting rocks and sheer stone wall looming far above—as a helicopter suddenly appears out of the dark with its deafening rotors rattling, "*Down,* Hagar, duck *down*! pretend we've never noticed, are fisherfolk trawling for *cod*!"

"In the *Thames*?"

"Of course—*Irish,* have no idea of direction!" The helicopter hovering low like a bright-eyed dragonfly, then abruptly whirling by. "See, see! Just 'cause I'm paranoid doesn't mean the whole world's not trying to *kill* me!" and dropping to his knees, Boyne quickly clambers down, holding on to his sou'wester. "Treacherous goddamn *voyage,* ha-ha! Surveillance from the skies, M15—probably *knew* I was coming by—Right, and I'll take over the wheel now, boy," toward this weird-looking bridge, "Ah, Albert's blazing Tinkertoy!" under we go, "and guide her *myself* to Ireland—"

"Like *hell* you will!"

"—Gene, get your bloody hands *off*!"

Wrestling with him for the wheel as I force it to the left—"No, we're going to your *show*!"—then lurching round to the right, "Seamus, your *Comeback* Show, greatest show of your *career*!"

"*No,* no need to *go*! Surrounded by that world of hyenas all scavenging and waiting to pounce—feeding off people like us, feeding off gossip, off fear and the bad news to salve their own *souls*—"

"But everybody'll be there—"

"*Precisely,* and that's just why going means pinning me *down,* and the point, whole point, of my life has always been *not* to be defined just by one's art—this's the *American* way, this's what happens to an artist, what's been happening to *me,* no other reality exists—" The *Wino* now floundering waywardly about. "—But Good *God,* there are far more aspects of a person that—as Courbet said, 'To be not only a painter but a man'—"

"Seamus, *goddamn* it, will you let *go*!" both of us still battling for the wheel through this fiercely surging current, heading once more toward those rocks.

"—And that's why you're coming with me—'cause in Ireland you can exist in *spite* of your art! You're a man *first*—the artist *always* more important than his work!"

"But you *are* more important, Christ, you've *always* been more important!"

"—Yea-ah, but if I fail now," his eyes shining with tears, "lose my daughter, that's it, nothing more for me to do but join *Turner* up there! Narrowed it all down to this—pinning my life on one bloody *vision*, one bloody *show*!"

"But there'll be *other* shows, other—"

"No, no, not if this fails, lose my girl—no *more*! And I can't go back to that house, to Ireland again without her, without success—I couldn't *face* it again, never paint again, can't take the solitude anymore, being alone—Gene, I *can't* go, I-I don't *want* to go! I don't want to *face* it!!"

"But what'll it matter if you face it or *not*? It doesn't matter to the reviewers, so you might as well go and *forget* about tomorrow, hell with it, and what happens, *happens*! Your appearance's not gonna influence the reviews one way or the other, it's your *work* that counts—and of course you'll paint again, you've been doing it all these years while I let the years drift *by*—"

WHOMP!! The sound of splintering wood!

"*Jesus,* what the hell'd we *hit*?" looking up at the long concrete pier, an oily zigzag of colors coating the lapping waves, "Seamus, you OK?"

"—My whole life wasted, gone astray—O *God,* Hagar, you just don't *know*!"

"Where the hell are we? What, what don't I know?"

"—and now they're taking my *girl* away, my *only* child!" tears glistening down his cheeks, "stealing her from me, I should say!"

"Though we seem to be staying afloat—Seamus, hey, easy, take it easy—"

"And I can't do a thing *about* it—*nothing,* not a bloody thing!"

"That's not true, going back next week—But how're we gonna get *up* there?"

"O Mother of Christ, Gene, had all these dreams and marvelous plans for her—"

"—nothing to tie on to—"

"—my wife leaving me when I needed her the most—"

"Maybe those ladders, all rotted away—Well so has mine—"

Boyne still crying and shaking his head, "—And the judge won't care—what the hell's a judge care for shows or lasting fame? Just a facade—thought I could evade it, not have to face it, always figured I had time, more time—O God, I *tried,* Gene, I did, I really did—"

"Seamus, will you *listen* to me!" The sky growing darker.

"—and now I've lost my daughter, lost her *forever*! You have any idea, Hagar, what it's like to lose a *daughter*?"

"Seamus—" easing the throttle forward and gliding on through the choppy water.

"And they give her everything, every bloody thing she wants back there, back where they cut your balls off with a smile! Gene, they're *killing* me! Those bastards back there are *killing* me—but she's *still* my girl and she'll come back—you wait, just wait, one day she'll come looking for me, come seek me out, that burnished little girl—'cause there's a card, have a postcard from her at my house, 'I'll never forget the Museum'—" Bumping hard against a piling, Boyne rapidly blinking and glancing up. "Jaysus, where the hell are we? Ah, Chelsea Embankment's up there—then this *has* to be Cadogan Pier—nobody ever find us here!"

"Right, and your show's in Cadogan Square, so let's get going! Though how the hell're we gonna get *up* there, use a pole vault?"

"No, there're ladders, Hagar, *always* ladders!"

"Yeah, all rotted away, pier's probably been condemned," rounding the far end, debris in the water and bollards above.

"So? So much the better—but you worry too much, always worried too much!"

"I'm worried about your boat."

"No fear, just back her in—Here, I'll tell you when to cut it—*Now!* There you go, right, perfect!" and he loops a bicycle chain round a piling, "Knew you were a born sailor all the time!" the boat knocking against these rotting timbers.

"Yeah, but how're we supposed to get *up*? We're still two feet below this ladder, which only has three rungs."

"Well then, I'd best scramble up and tie her down—"

"Scramble up *how*? It's way the hell above us! Listen, there's another ladder down there—"

Removing his slicker and sou'wester, "And I'd better not fall in—'cause you fall in that, Gene, you decompose—nothing lives in there except Godzilla or the Beast from Forty Fathoms, ha-ha!"

"Just be careful!"

The boat riding the choppy swells as Boyne in his tilted beret, Irish sweater, and gray seersucker shorts goes scrabbling up past the missing rungs—and onto that dark, deserted pier with Chelsea Embankment high above, cars zooming by—and not a sound.

"*Seamus*?" as I glance all around.

"—Right *he-ah,* Hagar! And gather up my paintings, would you, please, 'cause it's going to pour, really rain—Christ, any minute now!"

"Yeah, well you sure you want to leave the boat here, not worried about thieves, the harbor patrol?"

"Good *God* no, let 'em drink my wine, boy, good business there! Anyway, let me give you a hand, Gene, just lock the galley, douse the hurricane lamps—"

And with my blue raincoat slapping and flapping all about, he lifts me clear, "—So where the hell are we now, Chelsea?"

"Chelsea? Impossible, I wouldn't be caught *dead* in Chelsea, ha-ha!" moving quickly along the pier toward that corrugated tin fence, "Absolutely marvelous entrance, Hagar, sly, secretive, catch them unawares!"

"Yeah, 'bout the only ones who know we've arrived are the gulls and a few water rats!"

"Ah, there!" Boyne opening a narrow flap in the fence, "See, *always* a way out!" and up this covered gangway to the abrasive whoosh of cars and buses rumbling down the Embankment as we go trotting across the road and through these flower gardens, "Good *God,* we're on Cheyne Walk with Turner's pub, the Ship and Bladebone, less than an ass's roar from here—you feel like a drink now, Gene?"

"No, let's just get to your show!"

Flagging a cab to 62 Cadogan Square and round the corner into the Kings Road with Chelsea flying by outside.

"Isn't that Sloane Square up ahead?"

"Right, right, and I'm in and out: ' 'Lo, bye.' Whip in, wipe out—and just look at all those bloody *cars*!"

"Relax, that's only a taxi stand," streaking past Cadogan Gardens toward a high-windowed Georgian house with wrought-iron fences and a stucco and latticed facade, "That looks like it, people going in."

"All of 'em going *in,* ha-ha, then I'm going *out*! See you!" pushing open his door to hop outside—as I haul him back inside and slam it shut.

"—Seamus, *Christ,* I'm telling you it'll be over in a flash, give them the grand entrance!" and we pull up in front with a screeching splash.

"Grand, ha-ha, yea-ah!" adjusting his beret, "Well hell, Gene, bugger *all*!" and leaping to the curb, he swaggers flamboyantly in.

Lights glowing, faces gleaming, his paintings lining the walls—

"O he's *HERE,* he's *HERE*!!" "Mr. Boyne is finally here!!" "We wondered where you *were*!" "Please, *everybody*—Ladies and gentlemen—excuse me, please, but this is Seamus *BOYNE*!"

His manic grin, a wave of his hand, Irish music filling the air—

Jesus, what an entrance!

"Uncle *Seamus*!" a pretty girl kissing his cheek and taking the portfolio, "We've been waiting so long for these!" then introducing him to a host of admirers as I keep anxiously glancing around, feeling the excitement and glow, as though his show is actually mine—

"Ah, *Hagar,* m'boy, come here 'n' meet all these aesthetic people! Gene himself is a poet, a true poet—and my *friend,* which is *far* more important! God bless us, this is true! But you've already met Flynn's niece of nineteen, Jennifer Breen, who's off to Ireland on the champagne flight!"

"Seamus has told us so much about you—"

"And this is Herr Mumble and Dr. Jumble, and they've both come to *buy,* ha-ha! And that's the sensual bride of Dr. J from Roslyn, L.I.—Gloria, yes. Well Gene hea-ah is from Great Neck where the rich people live, came all this way to *guide* me!"

Jennifer's wide eyes staring at me, "Are you Irish also?"

"*Hagar*? Good *God* no, he's an Ivy League *Jew*!"

"O don't tell me you're *Jewish*?"

"All right, I won't tell you."

"No, seriously, I didn't mean it that way, it's just you don't look it at all, resemble the common stereotype, you know?"

"*Ah,* and here're my elegant patrons, Vi and Brenda—Gene, I'd like you to meet the sisters Sligo-Moeran, descendants of Normans, Elizabethans, and Cromwell's conquering army—and the owners of all you survey!"

These two sharply contrasting biddies: one wrinkled and matronly, in a gray tweed suit, with a flat, unblinking stare, tapping a riding crop in her hand, and the other clinging to her flaming youth, wearing a pinkish pastel print and trailing a wispy feather boa, exclaiming, "O Mr. Boyne, we're so terribly, *terribly* excited that you came!"

"Brenda, please!"

Lightly pianoing her fingertips across his cheek, "All this is so stimulating—"

"Brenda!"

"—for I simply *adore* your work," then frolicking merrily around him, "it just opens me up completely—"

Thwack! Vi's riding crop striking her thigh.

"And you still *look* so wonderful!"

Thwack!

"*Smell* so wonderful!"

Thwack, thwack!

"*Feel so—*"

"Easy, my dears, easy— But tell me, Jennifer, has the reviewer been here yet?"

"Well, John Russell and Terence Mullaly are due any moment, along with Brian Fallon from the *Irish Times,* Guy Brett and Nigel—"

"No, no, I mean the *LONDON Times,* Kenneth Clark, only one that *counts*!"

"O yes, well, he's on his way, taking William Gaunt's place, who's on holiday, and he said he would ring up later with his review—"

"*His* review, Christ!" and tossing back a drink from a passing tray, "The critics called Turner's *Snow Storm* a mass of 'soapsuds and whitewash'!" Boyne leads all of them away through the appreciative crowd with Brenda linking herself to his right arm and the busty Mrs. Jumble to his left—

"Gloria, please."

"Gloria, of course! 'For there once was a *girl* name of Gloria who was had by Sir Gerald DuMaurier, and then by six men, Sir Gerald again, and the band at the Waldorf-Astoria'—"

"Pardon, but I am Laetitia Marengue," an aging Zsa Zsa Gabor shaking my hand with her slim, beringed fingers, European accent, plucked eyebrows, and blue dirndl skirt, "And you are Mr.—?"

"Hagar."

"Yes, well we wondered, Mr. Jagar—"

"*Hagar.*"

"*Ha*gar. Terribly sorry. We wondered where you *were.*"

Draping my raincoat over my sleeve, "Well we came by boat, Donegal trawl—"

"By boat? O how charming, by boat. And here—Ordway? *Ordway*? (He is a little deaf, you see.) For Mr. Hagar, a drink, please? There you are."

My hand now holding—what, Ordway? Irish Mist—and down it goes with such smoldering bliss as I roam milling round this room filled with gawky, pallid-faced girls, the blood rushing up to apple their cheeks with a soft pink stain—and where the hell is Boyne? Where'd he *go*? Suddenly all alone as I glance about—and what am I doing here, back to my wild salad days, wayfaring Hagar aloft on the wind? Nostrils flaring at the heady gust of stud in the air, "There he goes, girls, get him!" Confidence waning, feeling so uneasy again, a shadow of my former self—No, younger girls love older guys, married guys, guys over thirty. So says Teri—and she ought to know—now faraway in Fargo! Once telling me of calling an old beau, unseen since college, just to hear his voice, and hanging up when he answered. And a whole *world* of girls out there, new generation hopping from bed to bed while I nuzzled, nestled into my wife's warm womb—these chance girls of Chelsea now smiling at me. But what do I say? Offering lines of the fifties? Have no idea how to talk to girls anymore, just grunt and Teri understands. Now back to small talk, the old savoir faire? Hagar, the fair-haired—Still, *whatever* I say and *however* I look, worn and musty in my carefree style, it sure beats the hell out of killing roaches!

And *there's* Boyne, moving upstairs beside Vi and Brenda—and Flynn's "niece," lithe Jennifer Breen, a slim colleen—Come live and dance in Carnaween! Christ, she probably would, too!—heading toward that office door. These slender, graceful girls in orange slacks and sandals, fine dark hair chopped at the collar, the gloss of natural make-up—and this passing conversation: "Hi, I'm Mary Rabbit." "What kind of name is that?" "It's Irish, actually, it used to be O'Hare"—as I brush by hopsack, tweed, and summer plaid—a turn of their gaze to suffer my Irish sweater, slacks, and these Adidas sneakers still somewhat damp—and if you've guessed Joyce, James Augustine, madam—no, merely a mask!

A bagpipe's distant skirling up there and Boyne's brilliant paintings here of lovers embracing in a shimmering swirl of sea greens and aquamarines—Jennifer and the stately Laetitia now placing all of Ciara's unframed lusty poses atop wooden runners on those bare alcove walls—And, Jesus, will you *look* at those poses! which no one has ever seen: spread like a centerfold upon a bed, amid a flaming sky of gold and magenta, stroking the insides of her thighs; another holding her girlish breasts, those firm, glistening globes; or playing with herself, eyes closed in orgasm, pubic hair, and nipples erect—I'm growing erect! And these BBC accents gasping in awe: "I say, frightfully blonde, isn't she?" "Indeed! Frightfully blonde." And all I did was *describe* her! as I turn away, raincoat cloaking my pants, and go brushing by these swishy men, light laughter, their high-heeled boots, buff-colored crushed velvet suits, dark glasses, and ascots of foulard, hands on hips, limp wrists dangling—can't get through. "Well first of all she was raped when she was thirteen." "By who?" "Freddie." "Then who'd she marry?" "Freddie." "And what does Freddie do?" "Just mooches around the Nag's Head with a boxer and doesn't say boo to a goose—O hi!" his liquid eyes drinking me in, "I'm Henri," offering his fishy hand, "*Enchanté.*" All their snickering smiles eager to play—but I'm off the other way—

Ordway tottering past with another Mist—and Boyne upstairs or already fled to the *Wino,* set sail for Erin? No, hearing that thunderous chortle and Dungannon's bagpipes bleating as I wedge on by these candlestands, people stepping aside with a polite shift of their feet—and I'd better go find him *now*! Someone trying to kill him? The crowd oohing and aahing before Ciara's carnal poses, re-created from my words.

Past the whitewashed walls and two-at-a-time up these carpeted stairs, knees thick with wine and Irish Mist, through a small, latticed-windowed room, and down this long passageway leading into a large organ loft and a sprawl of worn and upholstered chairs, floor-to-ceiling windows—and a rousing Irish jig gleefully pealing out over a circling crowd with Boyne and Brenda, Herr Mumble, Dr. and Gloria Jumble all in the center dancing away, bagpipes bleating, a *bodhran* beating, and someone with a brogue shouting my name:

"O Jaysus, Mary, and José, *Gene,* how the hell've ya *been*?" Flynn's freckled hands slapping me on the back over and over, orange curls and mustache reeling, "It's *grand* seein' ya again!" his chunky little body crammed into brown twill slacks and a tan turtleneck sweater (hasn't changed a bit with that same puggish face!) and holding me at arm's length, "Hell, yer lookin' more like a Paddy every day and we're only just arrivin' ourselves!" The crowd still carrying on, vigorously stamping their feet and clapping their hands as Flynn keeps thrusting people into the dance. "—And Gene, haven't seen ya since, where was it now, Dublin or Delgany years ago?" and glancing around, "And here, Lord love him's Dungannon again, the Iceman Coombeth with his bloody bags soundin' like the parrot house at the zoo!" Towering Dungannon glowering down, piping a two-note greeting à la Harpo Marx, then letting a shrill note sail, wheezing wail, and squeezing my hand with a strong meaty grip before getting back to his spirited reel—his bald dome shining, gray eyes smiling from the face of Eugene O'Neill, paisley shirt open at the collar, green kilt and sporran, and his left cheek ballooning as he inflates the bags, festooned with ribbons and a scarlet plume—"But listen, Gene," Flynn leaning close, "we'll have us a natter later, since this riotous throng's been clamorin' to hear me song!" and turning back to cheers and applause, he belts out "*I'll tell me ma when I go home, The boys won't leave the girls alone—*" as Boyne, jigging by with his tilted beret, Irish sweater, and those gray seersucker shorts—"Ah, Hagar, *there* you are! Come join the Irish frakaa!"—yanks me into this high-spirited dance and around we go, rapidly blinking, heel and toe, "*—They pulled me hair, they stole me comb, but that's all right till I get home—*" "Caught in this sensual music, Gene, like that marvelous sea-rider Oisín!" feet flicking, kicking out as we keep whirling and jigging about, "*—She is handsome, she is pretty, she is the belle of Dublin City—*" and somebody shouting from the wall, "Seamus, which is your latest work?" "—My 'latest'? Well Good *God,* right *here's* my latest—old Johnny Thomas, alias Wing Wang Wong, the father of 'em *all*—" and starting to lower his shorts, "give you a private showing—" "Seamus, *no*!!" grabbing his hand, "—of the longest balls in Christendom, a bloody glockenspiel!" "*—Out she comes white as snow—*" "—Genitalia *glorioso*!!" and guiding him into a do-si-do, "Ah, but modesty prevents—" as around we go, "—revealing my Etruscan fig leaf, for I must tap a kidney now!" the bagpipes bleating, "And Gene," Flynn grinning as I spin by, "here's a fine girl for you!" flinging someone into my arms—"Stop!"—Nordic cheekbones, tiptilted nose, straight blonde shoulder-length hair—*Jesus,* I *must* be dreaming—

"*Ciara?—*"

"My God, *Gene—*"

"—what're *you* doing here?"

"A girl by the name of Ciara Glasheen!"

"—Have you seen those *paintings* downstairs?"

"O that lying son of a bitch!" as we keep on jigging—bearded Celtic satyr, my ass!—staring at her yellow-sweatered nipples, tight blue denim skirt, and that same glorious hair!

"Let the wind and the rain and the hail blow high,

And the snow come travelin' through the sky—"

"—I mean I could not believe what I *saw*—" My dazzling girl before me! still so lovely, hardly changed—someone linking her arm and whirling her left—

"Ciara, just tell me what you're *doing* here!" the jiggling lilt of her breasts, my blonde poetic dream—

"—O I remembered his name from you years ago"—Brenda linking my arm and whirling me right—"but where is he?"

"She is handsome, she is pretty,

She is the belle of Dublin City—

"Gone for a sec—You never *knew*?"

"—No, of course not!" sashaying forward and sashaying back, "I have never even *met* him!" the crowd still clapping and stamping their feet. "—And those, those *poses*! Why would anyone *paint* me like that?"

"I don't know," the blonde down shimmering on her arms—Can't tell her, never believe I only described—and the sweat of health glimmering on her brow, what I've missed all these years, her ability to make it all seem possible, be anything I want her to be—and now a last chance to recapture the past? "But what're you doing in London?" as the bagpipes keep on skirling—

"—It is where I live. And what do *you* know about this?"

"Nothing, nothing—You *do*? Milo's here, too?" a fast glance over my shoulder—

"No, no—" Herr Mumble guiding her the other way, twirling a pearl-handled cane, "we are divorced. But Gene—"

"You *are*?" Fantastic! "Since *when*?" and linking our arms again—

"O not too long ago—"

Back to Carnaween with all I'd ever wanted, all I'd ever dreamed, writer, wife, "So you've never been to Ireland yet?"

"No," she smiling, "still not yet. Though Milo was once while we were married. But Gene—"

"And would you still like to go?"

"Yes, someday, I suppose—Is that *him,* is that the artist?" as Boyne comes whirling back into the circle, grinning like a horse with his lips curling away from his teeth, and jigging straight up to us.

"Ciara, wait—"

"How dare you—"

"O Suffering *Christ,* you must be *her*!"

"—how could you possibly *paint* me like that?"

"You're even lovelier than I'd *ever* imagined! a nymph in the flesh! wondrous and golden like Leda and the Swan, Deirdre of the Sorrows—"

"But I have never even *met* you! Why did you do this, paint me like that?"

"Paint you? *Good GOD,* I'm never going to *stop* painting you—"

"It's so, so—"

"Flattering, I know, captured you completely! 'Cause I'm going to paint you *forever* in the nude with your rosy arse in the air and a host of shamrocks *laced* through your hair—just wait'll you see my sketches!"

"*—What do you think you're doing*?"

And he goes dancing away with her hand in hand, through the crowd and down the stairs!

Boyne

"She is handsome, she is pretty,
She is the belle of Dublin City!"

"Will you let me *go*!"—dashing madly along under this showery drizzle, wet plane trees silverlimned in the lamplight—"Are you *crazy*?"—and on into Sloane Square, cars all impatient at the lights, squealing past over the dark glistening streets—"Where do you think you're *taking* me?"

"Down to my boat, my Donegal trawler, give you the grand tour along Old Father Thames by Greenwich and Gravesend and back to Carnaween!"

"All right, Mr. Boyne, enough is enough now—"

"Seamus, Seamus, the painter Seamus—"

"Yes, all right, Seamus—"

"—who tonight is famous!" as I continue waltzing deftly along the curb with the Astaire light step and spin, around and around and pop, pop the cane, the dancer set loose in the streets, "Bring back the dance, the old romance—Whee, ha-ha!" pirouetting round this zebra post with her in my grasp—and into a waiting cab, splashing down the Kings Road with this wondrous girl beside me, "And your hair, like silken sun sifting through my fingers, so like my daughter's, my lovely Tory—!"

"Your *daughter*?"

"Of course, the same childlike gossamer grain," and I can't keep my hands off her, caressing her taut, Modigliani nape—

"You have painted her also?"

"Absolutely! One of the essential ways we remain close. And your skin is, mmm, like strawberry shortcake, pink and beautifully smooth—"

"Yes, well, I am afraid I am not on the menu tonight."

Letting out a joyful guffaw, "*Marvelous, ha-ha!*"

"You think that is funny, do you? I am not joking."

To Cadogan Pier, down the covered gangway and through this corrugated tin fence, thunder rumbling in the distance—"Ah, the *Wino*'s still here!"

"Look, really now, Mr. Boyne—"

"You can climb on my shoulders or I could use the fireman's carry—"

"—why don't you just post me your sketches?"

"—no, better I take the lead on the ladder and then you follow—as long as you don't run away."

"And why would I ever do that? But really, I think this has gone far—"

As I go stepping gingerly down, the boat bobbing on the stormy swells and moored by that bicycle chain, rungs creaking, breaking—

"Watch out!"

"*O Mother of Christ*!" and plummeting feet first toward the Thames far below, high tide, suspended in time—rapidly falling—and crashing into the water with a cannonball wake! thrashing and heaving wildly upward—I'm still *alive*!—debris all around me, blinking and frantically dog-paddling—awaiting Godzilla or the Beast from Forty Fathoms—"*Help, help, help*!!" raising one hand above the waves.

And Ciara hesitating a moment before plunging in with a perfect swan dive, her blonde hair flaring backwards—a neat, nearby splash!—and finally reaching me, her splendid, radiant face growing clear as I let out another bellow of laughter, "*Ha-ha*!"

And she releases her lifeguard's grip, "But you—you *can* swim!"

"Why of course I can! I'm an Olympic freestyler, Junior Red Cross—"

"No, what you really are is a *lunatic*," pushing me under, "out of your mind!"

And grabbing my beret as I surface spouting like Moby-Dick, before scrambling swiftly over the gunwale, then hoisting her up—

"You really are insane!" sweeping blonde strands from her eyes with a quick, defiant gesture.

"No, just sensationally sane, dear girl, but come on into the cabin where there's wine and cheese and towels galore, key opens door!"

"Look at me! Look at *you*!" and she grinning ironically as I flop the soggy beret atop my scalp, water cascading down, "You don't even have any hair!"

"The surest sign of virility!" and I go ducking low toward the cabin below with boxes, bottles, and paperback books all piled together, "Here, just toss these out of the way, light the hurricane lamp, nice'n cozy, plenty of room," two flat foam rubber cushions on either side against the walls, long, pale blue, to sit on, "And there's even a loo back there, 'cause you'd best get out of your clothes."

"O really? And what do you suggest I wear?"

"Ah, well," gazing all around, "how 'bout my slicker and sou'wester? Love to paint you in those, like Winslow Homer, *Gulf Stream, Kissing the Moon,* or a Degas nude brushing out her hair—and meanwhile, I'll break open a case of wine!"

She shutting the door behind her with a huff as I strip briskly down to the buff and wrap myself in this soft quilted comforter, then shortly thereafter the loo door creaking open and—"*SWEET JAYSUS*"—Ciara shaking out her tawny tangles, "What a *vision* you are, like Venus on the half shell, sheer ripeness and bloom—you're all the inspiration I need!"

"*Inspiration*? And what was your inspiration to put me in all those *poses,* drag me away with you here?"

"Feel like Pygmalion with Galatea, Higgins with Eliza Doolittle, or Renoir with Gabrielle Renard—"

"But I have never *seen* you before tonight!"

"—which surely calls for, here, a toast of Irish wine!"

"No, I had too much at your show already."

"Nonsense, my dear! And anyway, it's what I put of myself in the painting that counts."

"Then you should have painted yourself, not me! Why didn't you use Irish models?"

"Irish models, Christ! Irish girls won't even take their knickers off! For as long as they remain on, they don't consider themselves nude—and therefore, as an artist, I have to imagine, if you will, their furry pubis, mons veneris, soft floral labia—"

"Good, well you go right on imagining because—"

"—and like Turner with Mrs. Booth, Picasso with Dora Maar, or Rembrandt with his beloved Saskia, I'm obsessed with the memories of sexual pleasure, a celebrator not a denier! But Jaysus, you look so cold just standing there, come sit here beside me, all nice'n cozy, Ciara, or nice'n Ciara, cozy."

"No, I'm fine," now sipping her wine, "But you are Irish, yes?"

"No one is more Irish than a Boyne from Valhalla, New York!" as I take a nervous breath, "Do you like the wine?" and she sits across from me, "I once owned the bloody vineyard."

"Yes, it is very good, but you still haven't told me how you could paint me without seeing me."

"I know, great gulping wine, frisky, coltish—"

"And where are these supposed sketches?"

"Would you care to gulp some more, 'cause you seem to be shivering—here, let me give you my comforter," opening it up.

"No, no, that is quite all right."

"O I'm sorry, sorry, I didn't mean it that way—for, really, the fact that you're finally here before me has me feeling so, well, so callow and ungainly, so outlandish and shy, like a, well, like an endangered species, a Block Island meadow vole!"

"A what?" her bewildered smile, "What is that?"

And hopping down on the floor, holding this comforter around me, "A frightened little mouse who goes whisking and frisking all about, seeking refuge from the world, shelter from the storm"—sniffing through a pyramid of boxes and bottles and paperback books—that come tumbling down on my head, she giggling despite herself—"and comfort for its paws!"

And resting below her, back against her legs, I take her hands and cradle them around me.

"And can you imagine, once I was so shy, afraid to let a girl touch me—now in this heyday of lust where I play at ram, goat-man, anything goes—for I was always a late developer, physically, athletically, sexually—though not artistically, never artistically—at four I could draw anyone who came into our house, exactly, unerringly so, an extraordinary boy with flamboyant charm, very recherché, as they say, used the same silky roundness to draw my daughter when she was that age, six years ago," sighing and snuggling warm within her arms, "and this feels so like my mother's tender cuddling while crooning Bach's 'Sleepers Awake,' forget my cares, despairs—this is the calmest I've felt since Christ knows where," and turning and staring up into her eyes.

Moored on the lordly Thames, the surging sway and drag of the tide, rainfall, seafare, wind's lash, girl's hair, a tawny shade in this hazy light—as turning, reaching forward, I gently kiss her wine-tasting lips, deliciously overripe—"I wonder how many people, Seamus, you've let see this side of you"—moving onto the cushions and hugging her close in this damp and flickering darkness, my hands fumbling under her chill yellow slicker, my breath in her ear, kissing the lobe, and caressing her hair, warm, intense kisses, roaming over the rise of her breasts, as pink and firm as I'd imagined and the nipple hard as I slowly nuzzle its round persimmon shape, sweet-tasting bud of a nipple, belly button and—*Good God*! after all these years and all those paintings, her warm sleek skin, waiting, working so alone with no escape from that feeling of black despair, and now here before me at last—as I hold her tenderly in my grasp, stroking my hands over her lissome body and kissing her knees, up her thighs, over her furry pubis like wild mountain thyme, mound of Venus, soft floral labia, the mingling aromas of blossom and brine as I keep nosing, cupping her succulent cheeks, and my finger moving inside her, spilling over, widening so, then two, all the while gently licking her clit, stroking her clit, taking it whole and sucking her clit, with her head now thrashing from side to side and she mewing, moaning, her thighs quivering, and she urging, "Come round," as I raise my legs over her mouth, both hands fondling my pulsing organ below, her thighs widening—and my cock now at full mast being softly nibbled under me, feeling her lips up to the hilt, her tongue taunting it, taking me whole in her mouth and sucking up and down and still whining, mewing, and feathering my balls, three fingers jammed within her as she starts to come, tensing and arching her spine as I hold on, my tongue probing deeper—and her mouth clenched tight, nip of her teeth, she whining louder and louder, nails digging into my pumping thighs—mind fading and I'm coming, too, pouring, flooding out of me, she still sucking, moaning, still coming as I collapse, still humming—and shift to the side under this smooth blue quilt, before cuddling closer in, her fingers caressing across my chest, bald dome—and O Christ, Ciara, you're even better in the flesh! The reality eclipsing the dream!

Turning the hurricane lamp much lower and fondling you within the nook of my shoulder as I cradle you in my arms, "God, you've been an image for so long in my life, and then suddenly here beside me—"

"Yes, and what will I become for you now?"

"—that all I can think of is what St. Augustine said, in that greatest of love lines, 'I just want you to be!' "

She staring with her lustrous eyes, then sighing and blinking, ". . . Curious, no one has ever wanted that from me," as we gently nuzzle and kiss, the rain outside increasing, thunder growing closer, the surging sway and drag of the tide, and I rise slowly to my knees, your thighs wrapping me round, drawing me down—and O Ciara, Ciara, *Christ,* what a wondrous woman you are! as I plunge wetly softly within you, deep within you, your teasing fingers gliding over my hairy chest, down my hips as I press you close, lacing your hair, silken sifting sun, and on and on—live with you now and paint like I should've every day, Turner and Bach, and the seas at Carnaween—faster and faster, side to side, rainwind spilling over the window ledge and the sounds of the river and Chelsea Embankment's road buckle, buses and bicycle bells, a pale light softwashing our soaking clothes, sneakers, and wool socks—O come live and dance with me there! *gallant lovers gaming in a gap of sunshine,* for you're all the inspiration I need, entwined, ensconced, enthralled with all the joy that lies waiting, there in that green, very special corner of the world, high among trees, overlooking the sea!—your cheeks flushed now above the blue eiderdown, wet denim skirt and yellow sweater, knickers and half bra (unneeded to hamper your sensual shape) cast across the wine: soft and gentle under the lily whites with candle lights and lemon tea and morning flesh under the summer me—as our limbs intertwine, suckling your breasts and thrusting away, getting closer, you grimacing, lashes fluttering, to the rhythmic slide and sway of this boat—rain falling all about us, raising you higher, and even faster now, though waiting, holding back with your shrieks and cries—"O Seamus, please, please, I'm so wet! O please, now, now, *now*!"—and come in a long, shuddering rush, the sperm spurting from me—your fierce spasms as they recur once, twice, again and again—and sink headlong together this muffling warmth!

Your hot, beating blood beside me, locked in each other's arms . . . To awake soon in Ireland on some rumpled green morning with the seas at Carnaween and paint you in a stunning variety of poses: like Matisse, in transparent Turkish blouses, or in purple like the Queen, rain lashing against the panes, flashes of jagged lightning—

A terrifying crash of thunder, my heart suddenly pounding with panic and fear, all of it returning: trains *roaring* round the bend! shotgun *blasts*!

And abruptly sitting up, "Let's get dressed!"

"Dressed? Why, is something the matter? Where are we going?"

Sifting through these excess clothes in the corner, "—O back to the party, of course!" tan slacks, stained black sweatshirt—

"You're not tired?"

"Not at all," pulling on a fresh pair of green-striped socks, "You've given me a second breath!" and kissing her tenderly, "a second life! Come, get dressed."

"But what will I wear?" watching her fingerbrush her hair, "I can't go as a vole."

Smiling, "Why of course you can, draped in my yellow slicker!" stuffing the fig leaf and black beret in my pockets, "You'll still look better than anyone there!"

"No, but wait, seriously, Seamus, why are you in such a hurry now," slipping on her damp sneakers, "what *is* the matter?"

As I hold her close, "Ciara, believe me, it has nothing to do with you."

And out to this driving thundershower, following her up another sturdier ladder, and along the covered gangway to Chelsea Embankment.

"Ah, here comes a cab!"

And guiding her swiftly in as he flips down the meter and we go splashing over the Kings Road's glassy sheen to Cadogan Square and this three-story brick town house with Dungannon's reedy bagpipes droning out the door, Flynn now singing, "*All you free-born men of the traveling people,*" and skipping up these gray-carpeted stairs through the smoke and whiskey-scented air, the room still wreathed with Guinness and Tullamore Dew, and this crowd of well-wishers lustily cheering my return!

Hagar

O Jesus, she trailing behind him, wearing his slicker—and nothing else underneath!! That son of a *bitch*!—as I go charging across the floor with my gut aching, eyelid really twitching, Flynn still singing—

"Ah, Gene—" "*Every tinker, rolling stone and gypsy rover*—"

"You fucking *liar*!" shoving him back.

"*Winds of change are blowing*—" "I never lie, you know tha—" "*Old ways are going*—" "Gene, please—" "*Your traveling days will soon be over.*"

"—knowing how much she meant to me!" and hauling off with a roundhouse right, snapping his bald head back—"Will you *stop*!"—my momentum tackling him down, a trickle of blood on his cheek, that manic horsey grin, "—Hagar, what on earth're you *doing*?" rolling over and over, "Phony fucking bastard!" bumping into these upholstered chairs, others shouting—"Mr. *Boyne*!" "Uncle Seamus!" "They're going to *kill* each other!" "Stop them, somebody, *please*—" Dungannon grabbing my arms, "Lemme go!" and people suddenly screaming—

"*FIRE, FIRE*!! *There's a FIRE in the GALLERY*!!!" "The gallery's all *ABLAZE*!!"

"*O Good GOD*!!"

Boyne quickly vaulting to his feet, then racing along the passageway to the bare second floor billowing with smoke and the glare of flames shooting up down there as the rest of us keep crowding anxiously behind, Vi and Laetitia pacing and wringing their hands, "The paintings are *lost,* they're all *lost*!" "Dear Lord!" "*All* of them?" "I-I don't know, we're not sure!" "But they *must* be saved, the new ones haven't even been photographed!!" and Seamus goes galloping down.

"Mr. Boyne, *NO,* you *can't*—" "Somebody *stop* him, *stop* him!" "He'll burn to death!"

O Christ! Nobody moving—*Son of a bitch*! heading after him—waving, coughing, eyes burning, sirens braying. "—I can't see a *thing*!

Seamus, get *OUT* of here, damn it!! All that booze inside him, he'll go up like a torch!" and retreating blindly through this thick, choking smoke, tears in my squinting eyes, fire engines pulling up outside—

"There he *goes*!"

And banging open this latticed window, rain barreling down, hoses blasting—as he leaps into the fire chief's car, a painting under his arm, swerving onto the curb below, tires spinning, blue lights flashing, then speeding off toward Sloane Street, "Where the hell're you *going*, you madman?" on the wrong side of the road!—and another car behind him? O Jesus!

Sprinting back along the passageway to take these stairs two-three-at-a-time and on out the door—really going to kill himself now or be killed, someone starting that fire!—over this rainslick pavement, a fading screech of tires, and into Sloane Square with no sign of him, traffic wheeling past—and where the hell'd he go? looking left and right, back to the *Wino*? Christ Almighty, my breath heaving so!—chasing my father in the rain, *Boyne wildly jigging by with his beard and beret,* everything falling apart in my hands, losing him again! traffic flying by—*O my father, raccoon eyes squinting in the sun, your double chin, reaching back for you, reaching out for you*—and I'll never catch him now, out on that stormy river—

Boyne

"*CRAZY,* Good *God,* Billy, I told you it was *crazy,* absolutely *CRAZY*"—the *Wino* seesawing desperately through these monstrous waves, thunder and jagged lightning—"nothing to do now but steer for the Tate and hang this last bloody painting *myself*!"

Force six winds and torrential rains—a steadily driving downpour—rising on white crests, cascading into dark troughs, "Never will I see my daughter again—" a stinging spray lashing across my face, "nor *Ciara* again—for as soon as I hang this portrait of her, now charred round the edges and freed from these stretchers (all those people rushing about in the smoke trying to rescue my work), Billy, I'll hang *myself* as well! Discovering my genius long after my death, but denying my struggles during my lifetime—*O Jaysus, Mary, and JOSEPH!*—"

A tidal wave of water knocking me sprawling! clawing and frantically clinging to the gunwale—

Down, down, we're going *DOWN*! *The Drowning of Seamus Boyne*—bells tolling at Lloyd's of London—and my helpless little craft hurtling round and round like the *Pequod*, farewell the Ancient Mariner!

Hagar

Trudging up this gray flight of stairs with the smell of fire still in the air as Flynn, Laetitia, Vi, and the rest all come hurrying toward me:

"Gene, what *news*?" "You *find* him?" "Is he *all right*?"

Shaking off this rainy spray, "No, no sign of him and the boat's gone, God knows where!"

"O dear Lord!"

"And where's Ciara?" looking around.

"Thought I just saw her."

"He's not dead! I'm *sure* he's not dead!"

"How do you know?"

"I just know!"

"Probably only gone back to Kew!"

"We've been calling out there—"

"O those bumblers!"

"The firemen?"

"No—I mean, yes, for nothing's survived, paintings, frames, furniture!"

"But I'm sure he's all right—"

"—has always had nine lives!"

"But he could really kill himself now—or be killed!"

"What?" "Who, Gene?" "What are you saying?"

"Someone's been trying to kill him," and slumping down into this upholstered chair, exhausted now and aching for sleep, legs lumpish, weighted, sleepy-needled feet, like a piece of old luggage flung around London as all of them keep milling about me.

"Gene, listen, why don't ya stay here for the night, 'cause there's a spare bedroom upstairs?"

"And the reviews should be comin' any minute."

"*Times* promised they'd be calling."

"Right, Clark, Kenneth Clark this is—" The phone stridently ringing, "That must be him!" as everybody goes chasing about helter-skelter for a well-positioned seat, Jennifer crashing into Laetitia, Vi colliding with Brenda, Gloria with Dungannon, Herr Mumble with Dr. Jumble, "Mother of God, will someone pick the blasted thing *up*?" and Flynn, bounding quickly over the sofa, plucks the receiver into his hand, "—Ah, Miss Binton, right!" reeling in the looping cord, "From the *Times,* of course! Ready with Lord Clark's review? Ah, that's grand, grand! And would ya be so kind as to hold on a tick?" then furiously signaling to Dungannon ("She's goin' to read it aloud!"), who flicks on a nearby intercom as the rest of them gather around.

"Ready, Mr. Flynn?" her echoing BBC voice.

"Right y'are, darlin'."

"'With a fiery light swirling in a great vortex of color, the paintings of Seamus Boyne's new show at the Sligo-Moeran inevitably call to mind the work of Turner again. Yet his paintings are realized with such an intense degree of feeling and control that their forms, though obviously derivative, acquire a vivid personal dimension and more than survive their influence—most notably the splendidly erotic nudes or the couples in naked embrace. Here is a similar explosion into color as a field of light and the treatment of paint simply as paint, many of the solid objects consumed in a brilliant, shadowless radiance. Yet the mood remains sensual and warm, shattered and melting and filled with the passionate breath of phantoms, his goals seemingly far more intimate than epic (recalling Turner's Petworth period and those private sketches that Ruskin burned). An altogether astonishing exhibit of a remarkably original genius.' "

"*O Jaysus, Mary, and José*!" Flynn ecstatically beaming—with the rest of them cheering and hugging each other—and his eyes growing glossy, "Well we've *got* to find him now!"

Boyne

Writhing, foamy seas and the *Wino* going down with this gray rain slashing across my bows—toss of the roaring main, run into another tanker bound for Bahrain or the pleasure boat to Kew!—rolling my portrait into a tighter tube and under my Irish sweater—as we keep listing and perilously drifting toward those jutting rocks and seething waves—fall in that I decompose, never paint Ciara or Tory again, my life turning out differently, ravaged by Godzilla and the Forty-Fathomed Beast!—must've sprung a leak—nothing left but to break into the Tate and hang this last bloody painting *myself*—then end it once and for all! Nearing the river wall, that emergency pier—not sure I can reach it, clutching her portrait in my fist and lifting myself onto the gunwale's sloping side—about a two-foot jump or watery grave—*Now*!

—and leaping out into space, over the darkling waves like that marvelous sea-rider Oisín—

My heels skidding, hand *smacking* the wall, the tide sloshing across my green-striped socks—but still hanging on to my painting!

And looking back as the *Wino* goes sinking and bubbling down like the *Pequod* in a surging wake!

And where the hell can I go? Cold and clammy and wet to the bone, have to find someplace to sleep, need to dry off—no idea where Ciara lives, don't even know her last name! *Damn!* Gloria staying at the Savoy, Jennifer flying out tonight, Vi and Brenda—?

Or Laetitia's Belgravia flat—handed me her address, here, somewhere on this soggy slip—and swiftly up these metal steps to hail that passing cab!

Hagar

—Boyne wildly jigging by with his beard and beret, nakedly swaying to an Irish reel—a massive wave crashing in, swallowing him up, he dying, my dream dying, can't get to him in time!—as I go racing out of my parents' house—God, don't catch me, old weathered walls, hollowed halls, stumbling down these steps, dark shadows right behind me, all my failures lost in his eyes, the aching weight of this pain and sorrow, so hard to breathe—O my father, images of you appearing, disappearing, reaching back for you, reaching out for you—fading away, flailing like a beached fish on the floor—heart pounding, bursting, running headlong through these dark, scary streets, so wet and cold—Daddy, Daddy! Where are you? working late in the office again, running to find you there, splashing through the puddles toward that blinking neon bug sign—And he's not there! I'm all alone, always alone, never there when I need him! huge black clouds closing in, disappearing—O help please, please, please HELP—

"No! No! No! No!"

Sitting straight up like a shot, panting with the sweat pouring off me and staring out at this dark, drifting room, grayish light, French windows drizzling—Boyne, Ciara? *Where the hell AM I*? Flynn, Dungannon, London—? Vi and Brenda's town house!—and still so scared, my heart hammering, been running away *all* my life! Both of them gone—and my fears of the dark, childhood fears, Teri holding me, hugging me all these years, but she's sure not holding me now!—and maybe never again! Ciara gone God knows where! with me fleeing to Ireland through flung nets, and the dream still back there!—as, leaning forward, soaked in sweat, I keep staring at my reflection on the drizzled panes: mop of floppy hair glistening in profusion, nose with its Roman bump (a wild and rowdy brown bear singed by the summer), and my father's raccoon eyes—Boyne convincing me to stay, he painting, me writing, "Christ, life is *leaping*, boy, never a lying down!" Finding other comforts, other joys—and not what others wanted me to be. The tyranny of their image, *their* fair-haired boy. So self-conscious, eager to be accepted, so busy, keeping pace. Everyone's favorite, the happy-go-lucky, All-American, glad-handing Haig. And my father saying, "When I was your age I had the same thoughts, the same ideas, but you'll see you'll change, everyone goes through phases like that. You'll look back later and see how silly your ideas were." My father, a slope-shouldered Ralph Bellamy with distinguished graying temples and double chin—could be a banker, a broker, a wealthy tycoon—with his six-in-the-morning-to-seven-at-night-and-most-Saturdays' dedication to the business, and golf his only pastime, mainly for business contacts. At Glen Oaks Sunday mornings feeling small among the rich Jewish barons: "I played in a threesome with Dr. Kronefelt of Mount Sinai Hospital and Lee Greenberg, who's vice president of Burlington Mills. These are big men." On his upstairs desk—now mine—three gold cups, one from Grossingers and two from Glen Oaks, Scotch Foursome winner, 1948, and Class C Driving Champion, 1949. His 150-yard-straight-down-the-middle game, thousands of lessons and just barely breaking 100. "They're having a cookout, Gene, next Wednesday night, a barbecue at the club. You wanna go?" Shaking my head no and my mother saying, "If he doesn't wanna go, don't force him." And rarely going, hating that garish, all-Jewish club. Like that scene at lunch last time I was there: gilded-haired mommas in gold sandals and peacock shades shoving each other aside to get their hamburger: "It's *MINE*! It's *mine*! I was here *first*!" All those aged women, tanned and wrinkled and looking like rhesus monkeys, calling each other "girl," and their husbands, financiers, captains of industry, in pastels and tasseled shoes, out on the links cutting strokes off their scores after another successful season of soaking blood from the dollar! And my father never quitting, coming back Sunday afternoons following a steam and a shower and a glad hand to all with, "They were all there. All the sons were out with their fathers. The only one who wasn't there was you." All those sons and friends of mine moving on from Jewish fraternities to the golf clubs with the same rules, segregated and holding away—and asking him once was he ever ashamed about being an exterminator and he answered, averting his eyes, "O sure. It bothered me, the jokes. But you get over it, you get over it." Really such a shy man, my father, underneath it all, starting Hagar Pest at twenty-six, married at thirty, and avoiding intercourse during the courtship because it wasn't the "right" thing to do, ranting if I came out of the shower without a towel, "Put something on! Cover up your business!" or hastily shutting the bathroom door whenever I found him shaving in just that old-fashioned undershirt, and thinking he would retire at fifty, then at fifty-five—

And *O God*! the tears now flowing out of my eyes and swallowing hard!—and I'm still sweating besides as I keep on crying—everyone crying at his funeral except me!—and all these years, the haunting fact of two lost children, one daughter, older than I, living a day and a half, and a younger son surviving with a frail heart and one hand for less than three months—and overly healthy me with 20/10 vision and never a broken bone, his "Teddy Ballgame," lone joy—and the criticism in his eyes when I didn't reach perfection, his list of expected achievements: going to Harvard first instead of Cornell, a four-letter athlete, marrying a beautiful, extremely wealthy Jewish girl, coming into his business, and settling down safe and secure in the suburbs, joining the Shriners, the Masons, the UJA, well-thought-of and religious in the community, and bringing up a brood of well-liked, good-natured children who at birth are enrolled at Harvard and at age three stroll across the ranch house lawn clad in crimson T-shirts—still crying, *Jesus*!—as I moved increasingly away from his dreams: the word "Dad" catching in my throat, always a wince when said, and those last few years in school searching for someone to spur me on, professors, writers, friends, till I finally ran into Boyne, his house of Carnaween, Ciara was coming over, following my dream, my father had his false-alarm stroke, and Ciara married Milo.

Boyne

Warm wet licking tongue, flicking slick pinkish tongue twining over my chest and groin, and all but bringing me, who's now sublimely erect in Belgravia, to the maddening, swelling, blissful brink of—"*Who? Where? WHAT the HELL—?*"

"O I am sorry, I did not mean to wake you, Mr. Boyne," Laetitia crawling up beside me on this hide-a-bed, "but you are so very beautiful when you sleep."

"—Laetitia, no, please stop!" Those falling gargoyles fading, along with Herr Mumble—

Her face foreshortened by passion: plucked eyebrows, wide mouth lustily grinning, her musky odor filling the air, "You have brought all the warmth and tenderness of your work into my home, Mr. Boyne, or Seamus, if I may call you that?" her hand still teasing across my stomach and down my thighs to fondle my cock once more. "And you are so immense now!"

"Yes, well as Flaubert said, 'I always salute the morning with an erection,' " sitting upright, "But listen, Laetitia, I need to ask you, where do I know Herr Mumble from?"

"Mmmm—see how he throbs! Herr Mumble, Mumble? You don't mean Herr Mündel?"

"Yes, yes, that's him! Who is he?"

"My second husband. Why?" still cuddling and stroking me.

"Well he may be trying to kill me."

"Otto? O no, no, no, never—though, yes, maybe that could be. He follows *me* around everywhere, so possibly he—"

"But I've never even *touched* you!"

"No, not until now, mmmm!"

The phone ringing—*Suffering Christ*! "Aren't you going to answer it?"

"Why? Should I?"

"Never know who it might be."

"So? These veins are so blue—"

"Well it might be your second husband or the police."

"O, all right. Yes? Hello, hello?" and she replaces the receiver.

"Who was it?"

"No one. They hung up."

"Good *GOD*!" jumping out of bed, "There's nowhere to hide!"

"Seamus, what is it? You're as white as a sheet."

"*Sheet, sheet*! That's *it*! Up, Laetitia, up!" and stripping the top one off with a bolero sweep.

"What are you *doing*?"

Then draping it all about me, "I've just had a *marvelous* idea—I must get to Harrods *now*!"

Hagar

The window goes blonde slowly, soft sleeves of sound—*Teri*? *Ciara*? looking anxiously around—and no one here beside me! as I keep on blinking and yawning with little if any sleep—running through the rain after Boyne, my father, things I can't control, accept, my fears, failings, own death—for what? from what? what the hell for? Boyne's art, success, what I've wanted all these years? To sell the business and write about what I know. But what do I know? My father, Great Neck, the world I grew up in? Or a second chance with Ciara? She and Boyne balling their brains out, she begging for more—but if he's dead, she's mine—no, no, what am I *saying*? Not even sure anything happened! Everything so bizarre, she naked under his slicker, like they both fell in the Thames? Who knows with Boyne! Probably just showed her his boat, went to a pub—then why'd she leave? Embarrassed at seeing me? Damn it, I'm not going to *lose* her again! Got to find her now, *both* of us find Boyne—but where the hell is she?—as I hop out of bed at 8:45 and go stumbling into the bathroom, hands on hips, pissing in the bowl—and a cold splash of water bristling me awake as I stare into the mirrored eyes of my father: raccoon eyes, which are my own—then quickly shrugging into yesterday's clothes, Irish sweater still somewhat damp, go hustling down the stairs to where Flynn, sitting at a long glass table with the morning paper spread out before him, nervously traces his orange mustache.

"Any word, Kevin?"

"Just had a call, someone saw the *Wino* go down—"

"Christ Almighty!" pounding the wall and pacing around.

"—but there was no sign of a body."

"So where the hell can he *be*?"

"Lord only knows! And to make matters worse, wait'll ya see this lot, all these critics, Russell, Goseling, Melville, Terence Mullaly, fallin' over each other in praise, all of 'em fuckin' sensational! Here, Russell, this is: 'Mr. Boyne's lusty chromatic fantasies yield brilliantly arousing effects,' or Mullaly: 'Nothing more to say except go see one of the wonders of the modern era!' "

"Fantastic, and now he's probably knocked himself off!" and I'm still pacing back and forth, "But if he *isn't* dead and wasn't out at Kew, where else could he be?"

"I haven't got a clue."

"You know where Ciara is?"

"Ciara? O I think I heard Laetitia say somethin' about her goin' to the Royal Court in the mornin'."

"Royal Court?"

"Royal Court Theatre in Sloane Square, just down the road—"

"Right," starting down the stairs, "well I'll be back later, so leave word if you've heard anything."

"I shall indeed, Gene!"

Nearly nine already as this taxi goes careering around Sloane Square toward the Royal Court Theatre, and there she is, wearing a tight white sweat suit—Just to be with her, any excuse to be with her now!—coming out the front with her sungleaming hair, and we swerve to a stop before her.

"God, you look incredible!" slamming the cab door behind me.

"—Gene, what are you *doing* here?"

"I didn't know you were acting. Did you get the part?"

"If I did?" Ciara seeming so edgy, embarrassed, "They will let me know. My accent may be too thick."

"Yeah, and where did you go last night?"

"Well, I left when you started fighting, it was so ridiculous!"

"And where's Boyne?"

"How would I know? Why, are you still trying to kill him?"

"Then you didn't see the fire?"

"Fire? What fire?"

"There was a fire in the gallery, Boyne's disappeared, may've drowned, his boat sank—"

"O dear God!"

"—all his paintings were burned, the reviews were sensational—so come on, you have to help me find him!"

"*Me*?"

"Yes!"

Ciara walking on, "Gene, I have not the slightest idea what you are talking about, but I had enough craziness last night and now I am going to jog, I don't want to think about it anymore."

"*Jog*?" hastily chasing after her. "Jog *where*?" and down the Kings Road, "Ciara, will you *listen*—" trying to keep up with her, "Where're you going?"

"Just up here there is a track at the Duke of York's Headquarters."

"But why?"

"To exercise, stay in good shape."

"But you're in great shape!"

"Not 'great' enough, apparently! I have still to lose another half stone."

"Sounds like you live in a quarry."

Ciara moving quickly through the military gate, the elderly guard waving her in—with me right behind her.

"Ciara, will you *wait*?"

She breaking into a leisurely trot, "And why is Boyne so *important* to you?"

"'Cause you can't let him die, have somebody kill him! Be like losing Picasso, Van Gogh, Cézanne—for Christ's sake, will you *stop* already!" coming around the far turn of this cinder track with the gulls soaring and the sun pouring down through the fluttering maple leaves. "—And why am I always running *after* you—in the Louvre, here—?" side by side down the straightaway, "—How many laps do you do?"

"Today I do three."

"Two *more*?"

"Yes, and sprint at the end."

"No way!" by this low brick wall, "OK, Ciara, I'll make you a deal—"

"I am not dealing, I'm running."

"—I'll sprint the end of this one with you if you promise to come with me after—?"

"You are insane!"

Along the inside lane, legs aching, arms pumping, all this running, playing, chasing—thirty-one now, not twenty-four!—And Christ Almighty, I'm never going to *make* it, coronary assault: *Found dead on Chelsea cinderpath, one Eugene Hagar, late of Great*

Neck, sprawled flat out, face contorted, in a tortured reach for his dream, beside him sprinting—

"*Now!*"

Toward the far turn again—and Ciara running so well, so love to see—a girl who runs well—not all awkward, arms and legs flailing—but girlgrace, flowing muscles, bulging calves—she leading by a yard—and I have to beat her, my competitive urge—"I haven't done this in years—" "Well, we are not who we were"—faster now, my heart really pounding with twenty yards to go, she still leading—and turning it on with my last lap kick, Roger Bannister breaking the four-minute mile—here I come on the outside lane, grimacing, gritting my teeth, straining—passing her down the straightaway—leaving her behind and crossing the finish line a yard ahead—as she continues on and—

O JESUS! gasping—heart pumping so *fast*! bursting through my chest!—and sinking to my knees, fear in my throat, eyes!—*I'm going to DIE*!—My father's stroke, flailing like a beached fish on the floor—this's how it *feels*? Can't breathe—heart totally haywire, slack mouth hanging open—salt taste, drenched in sweat—can't die now, have her see me like this—God, *breathe*! *breathe*!! *Keep* breathing!!!—and Ciara still running smoothly, her long lean strides, breasts' light bounce, blonde hair flaring in the breeze—and sprinting across—

"—O good, this last lap was—*Gene*?" she hurrying back, "What is the *matter*, you look so white!"

"—First time—" still panting, sweating, and kneeling forward, "—was ever scared—"

"You are not used to it, yes. Here, come sit down here and rest."

"I know—but no sleep last night and—always before—never worried and now—*Jesus*!"

"Just rest, rest," Ciara gently wiping my sweaty brow, "you can talk later."

"No—I'm all right now," so queasy—and still breathing deeply, "Christ—feel so stupid, like a fish, beached fish—gasping for air!"

leaning back on the grass, "Before—just pushed on, never say die, heart attacks, strokes—ridiculous, for old guys, but really, I thought, God—I thought I was going to have—*Wow*! have *something*! First time I ever felt, you know, thirty-one—don't know why."

"Because you *are* thirty-one. And it is very warm today and obviously you are not used to it."

"—No, it's more—" taking another deep breath and staring out at the blurry track—"it's more than that—" coming into focus.

"Are you feeling better now?"

"—Mostly fear, I guess—of death, thoughts about death, nightmares, everything exploding—*O Christ*!—let me just catch my breath!"

"Yes, well wait, Gene, take your time," and Ciara smiling as she brushes the hair from my brow, "Though you should never have run with me."

"Run after you is more like it, the Menopause Mile!"

"No, you did not do so bad, considering."

"Considering what? I almost died or that I'm old and paunchy?"

"O not so old, and maybe just a little—no, I am only teasing you now."

"God, Ciara, here I've been running, dancing, posing, even sucking in my gut—been trying so hard to look young for you, I'm going to *die* in the process!" as I finally stand, regaining my balance, "But now you'll help me find Boyne?" and we cut across the cinder track.

"Yes, yes, now of course I will help you find Boyne—though I am not sure what I can do."

And on toward the gate with my throat so dry and my blonde glimmering girl beside me again—O Ciara, so needing you now, right now, poetry and song, your life with me: halcyon days, Hagar whirligigged and ran his heedless ways, Aer Lingus lifting us away to—where? "And how long have you been acting?"

Ciara walking briskly along, "Since we were divorced. Remember I had been acting in Holland before I came to Paris?" and we go trotting across the Kings Road.

"Right, right, well we've hardly had a chance to talk, tell me about your life for the past seven years," back into Sloane Square, "So you live by yourself here in London?"

"Yes, though I am staying for the moment with the nuns."

"The *nuns*? You're becoming a—?"

"No, no!" Ciara giggling and laughing—brightly flashing, her front teeth's slight charming overlap—and going on to explain that her nearby flat in Pimlico is being painted, so temporarily she has moved in with two nuns who live below.

"Below? I see, well what happened with Milo?" turning up Sloane Street, my mind a blur, a swirling daze as I keep staring at her hair of Scandinavian shine—

"Well he is an executive now at ITT, we were divorced in June."

"What happened?"

"O, he wanted me to be his doting little wife and support his career, 'ascend the corporate ladder,' as he would say, while I suffocated in his stuffy world, that Bloomsbury flat. I was like a statue or figurine, something on the shelf to be dusted off during the day and then be all bright and cheery and precisely in place when he came home! Dear God, when I think now, I would sit for days on end on that damask sofa forcing myself to leaf through the *Tatler* or *Elle,* or doing crossword puzzles, clipping different recipes, until one night I said to myself, 'What are you *doing,* doing with your *LIFE*? I would much rather take care of someone than keep living like this!' I thought I would go out of my mind just sitting there, and finally walked out and left his dinner to defrost by itself, nearly burned down his precious homestead! And now here I am back at acting again, nervously waiting for my first part at the Royal Court, while breaking free from this ridiculous marriage."

"And all these years, Ciara . . ." approaching Cadogan Gardens.

"Yes. And you are how old now, you said, thirty-one?"

"Not as young as I used to be."

"Well you seem to be in fairly good shape for someone your age."

"Obviously slowing down, can't go to his left anymore, fans—"

"I know, I have seen how very slow you are!"

"—you young kids taking over."

"Shall I give you my arm, old fellow?"

"O get out of here! Anyway, would you really've come to Ireland then?"

"What? O, when I wrote you, you mean? Yes, I would."

"Were you sure I'd marry you?"

"I don't know, I suppose so. But that was before your letter that you had to go home, you didn't know for how long, and then Milo came back—remember he always was going off to Liechtenstein on those Intelligence missions of his?—I didn't hear from you, and all of a sudden he asked me to marry him, we went to Holland for the wedding, and then moved here to London. But now you are living in Ireland, too? I thought—"

"No, back in the States."

"And you have kept on with your writing?"

"Here and there. I'm in business, took over my father's—"

"But I thought you hated that."

"—I do, *still* do."

"And have you ever married, Gene?"

Nodding as we enter Cadogan Square.

"Do you have any children?"

"No," nearing the red brick town house, "Do you?"

"No, Milo never wanted them. And what is your marriage like—Dear God, I can smell the fire from here!"

"It's probably over," knocking on the front door—that opens—no answer, and on up the stairs, "Hello, anybody here? Flynn?

Dungannon? Vi, Brenda?" looking all about, "Guess they've all gone out—" The phone ringing. "I'll get it," hurrying across to the alcove, "Yes, hello?"

"Pardon?" a familiar, agitated voice, "Who is this?"

"Gene. And who's this?"

"O Mr. Hagar, please, I am terribly sorry I did not recognize you but this is Laetitia Marengue. Is Mr. Flynn there or the sisters Sligo-Moeran?"

"Nobody's here."

"O *no,* and Mr. Boyne has just left!"

"He's *ALIVE*? Just left for *where*?"

"Harrods—"

Ciara now whispering beside me, "Who is that?"

"(Laetitia). *Harrods*? But why—?"

"—dressed as a sheik and I am extremely concerned about him!"

"So am I! Listen, we're leaving for Harrods right now, so I'll speak to you later then."

The two of us hurrying back down the stairs—and nearly colliding with Flynn coming in the front door.

"Ah, Jaysus, Gene, Ciara—and will ya look at this girl, so pretty she'd make any hour sweeter!"

"Yeah, well listen," spinning him about, "we gotta get going—" and quickly outside again.

"Goin' where?"

Pushing him ahead, "We can take your car—Boyne's still *alive*—"

"Mother of Christ!"

"—and on his way to Harrods!"

"But stop, stop!" Flynn skidding to a halt.

"Why, what's wrong?"

"I just heard over the BBC that the paintings *weren't* destroyed but rather're bein' held fer ransom!"

"*Ransom*? What kind of ransom?"

"Didn't say. I know, 'tis all of it exceedingly strange!"

Boyne

Speeding through Saturday morning London traffic in the plush leathery comfort of this Austin cab and I'm unraveled, umbilical anew! with vibrant colors clashing, whirling textures massing across my mind as I apply a final smear of this bronze stain to my glossy cheeks—looking like Auda abu Tayi, sheik of the Howeitat and legendary Bedouin chief! Everyone trying to shed their own skins, cast off this mortal coil: Monet turning into a water lily, Cézanne a rocky landscape, Van Gogh the paint itself (the lead probably causing his madness)—and now me into Lawrence of Arabia, my headdress wound round with a gold sash cord and deftly fashioned by Laetitia, sunglasses, and one of her king-size sheets—she pleading with me to stay, "O please come back to bed!"—this Aer Lingus bag at my feet filled with a fast change of clothes, cold cream, napkins, her ten-pound note in my pocket (can't afford to be recognized, the need for disguise with all of London as well as assassins hot on my trail)—

And approaching Harrods now with its brightly flapping flags, huge six-story terra-cotta building crowded with customers as, cruising down the narrow block, we swerve to a sudden stop!

And I come billowing out with my bedsheet-robe flowing in the breeze and under the scalloped awning, by the Harrods guard, a beefy sergeant-major in visored cap—being ogled by children, women in flowered hats—and up these marble stairs to sample some figs and dates, past Wurlitzer organs and Steinway grands, Wedgwood blue and Doulton china, and into this world of hardware for a hammer, nails, and a coil of manila rope, then on through Kitchenware and Garden Care and a flotilla of Sporting Goods—

And Good *God*! that's it: Just look at this one-man *canoe*! Nobody ever suspect—perfect transport to the Tate! My Irish one knocked off by a shotgun's shattering blast—£35—But hardly any money left, so there's only one bloody thing to do—

"Might I be of service, sir?"

And nearly *leaping* out of my sheet!—as I glance swiftly around at this mousy little man in his gray pin-striped suit—and launch into my Iraqi accent:

"Ah yes, please, begging your forgiveness now, but I am interested, you see, in the purchase of this—how do you British say—canoe, yes? as in gnu, cuckoo, pooh-pooh, ha-ha, touch of Arabian humor there!"

"Quite."

A lithe, well-groomed woman in a bright orange suit passing by, "Any problems, Mr. Mortlake?" and adjusting her horn-rimmed glasses.

"No, no, perfectly all right, Miss Hynde. Proceeding quite nicely, thank you."

"Allah be merciful, such *a lovely* flower!" bowing with a flourishing kiss of her hand—and almost losing my tilting headdress! "Truly a splendid-looking woman. Older, yes, but as it is written, which of us can escape that, you know? As we say in my country, 'To meet a charming woman is even better than to trick the camel trader.' "

"Is that from the Koran?"

"If not, then it should be."

Miss Hynde nervously tapping her glasses into place and, with a lacquered smile, goes strutting away.

"But please excuse my babbling, sir, for I have chosen this six-foot-long, one-man, green fiberglass canoe from Twickenham here." Mortlake nodding and moving behind the counter. "Though there appears to be a slight defect with this particular model. I wonder, might you have another of the same design in stock?"

"Quite. And will this be a charge, sir, or—?"

"O yes, charge, by all means, charge! I delight in the charge, like your Light Brigade, ha-ha!"

"Certainly, Mr.—?"

"Tayi. Auda abu Tayi, of the Howeitat!"

"Very well then, sir, I'll just get a fresh one from the back, shan't be a moment."

"Words alone cannot express my gratitude—"

And he disappears into the stockroom—as I raise the canoe boldly over my head, burglar tools and collapsible paddle tossed in the bow, and frantically down these marble stairs toward a host of people veering out of the way, shouting. "Watch out, canoe— Heads up, canoe—Here comes a bloody canoe!" my heart doing its own soft shoe, any second expecting Mortlake's cry—and nearly decapitating a dowager, "My word, Aubrey!"—down this last slippery flight and right on by the sergeant-major whipping open the door and tipping his visored cap as I go striding up to the corner—Arab, of course, putting it to good use for those paddles up the Euphrates—and onto the back of this double-decker bus, knocking bowlers and monocles awry! "I say, what do you think you're doing?" that Indian conductor behind me, "Sir, this is not permitted—" and swinging round to confront him, fling him headlong into the street as we go roaring away and a flurry of people burst out of Harrods's door, arms waving, Mortlake and Hynde to the fore! Lowering my canoe and wedging up these narrow, winding stairs to the top deck—and into the open air! A sweet river breeze billowing my bedsheet and swiftly down the Brompton Road, leaving all that commotion behind!

Hagar

Flynn's silver Austin-Healey squealing up before Harrods with Ciara jouncing back in my lap—gripping her trim waist tight, "Thank you!"—and this chattering crowd, along with bobbies and reporters, milling about that dazed Indian conductor.

"What's going on?"

A photographer turning to me, "Some sheik just stole a canoe."

"Sheik—O Christ! Where'd he go?"

"Took off on a number 30 bus."

Flynn slam-shifting out onto Brompton Road, "Sure he's headed for the Thames!" whizzing ahead of this traffic, past the Victoria and Albert Museum and down Exhibition Road, grazing a passing cab—and a klaxon bleating somewhere, back there—a covey of pigeons fluttering white, scurrying gray, people dodging this way, that, bowler-hatted toff cursing after, and flat out into Cromwell Place toward an old woman in a polka-dot dress pedaling her two-speed bike—"*Flynn*!"—as she reins it up like a horse and we go zipping by, past this Church of Scotland, priest skipping the light fantastic, with Ciara's hand now clutching mine behind her and another klaxon joining the first, "Sure and they've got the entire flippin' Yard out now!" into the Fulham Road and Flynn switching on the radio, the BBC booming forth with traffic reports, weather reports, "*—The temperature currently twenty-two degrees centigrade,*" down Sydney Street with him changing stations, "*—and ironically, tonight at nine, the Tate is presenting a private Gala Retrospective of Mr. Boyne's work—*" "*WHAT?!*" "*—though the artist himself is presumed drowned—*"

"There's definitely somethin' fishy here!"

"Flynn, over *there*!"

On the corner a cabbie in Arab burnoose shaking out a bedsheet—screeching tires round the curve of the U, horns loudly honking, and we jolt to a stop before him.

"Where'd ya get that outfit?"

"None of yer bleedin' business!"

Flynn hopping out to confront the cabbie with a fistful of cash, then back in a flash, "Seamus hadn't the fare, so he bartered his clothes instead," for another wheeling U-turn, "then was dropped with the canoe at the Thames!" and off we go again!

Boyne

Like bloody Hiawatha paddling deliriously down the river!—starboard, port, God only knows! as I keep up this steady, splashing pace against the current—and on under Chelsea Bridge, staying close to the shore with the whole of London pursuing me—and that tour boat passing by, tourists waving—I'm waving, smiling back—always smile: Iraqi, of course, testing it out for those paddles up the—no, that was my last disguise! Just on vacation, off the reservation, over from Donegal trawling for cod, ha-ha!—clad as I am now in Laetitia's lilac, Oscar Wilde–like blouse, my tan slacks, green-striped socks, and the trusty beret—

"And Billy, as soon as I hang this portrait of Ciara, I'm joining you and my ancestor, King of Ireland in the sixth century, and farewell to the Celtic satyr!" under the blue arches of Vauxhall Bridge toward that gray, shingled shore—"Least I won't die arthritically like Renoir or blind like Mary Cassatt, be the same age as my father, thirty-eight, Van Gogh at thirty-seven, Modigliani at thirty-five—and all those wasted lives destroyed by drink and suicide of *my* generation: Pollock mangled in a car crash, David Smith in a truck crash, Arshile Gorky hanging himself, Frank O'Hara, Franz Kline"—as I go splashing onto the beach and, pushing the canoe back into this fast-moving current, skip up the river steps and on toward the Tate!

Hagar

Flynn's Healey careening across the honking Kings Road and left—grazing the curb—down Oakley Street. "Ah, but sure and Seamus is childlike, of course, knows no restraint—but ya shoulda seen him with that girl of his, Tory!" weaving in and out of taxis and between these red double-decker buses, "Granted, 'twas only over the short span, but still they were bloody marvelous together, never saw him happier than he was with her. O obsessed Boyne may be, but totally without malice, bringin' excitement and wonder into all our lives!" Ciara nodding (pining?) as we near the Thames—"Ah, but Jaysus, I just realized ya can't see a thing from the car along Chelsea Embankment, so I'll leave the two of ya here to search the river while I pop off to the Tate," past Cheyne Walk—Cadogan Pier down there—bumping onto the pavement, nicking the bollards, through these hedges—Ciara and I bounding out, stumbling, banging my knee—and Flynn turning to me, the klaxons growing louder, "Meet ya back at the town house at three!"

"OK—but listen, are any of Boyne's old lovers' husbands around?"

"Old lovers' husbands? Well there's Dungannon, of course."

"Dungannon?"

"O sure. Seamus had a fling with his wife—she was a flautist with Munich Bach Orchestra, who every night gave Percy the *St. Matthew Passion,* while Percy's passion waned. Lasted a year, before she fled with her flaut. Even tried the rhythm method, only his was a jig and hers was a dirge."

"And where's Dungannon now?"

"Well I'm not quite certain meself, at Kew, most likely, in case Seamus, ya know, should return—" and, with two fangs of vapor shooting out his exhaust pipes, zooming away he goes!

Ciara and I walking rapidly along the Embankment under the deafening traffic's roar—and no sign of Boyne down there!—a tour boat gliding by, tug on the far side—"God, we're never gonna find him!"

"Gene?"

Hurrying on ahead, "What?"

"You know you still haven't told me how he could paint me without ever seeing me."

"He said he painted you from my writings."

"Your writings? What did you *WRITE*?"

"No, no, just some descriptions."

"Descriptions? Descriptions of what?"

"Physical, poetic descriptions of you, and he took it from there."

"I never knew I had that sort of effect."

"Well obviously you did," nearing Chelsea Bridge, "Christ, where the hell *is* he?" Still no sign of him, the wall higher here—on my toes, "I can't *see* all the way over!"

"So climb up."

"Up *there*?"

"Why not?"

"—I'm afraid of heights."

"All right, I'll go then."

"No way!" Ciara gracefully scaling it like a lithe, sensual cat—"Well just be careful!"

The tide of her hair lacing against the pale shine of her face, toe-dancing atop the parapet, using her arms as a balance, wobbling slightly, high above the Thames—

"See anything yet?"

"No, nothing as yet."

Her tight-fitting white sweat suit snugly accentuating the sassy curves of her rump—and on her face, an expression I've never seen before: serene in this buffeting breeze, windlashing her blonde hair across her eyes, as I keep pacing anxiously below, "You're not afraid of the fall?"

"—Not at all."

"Christ, my greatest fear is acro—*Whoa,* watch it there!" grabbing onto her hand, "Acrophobia."

"Thank you—My God, what a view! You should *see,* Gene."

"I can see, I can see! Ciara, that's enough—"

"*Wait, wait!*" she leaning forward and to the side, "There's a *canoe* down there!"

Craning over the wall, "With Boyne *in* it?"

"No, there is no one in it—" her sneakers sliding, "—*Gene, hold me*!" fingers slipping out of my grip, windmilling her arms—

"*CIARA*!!"

—and headfirst she goes toppling off—

Christ Almighty!—disappearing from view—a distant splash!—as I go scrambling blindly onto the wall, no time for fears now!—and jumping straight out and holding my nose, falling fast, the Thames below coming up to meet me—exploding into the water! eyes popping, cheeks bulging, *Jesus,* I forgot I'm a lousy swimmer!—as I bounce gasping and blinking to the surface—and there's Ciara, already on shore! And I was gonna rescue her! Some hero, huh?—flailing hard against the current, and she helps me up onto this emergency pier.

Boyne

—And Good *God,* just *look* at that glorious, Victorian Tate! So damn excited, striding swiftly up Millbank and adjusting my dashing beret—all those blazing Turners inside!—that my hands are shaking, erection swaying, *Magnificat* echoing uproariously in my brain: *There was a young man from Iraq / Who played the bass viol with his cock / With tremendous erections / He rendered selections / From Johann Sebastian Bach*! Cézanne saying with an apple he'd astonish Paris, and soon they'll be saying—nay, surely huzzahing!—that with this radiant image of Ciara, I have astonished the entire planet!

And strange, how I can't stop thinking of her: a sunburst obscuring the circling of gulls, fringing their wings with a border of gold—

O Jaysus NO! Two bobbies patrolling the front—and spinning left down Atterbury Street, these black spoke fences, with my beret canted low—How the hell do I get *in*? Can't just pop in the front door, nowhere to hide. Have to secret myself somewhere till they're closed, all the guards've left—don't know how—these walls of Portland stone, grassy gardens, and vaulted basement windows—none ajar, metal bars—but I have to get in *now,* before I die or someone does me in! Staff entry down there, elderly guard with his froggy eyes, blue shirt, and black tie, leafing through his morning paper—while I'm passing by and pausing as he yawns, slowly standing, and goes waddling somewhere inside, his silhouette down the hall. Toward the loo? Looking left and right—the coast is clear—just say I'm Mr. O'Keefe from County Meath, needing to tap a kidney, too—

And with a glide, I go sidling quickly indoors! Must be a loo along here, white-walled corridor—that toilet flushing, guard coming out!—*O Suffering Christ*!—and nipping sharply into the Ladies beside it!

"Hellooo?" using my quavering Duchess falsetto—not a sound, glancing around—before locking myself in this stall! Another successful Irish crime: breaking into the Tate! (Though the reason the crime rate in Ireland's so low is 'cause nobody ever gets caught!)

Hagar

Ciara, having changed into Brenda's silky crimson robe, parading back and forth with her lithe and flowing stride, "Then what do you think happened to him?"

"God only knows, but I really doubt that he drowned."

"So do I," as she keeps on pacing.

"'Cause he was always a very good swimmer. And now the police're involved, dragging the river, all sorts of reporters, the Tate calling—it's suddenly become a *media* event!"

"Yes, and they don't even know him—but that also was a very brave thing *you* did, Gene."

"What?"

"Conquering your fear of heights to save me," Ciara's smiling bluestone eyes, "or let me save you," as she moves toward the rear, windowed wall.

"Right, well I think what we both need now is a shower, while our clothes're drying."

"Fine, fine."

"Where're you going?"

"I have to make a call," seating herself on an alcove cushion.

And I jog wetly up this short flight of stairs to the third floor and its black-and-white-tiled bathroom with that green, fluffy rug, hanging plants, and glass-enclosed shower stall. Peeling off these sodden clothes and wrapping a towel around my waist—make my move now or in a shower of sensual delights? This bar of Yardley, temperature just right, soaping each other up, the slippery feel of her firm wet flesh, lovely slope of her shoulders, tracing round her nipples and coming closer as we kiss, gulping kisses, under a hot steamy shower and kneeling down and lifting her back against the tile with her arms about my neck as I thrust deep inside, letting her slick skin slide—O everything falling into place, the two of us growing closer, like Paris again—and I go cantering down the stairs, by these worn and upholstered chairs.

Ciara still on the phone, listening and nodding, "—Yes? O you did, yes?" as she glances up, "No, no, I *do* understand, Arthur. Yes, of course I do, I know you are still optimistic."

Whispering, "Who're you talking to?"

She whispering back, "(My agent.) No, of course not, Arthur, and I will see you later then. Yes, yes, I am fine, thank you, good-bye," sighing deeply now and averting her eyes.

"Did you get the part?"

Ciara standing and still blinking, "No, they gave it to the producer's girlfriend."

"O Jesus!" and smoothing back her hair, the silky shimmer above her temples shading into a soft blonde shine, "I'm sorry, really."

"Though now they may want me for another play—"

"Well whatever happens," gently holding her by the shoulders, "at least Ireland'll be incredible—"

"—even though it is only a small part—"

"—Can't wait to show you Carnaween, Boyne's twelve-room house by the Irish Sea—"

"—Peter Brook now may be the director—"

"—Hell, you could even act at the Abbey, do Synge and O'Casey—"

"—and Albert Finney supposedly is playing the lead—"

"—'cause one thing for sure, Ciara, I'm not going to lose you again—"

"—and they need—'Lose me again'?"

"—finally start living our dream—"

"*What* dream, Gene? That I would run away with you as though I were nineteen again?"

"—'cause there's so much I want to show you—"

"But I hardly know you and you don't know me!"

"—all through Ireland and Dublin and of course Carnaween—"

"Gene, we knew each other seven years ago in Paris for how long, two or three weeks?"

"—follow the railroad tracks around to Kilcoole—"

"And it has never been *my* dream to go to Ireland, it has always been *your* dream to go to Ireland!"

"—meeting again like seven years never existed—"

"*Gene,*" Ciara suddenly pushing my hands away, "you are not even *hearing* me now!"

"—finally take care of you—What're you *doing*?" bumping back into the sofa.

"Well you have hardly heard a word I have said and you obviously have no *idea* what my life is like here, what I wish to *do* with my life, who I am!"

"What do you mean I have no *idea*? What're you *talking* about?"

"And maybe you can live your life just running away to Ireland or wherever, but I certainly cannot!"

"But we're *not* just running away, we're really going to *live* it now, 'cause everything's still the same—"

"But everything is *not* still the same, we have all changed!"

"No, not the way I feel about you! Nothing's changed except we can finally be with each other!"

"Gene, this is *your* fairy tale! I told you before I have had enough of being taken care of, of being rescued like Cinderella. Look, I have never been Cinderella and you have never been the prince!"

"But I've never been Milo, either!"

"No? Well you are certainly acting like someone who only hears himself!" moving past me round the room.

"So what'll you do," following after her, "just keep on acting?"

"Yes, I will do what I decided to do during my divorce."

"And what if you don't get this part?"

"I will get another one! I mean, who knows, it's possible I might not get a part until I am seventy-four, but I will go on trying."

"Ciara—?"

"No, you don't understand what I'm saying, do you, or what I feel? You're blind to feelings, other people's feelings—"

"Blind? You once told me how sensitive I was—"

"Yes, but it is a special sort of sensitivity. That is, you perceive and you analyze what other people feel, but you never really feel in their place. You know what they feel, but you never really *feel* what they feel. You won't allow yourself—Even in your writing, you observe and you watch, but everything that I read in Paris was always a reflection of what *you* felt. There was never one character who felt for himself. And now here you are doing the same thing to me, and running again. Though I am not quite sure what you are running toward, Ireland and Joyce and me, all part of your fantasy to be a writer? If you want to be a writer, write! All you need is a pencil and paper!"

"And that's *it*?"

"Gene, I'm sorry I am being so harsh, because I do like you and I didn't want to hurt you."

"Didn't want to hurt me? Why didn't you say that seven *years* ago? For seven years, all I've thought about, dreamed about, wrote about was you—and now I've given up my wife, my business, my whole life back there—It's *never* been a fantasy! Never! Not when I described you to Boyne, then meeting here again, you and he running off together—And what *about* Boyne, how do you feel about him?"

Ciara glancing away, "I'm not sure yet how I feel—I just hope he is still alive."

Boyne

Darting fast looks left and right out of the ladies' loo—before skipping silently across the hall like a leprechaun or bearded Celtic satyr, my painting gripped in one hand, Aer Lingus bag in the other, using my sprinter's speed, real quick—footsteps sounding—*O Suffering Christ*!—and nipping round this corner, swiftly out of sight—my head in a dizzying whirl!

This sinister shadow approaching—Herr Mumble? IRA? Laura's hit man? Who? Fee, Fi, Fo, Fum, I smell the blood of an Irishmun—and a large, portly guard in a suit of indigo serge comes harrumphing into view, thumbs vested within his watch-fob pockets—*can't* get caught now that I've broken in!—he's lumbering left, I'm cringing right, pressing flat against the wall—as he vanishes, still harrumphing, down the hall, and I hear him say good night!

Letting out a sigh, must be after six by now—Tory and I once hiding out in the Baltimore Museum till they were closed, then slowly emerging to see it the only way you should, by flashlight and alone! And God, so missing her now! Such a beautiful girl with her blonde Swede hair—for every child's an artist, as Picasso said, the problem is how to remain an artist once you grow up! And the critics overlooking all the agonizing struggle and mental planning that goes into a work of art, the seemingly never-ending, nerve-rending shape and reshape, reflection, and study—"Though I painted up a bloody *storm,* didn't I, Billy, with my worn brushes and palette knife! frenzied fingers and 'eagle-talon' thumbnail like yours gouging, scratching, and scrubbing aurora yellow across a field of green—till gradually and as if by magic that widening gyre of color turned into a wondrous Ciara (who's even better in reality!)—this work that'll never die!"

Outside, another driving rainstorm scudding over the Thames, those awaiting, darkling waves, while inside, there only remains this last act of hanging to do!

"And so few if any aware of what the artist goes through, denying our struggles during our lifetime and even recommending blood-letting for you, Billy, and a lobotomy for me to cure our diseased minds!" **"Aye, lad, took 'em till 1939 to find fifty of my greatest paintings in the cellars of the National Gallery, thought they were musty old tarpaulins!"** "O Christ, I know, the public forever losing sight of the man—Cézanne behind the apples and pears, on his deathbed calling out the name of the museum director who rejected his paintings, or you back of that whirling and radiant vortex, short and squat with your quizzical gray eyes, handsome beak of a nose, ruddy face, and rolling gait: a sexual rogue, never marrying, though seeking anonymity (even posing as 'Admiral Booth') to keep the demons at bay! Hell, remember the first time I heard you talking to me, it was here at the Tate, all gruff and thundering in your deep basso voice: 'My paintings are my children!' "

Good *God,* what a life! Leaving everything behind me now, Tory, Ciara, Sligo, my father, dying in that Rhode Island asylum. Loved to see him whipping up his own special béchamel sauce, velouté or mornay, under his framed photo of Escoffier, and that astounding Hong Kong curry, served in infinite varieties of mild, medium, and blast your bloody head off! Finally sneaking some in, rather than that psychiatric gruel, the night before he died and sharing his last meal with him—O my father! same face as mine, though smaller and Van Gogh-eyed. But Christ, we're *all* fathers, and you don't love anyone *but* yourself if you're afraid to love your father! Memories galore, Erin's green and fragrant shore—

And that first morning of land, the gulls cawing madly, balanced as they were on air, then swooping down the long slide and back to their tentative, poised hover. Spontaneously a thin shiver of earth out of the pitching sea, a lighthouse winking: Ireland. Green slice in a graygreen sea and I was so excited to be returning again, ten years after his funeral, drunk and awake all night with the gulls spearing my stale bits of cake that I let out a wild call from the side rail, my free fist pumping the air and shouting, "God bless Ireland!" while I pointed my erection toward solid land, "There're only two countries left in all this barbarous woe—Ireland and Israel—and they'll fight it out between 'em!" when tiny, heeled feet began descending the stairway above, a white, pleated skirt coming slowly into view as I spun about, hard-on in tow. She blinked. A startled gasp. She paused. Then fled up the stairs in the wake of my laughter—and two months later she became my wife!

O Laura, what a bewitching summer that was, no money nor cares, just living on air with my Sarah Lawrence grad, posing bare for my paintings again and again (but still so far from Ciara's vision of ripeness and bloom!) as I chased you round my studio! Or making love atop that hill in Kilcoole after watching a herd of ponies woo one another, nuzzling about and running down a glade with such exquisite freedom and ease, and a month later, when you found you were pregnant, you couldn't remember our lovemaking at all or where Tory was conceived, just those ponies running along—Sweet Jaysus, taking my newborn babe in my arms and humming "Sleepers Awake"—O *Tory,* the pain of your loss—tearing you from me—disappearing into the abyss!

More footsteps sounding—cane tapping? Herr Mumble, Mündel?—and holding my breath, making myself invisible!

That froggy little guard, a rotund toad with his bulging eyes, hardly pausing as he waddles by and tapping the floor with a pointer!

Waiting a few moments more, then scampering into this darkened kitchen, everyone gone for the day, and sneaking a look outside. Only when it falls suddenly past the dark, soaked wood, do you see it: pale rain falling into sight, the leaves a wet and smoky-green. Gray aftermath of rain, gurgling down the gutters or lacing the windows with intricate webs and woven designs. Those bobbies still there, guards departing—and the doors clanging closed with an echoing slam!

I'm all alone in the Tate!!

Ha-ha!! tingling in me bones as I cant my dashing beret, tuck in this lilac blouse, and head back the way I came, swiftly past the staff entrance and trotting up these empty stairs, not a sound and turning around—

Suffering CHRIST!! Light *bursting* out of darkness: *Sunrise, Snow Storm, Venice Skies, Self-Portrait*—

"Billy, I'm naked to the *core* before you! For to come upon your work again is surely to forget death and time with this *splendor* of seething light! And now *HERE*!!" unfurling my one surviving gem—O Ciara, to hold you once more and love you just as you are! *Golden haired and golden hearted / I would ever have you be, / As you were when last we parted / Smiling slow and sad at me*—and raising it high, "Billy, I'm finally going to hang *beside* you! For as you can see, like you, I'm even a better lover on canvas—though with Ciara I've never been so tender and passionate and lyrically warm! Such a shame it'll all end like this, during torrential showers, as I dive into the floodtide, ebbtide of Old Father Thames, that ancient, silty river!"

Opening my Aer Lingus bag and sifting through cold cream, stain, manila rope—Ah, my Harrods hammer, and taking it out along with these ha'penny nails. No frame, charred round the edges—Just have to bang it into a wall. But where's that marvelous spot? By your *Snow Storm* or *Sunrise?* Or what about round this corner? Strolling toward the main hall, these green curtains drawn. Wonder why? Peeking inside—

"*GOOD GOD!!!*"

And come face-to-face with my work—*ALL* of my work, old and new! *Must* be a mirage! Blinking, rubbing my eyes, and gazing in staggering amazement: No, it's true! *Everything* I thought was burned now before me on the walls!

And this accompanying brochure—

TONIGHT AT NINE
A Private Gala Retrospective
of the Works of Seamus Boyne

—printed a month ago! as I fling it high in the air, "O those *BASTARDS*! Well I'll give 'em a show!"

Hagar

"Gene? Ciara? Anybody about?"

"Yeah, we're up here," glancing uneasily at her as Flynn, with his orange curls and mustache, comes hustling up the stairs, along with Laetitia, Dungannon and his pipes, "Any news?"

"Well we still haven't got a clue about Boyne, but the Tate's paid the ransom to the IRA—"

"The *IRA*? What the hell's going *on*?"

"—though Percy here's been doin' some diggin', and 'tis high time we had us a bit of a natter with Vi and Brenda—"

"Vi and Brenda, why?"

"Well it seems that—" Those two phones shrilly ringing and Flynn bounding over to grab one, "What? No, Mr. Boyne hasn't been 'found as yet'! Yer like vultures waitin' to pounce!" then slamming it down, "More of them bloody reporters!" The phone ringing again and Flynn bellowing into it, "Will ya for Jaysus' sake go '*way*—Arson, is it? Police draggin' the river? O by the crucified fuckin' Christ!" and slamming it down once more.

"Shhh!" Ciara holding up her hand.

"What?"

"I thought I heard—Yes, there it is again. Did you hear that?"

Everybody listening intently, looking around.

"Sounds like shouting, a man's voice, coming from the gallery."

"But the fire, why would anyone—?"

"Let's go!" Flynn leading the way quickly down the dark corridor into this bare, lattice-windowed room, still acrid with smoke—then pulling up short with bated breath, "Jaysus, I'd know that voice anywhere!"

"It's Vi, screaming at someone down there!"

"—Confounded Ordway, you're becoming increasingly senile these days!"

All of us whispering, "*Ordway*?" "The butler did it?" "What did he say?" "Shhhh, just listen!"

"—and both of us know you don't deserve a penny—"

"But, m-madam, I only want what's r-rightfully mine."

"—since it was you and your bumbling Sinn Féin mates who caused this dreadful fire—"

"Jaysus!"

"—by knocking over those candlestands—"

"Scandal, m-madam? But you said the Tate p-paid the ransom and he d-drowned all by himself—"

"O those bloody *hags*!" and Flynn about to go charging down the stairs, "I'm gonna tear their arms right out of their sockets!"

"*No*!"

"*No*? Why the hell *not*?"

"'Cause they could lead us to Boyne—"

"Shhh, listen!"

"—but we'll settle this matter later, because now we must leave for the Tate."

And off they go, a taxi waiting outside.

"Come on!"

Down through the still smoking ruins of the gallery, doddering old Ordway, in his blue butler's suit, climbing slowly into the front of the cab, Vi and Brenda in back, as we all hop in: Ciara and I on either side of the sisters, Laetitia up with Ordway, and Dungannon and Flynn on the jump seats.

"Pardon me, ladies, but I'm sure ya won't mind if the lot of us share yer ride? Frightful London traffic, ya know?"

"*What*?—How dare you! What is the meaning of this? And Laetitia, what are you—?"

The driver pulling away.

"And I wonder now might we ask ya a few questions?"

"—Questions?—Why, what sort of questions?" Vi's terrified rhino face as Brenda keeps cowering beside her.

"Vi, you said no one would—"

"Brenda, *not* now! Driver, pull over this instant! This man is out of his mind!"

"Well our investigations have shown that you'd acquired considerable debts due to yer father's financial extravagance—"

"Sheer nonsense!"

"—and, therefore, devised this devilish scheme just after Sligo did himself in!"

"Driver, I demand—"

Dungannon glaring at the stubby driver, who continues silently steering.

"—knew ya'd receive no immediate rewards fer the Retrospective, so ya guaranteed the Tate the old work, then stole the new work yerselves and offered it back for ransom!"

"And worst of all, tried to kill Boyne so his paintings'd become invaluable!"

"*Exactly,* Gene!"

"Vi, is this true?"

"We demand to speak to our solicitor! *Driver*?" Vi raising her riding crop—

"Solicitor! I'll give ya a bloody solicitor, ya whore's melt ya!" and Flynn, swiping the riding crop out of her hand, is about to rain blows upon her head—when Dungannon yanks it from him, holding him at bay.

Flynn still pawing and kicking. "Will ya let *go* of me? They're worse than Goneril and Regan, they are!"

The taxi racing past Vauxhall Bridge, and there's the Tate shimmering in violet light, bobbies ringing the fences, as we come wheeling down Atterbury Street, lined with shiny limos, Jaguars, and Rolls-Royces, and swerve to a screeching halt.

"Yes, well I'm terribly sorry now that we can't discuss this further—Come, Brenda—"

"Yer not goin' *anywhere*!"

"—since we're already late as it is."

Flynn still clawing at her, "Jaysus, Gene, yer not gonna let 'em go!"

"No, we'll just escort them in."

Vi sliding by me, with Brenda alongside fluttering her boa, Ordway still muttering about "s-scandals," and the rest of us, Dungannon shouldering his bagpipes, right behind.

"How're *we* gonna get in?"

"Just follow along," Laetitia displaying a card, "they are with me," past the security guards, TV crews, a battery of press and photographers, and under the statue of Britannia, self-conscious now in my Irish sweater and Adidas sneakers, raking my fingers through my hair, Ciara in her tight white sweat suit—and inside the main hall, long tables of hors d'oeuvres and cocktails against the wall, and around a hundred formally dressed people seated before those dark green curtains, Vi and Brenda hurrying down to the front row as I rest my hands on Ciara's shoulders—letting me hold her, relaxing under my grasp—But hold who? *(You obviously have no idea what my life is like here, what I wish to do with my life, who I am!)* Losing her again? But how can I lose her if I never really had her? More than words and paintings—All part of my fantasy to be a writer! *(If you want to be a writer, write! All you need is a pencil and paper.)* But write about what? More dreams, romantic illusions? Or the reality of them and me? Joyce fleeing through flung nets past the pain of Ireland to write about what he knew. But what did he know in Paris, Zurich, and Trieste but himself, Ireland, his father? And here I've come all this way to write the story of my father, Great Neck, and the world I grew up in? *(Longest way round is the shortest way home!)* And the one way I have to really understand him (and maybe myself), though now he'll never read my work—as Laetitia keeps pointing out who's who: "That is Princess Margaret, of course, with Philippe de Rothschild, Francis Bacon, Armand Hammer is over there—" "*Quiet,* please!" "—and that is Kenneth Clark who is talking!"

"—Several years ago at Mr. Boyne's initial show, I shared with numerous others the feeling that here, in fact, was a talent of remarkable promise, an imagination absolutely vehement in its personal logic, in its determination to summarize all experience in the rhythmic flow of a swirl of pigment. Those splendid blazing outbursts served to remind us once again of the seduction and relish of visual language. He offered us then the possibilities of passionate commitment—someone willing to risk and to fail, someone willing to feel and to care, and finally, someone, now brilliantly fulfilled, I feel safe this evening in calling clearly the greatest artist of the twentieth century—"

"O just open the bloody curtains already before my *arms* fall off!"

HIS voice back there?! But how the hell could he—?

And a totally stunned Clark, fumbling and jerking the curtains apart, reveals a manically grinning Boyne standing naked (except for his beret, fig leaf, and those green-striped socks) with his arms outstretched like a crucified Christ or hung painting in the center of his stolen work as he comes leaping down from a pedestal amid a pandemonium of shrieking and screaming, women fainting, cameras flashing, and shouting as he goes, "Good *God,* you yahoos still haven't learned, have you, that there's never art without the artist?" Flynn breaking into rousing song, Dungannon's bagpipes bleating, "*All you free-born men of the traveling people—*" and bare-assed Boyne now bowing with a flourishing sweep before a gaping Princess Margaret—as Ciara goes rushing out of my grasp—reaching after her, *gone*!—and through the crowd to hug him and hold him, "Ah *Christ,* Billy, and here's my inspiration in the flesh!" kissing her wildly, "who just wants me to be!" and they go dancing away out the door to the echoing Irish music.

Taking another deep breath, my gut aching, as I watch them leave, and Laetitia, following, turns to me, "Are you coming, Gene?"

"No—I think it's time to go home."

"To Ireland?"

"No, *there* goes Ireland, home to New York."

Boyne's Lassie

September 1973

Tory

Raging Irish rain roaring down in windy buckets as I go slipsliding around, barely missing that bewildered old Guernsey and driving this British car with the steering wheel on the wrong side and a fake ID (making me five years older than seventeen)—a motorcycle splashing past doing a hundred miles an hour—and God, I'll probably smash this rented Cortina into a wall, kill myself, and arrive at his funeral in my own damn hearse!

And where the hell am I anyway?—squinting hard at this ridiculous excuse for a map (haven't been here since I was three!). If I've just passed Newtownmountkennedy and Killawhatchamacallit, I must be on the right road—not that I would call this narrowly curving stupid little cowpath a road! Windshield wipers wildly doing battle with this sheeting rain, blurring my sight as I nearly scrape that wall—O Jeez! And I've gotta be crazy, but I've missed my father so much all my life, damn it, that I'm not gonna miss his funeral!

If I could only find some *real* music on the radio, flicking the dial furiously back and forth and only coming up with this jiggy stuff and eerie harp music—Weird! Really weird! And I'm definitely gonna be late, feeling so alone and bummed out—though I don't suppose my father'll mind! And wonder what Mother must be thinking back in Baltimore now? *Everything I do is for your own good, Tory*—Yeah, right! Good for herself is more like it!—*and I won't have you flying across the world to attend the funeral of a man you barely even knew! How're you going to start Sarah Lawrence next week if you're off in Ireland?* So damn concerned about my happiness that she spends most of her time trying to keep her new husband, Tan Man Mark, convinced she really enjoys that phony-baloney life they lead of Republican parties, Reagan and Nixon, and still denying Watergate: *Every president did it, Johnson, Kennedy, you name it*—How could she ever *marry* Mark after my father? Though how'd she ever marry my father with her proper English background, so refined, no bosom and no behind? And whatever *I* do, it's never good enough for her, always finding flaws: too tomboyish, too skinny, too gawky, making me feel like a freak, writing poetry that no one else understands, royally screwing up!

Ashford looming just ahead—great, at least that's on the map!—and the only time Mother *ever* broke out of her strait-laced Sarah Lawrence world was to fall in love with an off-the-wall (and now world famous) painter! Though I really wonder what they were like then. What'd she see in him anyway? What'd he see in *her*? And why'd she keep me from him? Creating him in my mind out of newspaper clippings and magazine articles!

More cows and sheep out there getting soaked but not seeming to care too much, just munching down on those lush green grasses. And what kind of person was he, really? Strong-willed and domineering? Or poetic and sort of spacy? The last time I saw him, ten years ago, the two of us hiding in the Baltimore Museum of Art till after it closed, when I was given a private tour, sharing painting as he saw and felt it, and making me see and feel it, too. Later thinking he was like some rock or movie star, Roger Daltrey, Richard Burton, Dylan Thomas—

My God, if this road gets any narrower, I'm gonna have to get out and walk it! Hey, there's a sign. Now if I could only read it through this stupid downpour, slowing almost to a stop—Powers-court, Sally Gap, and Glendalough, green arrows pointing every which way, Devil's Glen back there, just keep going—And Mother'll never understand why I had to do this—how could she, when I don't even know myself! Though maybe she's right, maybe

I am just an "uncontrollable child," "alien oddball," I don't know. Maybe I should just fly home with my tail tucked between my legs and accept my Sarah Lawrence fate? Because things could be worse, Mark can be such a jerk, but he's really not such a bad guy in a slicky, Watergate way (even though he looks like he dips his face in caramel), incredibly jealous of my father, but he has been good to me (sure he'd give anything to go through a whole day without Mother's bitching and moaning, so would I)—turning down this bumpy drive and—

O Jeez, will you look at the *size* of that crowd!

And where the hell am I gonna park this stupid car? *Where*? What a joke! *How?* is more like it! Wow, what a ghoulish scene, hundreds of people standing around wearing black trench coats in an old country graveyard overlooking the Irish Sea, the tops of Celtic crosses clustered together in that gray coastal mist—and look at the media blitz! TV cameras, reporters, and film crews pressing forward, BBC, NBC, Telefís Éireann, as this shower keeps slanting down over angelic tombstones, soaking the crowd—and feeling even sadder now, so alone! Just stay here in this car, by myself? No, have to go and do what I came here to do, say good-bye and all the things I wanted to say to him when he was alive—as getting out and—

Spinning around, I nearly slam into this enormous bald man, seven foot tall, geeky-looking guy, towering above me, dressed in a green-and-black tartan kilt, the wheeze of his keening bagpipes flooding my ears—till his passing reveals a mahogany casket carried by four bareheaded pallbearers slowly leading the procession through the wet crowd and shuffling over that thick thatch of slick grass toward a waiting priest—

And I think I'm gonna *drown*! Cold rain dripping off my chin, soaking my blue waterproof (which obviously was never made for Irish rain) as I edge closer, the piper's dirge rising now, catching another glimpse of those weird pallbearers, two short, two tall—this's beginning to seem like some Three Stooges comedy!—nearing the open grave and that muddy patch—and they start slipping—*O my God*!—and sliding, losing their grip on the casket, and heaving it off to the side as they plunge six feet down, the two behind skidding in after, and all of them disappearing from view! The wheezy music screeching to a stop, the bald piper pausing head and shoulders above the gaping crowd, and then—can you believe this—bursting out with a lively rendition of "When Irish Eyes Are Smiling"! Half the crowd hysterically laughing, while the rest of us keep on staring, as the pallbearers come struggling and groping out of the muddy grave—

And I *know* my father would've loved this!

The ceremony finally beginning as the rumbling crowd quiets:

"Saints of God, come to his aid . . ."

The ancient words drifting off under the steadily falling rain as the casket is lowered—and so hard really to picture him dead, even though I barely knew him, his great energy and joy—"*You've gotta take life by the tail, lassie, and swing it round till it gives!*"—never have a chance to talk, to write to him again, find out what it feels like being him or tell him how it feels being me!—and my God! this gnawing ache out of the blue, I can't even *breathe,* catch my breath!—eyes prickling and my tears mixing with the chilly drizzle, stomach such a tight knot of pain as they shovel in the first spadeful of dirt over the casket with an empty thud. Someone tossing in flowers and still others crossing themselves, praying for my father's soul and—

"O *Jaysus,* I *do* know ya, don't I now?"

"—What?"

"I *knew* I did!" This dumpy little man appearing beside me in a tailored Burberry and green plaid cap, orange beard and scruffy mustache. "You've got yer mother's lovely hair and yer father's devilish blue eyes! *Y'are* his daughter, aren't ya? Yes indeed y'are, I *knew* 'twas you! Tory, is it not?"

"Yes, my name is . . . Do I *know* you?"

"And how long are ya here for?"

"I'm sorry—I don't think—Well I'm not really sure."

"And where are ya stayin'?"

"Uh, the Shelbourne, in Dublin, but—"

"The Shelbourne, is it now?"

More people gathering around us, the media, reporters pressing in, mumbling and urgently whispering, "Hey, someone said that's his daughter?" "His *daughter*? Never knew he had one." "Pardon me, miss, but might you be the daughter of Seamus Boyne?"

"No, ya whore's melt, she's Mother Fuckin' *McCree*! Come on, Tory, follow me! This way!"

And grabbing my hand, he goes darting off. "Wait!" This strange little man practically dragging me along, weaving rapidly in and out of the crowd, across the slick grass, slipping, nearly falling, and up the path—

"Have ya a car, Tory?"

"Yes, it's over there—But listen, Mr.—I don't even know your name!"

"Fine, then you drive, but hurry, *hurry*!"

Both of us hopping into the Cortina, banging my knee on this stupid steering wheel, the press hot on our heels—and off we roar, away from the cemetery and back toward Dublin down the rainy, winding road with this weird little man (*whoever* the hell he is!) giggling beside me as the sun finally breaks through the massing clouds—and a swarm of reporters tailing us now in the rearview mirror! "Look, Mr. Whatever-your-name-is, this may sound rude, but who the hell *are* you anyway?"

"Ah, Jaysus, saints preserve us, but I just assumed ya would've remembered! Well, I'm Flynn, Kevin Fl—*Left*, turn left *here*!"

"*Left*? *What* left?" Splashing across the road, the wet green countryside whizzing by.

"Bloody vultures they are, just waitin' to pounce!"

Another blind curve flashing past. "But how do you know who I am—and where the hell're we *going*?"

"Sure and you were always yer father's pride and joy, one of the most delightful children I've ever seen—"

Slamming on my brakes and careening to a screeching halt. "Fine, dammit, then tell me who you *are*!"

The line of cars swerving up behind us.

"Christ, Tory, what're ya doin now? *Go, go,* here they *come*!"

"No, I'm not moving till you tell me, for all I know you're some kind of crazy rapist or something!" The pounding of footsteps rapidly approaching.

"All right, I'll tell ya, I *swear* I'll tell ya, only get the devil out of *here*!"

And jamming my foot to the floor, as a hand reaches for the door—and we zoom away in a cloud of sunny spray.

"Jaysus, yer as stubborn as yer blessed father!"—the drenched reporters hustling after us—"But as to who I am. Ah, well, I fancy meself a singer, a winemaker, a poetic soul, and executor of the estate of me *great* friend, dear, departed Boyne, daft genius that he was!"

Speeding on toward this roundabout, Killiskey, Killoughter, Kilmartin, all these signs in English and Gaelic. "Which way?"

"Get off here!—good lass—and straight on to Bray! . . . O and listen now, we're havin' a grand wake at me castle tonight, just up the road from here, so I'm countin' on ya bein' there."

Splashing into Dublin and swinging up in front of the Shelbourne's sloping canopy.

"Me limo'll pick ya up at six on the dot."

"I'm sorry, Mr. Flynn, really, but I don't think so, I won't know any—"

"Nonsense, you'll be the center of attention, and it'll give ya a chance to hear all about yer da——"

A valet leaning down to open my door. "Shall I park your car for ya, miss?"

"Sure, thanks"—stepping out—"I really appreciate it, Mr. Flynn, but I—"

"Ah, there's a cab, so go on with ya now, off ya go, and we'll see ya tonight at the wake!"

"Well, I don't know"—turning around—"let me see how I feel, Mr. Flynn, it's been a very trying—Mr. Flynn?" But he's suddenly gone, with me still in midsentence—and blurting out, "God, doesn't anyone ever *wait* for an answer in this retarded country?" People staring at me like I'm crazy as they pass—and shaking my embarrassed head—maybe I'd *BETTER* take a walk.

But where? See my "da's" city?—as I glance about into the horsey, indifferent face of this decked-out doorman, looking like some kind of dorky Admiral of the Fleet—"Yeah, well I wonder could you tell me please how to get to the nearest art museum?"

"Why yes, of course, that would be the National Gallery, 'tis down Merrion Street, round the corner, near the foot, ya can't miss it."

"Right, got it, thanks a lot"—and around the corner through this hustle of people brushing briskly past me, sneaking a peek at the broody sky as they scurry by, offering up whispered prayers and mutterings about constant rain and meetings at Bewley's—when, with a thunderous rumble, the sky explodes, the crowded sidewalks clearing within seconds and—look at this, now I'm standing in two inches of water all alone! I quickly duck beneath the shelter of Halloran's Appliance Store and wait outside the window, hoping this downpour will soon slow to a drizzle. Glancing inside, there's a group of people standing before a TV set laughing and pointing at something blocked from my sight. I bob and weave and try to see, then hop onto this windowsill—*O jeez,* that's *me* on the screen! Feeling about two inches tall, embarrassed by it all, this scene of me being dragged up the grassy slope by Flynn, sopping wet and—

"O my God, I'm gonna *fall*!"—grabbing for something to hold on to, nothing here but slick glass—and tumbling down to the ground, wet pavement, right on my ass! Terrific, Tory! I scramble up and dash off into the blinding gale, practically running now—what a jerk!—hurrying along, my face thrust forward, eyes blinking, as I swiftly pass under the National Gallery's black iron gateway, through the brown, varnished door, and into this musty air. Feeling cushioned by the thick velvet silence, my heels click clack and I trip as they catch on a crack on the cold marble floor—recovering my balance and rushing past the Irish masters—Osborne, O'Conor, Orpen, and Leech, Paul Henry and Jack Yeats—not even curious as to their lives or their fates—and nearing the Boyne exhibit, still in awe of those bold black letters announcing: **SEAMUS EAMON BOYNE,** and whispering to myself, "Father? Daddy? Poppa? Da—or Seamus?" saying his name over and over and over again, loving its vibrant sound. At the entrance, a small display case with a short bio of my famous father, all those stupid stats, telling me absolutely *nothing* about the *man* who was my father, and at the end proclaiming him "the greatest poet of twentieth-century art." Walking on and staring at each painting with my fears growing, colors whirling round, reds and greens and oranges glowing, nothing here to take away that gnawing, knowing that for him I never was!

I move into another room filled with a whole wall of nude women in all sorts of erotic poses: this young girl in front of me, about my age, so perfectly groomed, her corn silk hair the same color as mine and—*Hey, wait a minute,* that's *Mother, my* mother! Far out! I wonder if she even knows that she's hanging here in the raw? All these swirling colors, and to her left, a whole series of portraits of my father's second wife, Ciara, beautiful Ciara, bright blue, teasing eyes peeking through her lashes, perfectly regal nose, and a feathery dusting of freckles blending with that tawny mane. Then back to my mother, her eyes shut tight and hiding that cool green gaze I know so well, her face contorted, lips parted, slim legs bent at the knee, butt pressing upward, her stomach taut and flawless, as she clutches at her furry pubic mound, snatches of pale hair escaping between her grasping fingers—and flushing hotly, I avert my eyes, 'cause, God, if Mother ever saw this, she'd just *die*!

Continuing on, I pause before another painting of Ciara, with her flirtatious smile, one hand cupping a full, high breast, while the other gently strokes between her thighs. Her flesh such pink and white perfection, kneeling at the center of these flaming colors, smoothly rounded hips and supple, dimpled tummy. I reach forward to trace her sensual shape—and see my own reflection in the glass: my body so thin and lanky, eyes wide now and full of pain, too big for my face, while hers are so serene—as I hurry off into the adjoining room—and there's a photo of *his* face, that same *Time* cover, and a sign boasting of the PAINTINGS FROM THE PRIVATE COLLECTION OF THE LATE SEAMUS BOYNE (boy, they don't waste any time, do they? Not even dead two weeks) and claiming they're FAVORITE CREATIONS OF THE ARTIST, NEVER VIEWED BY THE PUBLIC AND—O Jeez, that can't be *me,* can it? This giant, life-size portrait of a beautiful little girl about seven beside a shimmering blue sea, on all fours in the sand, unaware that the fringe of her pink, cotton panties is peeking out from beneath that frilly sundress as she holds in her hand a tiny, scalloped seashell—

And this fierce ache in my belly now clutching my throat—choking me!—as the pain keeps coming in waves and—*O my God,* I've gotta get *out* of here!—running, sliding across the polished wood floor, knowing I can't run fast enough or far enough—why O why, Daddy, please, please don't leave me, leave me again!—and out through the door—blanking my mind to this mass of memories—into a blast of cold, wet air—and taking another deep breath, shower having stopped—down the rain-stained street, not sure where I'm going, how long I'm staying, what I'm going back to—and slowing now at this crowded corner as a group of students pass, then a bearded monk in a brown robe and sandals, his cowl raised, hurries by with a strange-looking face, his face—

His face? Can't be, my wild imagination—

No, it *is* him, my father, it *is* my *father*!—who's just disappeared from sight!

Boyne

Hustling down Nassau Street toward the dusty gray splash and bustle of Dublin's fair city on this brash Friday afternoon replete with sailing clouds and a ruffling, shuffling breeze sifting through the trees—and, Jaysus, I must tap a kidney soon!—after that coronary feast in my private retreat of flagons of wine and jeroboams of bubbly and absolutely forbidden Hong Kong curry (which nearly blasted my bloody head off!)—as I go striding by these Trinity gates, raw, weathered doors, and divinity faces, and the pervading odor of Ireland: peat or horse piss fresh off the quays, those Clydesdales clip-clopping over the cobbles at a graceful, weighty trot, and this raspy, brown woolen disguise chafing my crotch, arse, and holy thighs—

"Ah, grand spell of weather we're havin', Padre—"

"Grand, grand, my son"—as I keep apishly scratching down my sides—

"—Sure'n even Noah would've drowned!"

—past oncoming lorries and vans, humming a Gregorian chant, and by those gawking tourists with their Nike sneakers, crew-cut hair, and Kodaks poised for future color slides as my deceptive two-step-and-glide surges me into the lead and—a braying *Garda* siren! *O Suffering Christ!*

Starting—quickly glancing—lights flashing—and splashing by.

Relax! No reason to be after me, a monk on the run, stately Franciscan, Brother Boyne having just pulled off his own bloody funeral and striding on—still, a strange feeling to be both alive *and* dead!—as I pop safely into Findlater's bright, cluttered shop for, let's see here, what's the worst thing I can possibly eat, ha-ha, that I've been denied all these years by my irregular heartbeat and sky-high blood pressure? Some killer cholesterol sweet to top off my celebration feast, like these jam rolls, Swiss rolls, *yum,* slashed to three and six—and I think I'll get me one. My private Hindu physician warning me with his squeaky Gandhi inflection, "You will live no longer than two or three weeks, Mr. Boyne, if you continue acting as you do, I surely promise you." And defiantly shouting as I shot to my feet—"And *I* promise I'll die on my *own* terms and bloody well *outlive* you!" Along this candy counter crammed with Dolly Mixture, Liquorice Comforts, Savoy Pastilles, and my favorite multicolored jelly beans (haven't had one since God knows when)—sampling a luscious handful: *O Jaysus, yes*! This cashier here giving me the eye, then averting her stare from my monkish glare as I go munching out the door and right into Grafton Street, by Goldsmith and his knobby poll, airily reading a book, and Burke with his chest (or is it his paunch?) flung out before him, under Trinity's dark granite arch, past the porter's lodge, and across a gray, cobbled courtyard toward the Book of Kells in there, gold volumes, a dusty gleam—and I just saw a flash of green go by—needing a breather now—down this slender path, smooth carpets, the smell of fresh-mown grass, quarter-mile track with a wooden bench or two for me to sit on alone under the trees and let the ache drain down my heels. A moment's pause beside this green field's shimmer before I devour my three and six bargain of a jam roll, Swiss roll, this Findlater gem as I nip open the cellophane with my teeth and ease back the wrapper—Up yours, Gandhi! Good crackling grains of sugar, sponge cake, and raspberry jam, yum yum!

And nothing quite like seeing Ciara, lovely in her ways, savoring a sweet. O Ciara, dear Ciara, still missing you so, your lissome grace, continuing support, and never-ending inspiration I've lost: the creamy sheen of your wondrous skin and those keen bluestone eyes with their flaxen lashes—*Good God*! But the noose of fame kept crowding us in on that dark March evening, the night of my show at the Douglas Hyde Gallery, with me absolutely refusing to go, couldn't stand another bloody minute of fame and fawning—but you said no, someone had to be there to represent us, so—*O Mother of Christ*! tears welling, clouding my sight—off you went, never looked lovelier, to be blown to bits by an IRA bomb that was meant for Louis Mountbatten—who never *did* show!

And here, on this day of *my* funeral, leaving my home forever, rambling seaside estate of Ballyduff, bright green-painted Georgian domain (though since Ciara died, I was never home when I was at home with my entourage of housekeeper, secretary, and chef, gardener, nurse, and chauffeur)—Rothko once telling me as we went bouncing around Long Island in his dilapidated old Studebaker, its door shut tight with rope, that "fame'll estrange you from yourself. It's like far too much light on a film negative, instant overexposure."

And—*O Jaysus*!—still so on edge, taking several deep breaths in a row, as I rise to adjust my cowl. This Irish air so fresh after rain with its splendor of seething light, now dying, deliquescing into pale pastel shades, and the clouds slowly drifting along with dark blue centers, floating westward out to sea—

And could I ever capture it again, paint another masterpiece? God only knows, but I'd best be on my way!

Up the slope and onto the gravel path, close by that high-bouncing soccer exchange, reminiscent of my old warm-up sessions at school. Have a go at it? No, not in this disguise, can't be discovered now, just passing by—But ho, what's this? A loose ball rolling toward me—All right, lads, circle around to get the good right shooting boot on it, as they say (or, in my case, damp monkish sandal), toe down, show them the old flash, quick skip and—

Whomp! Soaring off, rising now and fading into an airy float—awe in their eyes, wondering who I am, where I'm from, Divine Order of Tottenham Hotspurs, ha-ha!—as I go grinning out the back gate and on down to Poolbeg Street. Still, no way I could've *kept* living like this, a prisoner of my fame and strained Gauguin heart: last two years've been a hell on earth, with water pills, beta-blockers, the Mahatma's cattle fodder diet—and a talent that's all but dried up, though the public keeps buying, prices keep rising—too much publicity, too little privacy, wanting out of the limelight, freedom to come and go, recapture my prime, my passion once more!—and dashing now toward this cozy pub, Mulligan's mahogany snug, and through this opaque cut-glass door with its embossed embroidery, past the boozy stares, to wedge my hand toward a tall, frothy Guinness.

"Ah, 'tis on the house, Father."

"Bless you, my son."

Bartender pulling the brown billy clubs and the dark brew rising in the glass, creamy foam gushing over—O gulp down this Guinness and lick off the lips! And behind me the huddled, heavily coated men jammed, jostling together, pints in fists, belching out laughter through the thick Woodbine smoke and stout smell. Such sad, flat faces grouped about this bar, gleaming with thirst on a payday in Dublin—

"Same again, Father?"

"Please."

Ah, Seamus, you may be on the road to forty-five, a rather grizzled evergreen, convalescing tosspot with the air knocked out of your sails, but the wild dream still sings in your veins, a lusty, brawling legend in your time! And back there, someone's getting up, sorting out his change, and shrugging into a rumpled mac. And I'll wedge a path through here, escorting my glass carefully over to this dark corner table—tumbles of ash and the stain of wet drink—coming around and slowly lowering myself into the seat, leaning back and gargling down the bitter brown foam of an almost cold Guinness, copies of the *Irish Press, Independent,* and *Time* in the corner—my bearded photo adorning the cover of that recent edition (and estimates inside of my worth having surpassed

Picasso's now, at nearly 200 million pounds: that Sotheby sale last spring for 3 million skyrocketing me into the forefront of contemporary painters, McCartney and Olivier buying, art market becoming outrageous, a hedge against inflation)—

And it's *all* such a fucking sham! *I'M* a sham: Boyne, the reigning flimflam man!—while *Time* lets me hail and climb above the Fords and Guggenheims, and that horde of flattering hangers-on, whorish critics feeding off me—dried-up me—and forever praising me to the skies: *How dare you criticize Boyne, the current king, whose brush is truly sublime!*—but who's been living, face it, on reputation, having lost my inspirations: wives Laura and Ciara, and my daughter, Tory (so many years, denied visitation)—as these seedy-looking men come swaggering through the door, reporters all, some of whom I've met before—and that tweed-capped, runty yahoo spotting me, doing a double take and—

O Christ! The jig is up, nowhere to hide!—as I glance away, tucking my cowl tighter, and he struts across the floor, thrusting his weasel face in mine. "Pardon me, Father, but I wonder now has anyone ever told ya you bear a strikin' resemblance to that famous painter what's-his-name, who was buried today?"—and chuckling smugly to himself—*odious little pest!*—as I remain silent and tense, anxiously twirling my glass and jiggling my knee to keep my teeth from floating. "And since his mug is now, in this year of our Lord 1973, bein' plastered all around the world, how's about puttin' yours as a look-alike in one of our local papers? Micksey, bring me camera—"

"O hell and *damnation*, man!"—leaping to my feet—"a curse on your local fish-wraps!"—and flinging the table brusquely aside, sending jars of Guinness flying, chairs crashing—

"Jayz, the monk's a fookin' psycho!"

—I escape like a wheezing Houdini, bounding out this cut-glass door with a burst of speed toward my secret studio-flat—heart pounding, bladder aching, dark rain clouds drifting over—and round the corner into Anne Street, with its gray, four-story building, a restaurant sign hung from the second floor—REGEEN S, FINE CUISINE, LUNCHES, WINES—as I lurch breathlessly on inside, along this hallway barely lit by a tea-colored bulb tucked against the ceiling, dust sagging down from these concave walls—and I always feel as though I were in one of those trick circus halls and that suddenly all the plasterwork will vanish and a bevy of wild Irish girls with their flaming ginger hair, shamrocks laced across it, will come prancing gaily out to welcome me to Dublin—panting up these narrow, creaking stairs with their worn red linoleum toward this bleak yellow door, my old Samoyed dog now barking and howling to beat the band, and into my secret retreat with—

Good God!—Poldy *pouncing* upon me and knocking me sprawling, a flurry of white fur, licking briskly over my face, nose, eyes, and beard, and shimmying his snowy rump, his plume tail swishing, still barking and wolf-howling loudly away—"Easy, doggie, easy—I know, I know, I love you, too!"—Poldy still licking, his tail wagging to and fro—as I finally stagger up to one knee, stroking his thickish ruff, and he continues nuzzling in, his cold nose urging more—"Can't get rid of me so quick, ha-ha! my great white Samoyed beast!"—spitting out his wispy hairs and fishing into my pocket—"See if I can find you a canine yummy, then off for a brisk romp round Stephen's Green—*Ah*, and look what I've got for you here!"—two blues and one red jelly bean popped in his mouth—"But first I'd better tap this kidney before I explode!"

Into the lav for a long, arching pee, and on the wall, my painted arrow winding upward from the floor and the words "As you follow this arrow with your eyes, you're probably pissing on your toes."

Then rummaging helter-skelter through this closet clutter of various disguises for a dry pair of socks and a spare pair of sandals—and where the hell did I hide them?—Ciara once calling me a Celtic pack rat—"You never throw anything away." Even tried my hand at cleaning the lot, but all I could do was shout orders:

"Towels, fold thyselves! Dust, be gone!" Half a case of Chinon '69 back here, along with tins of Buitoni canelloni and Danoxa Irish Stew, Guinness bottles and paperback books, sketch pads and still lifes—Just after World War II, Picasso buying a home in the south of France and paying for it with a single still life, and now with his death, there are Minotaur bath towels and Blue Period coffee mugs and—*O Mother of Christ!* here's that sketch I gave Ciara, my wondrous, golden wife, on her last birthday two years ago, when she turned thirty-one. Wanting to buy her a brand-new XKE, but forgetting my wallet as usual, so I dashed off this fast pen-and-ink sketch of her in the showroom, and she took it instead, adding, "I would rather have this as a gift from you." And after she died, hiding it away amid the clutter, avoiding all those painful memories, her last letter to treacherous Hagar—

Ah, and here they are! Behind these boxes and masks I'd only recently stashed from O'Callaghan's Costume Shop! Then sitting down on this green, rumpled bed, where Ciara and I once had that stormy fight early on in our marriage about my need for privacy, which nearly ended it before it began. The two of us getting jarred at the Shelbourne one night, and I decided to stay over here, put her in a cab, but five minutes later, she came raging through the door, proclaiming this was the final straw—"I have had enough, Seamus, of you and your 'off-limits' flat, your precious time for yourself!"—and stalking impatiently around, searching from room to room.

"Ciara, there's no one else here—so you have to leave right now!"

"You are such a hypocrite, saying always how much you want commitment in our marriage—"

"Yes, but freedom, too, time to be alone. Ciara, will you come on—"

"Freedom to roam whenever you like?"

"No, to breathe, be on my own. Ciara, I mean it now—"

"But why?"

"O Christ, who the bloody hell knows! Goes back to my mother, I suppose, suffocating me with mother-love, no privacy, hovering over her only child—'No locked doors in this house,' so—"

"Yes, yes I *know*, opening your mail, your sketch pads, notebooks, fearing her control!"

"Right, the fear of being swallowed whole—and those fears always returning—anyway—"

"So now you want your cake, as you say, and to eat it, too? And I am just around to provide you with a cheery little screw, the doting little wife who wants nothing more than to wait on her genius husband?"

"OK, Ciara, fine, fine—"

"No, it is not fine! Let me tell *you* something, Mr. famous Seamus Boyne, I am going to grant you your wish of having all the freedom you desire, because this is not *my* idea of a marriage!"

"Really, and what exactly is *that* supposed to mean?"

"It means that I have already gone through one marriage of leading someone else's life, so I am certainly not going to go through it again."

"Marvelous! So you just leave, pack up your bags and go? You knew what you were getting into when you married me—"

"O I did, did I? That is not what *I* remember you saying! How finally you had met someone who truly understood you, accepted you as you are, your 'easy give-and-take.' Well, all I see is that I give and you take nearly all the time!"

"I give you quality time, the best time I can—"

"Yes, fit me in between your busy social schedule, your interviews with the press, your painting sprees—I am more than just your model!"

"Christ, Ciara, you twist *everything* around, don't you? And, whoa, what're you doing *now*?"

"I am staying here!"—taking off her coat and unbuttoning her navy blouse.

"No, you're not, you're going, this is *my* private flat—"

"I am *not* going"—kicking off her shoes—"I'm staying here tonight!"—and wearing only her scanty satin slip.

"Ciara, you're acting ridiculous—"

"You are not going to make me leave!"

"Come on, I'll drive you home—"

"Don't *touch* me!"—swatting my hand away—"I am not going anywhere, I have had too much to drink and I am going to sleep here tonight"—and she slid stubbornly under the sheets.

"What're you doing? Ciara, will you get out of my bed!"—and she shook her head. "O, so that's what this is all about?"—and smiling, I started stripping off my clothes to crawl cuddling in beside her—

"*No!* Leave me alone, just leave me alone!"—and she rolled defiantly toward the wall. "This has nothing to do with us getting back together, it is *over*!"

"OK, *fine* with me, if that's what you want!"—and I rolled the other way—her sleek satin arse tipping mine, driving me crazy, couldn't sleep beside her without touching her, loving her, holding her through the night—God, I was *seething* inside, but enough was enough, invading my privacy, this place of my own—and suddenly all my fears returning, washing over me, the need to flee, being swallowed whole! But caught halfway, tightrope walking—togetherness or freedom? Sharing or solitude?—she ruining my life! But what was she ruining, my loneliness, misery? Hell, she was the best thing that ever happened to me!—as that panic came crushing in, suffocating me with the prospect of *losing her* then! All those terrifying images: So alone all those years, divorce, denied from seeing my daughter, suicidal—couldn't breathe, that pain in my chest, in my heart, couldn't quench the need for Ciara—like a starving man who can't get to the food that'll save him, I was *screaming* inside, needing her so—her lips, her hair, her eyes, her tongue, her skin, her smile, her sunny, joyous ways—so needing her in my life, the deep core of my life!—O Christ, waves of panic were flooding over me, that fierce, suffocating pain, barely containing it, wanting to cry—I *was* crying!—or end it right then! That fear of losing her, of never finding her again, and starving till I die!—and finally seeing there was no need to fear with Ciara, to protect myself from her, for only when we shared, became one, was there love like I'd never known, such calm, so tender and caring, and that sweet sense of exhaustion when we'd fall asleep spent and secure in each other's arms, and I groaned. "O Ciara, *PLEASE* . . ."

And she slowly turning over and sliding sensuously onto my back, wrapping herself around me like a satin glove with the creamy sheen of her skin, nuzzling and kissing my neck and shoulders as her hands went gliding across my chest and belly and down my thighs, my hips revolving, arching my spine, and she pressing her mound of Venus into my tailbone, grinding it round and round, holding me rockhard in her hand and stroking me up and down, both of us thrusting faster and faster, in sync, about to explode, and crying out together, "O Jaysus, Ciara, I love you so!" "O yes, dear God, yes, Seamus, yes!" as we came in a shuddering and shrieking frenzy, with her holding and hugging me as tight as I've ever been held, my sperm hand-handled all over the white, warm sheets!

And next morning making love again in the shower, then under my easel—as I gaze abruptly around my black-walled studio at those tubes of Winsor & Newton, cracked water glasses full of long, slender brushes, paint-stained rugs, rags, palette knives, and this half-finished canvas of a girl I'd given up working on with her ripe, Gauguin-like arse: Gauguin dying at fifty-four (only nine years older than I), broke, of a morphine overdose in the Marquesas Islands, ravaged with heart disease, eczema, and syphilis—

And sighing and blinking now as I rise for a final check of my Franciscan disguise: grizzled beard, cowl, and a deceptive glaze to my hollow eyes—denying death, preserving my prime—O and to *hell* with all doctors, lawyers, and publicity chiefs, greedy dealers, hounding fans, and autograph seekers!—as I tighten Poldy's pet leash around his ruff, "Ready, doggie? Time for your run, then I'm off to my wake in Bray!"

Tory

I can't believe how small this room is, sitting on this Shelbourne bed with its Swiss dot patterned spread and still feeling so lonely and shivery inside now that it's finally over. And what a change from Mother's grand hotels of Washington and Baltimore, the Jefferson or Peabody Court, with their huge, lavender and gray suites. The grandest thing about *this* room, as I pad barefoot across the floor, is its gigantic bathtub with its brass-handled spigot that I keep twisting with all my might, till the steamy water comes gushing out, then slip off my clothes—and no way that could've been my father outside the museum, my mind had to be playing tricks. Though who was that weird little guy I saw before leaning against the lobby door? I could've sworn I felt him watching me everywhere I went, but when I glanced at him, he ducked behind his newspaper. Or maybe I'm really going crazy, first thinking that I'd seen my father as a monk and now imagining that someone's following me. Come on, get ahold of yourself, Tory, probably just some horny old pervert, but he really did look strange, with his shaggy head of sandy hair and that long, craggy face, like some seedy detective out of an old B movie.

And, God, sinking down into this hot, steamy bath, leaning back and soaking. Why do I keep missing my family so, my home, and my own cozy bed with its rose-pink, satin spread that I picked up last week in Ocean City? Ocean City . . .

Ocean City's evening breeze chilling my bare knees as I sat hunched out there on that deserted pier, feet dangling above the stormy tide, lost within my fears of *never* finding my father, never finding myself—even thought of sliding off—ten *years* since I've seen him, and all those lonely summers, how could he just leave, *die,* did he even *think* of me, dreaming of a faraway father across the distant Irish Sea! And sinking even lower now in this scalding bath, submerging my bossy toes—and I kept recalling that time when I was seven and he suddenly appeared out of the blue as usual, finger to his lips—"Shhh!"—and snuck me away from our summer house down to Ocean City's beach, the two of us feasting on clouds of cotton candy, exploding ripples of laughter ringing in my ears, tender touch caressing my hair, and his joyful, booming voice telling me those incredible Irish tales of changeling fairies, wizard animal sprites, comparing himself to Cuchulain, Erin's greatest mythical knight, so like a shooting star, brilliant but short-lived, then passionately shouting, "You've gotta take life by the tail, lassie, and swing it round till it gives!" And when he finally took me home, I fell fast asleep in his arms with my birthday seashell still clutched in my hand, and was jolted awake by Mother's screeching, "Damn you, Boyne, don't you ever come here again! Kidnapping *my* daughter, I'll get a court order"—as he went charging out the screen door, setting me quickly down on the porch, one brief kiss good-bye, and then took off. I wanted to run after him, beg him to take me with him, beg him never to leave me—

And crying—*damn!*—throughout the rest of that summer and into September, as we packed for our return to Baltimore, and I knew he'd gone away, though I still held on to my dream that he'd be back again someday—was *supposed* to be there with me!—till that final straw when Mother married Mark, went flying off to Rome on her honeymoon and left me all alone my junior year of high school, just before that so-called scandal with my drawing instructor that she's never let me forget, along with her nonstop bitching about my "obsession with your 'supposed' father, who's out of sight, Tory, out of mind."

But when I read that story in *Time,* it seemed like I was reading about a stranger, so much about him I never even knew—and not one mention of me—as those tears kept streaming out of my eyes and I jumped to my feet, swaying awkwardly, and began to run, faster and faster away from that pier, running toward home, the pain hurting so—'cause there was only one thing to do—as I came bursting into our beach house and that crazy scene with Josie vacuuming, *The Brady Bunch* blasting over the TV, and Mother, with her platinum hair pulled back in a tight French braid, marching out of the glass and chrome rec room's glaring light and directing that swishy fag and his muscle-bound assistant with his pad and pencil down the hallway and into the sunken living room.

"Mother, listen, could I—?"

"—O hi, dear, you're out of breath—"

—the story of a man named Brady—

"—were you jogging?"

"No, listen—"

"Just a moment, Leonard."

"—I need to talk—"

"But I thought you were on the beach—Leonard, be right there. Tory, I'm dealing with the decorator—"

"I can see that, Mother—"

"—this is Leonard, Mr. LaMarre—"

"—but I need to talk to you right now!"

—and that's the way we all became the Brady Bunch—

"Hello"—almost tripping over the vacuum cleaner—"it's really important—"

"Keep this sylvan urn, Mrs. S?"

"Sorry, in a minute, Leonard. Yes, that, too."

"*Damn* it, Mother—"

"O sorry, what were you saying, Tory?"

"That I'm leaving for—"

"And have you decided, Mrs. S, on the Ming?"

"—leaving for where?"

"Ireland."

And she whirled about, her green eyes gleaming. "O no, you're *not*! Leonard, I'll be right there. Please, Tory, come in here! Excuse me, Josie, can you turn that *down*?"

"*Say what?*"

"*Turn that*—O never mind! Can't even hear yourself *think* in this madhouse! Anyway, Tory, no, you are *not* going to Ireland, and that's that!"

"Mother, I'm not asking you to pay for it or anything, I'm using my own savings—"

"This has nothing to do with money. Tory, I won't have you flying across the world to attend the funeral of a man you barely even knew! Why don't you go down to the florist now, pick out some flowers, and wire them to Ire——"

"That's 'cause you never *allowed* me to see him, to get to know him—so at least I can be there when they *bury* my father! God, Mother, can't you understand I *need* to be there?"

"And can't *you* understand I won't allow him to wreak havoc on this family again? And furthermore, how're you going to start Sarah Lawrence next week if you're off in Ireland?"

"Mother, you keep forgetting I don't even want to go to Sarah Lawrence. That's your plan, not mine!"

"So what're you going to do all year, just sit around the house and write poetry in that dreamworld of yours?"

"Look, Mother, I'm going!"

"Well, I think you'd better talk to your dad about all this—"

"Talk to me about what?" The screen door banging shut and Mark, flashing his George Hamilton grin, came loping in with his gray, lacquered hair, sunbaked tan, and blue and white tennis outfit, carrying a grocery bag in one hand, his Slazenger racket in the other.

"Well, maybe *you* can talk some sense into that seventeen-year-old head of hers, since she's just informed me she's not going to Sarah Lawrence and—"

"Mother, I never *said* that, all I said was I don't want to go *now*!"

"All right, all right, you two, let me put these away, then we can discuss this calmly. What a day! So much pressure lately, politics, money meetings. So what's this all about?"

"What this is about is that Boyne passed away last night and she has this crazy notion of flying to Ireland for the funeral. It's an absolutely ridiculous idea, what with school starting—"

"You're not going to Sarah Lawrence, Tory?"

"I didn't say I'm *not* going, just that I don't *want* to go! Really, can you see me fitting in with those artsy-fartsy kids whose only thought is who's got the best nose job, the biggest boobs, or the newest Gucci-Pucci?"

"O come on, they're not all like that! After all, I went to Sarah Lawrence."

"Well, that's hardly a glowing recommendation, Mother!"

"And what exactly is that supposed to mean?"

"OK, OK, fine, I promise as soon as I get back, I'll go to your precious *Sarah Lawrence,* I swear I will, but this is my father's *funeral,* damn it!"

"Tory, believe me, your mother and I *do* understand what you're saying, but still, there are other things to consider."

"Such as?"

"Such as more than likely you'll be coming into a great deal of money—"

"Mrs. S, one word?"

"I don't *care* about his money!"

"Well, don't be so quick, Tory, to dismiss—"

"*Mark,* this whole thing is—"

"Mrs. S, please, about the Ming—"

"O shut *up,* Leonard! Mark, this whole thing is absurd! She is *not* going to Ireland, and that's that!"

"Well, I have Irish contacts, law friends—"

"Look, Mother, I've got plenty of extra cash and my

passport, I'll be fine, and I promise I'll call you as soon as I get there—"

O Jeez!—that sharp twin-brrrringing sound!—nearly jumping out of my skin! She's calling here since I haven't called?—as I go slipsliding across the floor to fumble with the phone, untangling this damn cord, "—Hello?"

"Ah, sorry ta bother ya now, Miss Boyne, but yer limo's just arrived."

"My what? O my limo, right, right, uh, OK, well, I'll be right down."

And that's all I need now, my father's wake filled with loony Irish artistic types droning on about what a fantastic man he was! But hell, briskly toweling myself off, I guess I might as well go (whatever I look like now: paler than usual with these bluish smudges under my eyes), since, face it, anything's got to be better than sitting around here moping! And what exactly are they wearing to wakes this year? How 'bout this black Bergdorf number? Suitable for mourning? No! And hastily grabbing a bright blue party dress instead—'cause *I'm* not dead, and I'll be damned if I'll dress as though I were.

Boyne

—Rocketing full bore out of this hairpin curve on my sleek Harley with the brown hood rippling and whipping off my tonsured dome and—*Good God,* what a wonder of speed, careening down the Stillorgan Road, eyes slitted, teeth gleaming and gritted as I weave in and out of these buses and cars, leaning forward into the engine's shuddering roar—and *Christ, what a high!*—splashing through these twists and turns, flashing toward that leafy crest and passing all my cherished watering holes long denied me: Slattery's in Ballsbridge, Purty Kitchen in Dun Laoghaire, Druid's Chair in Killiney, and soon the Pipers Lounge in Bray—the sun setting across the darkling sea as I come squealing round this bend, needing to fight off that black despair one final time and not end up like drunken Pollock catapulting ten feet off the ground and fifty feet through the air out of that pinwheeling car and slamming headfirst into a tree!—for *everybody's* dying these days, Steichen, Tolkien, even Picasso this April—and all the artists of my generation, Arshile Gorky, David Smith, poor Frank O'Hara, losing their lives, freaky car and truck accidents—and three years after I broke into the Tate, my dear friend Rothko, that scruffy, irascible bear, always talking about fulfilling his lifelong dream of having his work shown in the same museum—and on the day his paintings were being delivered at the back door of the Tate, a cable was arriving at the front announcing his suicide!

Tory

This long white limo zooming smoothly onto a slick back road somewhere close to Bray and up a deserted driveway that keeps bumping and winding through a pitch-black forest—what the hell've you gotten yourself into this time, Tory? Feeling like an oddball even here, never quite fitting in no matter *where* I am—at school, at home, and soon at Sarah Lawrence. Guess I'm just lopsided, as Biggio said, a skinny, spacy tomboy (who can sometimes sound far too sophisticated for a seventeen-year-old: "You've got the words, but your emotions haven't caught up yet."). Always getting A's in English (710 on the Verbal SATs), but screwing up everything else, failing math, C's and D's in science—and, O yeah, A in art, too. Though Biggio had a bit to do with that. Arlo Biggio: half hippie, half scholar, with his Jim Morrison mouth and Modigliani eyes. And sure I flirted, buttered him up, after we went joyriding on his Honda, till he started coming on like crazy—and I stopped him from going all the way. Why he ever told his wife, I'll never know!—and he got booted and I got suspended. But he really was such a passionate kisser that I just wanted it to last forever, so of course I kept on kissing, opened my mouth, sucked his tongue as his hands fumbled with my breasts—but suddenly the little girl popped out and I got all flustered and scared—and I stopped, which made me feel like a tease—

And—*Wow!*—will you just look at that really cool castle straight ahead with its towers and turrets, battlements and bastions right out of my childhood's Irish fairy tales as we glide to a stop and this chivalrous chauffeur hops spryly out to hold the door open for me—making me feel like a princess gracefully stepping toward him and—*damn!* slamming my head hard, practically cracking my skull—so embarrassed, holding back my tears as he turns to go, and I'm left standing here rubbing my aching scalp in front of this shield-shaped, oaken door.

Lifting the iron knocker, I let it clank a couple of times, before the massive door finally creaks open and this pie-eyed W. C. Fields, wearing purple paisley suspenders, orange-striped pants, and cradling a glass of stout—"God help all tinkers and poor wanderin' folk!"—drunkenly waves me in, then goes waddling off as I follow behind his Humpty-Dumpty shape, through the dark foyer toward that ear-shattering chatter, Irish bagpipe music, and this motley crew toasting one another—"Drink up, Brian, sure 'tis the water of life!" "*Water*? Good Chroist, man, Oy never drink *water*!" "And why's that?" "Fish fook in it!"

Maybe I should just leave, tiptoe out of here—

"Ah, *Tory,* me dear"—Mr. Flynn roughly kissing me on both cheeks—"so glad ya could make it!"—his whiskey breath and the rasp of his ginger mustache—"But let me introduce ya to all yer father's friends"—and taking my hand once again, he guides me ahead, round the curving castle walls, toward that same seven-foot geek playing the bagpipes, Percy Dungannon, and the rest of the guests crowding closer now in a gushing whirl of Maureens and

Noreens, Doreens and Dermots, Liams and Seans, all going on about my dad—"O he was mad as a hatter on a good day, he was, but he painted like an angel, he surely did, afflicted with a brilliant talent—" "Oym in desperate need of a wet!"—and this blonde bombshell with the boobs of life, who looks about ready to tip over—"Must be terrible sad to lose a father." "—Shattered, really." "Wasn't it Janis Joplin said the hardest ting about bein' an artist was makin' love to twenty-five thousand people onstage, then goin' home and sleepin' alone?"—as W.C. Fields, with his clowny, road-mapped nose, drapes a hairy arm around my shoulders—"O Jayz, I recanize ya now from the picture on yer father's walls, and I just wanna tell ya that the rumors are definitely true."

"Which ru——?"

"That he was the besssst fookin' painter west of the Liffey! Did grand tits he did, so don't ya ever forget it!"

Have to get out of here. "Is there a bathroom upstairs?"

"Right y'are, Tory, second door on the left, past the sitting room."

"Thanks."

And wrenching myself free, I duck under WC. and dash for the hall, up these winding stairs, and away from this crazy wake, W.C. and the Irish boozers (sounds like a local rock group!)—because if I don't get some peace and quiet soon, my aching head's gonna explode!

Boyne

Breezing full speed up Flynn's dark, sloping drive with my brown gown still billowing behind me and sweeping to a skidding stop on the damp fringe of these woods—glee wildly humming in my veins, what a surprise in my disguise! recapturing my prime in the brief time remaining, one last sniff of the rose—and fitting this rubber mask over my eyes, grizzled beard and mustache, go darting off like an Irish commando, keeping low to the ground toward that shimmering, vine-covered castle—ready to react at the slightest sight or sound with my split-second reflexes that still allow me to stop on a dollar, turn on a dime, and sprint faster than a bloody cheetah, ha-ha!

All those luxury cars, wheezy music blaring forth, and swiftly reaching this wrought-iron trellis, cat burglar Boyne scaling the heights, pop in through that second-story window, hand over hand, up we go and—*Jaysus!*—slipping, nearly falling (no Flying Wallenda I!)—above these vines (my heart ceasing at any time!)—and pausing, loudly panting—to glance in at this gray, dimly lit drawing room: a scene of carnage and repine? No, plush of carpet, armored of wall, and leathery of chair—as suddenly a fair-haired girl comes rushing through the door with coltish grace and an angry scowl on her pretty face—

Tory

O my God! someone's breaking in!

I take one step forward, one step back—what'll I do?—spinning desperately around and spying a knight's suit of armor with his spiky silver mace held out before him and trying to wrestle it from his grip—this damn thing weighing a ton!—as it flies free with a jolt, sending me reeling back and screaming, "Don't come any closer!"—

"No, no, really, listen, miss, I'm not a robber, I'm—"

—when Flynn bolts through the door—

"O Suffering *Christ,* Kevin, tell her it's *me, Boyne, Seamus* Boyne!"—and stripping off his freckled mask—a *Howdy Doody* mask?—beard, mustache—?

"*Boyne*? *O Jaysus, Mary, and José*!"

My *father* Boyne?

"*Holy Mother of God!*" Flynn grabbing him in a bear hug and swinging him round and round, laughing and pounding him on the back—"I can only suppose that you've taken leave of yer bloody senses—"

Father, Daddy, Poppa—?

"No, quite the contrary—"

"—though I'm beginnin' to see a certain ruthless logic about yer schemin' mind!"—as Flynn grins back at me, still holding this weighty mace and staring—"Well here, Tory, come meet the recently late, but no less great, Seamus Eamon amazingly resurrected Boyne!"

"My *daughter* Tory?"

"Yer lovely teenage daughter!"

"What the hell're you doing *here*?"

"What am I? What am *I*? But why'd you *lie*, fake your own *funeral*?"—as W.C. stumbles pie-eyed into the room.

"—Ah, pardon me intrusion, Padre—but the press's just arrived, and they're all of 'em askin' after Miss Boyne!"

"O those bloody vultures!" Flynn gruffly shoving my father and me toward this open window—"*Wait*! What're you *doing*? *Stop!*" and the next thing I know, I'm being half-carried down a trellis and through these tangled vines—"Damn it, will you let me go?" "Just hang on, Tory—but why're you *here?*" "—I came for your funeral but—" "O right, right, well that makes sense—watch your footing there—got it?" "Got it—*Ouch!*" "You OK?" "Fine." "And where're you staying?" "At the Shelbourne—" "Ah, well, not the safest place with the media hounding you. Ready, we'll jump together—*now*!"—down, down through the breezy air—*thump!* "Well done, lassie, follow me!"—and running across the lawn—"We'd best go back, get your stuff, and you can stay at my place." "Stay *where*?" "Ballyduff, my estate in Rathnew, no one'll suspect you there!"—and racing for the woods toward that monster motorcycle—no way am I gonna ride on this Harley—

"Hop on behind!"

And I reluctantly squeeze myself onto the seat back, holding tight and squealing as this hunk of metal roars into life and we pop a wheelie, much to my father's delight, and go shooting off down this dark, winding road, leaning sideways left and right along these blind, tree-lined curves, the wind whipping my hair into my eyes and mouth—quickly wiping my sweaty palms on my dress—and I think I'm gonna be sick to my stomach! clinging to his back for dear life—and I can't believe it's really *him: my father and me on a Harley!* faking his own funeral? Howdy Doody mask—And maybe Mom was right after all, 'cause he *is* so weird and *really* off the wall!—speeding past these tall, swaying trees, doing at least a hundred miles an hour! and squinting briefly at the black blur of pavement beneath my feet, thinking how easily it could grind my skin into raw meat—and keeping my eyes shut, tentatively feeling the warm flesh of his waist through the coarse cloth of his strange monk's robe (afraid to squeeze)—and, God, I hope he knows what the hell he's doing!—as he yells something back to me now—losing his words in the wind whooshing past my ears before catching a bit about "—popping in the pub for some fags." "Some *what*?"—and into town as he screeches to a stop in front of the Pipers Lounge.

"Be back in a flash!"

"Wait, where're you going—?"

But he's already inside the door, and I'm left sitting here on this stupid motorcycle in this stupid dress, feeling like a totally stupid jerk! And why is he looking for *fags*? O my God, don't tell me he's queer, too, queer *and* weird?

No, here he comes now, sauntering out of the pub alone, wiping his lips with the back of his hand and tossing me a bag of—what the hell're these? *Cheesy Wedges?*

"Thought you'd like a snack."

Yeah, really! I didn't even realize how hungry I was, haven't eaten since—ripping open this bag with my teeth and about to feast on these—"O *yuck!*"—spitting them out—"These things taste like Elmer's glue!"—as my father erupts with a bellow of laughter and once more we're on our way—"Off to Harold's Cross!"—popping another wheelie out of Bray.

And what the hell's Harold's Cross? Another fag stop or what? "Hey, I thought you were taking me to the Shelbourne"—but my words're again lost in the wind as we go whizzing along these narrow roads and under the neon's night-slitting light—and last time I rode a motorcycle like this was with Arlo Biggio—and look where the hell that got me!

Quickly passing signs for Donnybrook and Rathmines, my cheek pressed against his robe, and feeling the machine slow, I cautiously open my eyes and, much to my surprise, find we're pulling into a parking lot: the Greyhound Race Course? O Christ, *now* what is he up to?

"Just stoppin' in to place a fast bet on a real hot tip, ha-ha!"—and he hurries off, leaving me standing here looking stupid again in this blue party dress and tangled hair, windy tears still burning my eyes as I go scampering after him, shouting his name through the crowd and dodging between hordes of scuzzy-looking workmen with broken teeth and stained lapels, jeering at me as I pass, the women dressed in drab skirts and god-awful shoes, clucking their tongues in disapproval—and, *damn*! breaking the heel off my shoe—this group of teenage boys cheering me on with catcalls and wolf whistles as I slow to a hobble—and *now* where'd he go?

Finally slumping down on this wooden bench as the gravelly Irish announcer thunders, "And they're *off*!"

All about me the crowd standing and roaring as one at the lean pack of dogs racing around the dusty track chasing some kind of fur and metal contraption—what a bunch of dumb dogs! And then it's over in a blink and I'm caught in a confetti swirl of worthless, losing tickets flung in the air, people cursing and grunting their despair, while those few winners whoop and cheer.

And sitting next to me, this pasty-faced, courtly old man, with his rumpled, mismatched suit and crumpled tweed hat, leaning over with a powerful B.O. reek and throaty brogue, "Might I be of some assistance, miss?"

Yeah, try taking a bath! *God,* Tory, he's trying to be nice! "Well, see, the thing is—"

"Lost your way?"

"No, no, I'm, uh, waiting for my father"—and there he goes, dashing by!—as I jump to my feet and catch him from behind. "Where the hell *were* you?"

"Ah, Tory lass, I won a bloody *fortune,* fifty-six Irish pounds, that's *all* for you—must've coked up my dog's Kal Kan! But, Jaysus, this is no place to be out gadding about, so come on with me!"

And away we go again, following him through the crowd like a puppy, wanting to leave, to run, to tell him off—but I can't quite figure out what to call him—Seamus? Daddy? Papa? Dad?—then zooming down the narrow roads on the Harley, along the canal, barely missing cars and buses and on through these traffic lights—I'm never gonna make it off this machine *alive*!—up ahead, a sign pointing left toward Dublin, the Shelbourne, and safety—but my father takes a sharp, skidding right—as I scream in his ear, "Where the hell're we going *now*?"

"Just want to pop into Slattery's, it's merely a stagger away on the quays."

"Look, this is crazy, enough *stops*—"

But my voice cut off as he screeches to a halt in front of this seedy-looking pub, telling me to wait right here for him.

"Be out in a jiff!"

No, not again! And hopping down from the seat, tearing my dress, I shout at the top of my lungs, "Damn it, if you won't take me back to the hotel right now, I'll walk there *myself*!" Then slipping off my broken heel, trying hard to stare down this crazy man—who no way could be my father!

"What on earth's the matter?"

"'What on earth's the matter?' What on earth's the *matter*? You fake your own funeral, scare me half to death dressed in a stupid Howdy Doody mask and that retarded monk's robe, drive like a maniac, stop for some *Cheesy Wedges*—Why don't you quit being such a *jerk*?"—and I go stomping off, barefoot down the street.

Boyne

Daughters—*Jaysus!* what can you expect? Her head still high and cocked at an arrogant tilt, walking swiftly on—when from out of the darkness under those eaves, three Teddy boys, all with long, greasy hair, spiky shoes, black leather jackets, begin following her now, teasing her, hemming her in, forcing her toward that shadowy alley—

"Hey, Yank, how 'bout comin' round the back lane wit us?"

"O go to hell!" Tory still walking fast.

"Come on, empty fork, ya wan' me to fill it fer ya?"

"Look, were you born retarded or do you have to work at it?"

The tall one shoving her hard into the other one's arms.

O Suffering Christ! And I'm off in a flash, flapping after them all in this ridiculous brown robe, my heart wildly pounding—"Wait, hold on there!"

The tall one whirling around to face me. "Fook off, Friar!"

"Listen, you don't want to mess with me, I know karate, judo, kung fu, haiku—"

"Ah, go rattle yer fookin' beads!"

Whack! And unleashing a savage left hook snapping his greasy head back—

"He *hit* me!"

"Right, and I'm about to do it again!"—faking the jab, then karate-spinning around, toe down, and—*Whomp!*—booting him in the balls as he falls straight back, his head smacking the pavement, probably cracked his bloody skull—"Any more tough guys about?"—the other, shorter two fleeing at my manic stare as I gently guide Tory up the road, her blue eyes blazing, with me breathlessly saying, "Listen, I'm awfully sorry for all this—I was wrong, you were right—so, please, let me buy you a drink, whatever you want"—on into Slattery's—"but you've sure got a hell of a mouth on you, don't you? Your mother taught you well."

"Yes, she did. And are *you* OK?"

"I think so, though I'll never play the violin again—No, no"—flexing my fingers—"really, I'm fine, fine, never better."

"O you *are* left-handed! I was certain you were. Everybody tried to change me—"

"Me, too!"

"—but I wouldn't let them."

"Ah, then a toast to the two survivors: Tory, my lovely lassie, and her resurrected da!"—and sitting across from each other in this dark snug and letting out a weighty sigh—"Jaysus, nothing like a little physical violence to make a man feel young again—though my blood pressure's probably skyrocketing straight out of sight!"—this white-aproned waiter before us—"Is Guinness all right?"

"Uh, sure, sure."

"Two stouts here. Anyway, Tory"—broadly grinning—"walking back to the Shelbourne yourself would've been a bit much now, don't you think?"

"Well, what'd you expect, you *always* do that!"

"'Always'? What're you talking about?"

"Don't you remember?"

"Remember what?"

"When I was seven and you did the same thing, came to Ocean City, dumped me on the porch, and then took off?"

"I did?"

"Yes, you did."

"Well never again, I swear, 'cause *Good God,* I haven't felt this alive in I can't *remember* when, and I'm going to draw you now, paint you now, 'cause *you're* my inspiration! For as Gauguin said, 'In order to achieve something new, you have to go back to childhood.' And the question now is how? How? *How*? A whole new direction now? Abstract? Pollock drips? Or Rothko expressionistic? Well, we'll see, we'll see! Ah, but here we go!"—clinking our foamy jars together—"To the *two* of us, Tory! *Slainte*! But you don't really like it, though, too warm, too bitter, eh?"

"No, it's fine, really."

"You have to acquire a taste for it. But I can still paint the *spirit* which shines through your face—'cause Christ, you're so wondrously, *expressively* pretty!"

"I am?"

"With marvelous bones and glittery eyes—"

"You don't think I'm too skinny?"

"*Skinny*? *Sweet Jaysus,* you're like a slender ash on the coast of Ireland! Hair like silken sun, a childhood gossamer grain!"—draining the last of my jar with a flourish—"Would you care for another?"

"Uh, yeah, sure, why not?"

"Though it really shouldn't surprise me, Tory, since you were such a beautiful, shining child!"

"Well, I still can't believe those paintings I saw in the National Gallery today. It made me think of our sneaking into the Baltimore Museum—"

"The Baltimore Museum—O that's *right, right,* never forget that!"

"Remember you told me, 'You've gotta take life by the tail, lassie, and swing it round till it gives'?"

"Yeah . . . well, it's certainly been giving these last few years. You OK, Tory, feel all right?"

"Just a bit tipsy."

And finishing off this final round myself, then arm in arm out the door into a whack of wind as, hopping back on the Harley, we roar out of Ballsbridge with a snarl of blown exhausts, her slender hands now clutching my waist, popping another wheelie and careening at top speed down Baggot Street past cabs and cars with that zany rush of energy once more, toward Merrion Row and swerve to a screeching stop before the Shelbourne—"Want me to come up, lass?"

"No thanks, I'll be out in a minute."

"Fine, then I'll wait for you down here."

Tory

Hurrying through the hotel lobby, I glance back with a grin at my "monkish" father sitting astride his monster motorcycle, then keep pacing before the slowest elevator ever made—be here forever if I wait for this stupid thing!—and dashing barefoot up these three flights of stairs—footsteps behind? Getting paranoid now like my da with his media fears—quickly down this creaky corridor covered with paisley swirls of ugly green and purple, passing 325, 327, 329—to 333, and fumbling for the key, I jam it in! My clothes scattered all about the room, and pulling out a pair of blue jeans and matching sweater from the pile—No, wear these jeans now, white sweatshirt, and Nike sneaks, then stuffing the rest into my bag—and someone's knocking loudly on the door.

Who the hell's that?—My father changing his mind, doesn't need a daughter along, interfering with his pubs and wakes or whatever else he does! No, stop being so negative—as I swing it open—"Uh, yes?"—and a weird little man standing there in a bright yellow slicker, the hood pulled tight round his head, his eyes and half his face concealed by those huge aviator sunglasses—"Miss Boyne, you'd better come along with me right now, I'm afraid yer father's had a heart attack."

"*O my God*!—where *is* he, in the street, the lobby—?"

"No, no, gone to hospital, hurry! I'll take ya there!"—and racing down the back stairs—"I'm parked outside, this way!" He guides me through the kitchen, banging into pots and pans, this pissed-off cook screaming and waving a carving fork at us—"Just out here"—this narrow alley, where he practically shoves me into a rusty green Volkswagen and slams the door.

"Hey, what the hell's going *on*? Who're you anyway—and how'd you know he's my *father*?"—and reaching for the door handle, I find only a hole where the handle used to be—"Wait a minute, what *is* this?"—as he revs the engine and we go veering crazily out into traffic, horns honking, just missing an oncoming cab, with me shrieking, "What the hell're you tryin' to *do, kill* us? Let me *outta* here!"

"Sorry, Miss Boyne, but I'm afraid I can't do that."

"Just what do you mean you *can't* do that? Dammit, you pull over right *now*!"

And he squeals sharply to a stop by the curb, grabbing my wrist with one hand and stretching behind his seat with the other for a dirty green dish towel—"I really don't want to hurt ya, Miss Boyne—" "You son of a *bitch*!"—pressing it into my face—"Where's my *father*?"—this sweet, sickly smell—"What're you *do*—?" The rag blocking my mouth and nose, squirming hard as I can to breathe, his voice growing fainter, seeming a thousand miles away—

"Believe me now, Miss Boyne, ya won't feel a ting . . ."

Boyne

Ah, and how marvelously bizarre it is to see my only child blooming into a lovely, feisty lass, same eyes and nose as mine, her mother's mouth and sensual arse—

"*Boyne buried!*"

—and whirling about to that raucous shout: newsboy hawking the *Irish Press*, and below the headline, deceased me with that glazed yet piercing royal blue gaze staring devilishly back—as, sighing, I sink down on my Harley, drawing this dark cowl around my face. And Tory certainly taking her girlish time, better go hustle her along—and run the risk of being recognized.

Under the awning, behind these posh men, shoes slicked to a blinding shine, up to the elegant front desk.

"Yes, may I help you, Father?"

"Tory Boyne's room?"

"Tory Boyne? Yes . . . three thirty-three. I'll ring . . ."—keeps ringing. "No answer, I'm afraid, Father."

"No *answer*? Has she come down?"

"Not to my knowledge."

"Then I think I'd better check"—and scampering toward that closing elevator door, one of those slickly shiny men holding it open for me—"Ah, bless you, my son!"—I squeeze inside under this sign MAXIMUM 10 PERSONS ONLY, cheek to jowl, chin to cowl!

And up we go, so incredibly slow, finally reaching three, the group parting like the Red Sea to let me pass—and rapidly down this paisley-carpeted corridor to her room—odd, her door ajar—"Tory?"—leaning in: no sign of her, clothes strewn, Levi's and sweater left on the bed. Rushed out without telling me? But why? Press corps whisked her away down the back stairs? I'll give it a try.

Now where? Kitchen straight ahead, reeking of olive oil and thyme—and this chef-hatted hippo steaming toward me—"Sorry, please, no one's allowed in here!"

"Just one quick question, did you happen to see a young lady—?"

"I said *no one's* allowed—"

"Yeah, well, Oy did, Father"—that pastry boy lifting his carroty head.

"Dennis, this is not your—"

"Alone?"

"No, wit a short man in a yellow mac who went runnin' tru."

"*Dennis!*"

And swiftly by their shouting match into this alley leading onto Kildare Street filled with Dubliners out for a Friday night—and of course my daughter and this loony now *nowhere* in sight.

Tory

My poor head—*Wow!*—feeling like it's been run over by a fleet of eighteen-wheelers—and where the hell *am* I, anyway? Blinking hard in the pitch-black darkness, can't see a thing, must have fallen asleep—but where? At home, Ocean City? No, dummy, Ireland, Dublin—*duh!* Right, right, so I fell asleep—yeah, must've been a dream, that crazy little man in his yellow—*Brrrr,* it's so *cold* in here, feeling around for a blanket—*hey,* this isn't the Shelbourne spread! Then it *wasn't* a dream, it really did happen—*O my God,* I don't believe this, I *have* been kidnapped! But *why*? My panic rising—terrorists, IRA, and that Lindbergh baby turning up dead—about to scream—*no,* don't panic, Tory, don't panic, just calm down, take a deep breath—

OK, OK, so *now* what? Find the lights.

And cautiously reaching out, there's gotta be a wall here somewhere! What the hell *is* this place anyway, a storage room? Brushing past piles of God knows—*ouch!*—and slamming my shin into something sharp, rubbing my leg and feeling warm, sticky wet—Terrific, now I'm bleeding, too! Stretching my arms before me—and what the hell am I doing, playing some stupid game of blind-man's bluff? Touching something cold and rough—the wall?—and timidly running my hands along its bumpy texture, imagining all sorts of creepy crawly things—can't even see my own hands, a rattling noise growing louder and—

The door flying open, bright lights streaming inside, hurting my eyes—and this evil-looking hook of a woman in a white nurse's uniform shoving a stainless-steel food cart toward me, then turning to leave as I rush after her, screaming, "No, *wait,* who are you and why am I—?" and she just glaring over her shoulder with those steely gray eyes and slamming the door in my face—"What do you *want* from me? Tell me, will you at least *tell* me?" And, *God,* I feel like such a dork standing here in the dark, screaming at myself as her footsteps fade away.

Boyne

Swiftly up these creaking stairs, my old Samoyed barking and wolf-howling even louder than before, and into my secret retreat with—"*No, Poldy!*"—he *pouncing* upon me as usual—but this time catching him in midair, staggering and waltzing dizzily about (not quite Rogers and Astaire)—then falling backward onto this couch—"O *Christ,* doggie, can't dance now, maybe later—got to find my daughter!" Poldy still licking briskly over my beard, nose, and blinking eyes, and shimmying his rump as I spring to my feet and start pacing round the room, past my half-finished painting—and *Suffering J!* Who the blazes *is* this thieving bastard, pervert, kidnapper, greedy wheeler-dealer, IRA henchman (though, with my usual flair, I've managed to enrage *both* sides over the years, Provos and Paisley knaves), who's obviously recognized me, knows I'm alive, and is holding her for ransom?

All these years, and such a wondrous daughter, with her gamine smile and hair like silken sun, my inspira—And *Christ,* what the hell am I *saying*? Haven't seen her since she was seven—for there's more to her than just a model for my bloody paintings!

So what do I do, what *can* I do? Need help—seething inside, mind spinning! Can't call the police—so whom *can* I call, who knows I'm alive?

Flynn, yes! yes!
He'll know what to do!

Tory

A bare lightbulb swaying from the ceiling of this cramped little room—finally finding the stupid switch—filled with buckets and mops and stacks of cardboard boxes—and in the corner, a narrow bed jammed against the wall and covered by a red wool blanket tossed across that—*gross*!—pee-stained mattress as I keep weaving past this serving cart and delicately lift the lid to find a pile of boiled cabbage and potatoes and a pot of lukewarm tea. Well, it's certainly not Maxim's, folks, nor even McDonald's. But God, I'm so hungry, famished, really, eyeing this plate of soggy veggies—though not *that* hungry, I'd rather starve than eat this stupid slop! OK, well, maybe just some tea then, pouring it into a cracked china cup— Hey, wait a minute, maybe they drugged it or something! And shoving the cup aside, the tea sloshing onto my feet—This is really *sick*! then slumping to the floor—I mean, what the hell did I *do* to deserve this? Fly to Ireland? Defy my mother? It's so absurd, totally crazy—I don't know *why* I'm here, *who* brought me, or where the hell I *am* for that matter! But I'm sure my dad *must* be hot on their trail by now, finding my wallet back at the Shelbourne (along with my fake ID), the empty room—

But wait, wait a second, why can't I just escape myself? God, what a dork, I should've at least checked the door first thing, you never know—as I grab the knob and pull with all my might—O come *on,* please come *on*!—and it's starting to budge! Pulling even harder and the door suddenly gives—as I go hurtling backward on my butt, then look up to see that weaselly little creep who dragged me here in the first place!

"Hey!"—getting to my feet—"you're the same guy I saw hanging around the Shelbourne lobby—so you *were* following me! But *why*, what the hell do you *want*, huh, what's going on?"

"Now if you'll just calm down, Miss Boyne, nothin' a'tall will happen t'ya—"

"Calm *down*? O right, I'll just *do* that! You spy on me, *drag* me out of the hotel, *lie* to me about my father having a heart attack, *drug* me, then throw me into this dark, *scuzzy* room, and then tell me to *calm down*"—and flinging myself at him, I'm waylaid by some monster nerd in hospital greens, who slaps me hard across the face, then slams me back against the doorjamb!

"Ah well, Miss Boyne, I see ya need a bit more time to yerself, so we'll just leave ya be fer now"—and with a nod to his ten-foot goon, who dumps me on the bed like so much trash, he walks out of the room, with his plumber's butt, locking the door behind him—and I fire the plate of cabbage at the door, followed by the teapot and half-full cup, which shatters on the floor—"*You creepy, sicko bastards!*"—crying now as I glare at this scummy mattress, yank the blanket from the bed, and sink down in a clammy corner!

Boyne

Dialing Flynn's castle again and again—my drunken wake'll probably never end!—as I keep frantically pacing with this phone in my fist, been busy forever and—*Ah*, thank God! finally getting *through*!—ringing and ringing—

"—'lo? Flynn's summer home—"

"Who the hell's *this*?"

"—some're home'n some're not! Godfrey Daniel at yer beck'n call, m'lord."

"Right, well, listen—"

"But yer not that fella's been tryin' to sell me T. S. Eliot's false teeth, are ya, wrapped in a toilet roll?"

"No, no, will you let me speak to *Flynn*?"

"Who?"

"*Flynn, Kevin* Flynn!"

"Ah, Flynn is it now?"

"Yes, Flynn, Flynn, whose bloody *castle* you're in!"

"Well, Oym afraid somethin' has come over himself lately, wherein he seems to prefer women now to Guinness and, when last seen, was astride the busty Jennifer—"

"I don't give a *damn* about that, just get him on the phone *now, 'cause* this is a fucking *emergency*!"

And still furiously pacing back and forth—till Flynn, footsteps finally arriving, drops the clattering receiver—"And, Jayz, who the blazes is *this*?"

"*Boyne, Boyne*! Will you lis——"

"*Boyne*?! Holy Mother of *God*, is there *no* killin' ya off?"

"Flynn, will you *listen* to me, they've kidnapped Tory!"

"Tory?"

"My *daughter* Tory!"

"Yer not *serious* now?"

"No, I'm joking—*of course* I'm serious!"

"Well Christ, *when*? *Where*? Who the hell *was* it?"

"That's what we've got to discover! So meet me at my flat as soon as possible—"

"I shall indeed!"

"—'bye!"

And pacing rapidly past my windows, Dublin out there, chimney pots and rainy lights—a city which, as Behan once told me, will give you the loneliness but no solitude—reeking as it is with envy and guile, and vandals galore! This blasted habit still itching so—'cause they've already kidnapped Getty's grandson and sent back his ear as a souvenir—*O Suffering Christ, no!*—all my nerves exposed, that ould terror raging in my soul—as I keep on madly pacing—needing a drink, Guinness, wine, or a fizzy split of bubbly—but drink no longer doing it, calming me down, revving me up—though once making painting possible, releasing the tension, keeping the demons at bay—yet I *never* painted when I drank and only came alive with the work, fame like a second childhood—till Ciara taught me different, that art wasn't life and death to me, defining who I was, all I was, and all the while I was screaming, shrieking inside just to be accepted whether I succeeded or not—till one day she hugged me and said, "You don't have to be a genius for me to love you, you know, you can 'just be,' as you once told me, quoting someone or other." The same way she accepted herself, enjoyed the childlike play of acting—and unlike Picasso's women, who only loved him *for* his genius!

And *Good God,* here I open myself up and look what happens again! These suffocating waves of panic now *crushing* in on me, being cruelly and physically *stripped,* like losing Ciara anew! The loss of a child unbearable: loss of daughter, loss of wife, wives—losing Tory once, now once more—how much loss can I *take*? Thought I'd evade it all, have these last few days to recapture my past before fame and fawning—and now, *damn his eyes,* whoever the hell he is, if he harms one hair, even *one* silken hair on her precious head, I'll skin the bugger *alive*!

Tory

So afraid to open my eyes, squeezing my lids even tighter, to find that I'm still lying here in the same clammy little room clinging to that scratchy wool blanket and trying my hardest to hold on to my will (since headstrong and feisty can only take me so far and then I get *terrified*!*)*. Now easing them open to narrow slits: and all I can make out under the swaying ceiling bulb are stacks and stacks of blurry cardboard boxes. What am I, a prisoner in some kind of stupid Irish box factory?

And jumping to my feet, I jog twice around the room, then begin bouncing on my toes—all this nervous energy! This's really like an obstacle course, with boxes everywhere I look—and grinning to myself, I leap atop one and hop across to another—"Here we are, folks, with the Olympic champion box hopper, the infamous Tory Boyne—the crowd going wild '*Ahhhhh!*'—who will now attempt to break the world box-to-bed long jump record before your very eyes!" Precariously perched on this cardboard ledge, I take a deep breath, squat, then jump high and far—and land with a splintering *crack* in the middle of the mattress, the frame collapsing beneath me (which is really funny when you think about it)! And imagine what Mother would say: *Tory, what on earth are you doing*? "Why that's perfectly obvious, Mother, I'm going *crazy,* talking to myself! Yeah, *stir* crazy, cabin fever and claustrophobia setting in—besides, can you think of something better to do, my nails maybe, or perhaps my hair? Hey, how 'bout we just rip it all out, eh? Or paint it Day-Glo green? Yeah, right!" and totally cracking up now—as the door flies open once more and that bitchy nurse comes marching in with another food cart and a smug look on her hatchet face—which abruptly changes when she sees the mess on the floor and me now hysterically giggling!

Boyne

Flynn bounding breathlessly up the stairs and lurching into the flat.

"Good *God,* man, what the hell *kept* you?"

"What kept me, is it—O Jaysus, Mary, and *José,* and will ya *look* at this great giant woof-woof!"—as Poldy, suddenly displaying his best behavior for strangers, sits back on his haunches and offers the kneeling Flynn shy licks across his nose, eyes, and elfin ears—"Ah, Mother of Christ, Boyne, see how he *takes* to me, start a bloody relationship goin'! Well hell, y'know the Brits do this all the time, bed down with their hounds, bugger their sheep!"

"Fine, fine, but what do *I* do about my *daughter*?"—still pacing across my studio—"I was so afraid to come back here and find a note from her captors or even an ear—"

"Ah, Boyne, well there's no need to panic quite yet, not even certain what occurred, might be a reasonable excuse behind it all, could be any one of the local Neanderthals of criminally psychotic stripe, hue, or kidney—"

"Don't you understand, I *know* who it was, she was kidnapped by a short man in a yellow mac, *goddamn it*!"

"Ah, right y'are, well then, just hold on a tick and we'll tap into the Irish Mafia, me own personal network, get out me trusty black book here and see if anyone's heard—'cause Liam surely would know, was once an informant for the Special Branch, cousin of mine, Liam Coddle."

And he quickly dialing as I sweep my monk's robe around me, uncapping another stout and swilling down this bitter brown foam—"Terrorist scum think they can get away with *anything* these days, take Ciara from me, now Tory, well, let me tell you something, *not again, no, never again*—!"

Flynn waving for quiet. "Ah, Des, ould son, Kevin here, and we were just after wonderin' now if yer brother'd been released? Liam still up in Portlaoise, is he?"—and babbling on as I drain my Guinness, then swiftly uncap another—"I shall indeed. And have ya heard anything about Boyne's daughter? *Seamus* Boyne? The painter, right y'are, dead he is"—and winking at me—"buried 'im this very mornin', we did, brilliant artist, simply brilliant—O Jaysus, wasn't he now, had all the bleedin' tools to charm the cross off an ass on its way to Calvary! But ya haven't a clue—Do ya now? Right-right, off Arran Quay. Ah, that's grand, grand! And me best to Liam, God bless!"—hanging up—"Come on, Boyne, let's go!"

"Where?"

"Arran Quay, cousin of theirs runs a private club, and if anyone'd know!"—kissing Poldy on the nose—"Bye-bye, beastie, bite first, ask questions later, the villa's *all* yours!"

And taking the stairs two at a time in a desperate hullabaloo, lickety-split, and out onto rainy Anne Street, knees thick with stout, calves close to the pavement, and my rotating head of Guinness now as we go hustling down Dawson, Bective's Electrical clock reading quarter past twelve, and my stomach noisily unwinding—"O Christ, Flynn, I can't *lose* her again!"

"Ya won't, Seamus, *believe* me ya won't!"

"I mean, here I finally discover my daughter again, 'cause I was far too young back then, knew nothing about marriage and babs—and when you have a bab, you *know* you're married! Reaching out for a family life I never had, but I never knew *how* to do it, to *sustain* it, so I always ended up leaving, tossing it aside!"—through this dark maze of streets—"But, Flynn, listen to me now, we're not heading for women at this club, to take my mind off—?"

"*Women*? Good *Christ*, man"—whipping over the Liffey—"me cock's so worn to the bone at the moment, it's currently on loan to the Smithsonian!"—gulls wheeling between gaunt quay walls.

By blear-eyed men in alley corners, and an orange cat, after a reconnoitering sniff, silently padding across the road, one delicate paw after another, tail curled high—as a white Austin-Healey comes streaking down Arran Quay, zigzagging through the rain and heading straight for us—then veers violently into the cat—who goes somersaulting through the air—the Healey swerving to a skidding stop—"O that bloody *bastard*!"—and I'm off in a flash!—"Boyne, what're ya *doin'*?"—edging the dead cat tenderly onto the curb as I approach the driver, a wavy-haired toff sporting a lemon-yellow ascot, who glances up at me with a whiskey grin.

"Sorry, Father, never even saw the bugger—"

"Like *hell*! You deliberately killed it!"

"Ah well, 'twas only a cat."

"Right, and that's only a steering wheel!"—*Wham!* ramming his head hard against it, then gently cradling the limp cat in my arms—who, amazingly, blinks up at me with a rusty meow, clawing the air and, springing down, scampers off round the corner.

"Eight lives to go, Macavity!"

The driver staring groggily after as we scoot through this filthy alley, up a sinister lane to a red, peeling door, with Flynn rapping impatient shave-and-a-haircut knuckles upon it—not a sound, he rapping once more—and the dark door creaking open, a timid, bifocaled soul peeking out, blocking our path, then meekly asking: "What's the password?"

"Get the hell out of our way or we'll smash yer fuckin' head in!"

"Ah well, that's close enough."

Tory

Still worn out from my giggling anxiety bout, holding on to my aching sides, and realizing now how badly I've gotta pee! Not even a chamber pot in this stupid room! And you know, it's *really* getting weird in here, 'cause I feel like this place is lost in space, a Twilight Zone, just floating around, locked inside—and my jailer is *the Nurse from Hell*!

Have no idea what time it is. Should be getting light soon, craning my neck toward that dirty little window up there. Peephole, really. And, who knows, maybe I could just slip through, inhaling all the way—reaching for that high ledge. But *damn,* I can barely touch it with my fingertips—Aha, but the champion box hopper now using that brain she was born with and grabbing a couple of sturdy cartons, stacking them along the wall, then slowly climbing up, swaying slightly—*O please hold!*—starting to give way and—*Whoa!*—I go sliding and bumping back down and land on my feet—as the door swings open and that same weaselly-looking creep walks in with his lopsided grin, and that monster goon with those Lucifer eyes lurking right behind him.

"Hey look, mister, I don't know what you want with me, or why you brought me here, but do you need to treat me as if I were some sort of animal, for God's *sake*? I haven't eaten a bite of decent food since I arrived, and I don't think I'll be worth a dime to you"—shifting from foot to foot—"if I starve to death or my bladder bursts, for that matter!"

"Ah well, I'm glad t'see you're ready to talk some sense now, Miss Boyne."

Still squirming—"Right"—and gnawing my lower lip—"well, I really *do* need to use the facilities."

"I'm sorry, the what, Miss Boyne?"

God, what a retard! "You know, the ladies' room, rest room—the john?" But the jerk just stands there with this dumb expression on his craggy face. "*The loo*?"

"Ah yes, a-course, Miss Boyne, the loo, the lavo."

"And do you think maybe I could have a decent blanket, a pillow, and some food that's edible while you're at it?"

"Fine, fine, I'll see what we can dig up, and Bruff here will show you to the loo. O, and by the by, I wouldn't go tryin' any more funny stuff now"—glancing toward the window—"since all the windows here are double thick and barred from the outside."

And I follow the giant geek down a corridor—what the hell *is* this place?—identical doors to my right and left, the white linoleum floor all shiny and slick. And I'm trying hard to remember the way we're going, left then right—and this anesthetic smell making me sick—then left again, up some tiny steps—and if we don't get there soon, I'm really gonna burst!—trotting now to keep up with his elephant feet—looks kind of like a hospital, loony bin, or home for the terminally ill—as he suddenly stops before this battered black door, indicating that he'll wait outside for me. Thank God! For a minute there, I thought he might be planning on escorting me in!

Closing the latch behind me and that stall on the left looks OK, as I hurry toward it and barely get my panties off in time—*O God,* what a relief! Looking around for some toilet paper, and, of course, the roll is empty—figures in this dump. Well, I guess old Bruff, the moron, will have to wait for me to drip dry—

And what was *that*?

A plinking sound from the far stall, and something rolling out from under—what the heck?—as I bend down to pick up this white gleam from the concrete floor: *a pearl*? Another plink, followed by two more plinkity-plinks.

And quickly dropping to all fours, I peek beneath the stall. O Jeez! Here's this teeny tiny little lady, about a hundred years old, with these plucked eyebrows and Coke-bottle glasses, crouched upon her stool, her hands fumbling with a broken string of pearls and mumbling away in a singsong brogue:

"Ah, sweet Jaysus, what'll Oy do now? Can never find a daycent stringer in Dublin these days . . . not since dear sweet Paddy Laferty passed away—not that Oy could even *get* ta Dublin. Poor Paddy, God rest his soul. Heart attack, me arse! Neglect 'tis more like it! Though Oy can never recall whether these are me anniversary string or those bluddy imitation ones that cheap wife of me son's gave me last year—O me glasses, where the fook are me glasses?"—and looking up, tapping her blue-rinsed hair, then down at me with a start, she drops her remaining pearls—which go plinking and scattering all across the floor—"Where the devil did *you* come from?"

Boyne

So drowsy now, my eyes fluttering, slowly sliding closed, feigning sleep like I used to when I wanted to hold on to a dream, after that strange early-morning scene with Flynn's own Irish Mafia, and trying hard as I possibly can to take my mind off this hollow, helpless ache and think of something positive, a sunrumpus of shapes, memories of sexual pleasure: Ciara's moist, bluestone eyes ringed with shadow and her just-washed, just-now-dry blonde hair laced across the pillow following our last lovemaking spree: earlier, she bathing me with a sensual scrub-a-dub-dubbing in our huge Victorian tub the size of a bloody dinghy out in Ballyduff, with its brass claw feet and my plastic yellow submarine. (Ciara always saying that *all* artists were children who need women to take care of them, feed them, nurse them, "even *bathe* them, like silly you!" Picasso, Turner, Modigliani, Pollock, and, of course, old Rabbi Rothko, who was so myopic, he could barely see, much less bathe himself.) Ciara's soapy hands gliding over my back and wooly chest—"God, so much hair"—she smiling—"and so little on your head"—across my stomach and down my thighs to gently fondle my cock and balls, foaming with suds like a codpiece of lather (so loved her gentle, fondling hands)—"But you could lose a few pounds, my dear, especially around your middle—"

"I'm still mad about *your* body."

"—too much of your Hong Kong curry—No, my thighs are too fat, and my behind is—"

"What legends are made of! O I *adore* your arse, *covet* your succulent butt, going to bronze it straightaway like a Matisse or massive Henry Moore!"

And Ciara grinning and coming closer, her hands still sensually scrubbing as I kissed along her nape, the lovely wet collision of her breasts, jiggling their lilting weight, till she finally disrobed, slipped gracefully into the tub, and handed me the soap—"Here, well, you can do me now."

The creamy slope of her shoulders, islands of soapy foam dissolving as she lowered her hair, nimble swirls of blonde flaring and cascading, and I went nuzzling down the firm hollow of her spine, across a meadow of freckles, and began softly gnawing—O

Christ!—those sleek, melonous globes, she leaning forward on her knees and me licking lower, over her slick lips with their brine-winey tang, my fingers easing deeply inside her, her head thrashing, bathwater splashing, then sucking her clitoral pearl, up one side and teasingly down the other, till it bloomed to the size of a grape as she kept on rotating her smooth, buttermilk rump (so loved giving her pleasure) and moaning, "*O don't stop, don't stop, please don't stop!*"—gripping the rim of the tub with one hand and my swollen cock with the other—"*Dear God, you are driving me insane!*"

Tory

And how's *this* for totally weird: lying here with my face pressed to the scuzzy tile, the air reeking of stale pee and ammonia as I peer upwards at this Irish Grandma Moses with her plucked eyebrows and blue-rinsed hair, who asks: "Yeh, well, what is it ya *want*, dear?"

How about a dry Rob Roy, straight up, with a twist?

"And what're ya doin' down *there*?"

"Pearl diving?"

"Ah grand, ya got 'em then!"

"Some of them, but wait, let me get up and I'll meet you outside."

And coming out—she's half my size!—handing her these pearls.

"O tanks very much, darlin' "—adjusting her owly glasses—"But Oy haven't seen ya here before, have Oy now? Are ya new on the staff or one of them visitors of Hazel Mulqueen's?"

"No, I've been kidnapped—"

"Yer jokin'! But why?"

"That's what I'm trying to figure out. But what *is* this place?"

"A nursin' home, and Oy'm Cathleen Coddle."

Shaking her tiny, veined hand. "Hi, I'm Tory."

"Tory is it now? Such a lovely name, like the island. So what d'ya intend to do?"

"Escape, if I can! Is there a quick way out of here?"

"Ah, well, let me see, luv, though Oy've never really explored it with that in mind. There *is* a storage room, I tink, down the back."

"Right, that's where I've been staying"—looking anxiously around—"But listen, listen, I have an idea, Cathleen: if you start screaming and Bruff races—"

"Who?"

"Bruff, the big guy?"

"Ah, Bruff, the handyman, yeh?"

"Right, well, if he races in, then I'll race out—"

"Ya won't get very far."

"Well, I can at least try—You *can* scream, Cathleen?"

"Ah, bluddy sure Oy can. Wasn't Oy first soprano at St. Brigid's in Killester now? But are ya certain he's still out there?"

"Let me listen."

I listen.

No sound. He still waiting around? Then whispering, "Bruff? . . . O Bruffy?" No reply—and slowly opening the door—

He's *gone*! For a pee of his own? *Yes,* I hear him in the men's room flushing. *No time to lose!*

"Cathleen, listen, lock the door, then scream as loud as you can, 'I can't get *out*!' That should keep him occupied for a while. OK? Thank you, 'bye!"

"God bless, Tory—*Oy can't get out, Oy can't get out, the bluddy door won't budge—Eeeeeeeeeeee!*"

And with her high-pitched shriek ringing in my ears, I go sprinting down the corridor—hear Bruff back there slamming out of his loo and bursting through her door—round this dark corner, his heavy feet now hot on my heels, up these stairs—and what is this,

Road Runner and Wile E. Coyote? Christ, Tory, it's not *funny*—you're running for your life at full speed and those French doors straight ahead—misty morning light, green shadows out there—and in here, everybody's in white: a sunroom filled with women in wheelchairs. Have to hide—but where? No way out—There, linen closet!

Beatles music blaring, "*I should have known better—*"

You're telling me—*the Beatles*! What is going *on*? Here, live, making their long-awaited comeback at the Kidnappers' Nursing Home: John, Paul, George, and Ringo—and breathlessly peeking out, the only thing I can see is one old woman (they're *all* old!) who *does* look like George (with her sheepdog bangs), and beside her, twenty other ancient biddies in their wheelchairs all twisting and shouting and waving their bony arms in the air—

Unbelievable! This is *hysterical*! Maybe next they'll flip on some of *my* favorites, Moody Blues, Zeppelin, or the Who—

O Jeez! And there's panting old Bruffy weaving and bumping in and out of the wheelchairs like Karloff in *Frankenstein*—music loudly pounding—

"*Gotcha!*"

Damn! "Look, Bruff—*Ow!*"—my arm snapped back into a painful hammerlock as he parades me quickly by these wrinkled faces—all of them grinning with gold teeth, false teeth, no teeth—and shrugging at Cathleen, who flashes me a wink, I'm hustled gruffly down the corridor and flung roughly back into my cell or dungeon—"OK, OK, I mean, hell, all I was doing was stretching my legs."

Boyne

Two million pounds by Tuesday noon! "O those *swine,* those *scum*—with their tidy little *sum*!" Still, means they're Irish or English—and this ransom note must've been slipped under my door when I was out for Poldy's run!

But how'd they *know* I was here? And alive? Tory and I were followed all along—and now they're watching me? Peering out the bluestone drapes: Warm sun spilling over the roofs and M. Deegan's window, men glancing at the headlines as they go past—BOYNE BURIED already yesterday's news—and downstairs P.J. Kilmartin, Turf Accountant, with that sign outside: SHOES STRETCHED, LONGER, BROADER, OR BOTH, COMFORT GUARANTEED—and not a suspicious soul in sight—or rather *every* Irishman nowadays has a smoking gun in his pocket or a stick of dynamite!

This handwriting like a drunken crab on his cheap stationery, ballpoint pen:

> *If you want your daughter to live and you to remain "dead," put the sum of £2,000,000 in a locked toolbox no later than Tuesday noon at the Monkey House of the Dublin Zoo and leave it with the keeper. Don't call the police or your daughter will die and you will "live."*

"And the hell with my bloody cover, revealing myself, Tory's far more important, I can't lose her now! Easy, Poldy, easy—not mad at you, doggie! But *how, how, how?*" The clock already ticking! *O Suffering Christ*! Now Saturday, 2:15. Have to call Credit Swiss, only way, and instruct Rolfe (one of the few who knows I'm alive) to wire the funds to the Bank of Ireland here—as I keep striding back and forth across the room—wire directly to Flynn, who can make the pickup and deliver them to the zoo.

But why the hell am I staying here anyway in my "off-limits" flat, secret hideaway, rather than sneaking back into Ballyduff and scaring the bejaysus out of my staff like the Canterville Ghost? Give up this absurd charade of dying on my own quixotic terms, recapturing my prime, and touring the length and breadth of Ireland, swimming nude in Gweebarra Bay, camping out in the wilds of Donegal, staring straight down the Cliffs of Moher, and lustily carousing to my high cholesterol heart's content—'cause I may expire at any moment no matter what I do—but damn it to *Christ*! one thing's for sure, *I will not die before my daughter's found or have my daughter die before me*!

Right, right, but what the hell do I do *now*? Since they know where I am, watching my every move—Call the Garda? No, can't take the chance. Flynn? His Mafia? Hire a detective?—No, *Laura*! *Exactly*!

Call *her* now! And reveal I'm alive? *Have to*—'cause she may've heard, been contacted, might have a clue, know Tory's itinerary, others she could've met or was planning to meet—Have to! Even though it's been, what? seven or eight years! Surely grieving me now, regretting her loss, so wanting to possess and keep me then in her Sarah Lawrence world—though as she'd often say, "Marriage to a madman is hardly a recipe for domestic bliss!" And what's that yahoo's name she remarried, Republican fund-raiser? Salzman, Saltsman, *Salzburger—Yes, yes!* Mark Salzburger in Baltimore, U.S. of A.!

Punching out Operator for Baltimore information and getting the bloody number, area code 410—2:20 P.M. here, 9:20 A.M. there—

But it's busy. *Blast!* Talking to the police? Tory? The kidnappers? Who the hell knows!

Try again. *Still* busy! Get off the fucking *phone*, will you, Laura! Always could talk a bloody blue streak! Trying to see her in my mind's eye, a sophisticated blur O so long ago, memories jostle and fuse: our musky lovebed the morning after as she reclines in my mind—a blizzard of gulls mulling in the morning light, gray pigeons ruddering down, fantails white—and her flaring, pear-shaped arse of a South Sea maiden, Gauguin wench that I placed, while sublimely erect in Holy Catholic Ireland, in many of me early paintings. Living together initially in that easygoing solitude that all artists crave but soon grow restless of, as time goes by—and nothing happens except art. And she so wanting to possess me, keep me then—and though I admit I needed to be kept, I needed far more to be free. And you think we knew each other? Good *God* no! Just a madcap fling, fleeing our separate worlds, till we became islands drifting apart.

And so unlike Ciara, who's always with me, beside me, the blonde friction of her still under my skin. O she was the juice in a world gone dry! The thrust and quiver of her thighs, warm mouth, breasts of a silken hue. *Never think she loves him wholly, / Never believe her love is blind. / All his faults are locked securely / In a closet of her mind.* "For I was Ciara Boyne's lover, a bloody painter that's me, I love old Bach and Turner, but none like Ciara B!"

And I'd better try Laura again—it's *ringing, ringing*! *Marvelous,* finally getting through—pick the damn thing *up,* will you!

"Hello?"

"Laura, listen—"

"Who's this?"

"It's Boyne!"

"*Who* is this?"

"Boyne, Boyne, look, I'm not dead, *still* alive—"

"What are you talking about—*who is this*?"

"—faked my own funeral and Tory—"

"Tory? Tory's in Ireland. Look, whoever you are—"

"Tory's been kidnapped!"

"*What? How*—?"

"We met at my wake, I don't want to go through the whole story now, it was crazy, I was in disguise—Laura, I swear on my mother's Galway grave—"

"Look, this is not *funny* anymore!"

"—and I'm *hysterical*! Haven't seen Tory in ten years, and here's this two-million-pound ransom or she'll die—I'm *frantic*! Have *you* talked to her, to the police, to the kidnappers?"

"No, I haven't talked to her, or the private detective we hired either."

"*What* private detective?"

"When Tory left here, she was furious with me, so we hired an Irish private detective there, someone Mark knew, to keep an eye on her."

"Have you heard from the detective?"

"I just told you I haven't heard from *either* of them, but this whole thing—Boyne, you are so *sick*!"

"Could be, but I'm not going to lose my daughter!"

"*Your* daughter? Since when? Never mind, I'm taking the next flight out—"

"Why, what for?"

"Well, I'm certainly not going to let *you* wreak any more havoc—"

"But—"

"I'm on my way."

Tory

"Try picking on somebody your own size!"

Whack! And I'm slapped once more against this bumpy wall—and dizzily reeling, tasting my own blood—his monster paw about to slap me again—and I kick him in the shins!

He blinks, looming huge above me and giving me his nerdy grin, before emitting an unearthly roar and—*O Jeez!*—punching me in the stomach, and I go crumbling to the floor face first into this scuzzy mattress—as the door flies open.

"Bruff, enough now, enough, let her alone!" The weasel dragging him off. "Miss Boyne, I'm terribly sorry—"

"—You're always terribly sorry—"

"I'll have someone tend to yer wounds. Bruff, out now, out! No need for violence."

"—You could've fooled me!"

And he slams the door behind him as I finally catch my breath, sitting and shivering now in the center of this red wool blanket with my hands tightly wrapped around my drawn-up knees, my cheek and lips stinging, stomach aching like I've been hit with a damn sequoia.

Enough of this hostage crap! Where's my father? And how long have I been here? Two days, three days—a week? I'm going to *die* here! Never get out alive! Scared, really scared, sweating and shivering and feeling so small, little girlish, like I'm shrinking, disappearing—Calm down—I *can't*! Don't panic! Think positive, positive, soon free, *out* of here, escaping, and my father believing in me (so where the hell *is* he?)—No, positive, positive: like kicking Bruff in the shins. *That* was pretty positive, huh, if I do say so myself. You've come a long way, baby! from that school report I once saw, took home with me, that "Tory is timid, lacks confidence, and doesn't mix well with other students." Friends quickly made, quickly lost. Only close one I had was Nina Jaccalone, another introverted bookworm, closet hell-raiser—and awesome volleyball smasher—who first brought Dylan Thomas's poems into my life, then got killed in a head-on collision. So lonely after that, no friends, nobody to talk to, switching from school to school. Alien oddball, uncontrollable child, so different from other girls, "the gawky gosling," I called myself, a skinny, spacy tomboy—

And he sees me as a swan, his lovely lassie, with marvelous bones and glittery eyes, like a slender ash on the coast of Ireland, so wondrously, *expressively* pretty!

"Fine, then get me *out* of *here—Ow*!" My stomach still hurting so—

And that bitchy nurse now marching in with that smug hatchet face and holding a bowl of water and a washcloth.

"O look who's here, the Nurse from Hell! Terrific! Is that my dinner or a douche?" She keeps staring at me with that steely gray gaze. "Hey, don't you and Bruffy speak? Or are you both mutes, or mutants?"

She dips the washcloth in the bowl. "Let me see yer face."

"O she *does* talk! and walk and crawl on her belly like a reptile—Hey, not so hard there!"

Finished, she takes me by the arm and ushers me out, down the corridor, to the john, loo. "Yer probably wantin' to use the lavo."

"Do I ever!"

"I'll be right out here."

"Wouldn't have it any other way."

Through the battered black door I go and into my favorite stall—when suddenly Cathleen appears out of the blue, a tiny finger to her lips, and leads me to a corner.

"We've got to stop meeting like this!"

A glint of her gold teeth below her owly glasses and blue-rinsed hair. "Dear God, Tory, what happened to yer lovely face?"

"Bruff hit me."

"Selwyn did?"

"Selwyn?"

"Ah, well now his real name is Selwyn Bruff Bouteiller—Bruff they spell B-r-o-u-g-h. Actually he's French."

"No, actually he's a butthole!"

"Well, he's that, too, Oy suppose ya might say."

"And pardon *my* French."

"Yeh, yeh, but here's the ting, Tory, Oy've got an idea."

"Least that's one of us."

"Oy'm goin'ta call me nephew Kevin, *he'll* know what ta do."

Boyne

Havoc? Well, I'll wreak you havoc—devastating, avenging, annihilating havoc like you've never bloody seen!

Speeding along on the Harley with Poldy behind me, wearing that Snoopy World War I leather flying cap and goggles and sitting up, his paws on my shoulders, in my specially designed basket-seat as I keep twisting the throttle hard and veer sharply into this tight turn, right turn, then straightaway through the gathering Dublin dusk!

And I *had* to take Poldy along, needing him with me in this hour of greatest peril, after Flynn's call ("Me Aunt Coddle phoned and they're holdin' Tory out at this nursing home atop Bray Head")—and I was off in a shot. ("And once ya get in, Boyne, me aunt'll guide ya to yer daughter, she'll be waitin' at the top of the back stairs when ya come in the main entrance." "How will I know Aunt Coddle?" "She'll know you, believe me! Told her to be on the lookout for a mad-arse monk.")

Flynn flying to London tonight, be back a week Friday. And now Laura coming over—Coming over *where*? Doesn't know my Anne Street flat, so she'll go to Ballyduff and they'll tell her I'm dead, or see her Irish private eye, whatever, that's her worry—first things first—though I wonder what she looks like now. Held up over the years? Had such lovely, muscled thighs in our salad days, she with her smooth lewdness, my green madonna, performing what used to be racily referred to then as unspeakable acts—as I go speeding fast, speeding past Ballsbridge and Booterstown, rocketing in and out of buses and cars on my black metallic stallion, the hot pavement whizzing by a few inches from my heels and—*O Jaysus!*

"*Hold on, Poldy!*"

Skidding straight for that concrete wall on this slick spot, grease spot, overhanging branches—ahead a dry patch, only chance—kicking it into high, a berserk screech and shuddering thrust, the wheel gripping, knifing, and righting itself down this sloping straightaway—now steady as a rock, Poldy grinning, the wind buffeting his silky fur:

"Sorry, old doggie, nearly bought it, I know—end up like Pollock slamming headfirst into a tree!" as we go careening round this leafy bend—And first meeting him in '53, when I was fresh out of art school, the most promising painter of my generation, as well as Rothko's buddy, and down to the Cedar Bar we went, where Jack the Dripper was holding court with his macho cowboy swagger and shouting at the crowd, "Who's the greatest painter in the world?" and they all replied, "You are!" calling him Picasso's heir (what they now call me), and asking him when he was going to paint another masterpiece—caught in that destructive tide of celebrity not to repeat yourself, yet be as good as you once were: a bloody *suicide* cycle!—while bald Rabbi Rothko in his long brown topcoat kept buying us drinks and mumbling behind those thick accountant's glasses that in the States "no one ever permanently makes it" and telling me, nine months before my first major show, "You're going to top us all, Boyne, the best of the lot, with your erotic fury, no one's used color like that since Gauguin in his prime!" when Pollock abruptly asked if I'd sucked any good cock lately, then punched me in the mouth—and I flung him across the bar into a shatter of bottles—and this free-for-all broke out, everybody swinging wildly, Rothko bear-hugging a longshoreman, Pollock cracking a knuckle, and me booting several bruisers in the balls, before we three went tumbling and roistering out through the streets of Greenwich Village, where the air nightly smells of lightly roasted coffee or slightly toasted rusk, Pollock circling his arm around me and yelling at passing cars, then pissing in the gutters, spraying it from side to side over the cobbles in a glinting golden stream and bellowing, "I can *still* piss on the whole world!" stumbling down the long, dark length of Hudson Street and into the jam-packed White Horse, gargling black and tans, and Jackson looking up at that dreadful portrait of Dylan and urging me to fucking rage, rage against the dying of the light and sell out, if you must, with a bloody bang not a whimper—though, *Christ,* Pollock in his lifetime only sold *six* of his most important works for a total of twenty grand!

On past Sallynoggin and Dalkey, soon be in Bray—but still the question remains: How the hell will I get in and rescue Tory? A new disguise? No more Howdy Doody? Just the element of surprise—

Abso-fucking-lutely! Shock the bejasus out of these buggers, an ancient Celtic assault, charge naked into the fray with "The Garryowen" blaring, slingshots whirring, swords clanging, and Boyne in all his roaring glory!

Tory

A whisper from the hall. "Can Oy come in?"

"Cathleen?"

"Aye."

"How? You gonna huff and puff and blow my door down?"

"Got t'key."

"Where's—?"

"They left, both left, probably went to the shop in Greystones or Bray." The door easing open and teeny Cathleen blinking in with her Coke bottle glasses—"Jaysus, 'tis foul in here!"—as I stand, rubbing my tired eyes—dark out, dusk—and flicking my musty hair off of my face.

"How'd you get the key?"

"Thrickery. Ah, ya been nappin' now, have ya?"

Nodding. "What time is it?"

"Just gone half six, quarter to."

"Did you reach your nephew?"

"That Oy did."

"And is he coming?"

"No, no, yer father'll be."

"My *father*?" Weaver of dreams and legendary schemes!

"And Oy told me nephew we'd meet 'im at the top of the basement stairs."

"What about Nurse Hook?"

"'Tis her evenin' off."

"But what if Bruff or the weased come back before—?"

"Ah, then we switch to Plan B."

"Which is?"

"Nursin' home revolt!"

Boyne

Roaring over jutting ruts and craggy potholes at eighty, eighty-five—giraffes've been known to copulate at eighty miles per hour—and up this narrow, curving lane toward the top of Bray Head, Poldy still bouncing behind, by pale heather and gorse, the shaving of a moon—and soon stripping down to the buff, Boyne in all his glory like those hot-blooded Celtic warriors fighting naked in ancient times, strutting before their foes and hurling frenzied insults and taunts—as we come jouncing onto the summit, downshifting, and whispering over my shoulder, "Shhh, Poldy, quiet, no barking now."

Coasting into the dark parking lot, only two cars here. The distant chiming buoys, flapping inshore breeze, music floating out from somewhere, pine scent and fierce tang of the sea—and that weathered, whitewashed building just across from me. Cutting the engine and hopping off (kidnapper nailing me in his sights)—No, can't stop now! Hoisting the habit up over my head, draping it across the seat, slipping off my socks and sandals—then standing erect in the breezy night.

Well, not quite that—though I do feel, I must say, like one of Rubens's naked satyrs, stark raving bald, with my hairy paunch and curly beard as I keep inhaling deep lungfuls of air: Breathe, Boyne, breathe! And one last stroke of Poldy's fur for good luck—"Guard the Harley, doggie!"—and away I go on cautious tiptoe, that breeze laving my swaying scrotum, and nearing this low, glassed-in porch with its wicker chairs inside and lights blazing behind it. Ducking down! A large sunroom filled with figures—and music booming out:

When I was younger, so much younger than today—

"What the hell is that?"

I never need anybody's help in any way—

"Sounds like the Beatles' 'Help!'" as still breathing deeply, I charge shrieking like a banshee in the buff through these French doors into a room of wheelchaired old ladies all shaking and gyrating to the music—and freezing at the sight of me, their eyes still bugging, mouths gawking, spittle and drool—then shouting and applauding, "*Bravo! Bravo! Encore! Encore!*"

And that pint-size biddie by the door—must be Flynn's aunt—signaling me the coast is clear. "But get this on ya or you'll give most of 'em a bluddy heart attack! Can't let yer daughter see ya like this"—and she tosses me a towel—"t'cover yer family jewels."

And suddenly *Tory,* in sweatshirt and jeans, is before me, "Glad you came!"

"Never resist a touch of the dramatic, lass."

"I know."

"Let's go!" and one of the pink housecoated ladies kissing my hand as I pass.

"Ah, 'tis a grand man y'are."

"Thank you, thank you *all*!" The applause continuing and following us out, quickly through the French doors, across the parking lot, Tory behind me, to the Harley—

"What's with the dog?"

—as I slip on my monk's robe, letting the towel fall, socks and sandals, crucifix swaying—"Poldy, Tory. Tory, Poldy"—then kick-starting it—*vrroom-vrroom!*—and sliding forward, Poldy behind her. "We're off!"

"I already knew that!"

"What?"

"Nothing, nothing—"

A surge of power, spinning around in circles before leaping into the air and flying out of the lot—and narrowly missing an oncoming green Beetle—

"It's *them*, it's *them*, Dad! *Step on it*!"

Tory

The weasel and Bruff squealing to a stop, the weasel's arms wildly waving, backing up their car, stalling out—what a pair of goons!—and we go shooting down this windy hill at breakneck speed, the motorcycle splitting the night, and around this bend, wedged as I am between this crazy dog, his paws on my shoulders, and my mad-ass father—sorcerer, necromancer, weaver of Celtic dreams—trees, hedges racing by in a blur and *screaming*!—bouncing high over that pothole in the road and slamming down—my stomach up in my throat! and glancing back—barely make out the Beetle's sweeping headlights—down, down, down this darkened slope, leveling out, across a smooth ribbon of road, traffic coming and—*whoa*! like Steve McQueen in *The Great Escape*—blowing my mind!—blasting through these high hedgerows, a storm of grass and dust, dark undulating fields—*anything* could be in front of us! just missing that boulder, underbrush whipping my calves, knees and—*O Jeez*! hit something:

Catapulting through the air, I somersault over and over, and finally land, scraping my shins, chin, spitting out weeds and blinking in the dim light of that slice of moon—and Poldy, his goggles now gone, licking my nose, eyes, cheeks—

"Tory, you OK?"

"Yeah. You?"

"Fine, fine."

"Where *are* you?"

"Over here, behind this hedge. Harley's smashed, totaled. We'll head for Little Sugar Loaf—think we've lost 'em. And here, brought a blanket for you from my saddlebag."

"Thanks."

"But listen, hardly had time to talk, Tory—did they hurt you back there?"

"Uh, no, sort of, not really."

"Well, now you're safe"—and he gives me a big hug, wrapping his arms around me and kissing my hair—"Right, but come on, we'd better get moving."

Poldy trotting ahead through the heather as we weave stealthy and fast over this thick grass and up a woody rise.

"Stay here for the night, hide out under the trees"—into a small clearing—"and I can curl up with Poldy, keep a vigil"—and kneeling down, he lets out an enormous sigh, then a throaty chuckle. "Suffering *Christ*, we've logged more miles today than the wandering tribes of Israel!"

Boyne

Awaking several hours later to this feathery drizzle being swept by the breeze and now steadily falling.

"Tory, listen, looks like we're in for a bit of a shower, best be moving."

"Why?"

"'Cause it's going to get worse, and this cover won't be enough. And besides, I'm not sure your captors aren't still mooching about. Most likely they figured we headed down the main roads, but just to play safe, we'd better get going."

"Going where?"

"Inland, head west"—shoving this blanket under my robe—"never make it to Flynn's castle now, just try and find some shelter."

"A Holiday Inn?"

"Not likely"—smiling and squinting as I lead the way out of these woods, across a dark meadow—spray lashing my face, soaking my feet—and the rain keeps growing harsher, a torrential squall coming down in slanting, windy sheets, a steadily driving downpour—the moon abruptly breaking through a brief gap in the clouds—and it must be at least an hour, hour and a half to Flynn's.

"Where's *your* castle?"

"A long way from here, Tory."

"And what's that, down there?" Poldy ambling beside her with his sopping fur. "Looks like a ruin or—"

"Or an abandoned cottage. Come on!"—and we hurry down the throat of this ravine, well-worn path, crushing wildflowers and ferns and bounding over boulders—my heart pounding sixty to the dozen, going like ten bells, slipping, panting, sliding—and through these thorny hedgerows—"Watch your eyes, Tory"—and out the other side—"OK?" "Fine, fine!"—to come face-to-face with a crumbling stone cottage with three standing walls and a partial roof as I vault over the threshold, "—Ah, *marvelous* refuge! Shelter from the storm!"

Tory shaking out her tawny tangles, wet blonde tendrils (so like Ciara's in the rain)—

"Jaysus, you must be drenched to the bone, but this corner seems dry—as is the blanket, I'm happy to report"—flopping it out and spreading it over the ground. "Hell, Wolfe Tone probably hid out here."

"Who?"

"Irish hero, tried to unite Ireland in 1798 and throw out the English. But he was caught, and cut his own throat to avoid the hangman's noose."

"Terrific!"

"The Sugar Loafs were used as hiding places after his rebellion, filled with insurgents"—drying Poldy now with my robe. "Tired, Tory?"

"No, still wired, really."

"Yes, yes, of course. Well, in the morning we'll head to Flynn's—"

"If it stops pouring."

"O it will, it will, a passing shower." The rain still drumming hard on the partial roof, chipped and dripping above.

"Then what, call the police?"

"No, not quite yet. First find out *who* these blackguards are. I'll make a few inquiries. Anyway, lass, why don't you try and get some sleep for now and I'll keep the vigil."

"Can't we split it?"

"No, no, I don't require much sleep these days—and you must be exhausted."

"Well, all right, but if you start dozing off, just let me know."

"Ah, I will indeed."

And she curls up with Poldy at her feet, then raises up on an elbow. "By the way, I meant to ask you, why did you burst in naked?"

"Where? O at the nursing home, you mean: Shock effect, ancient Celtic custom."

"And when you got in, what was your plan?"

"A bit of Bruce Lee and grab a sheet before I saw you."

Tory grinning. "You're really far out, you know"—then suddenly twisting about—"*What's that?*"—as Poldy barks and bounds to his feet.

"Shhhh!"

Dog ears up, plume tail raised, checking round the cottage, into the dark rain, sniffing along the walls, the moss, the overgrown hedges—before he pauses to pee on the threshold, then, wandering back, settles down again, swiveling from side to side till he finally rolls over, four paws in the air, and heaves a contented sigh.

"Doubt if they're out in this rain, especially in these wilds. But anyway, enough nattering now, get yourself some sleep, lass, and we'll be all set to go in the morning."

Tory

And my father tucks me in and kisses me good night with his bristly whiskers, smoothing down my hair and caressing my cheek. Just like when? Ten years ago, when I was seven and he'd tell me those bedtime tales of Cuchulain and wizard animal sprites . . . Have him tell me one now? No, tomorrow'll do—if Bruffy and his plumber's butt don't appear out of the blue. But my father's here to protect me—Erin's greatest mythical knight—and kick the crap out of old Selwyn and that creepy retard weasel!

Blustery rain still raging out there . . . and if I don't get a bath or shower soon—feel so scuzzy. Been wearing the same sweatshirt and jeans, not to mention panties and bra, since I was kidnapped, however many days ago that was. And so drowsy all of a sudden, my eyes blinking, slowly sliding closed . . . Poldy lightly snoring and sprawled over on his side now, white lashes drawn shut, ears back, dreaming of frolicky romping, feet flicking through lush green fields. And this strange, ancient cottage once housing Wolfe Tone and his insurgents (sounds like another local rock band). Soft hills all around us, yet *over Sir John's hill, / The hawk on fire hangs still.* Glinty Lucifer eyes and his monster paw—my muscles so sore, bruised from that Harley fall and Bruffy's slaps and punches—as I peek once more through my lashes just to check: my father's head slumped upon his chest and looking like Friar Tuck leaning against that wall . . . And a week ago, who would've guessed? Weird, really weird! This man, stranger, father of mine still alive, and rescuing me . . . So many questions to ask: like who'd they bury in his Wicklow grave . . . ?

Boyne

"Awake to the ramshackle sweet green that is Ireland, Tory, with the sun blazing a Turner gold, and your eyes a hyacinth blue!"

She grinning and stretching now like a sleepy-eyed, immaculate cat. "I *am* awake—I tucked *you* in last night."

"O you did, did you?"

"Indeed I did."

So fresh and childlike she is with her blonde Swede hair, satiny skin, wondrous bones, and wide, glittery eyes. "O I'd love to paint you this very second, I would, I would!"

"Fine, but what's the plan this morning?"

"A quick sketch, few fast strokes like a Picasso drawing, the simpler the better—Ah, the plan, yes, of course"—as I stand, apishly scratching the top of my head with my left hand, my ribs with the right—"Well, Enniskerry's just an ass's roar from here, we'll cross the N11—main thoroughfare—grab a bite in the village, a bit of a wash, poop and pee, then hightail it over to Flynn's."

"Sounds like a plan." Tory heading out of the cottage and blinking at the verdant sheep pasture before us shimmering in the breeze.

"Off to 'rope the blowing wind,' to quote Dylan." Poldy prancing on down this slope, his nose high, tongue lolling, and through a sheen of cobwebs.

"Did you know him?"

"Know who, Tory?"

"Dylan Thomas."

"Of course I knew him, I knew 'em all! O not intimately, but I *knew* him, I *met* him."

"What was he like?"

"Well, I really didn't know he was as much of a celebrity until *after* he died, only knew him as a person."

"Did you know Joyce?"

"*Joyce*? Christ no! How old do you think I *am*? Though apparently I *did* meet him when I was a boy with my father by the sea in Brittany, summered there right before the war"—past heather and gorse, scree stones and cushions of moss—as I abruptly catch my breath, the light igniting her windblown hair, Ciara's tousled, silken sun. "Lassie, I swear, as soon as we get to Flynn's, I'm never going to *stop* painting you!"

She glancing over her shoulder. "You know, I'm beginning to feel as if that's the only reason you rescued me."

"What is?"

"To use me as a model."

"Well, that definitely was *one* of the reasons."

"Is that all I am to you?"

"No, no, of course not, Tory! For only last night I was thinking that the most significant relationship of all, no matter what anybody says, lass"—skidding down this rocky slope—"is *ours*!"

"Ours, huh? How do you figure?"

"The father-daughter relationship surely being the most haunting, the most mythological of all relationships known to man!"

"Why, because imaginary fathers are never around?"

"Precisely right! Absence and distance *creating* images larger than life. Well hell, how 'bout all those phrases of expectation: 'Wait till Daddy gets home, then we'll go to the park, and on Sunday to the circus—' "

"Or the beach?"

"O absolutely—Poldy, get over here!"

"But how often did that happen? Think about it, how many times did you say you were coming and then never even *show up*?"

"Yes, but how many times did I appear right out of the blue?"

"Do you have any idea what that does to a child? How painful it is when her own father keeps missing birthdays and most holidays?"

"I gave you quality time, not quantity—Which birthdays?"

"My sixth, seventh, how 'bout the last *ten*!"

"Yes, well, your mother made it extremely difficult—"

"O don't blame it on Mother—"

"And why the hell not?"

"Because it wasn't just *her* fault, and the courts must've had *some* reason to deny you visitation."

"The only reason, Tory, was that I was an unpredictable, unsuccessful painter then—"

"But what I still don't understand—"

"—hiding out with you in the Baltimore Museum till they were closed—"

"—is how could you *leave* me?"

"Well, I believed that it would be far better if you remembered me as I was, what we were *together*—"

"Never calling, never writing—"

"—and I've always loved you."

"O yeah, *right*!" She whirling about with that fiery blue gaze—"Loved me *how*? *When*? *Where*? The last time I saw you I was seven and you gave me a seashell at the beach and then took off. You never called, you never wrote me *once*! So how can you possibly say you *loved* me?"

"'Cause God knows it's true! And I've never stopped thinking of you, painted you so bloody often—"

"Well, if you could take the time to paint me, why couldn't you take the precious time to pick up a bloody *phone*?"

"Tory, I'm truly sorry, I really am."

"Well, why couldn't you have said that then—*O Jeez,* just forget it!"—she abruptly turning away, sobbing and walking on, her shoulders shaking, then loudly sniffing and drying her tears with the back of her hand as I follow behind and, reaching out, gently stroke her hair.

". . . Do you love *me,* Tory?"

"What's that supposed to mean?" She still striding ahead. "Of *course* I love you!"

"Why?"

"How the hell should *I* know! Maybe 'cause you're the only father I've got!"

"Yeah, well, you're right and have been all along."

"I have?"

"Absolutely. I *was* more the painter of you than the father of you—and Tory, damn it to hell, now I want to be both."

And nearing the highway, the N11—cars, trucks speeding toward us, whooshing by, and taking her hand—"Come on, Poldy!"—and the three of us go racing across into a shadow of Scots pine, Poldy pausing again to pee, more cars passing, and Tory suddenly screeching:

"It's *them*!"

Tory

"Hide!"

And we scurry deeper into these woods, under this leafy cover of shrubs, and I stare hard at the departing car heading down the highway.

"Uh, listen, dad, guess what."

"What, lass?"

"It's not them, false alarm—just thought it was."

"No, that's OK, better safe than sorry. Anyway, we should be in Enniskerry shortly."

And I follow him through the trees and that pinewiney aroma as he sharply cuts to his left and, bending over, plucks something—can't see—from that shadowy patch.

"Just *look* at these beauties, Tory! Here, have some gooseberries!"

"Gooseberries?"

"Right, tart and lovely gooseberries—O they're so bloody good! Here, taste."

And I cautiously bite, then wince when I swallow.

"Too tart, Tory?"

"A bit, but actually they *are* good."

"And be careful, watch the thorns when you pick 'em, gooseberry stems bristle with vicious spikes—yes, doggie, some for you, too."

"You realize you don't *say* gooseberries."

"What do I say?"

"You slur the end, so it comes out goosebreeze."

"Goose-breeze? Goose-breeze! Yes, right y'are, I like that! The same way we say straw-breeze and blue-breeze and black-breeze—*Goose-breeze,* ha-ha! That's *marvelous*! And you know of course that your Cherokee Indians ate 'em, as well as Hitler, gooseberry pie a favorite of his, and then there's Chekhov's brilliant story of the man passionately plunging into that rainy Russian river. But I like 'em best baked in earthenware pots and drenched in sugar like my father made. O *Christ,* this is what I've truly been after—mmmmm!—since I learned I was dying!"

"You're *dying*?"

"Well, according to my Hindu physician."

"You're kidding, right?"

"But I'll bloody well outlive 'em all, die on my own terms, and truly recapture my prime! More goose-breeze, Tory?"

"No, I've had enough. Then who's buried in your grave?"

"Flynn's uncle."

"Flynn's *uncle*?"

"He always wanted to be buried in that cemetery."

"Gimme a break!"

"No, lass, actually bags of sand."

"How'd you manage that?"

"Brendan McCabe's an ould butty of mine."

"Brendan McCabe?"

"McCabe's Funeral Home, he owed me one. Though maybe when I eventually rise like a phoenix, I'll place an ad in the *Irish Times*: 'For Sale, secondhand tombstone. Excellent buy for someone named Boyne.' "

Moving across this green and rocky pasture. "But why'd you fake your own funeral?"

"'Cause I'm not half the man I used to be—"

"No, you're an Irish loony!"

"—there's a shadow hanging over me—"

"And you like the Beatles, too?"

"O absolutely! Especially the late Beatles, when they discovered Bach and B flat. In fact, McCartney and I did business a few times, bought some of my work, Harrison as well. Actually, there's one tune I prefer above the rest."

"Which one?"

"Don't know the name."

"Well, how's it go? Hum a few bars."

And he grins—great beaming grin!—my grin, and begins . . .

"O, 'In My Life.'"

"What's it called, lass?"

"'In My Life.'"

"But keep going, I'll harmonize."

And we sing it together in, I must say, pretty good harmony, weaving through the trees, a stand of beech buffeted by the breeze, as Poldy pauses beside a shallow stream to gulp down water, biting and loudly slurping it, then, looking up, joins us with a plaintive howl of his own that has me laughing, tickling my funny bone—*O Jeez*!—and I can't *stop* laughing and giggling, my dad guffawing, tears spilling out of our eyes—till I cry, "I'm gonna pee in my pants!"

"Me, too!"

And he hugs me again, holds me tight—Poldy shimmying, wriggling in—while we catch our breaths beneath these shafts of morning light. "By the way, dad, how'd you say you died?"—walking arm in arm now under the leaves and over the sloping ground.

"Heart failure, supposedly."

"How *is* your heart?"

"I told you, I'm not half the man I used to be—This way, Poldy."

"No, really, what's wrong with you?"

"Nothing, nothing, touch of high blood pressure."

"What's *that* supposed to mean?"

"Means if I keep acting as I do, to quote my Hindu M.D., 'You will live no longer than two or three weeks, I surely promise you.'"

"O *terrific*!"—breaking away.

"But I've never felt better—"

"It took me ten years to find you, and now you're gonna leave me *again*?"

"I'm not *leaving* you! You're the best thing that could've happened to me, this frenzied chase and escape—I told you, I haven't felt this alive in I can't *remember* when! Believe me, Tory, I'm fine, fine, in tiptop shape!"

Silent now as I continue walking ahead with this gnawing ache, across a river bridge, bells sounding—and, really, who would ever *believe* this? This man, stranger, father of mine, barely alive, rescuing me—a dream, fantasy come true—and now *deserted* again?

"Ah, there's Enniskerry."

Boyne

Sneaking another safe look from the fringe of these woods at that quiet, twisting street leading down to the town square and green-domed clock tower. "Coast looks clear"—a few church-goers and tourists calmly strolling along as I adjust my rope belt and cowl.

"You wait here, Tory."

"But I need to go to the bathroom *now*!"

"All right, then use that one over there."

"Where?"

"In that hotel, Glenwood Inn, and I'll wait with Poldy till you return. Go on."

The sun grimacing through those clouds above her coltish gait, a shimmer of blonde, my only child, vulnerable and feisty daughter of mine ("How 'bout the last *ten*!"), who hurries into that hotel—use a Naples and Cad Yellow for her hair (like Turner's paintings late in life shifting from sunset to sunrise, those splendid blazing outbursts), and a Prussian Blue for her deepest shadows. Here in this wooded hollow of Enniskerry, green hills resplendent about us, and Tory conceived on a hill in Kilcoole exactly like this. Hers such a silvery delivery, out she popped smooth as silk—and now she pops up here, her mother on the way (if she can ever find us). Remember Laura, at eight months pregnant, rising early to take a morning dip in the nude, her huge belly and swollen breasts, wading out past the gray shingle into the Irish Sea—when suddenly gliding into view came three canoes crammed stem to stern with a host of Jesuits—and Laura, frozen with shame for a moment, let a giggle escape and then a guffaw, her huge belly jiggling in the dawn's early light, and the gawking Jesuits practically falling into the water.

Yet all the arguments we had, again and again: "*Hell, Laura, the artist is always more important than his art.*" "*Than his art?*" "*Absolutely! The public forever losing sight of the man: Beethoven going deaf but still composing; Joyce almost blind but still writing; and Gauguin, ravaged by abscesses and heart disease, eczema and syphilis, still painting right up to the day he died!*"

And now here am I, having just breathed thirty miles of the sweetest Wicklow air, feeling more alive than I can't remember when—as Tory, bladder free, comes bounding back across the road, down the slight slope, and Poldy shimmies his rump in welcome.

"Better, lass?"

"Much."

"OK, well then, I'll go get some food, meet you back here in say, O five or ten minutes. You hungry?"

"You kidding? I'm *starving*!"

"All right, what would you like?"

"Whatever. But definitely something cold to drink."

"Fruit juice?"

"Fine, O and some snacks, too, candy, I could use a shot of energy"—she grinning—"and maybe throw in a cheeseburger while you're at it—No, no, only kidding, whatever you bring back is fine."

"Is that your favorite food?"

"O yeah, a Gino's double cheeseburger—far out!"

"Gino's?"

"In Baltimore, named after the Baltimore Colts football player, Gino Marchetti. Thick, juicy burgers, best burgers I ever had."

"Right. Well, Poldy'll stay here with you, and after I get back, we can parallel the Bray Road straight to Flynn's."

"And when we get there, will you call the police?"

"After I make some calls of my own. 'Bye."

And trotting on into town, with my blood pressure pounding in my ears, curling my side whiskers and stroking my mustache and grizzled beard—footsteps shuffling, cantering behind me, hand on my shoulder, and a voice proclaiming: "All right, come quietly now, sir—"

O Jaysus!

"—Yer under arrest fer impersonatin' Seamus Boyne!"

And whirling around to see a small man in a stained brown mac laughing from the tip of his ginger beard to his bald walrus dome, his breath a powerful Guinness reek.

"Only kiddin', Father, only kiddin' "—he blinking and swaying—"sorry fer scarin' ya—saw ya from across the street—but yer the spittin' image of himself, so y'are, of that artist fella who died."

"Artist who died? Look here, I think you're operating under a misconception."

"No, 'tis just a lamppost, Padre!"—and chortling three sheets to the wind, he goes weaving down the narrow street.

Christ, if the Irish don't kill me, nobody will—past the clock tower surrounded by a florist's storeroom of color, marigolds and asters, burnt sienna and velvet rose, and into the cheesy scent of this grocer's shop—and that huge, hulking figure passing outside, rather tall for an Irishman—

"Father?"

"O, so sorry, yes"—and moving up to the counter to place my order with this wisp of a woman in a dark blue smock, so frail and wafer-thin that if you put a stamp on her, you could probably mail her anywhere in Ireland.

Tory

O Jeez, what a sight! My father, like a weird vampire with his monkish brown robe darkly flapping around him, comes prancing over the grass—"Here, lass, goodies galore!"—to open a plastic bag and pluck forth "a Nestlé Milkybar, finest white chocolate on Erin's green and fragrant shore, a half pound of Irish Swiss, Bolands biscuits, Colman's English mustard—and yes, Poldy, yes, got your favorite Milk-Bones, fresh from the States!—and last but not least, a special treat, the legendary drink of Ireland, Mi Wadi Orange Quosh! Somewhat similar to the French Pschitt, but the Mi Wadi is vastly superior, far more body, a bolder bouquet!"

And we all dig in, with me making a pig of myself and brushing the flies aside—"O my God, this is *so-o-o* good!"—as beaming, I keep on eating. "I never knew the Irish made Swiss cheese."

"Just started, Tory. And you like the Mi Wadi?"

Gulping it down, "Bit syrupy but—"

"I know, needs a bit of diluting."

"But the cheese and mustard are fantastic together! And it's amazing you're left-handed, too."

"Of course I'm left-handed, who was beaten into being right-handed by the rulers of those bloody nuns who broke my pinkie and cracked three other knuckles to boot. Remember what the last words of the Quare Fellow Himself, Brendan Behan, were to that nun on his deathbed?"

"I don't."

"'May all your sons be bishops, Sister'"—and he tosses Poldy another Milk-Bone—"But it's the left and not the academic's right where the creative juices flow! Leonardo, Michelangelo, Picasso, Klee, you and me, *all* of us left-handed!"

"Is that really so?"—sighing and stretching back now on the soft grass.

"You stiff, lass?"

"A little."

"Why're you smiling?"

"O I was just thinking I so wanted to be a gymnast when I was little. All my friends were tiny, and I was so tall and lanky that when I would do somersaults, I'd get all tied up in knots."

"And when did you start dating?"

"O, fifteen, sixteen, I kept waiting to develop. But I was so unlike most of the girls my age, who only wanted a guy with messy blonde hair and six-pack abs"—taking another long gulp—"The Mi Wadi grows on you," and looking up—

"I know."

—as that green Beetle cruises through the heart of town—"*O no*! We've gotta get going *now*!"

"Why? What is it, Tory?"

"This time it *is* them, I *swear*!"

"Here, this way!" The Beetle pausing to let people cross—don't think they've seen us.

And we scurry onto the road, around this bend, Poldy romping alongside my father's flapping robe, and toward these entrance gates, Powerscourt, those tour buses filling up—*O Jesus*! *O*

Christ!—the Beetle bearing straight down on us, Bruff jumping out, already running, his elephant feet thumping down the tree-lined street—

And my father, Poldy, and I scramble aboard this bus jammed with Japanese tourists all wearing white fishermen's sweaters, and my father shouting, "*Arigato, hai, hai!*" and to the cowed Irish driver, "In need of a lift, my son"—the tourists now bowing and grinning, Nikons and Canons wildly clicking away, and Poldy licking their faces, his tail wagging a hundred miles an hour, while I'm wrestling with the driver to shut this goddamn door, Bruff groping and shoving his Karloff paw inside, his sinister, goblin eyes—"Let's go! He's trying to kill us!"

And with a jerk, I *slam* it closed!

Bruff shrieking, wincing at his mangled fingers, and we roar away, back to Enniskerry.

Boyne

That huge, hulking galoot (same one I saw) hobbling into the Volkswagen beside the driver—glinty sunglasses obscuring his face—and with a rattling lurch, we squeal around this bend—they whipping a fast U-turn, hot on our tail again.

Tory swaying against me—"Now what?"

"I'm thinking, I'm thinking"—bouncing down the twisty street, the clock tower looming ahead with its town square spoking off into three directions—"Driver, here, stop here, we'll get out right here!"—then back to the tourists, "An *arigato* to you all and to all a good night!"—cameras still clicking, hands waving, and—"Tory, this way!"—into the grocer's cluttered shop as the bus goes bumping off to Bray.

"Forget somethin', Father?"

"No, no, my child, not at all, only a bit of relief from the blazing midday sun."

Tory peeking out the lace-curtained front door panes as I join her in the shadows—and the green Beetle abruptly appears, pausing—then zooms off in the wrong direction—as we both sigh and head outside, swiftly across the street and on through this meadow, back into the woods, between these trees, moving at breakneck speed down this grassy path, gliding and sidestepping and slowing to a jog, paralleling the Bray Road, keeping our eyes peeled just in case—and Flynn's Gothic castle beneath those billowing clouds ahead on the blue horizon!

Tory

This same shield-shaped, oaken door opens wide with a creak:

"Flynn? Hello? Anybody to home?"—and my father cautiously enters, talking over his shoulder, "Always leaves his doors open, especially when he's gone to London, sure he gave his servants the entire week off"—then striding along the corridors, down these dark castle halls, with Poldy following—"Hello, hello?"—through drawing rooms and dining rooms, sitting rooms and dens, past tapestries and busts, paintings by my father, and books from the floor rugs to that ornate plasterwork ceiling as he turns back to me, "Empty as a tomb, so you ready for a bath?"

Smiling. "I thought you'd never ask. Though actually, what I'd really love is a shower."

"Top floor, to the left, towels in the closet—and you know what, lass?"

"What?"

"I think I'll have a bath myself and get out of this blasted habit! Been driving me up the wall. Anyway, that was a brilliant idea, Tory, shower for you, bath for me, then we'll both be ripe for a snooze."

Grinning. "Couldn't be any riper."

"'Cause I think we're safe here for the moment, they probably assumed we continued on to Dublin or back to *my* castle. Anyway, after a wash and decent sleep, we'll figure out our next best step, make some calls. And if you need anything at all, give us a shout, and I'll see you when you wake."

Up these winding stone stairs and down this long corridor—I can't believe a real shower!—and into this lavish loo, lavo, sumptuous bathroom with hanging plants and silvery fixtures. I stop before this mirror: *Wow!* Really sunburned now, and staring at my staring, freckled face, nose peeling, hair a mess, a windblown mess. And so much of my thinking seems to be what do I look like, when I seem to be thinking. And, let's see, he's gotta have some shampoo here. Yes! Pears. Swiveling it open. Smells nice, like pears. Duh! No, really—laughing—Bartlett or Comice? Whirling around: No, just thought I heard, my nerves so raw, but Bruff and the weasel long gone. Feel safe here, with me da (my two-bit brogue) and his quicksilver tongue, an eloquent rogue. Hilarious aboard that Japanese bus. And my fantasy come true, to finally have a relationship with you, dear father of mine, Seamus Eamon Boyne. But so afraid of being deserted again, high blood pressure, he dying. Don't know *how* to feel, what to do, totally confused. *I haven't felt this alive in I can't remember when! In tiptop shape!* We'll See.

And quickly stripping, I pop open this opaque ripple door and step inside. Shiny black tile, smooth and cool to the touch, a monster showerhead—and "*Whee!*" Hee-hee! A blast from the past, folks, like that one at the Peabody Court, and I'll scrub till I'm blue, then pour on the Pears, lather it into a halo, a bubbly crown, sudsy tiara—

Someone whistling?

Who's *that*?

"Dad?"

The whistling continuing—sounds like "It's a Long Way to Tipperary."

"*Dad?*"

O Jeez no! As I step up on tiptoe to sneak a peek over the shower door and see: a tiny, whistling man with a monocle and spats.

"Uh, excuse me?" Could be deaf. Louder, "*Excuse* me, do you work here?"

He keeps on whistling—then walks right *through* the closed bathroom door!

"*Dad! DAD!*"—screaming at the top of my lungs, turning off the shower—and my father racing headlong into the room.

"*What*? What *happened*? What's going *on*? Still in his habit as I turn aside.

"Did you see that *man*, or am I dreaming, flipping out?"

"What man?"

"That little whistling man—"

"Where?"

"In here! He just left, walked right *through* that closed door!"

And spinning about, my father charges out—hear him sprinting up and down the halls, opening and shutting doors and calling, "Hello? Anybody here?"—down the stairs, up the stairs, and finally back in here, panting and leaning against the wall.

"—Know what, my dear?"

"What?"

"—You saw a ghost."

"Yeah, right!"

"No, really."

"Then how come *you* didn't see him?"

"Some of us can, Tory, some of us can't—but Flynn does have a few about."

"A few ghosts?"

"O sure, castle's been haunted for centuries."

"And he talks to them?"

"Absolutely. Talks to them, has a Guinness with 'em."

"Do they speak?"

"You mean verbally, the way we speak? O no, though apparently they speak more here in Ireland than, say, in the States."

"Well, I read where Yeats's wife supposedly spoke to Yeats."

"I wouldn't doubt that. Anyway, lass, I'll be right downstairs, so relax and finish your shower. Though, come to think of it, you know, I've always wondered why they wear clothes."

"Who, the ghosts?"

"I mean, why aren't they naked, or still wearing the same clothes they died in? No dry cleaning? Or modesty even in the afterlife? Anyway, call me if he returns."

"Hey, in a fucking New York minute!"

Boyne

—Through the Wicklow Hills, a silken blaze of sun over the meadows as the green hedgerowed fields shimmer and dim—and a white flock of gulls suddenly erupt, rising in startled flight, the interlacing flap of their wings across the sea, the shadow-dappled, gull-wheeling, green-shimmered sea—

Wrestling myself out of a wheezy sleep, a shivery blur, and slowly blinking my eyes . . . so very tired, lying here in the dark wrapped in Flynn's wine-colored Turkish terry-cloth robe, blue-flecked fleur-de-lis wallpaper surrounding me and this king-size, downstairs bed. Must've slept awhile, after that reviving bath in his contoured reclining tub. And no more cries from Tory. Ghosts merely checking her out, putting their stamp of approval on who comes and goes. Well hell, it is their house, you know. Still, what to do with these kidnappers, captors, villainous scum? (Poldy on guard outside, tethered to a tree by his braided green leash.) Hole up here for a few more days till Flynn returns and call the police, or the Irish Mafia, and nail these bastards to the wall like I should've done last night? Right, shrieking like a banshee into the fray!

Then, as soon as I can, begin turning my sketches of Tory into marvelous full-length portraits. So missing the physical act of painting now, that first brilliant assault, almost without effort—and it's those bold, initial strokes, born of endless practice, that inevitably create great art, touch the deep core of my life, or like Pollock said, prevent you from ending it all—

Mother of Christ! That blinding shaft of light from the hallway as the door creaks slowly open, a silhouette framed within it—

Another bloody ghost! My very first as I bolt straight up, holding my breath—

"Is anyone here?" A woman's familiar voice.

"Uh, yes—yes, there is—"

"Boyne?"

"Right, but—*LAURA*? Jaysus, how the hell'd you *find* me?"

Her hand searching for the light, flicks it on—and actually she's aged rather well—as I keep blinking and panting—in a tan London Fog, short black heels, her hair swept back into a brassy, no, platinum twist, and those vivid green eyes roaming over my face, the wallpapered room—

"I went to the Shelbourne. Any further word?"

"She's fine, safe, is upstairs sleeping."

"Why didn't you *tell* me, *call* me?"

"Couldn't, been on the run since I found her—"

"Where?"

"—at this nursing home in Bray, the kidnappers are still chasing us. But, Laura, how'd you ever find us, why come *here*?"

"I went over to the private investigator's office—it was closed on Sunday, of course, then called your home, you were dead, and remembered Flynn, thought I'd take a chance, saw the lights on and—"

"Scared the bejaysus out've me!"—as I slowly stand and follow her into the hall, scratching down my sides and thighs.

"My God, Boyne, what on earth are you *wearing*?"

"Flynn's robe. Why?"

"Because it looks ridiculous on you!"

"Well, I'll take it off, if you prefer."

"No, that's quite all right."

"Though I must say, *you* look very well, Laura, very well indeed, far better than I expected."

"Thank you—I think"—she sweeping a strand of hair from her eyes with a quick, defiant gesture. "And you have no idea who these people are?"

Turning into this den—"Not a clue"—with its studded leather sofa and chairs, and by the latticed window.

"Is that your dog outside, Boyne?"

"Right, surprised he didn't bark."

"Because I petted him"—she sighing deeply now as she marches about. "And to come all this way to Ireland for you and your crazy prank—I won't even ask why, make a three-thousand-mile journey back—"

"Well, all journeys are return journeys, aren't they?"

"If you say so."

A momentary pause, the two of us staring uneasily at each other after all these years—she suddenly shutting her eyes, wrinkling her nose, and turning away with a shy—

"Ah—*choo*!"

"God bless you."

"Thank you."

"Have you a cold?"

"No, just a sneeze"—her eyes tearing as, still sniffling, she begins strutting again, opening her raincoat to reveal a black wool pants suit and cream silk top. "Anyway"—heading back into the hall—"I'm going to wake Tory"—veering toward the stairs—"and take her home and away from all this craziness—"

"*Mother*? What're *you* doing here?" Tory coming hesitantly down in her dry sweatshirt and jeans.

"O *darling*, are you all right?" giving her a stiff hug and kiss, "Did they hurt you, torture you?"

"I'm fine, Mother, fine, but tell me what you're *doing* here"—then glaring at me. "Did *you* call her?"

"Yes, he called me, but *before* he found you. Anyway, dear, get your things, you're coming home with me."

"What're you talking about?"

"Look, you're still in danger, and you don't fool around with kidnappers, who knows what these lunatics have in mind, the IRA kills people all the time, and they could certainly kill *you*!"

"Who said anything about the IRA? These creeps just want the money."

"Look, I'm not going to argue with you now. Are any of your things upstairs?"

"No, back at the Shelbourne."

"Good, then we're leaving right now."

"Mother, I'm *not* leaving."

"Tory, don't start."

"Why don't you listen to her, Laura?"

"Just keep out of this!"

"Why should he? He's still my father, whether you like it or not, and whatever else you may think of him, the point is he did *rescue* me, risk his life to save mine."

"Fine, and I'm very grateful, but the fact remains *I'm* your legal parent now."

"And what about me, Mother? Don't I have a say in my own life?"

"No, you don't, you're still underage."

"Laura, listen, I don't think she's in any real danger now—"

"What're you *talking* about? Here she was kidnapped, held for ransom, God knows what they did to her—"

"Mother, they didn't do—"

"And, Laura, we're both with her now, and I'll take care of the kidnappers."

"O I'm sure you will! The same way you let them kidnap her in the first place, got her over here on false pretenses, faking your own crazy funeral! O I'm certain you'll take care of it! Anyway, Tory, like I said, I'm in no mood to fight with you now."

"Well, neither am I."

"You've gotten yourself into enough trouble—"

"So now it's *my* fault?"

"I didn't mean that, sorry."

"O Jeez!"—and grinning and shaking her head, Tory leans back against the stairs. "You know what's really wild?"

"What?"

"I just realized this is the first time we've all been together since I was seven—and that was for ten minutes, tops, before Dad took off."

"That's exactly right! He was never there for you—"

"O and you were?"

"Yes, I was."

"Really? Tell me, *when* were you there for me, Mother?"

"*When, when*? I'll tell you when!"

"Tell me, Mother."

"All right, who was there, matter of fact the only one who *was* there for you, when Nina Jaccalone died?"

"Yes, but—"

"And when you went through that thing with your art teacher your junior year in high school—?"

I stare at Tory—"*What* thing, lass?"—as she glances away.

"OK, Mother, OK, you made your point. I'm sorry, but the fact remains, he did save my life."

"And got you here on false pretenses."

"He didn't 'get me here'! I came on my own. And we really do make a great team."

"Actually we do, Laura, but anyway, listen, the point is we're perfectly safe here, and it's nearly, what seven, seven-fifteen, and I'm sure you're all really hungry, so why don't I—"

"I'm not very hungry."

"—crack open a bottle of Irish wine"—as Poldy starts loudly barking outside. "*Uh-oh!*"

"Now what?"

Rushing to the window to see that dark shadow flitting like a grainy silent film figure across the lawn, with Poldy straining hard at his leash. "*Damn*! Looks like somebody else knows we're here! Quick, Tory, make sure all the doors are locked, and, Laura, you come with me!"

"Where? Why? Who is it? What on earth is *happening*?"

"Just come on!"

Tory

Racing in and out of drawing rooms and dining rooms, flicking locks, shooting bolts—and into this monster kitchen with its shiny copper pans hung from the walls—and any second expecting Bruff, with his mangled claw, Karloff paw, to come smashing through the door.

O my God, now he'll really kill us *all*!

No way, José! Over my dead body!

Poldy still barking—and so strange: she flying three thousand miles, for me? Will wonders never cease? Though part of me *is* happy to see her, relieved in a funny way.

And how many damn doors does this stupid castle *have*?

Boyne

"Look, will you kindly tell me what's happening, Boyne, what is going *on*?"—as I reach around Laura and lift this long-handled, cast-iron, antique popcorn popper from the hearth.

"Not sure yet, but it doesn't pay to take any chances. Here, you get behind me, and we'll both stand back of the front door—give this whore's melt what-for."

"You really think it's the kidnappers?"

Another furtive glance out the latticed panes: someone or something still flitting there, there, across there—"Can't be certain"—Poldy madly barking and—"*O Christ,* here he comes!"—with slicker, hat, and pointed gun! Where's a bloody ghost when you need one? (Right behind me, clutching my waist!)

"Call the police, Boyne!"

"Too late, Laura, have to get rid of the bastard myself!"—tightly gripping this long handle and whipping the popper back over my head like a mace—Laura falling—just as the door bursts open and a small man hurtles in, knocking me sprawling, the gun clattering across the hall—"Run, Laura, scatter and hide!"

And I fly up the winding stairs—no shots behind—these slick stone steps, past the second floor, third floor, and on toward the battlements!

Tory

What's all that racket, pounding feet? as I ease silently down the hall, around this corner: no Bruff, father, or weasel—*O my GOD!*—Mother—black and tan and tumbled hair—lying zonked behind the door!

Her heady scent of Joy—still breathing, but out like a light—as I grab this cushion, gently cradle her head, and slip it under, thank God she's not dead, as she softly moans, groggily coming to, her green eyes blinking.

"Boyne is such an *idiot*!"

"Are you all right?"

"*Damn* that blasted man!"

"Mother, who else is here?"

"Who knows? I never got to see them, your father knocked me cold!"

"OK, well, don't move, stay where you are, and I'll be back in a moment."

Quickly outside the castle to let Poldy go, the poor dog still wheezing and straining—then romping free with his trailing leash and the cantering click of his nails on the floor as he rushes up to Mother, with his swishing snowy tail, and starts licking all over her face—

She flailing, "Will you get him *off*—"

"Listen, I'm gonna find Dad."

"—and—*God!*—take this stupid dog with you!"

And she loudly sneezes as I grab onto Poldy's leash and make my cautious way up to the roof, uneven steps, this damp castle smell.

Two voices talking—"Shhh, Poldy, easy, easy!" Can just make out what they're saying:

"Look, Mr. Boyne, I don't want ta kill ya, but I will if I have ta now."

The *weasel*! Bruff with him?

"That's good, 'cause I'd prefer staying alive."

"But I'm not goin' ta jail fer this."

The door slightly ajar as I slowly reach the top stone step and drop to a knee, Poldy panting and straining hard . . .

A silvery moon, fleeting clouds out there—and the weasel's back to me in that bright yellow slicker, shaggy head of sandy hair—and no Bruff about that I can see. The weasel pointing a stubby gun at my bathrobed father, framed against the battlements—when Poldy lurches forward—

"*No!*"—yanking me up and onto the tar and gravel roof, the weasel whirling.

"Don't move!" His teeth clenched and the artery on his neck pumping.

"Where's Bruff?"

"Gone ta hospital. Ya broke his hand in the bus. Just get over there!"

"Tory, what on earth is going on?"

Glancing behind as Mother comes stumbling up. "No, *back*, go *back*!"

"Who's up here—Wait a minute, I know him! You're, yes, I saw your picture—you're the private detective we hired—"

"Private detective?"

"So *that's* who he is, Laura!"

"Mulcahy, right, Finbar Mulcahy! Yes, same shifty eyes, craggy face—"

"You hired *him* to watch me?"

"Exactly!"

"O Mother!"

"Mark had a contact in Ireland, from his law firm. But what I don't understand—"

"All right, ladies, get over here where I can see the both of ya."

Finbar's gun shaking in his hand—he looking more like a fidgety Don Knotts now than a professional private eye as Mother, Poldy, and I move around the roof toward my father.

"So, who're you going to shoot, Finbar? Me? Her? Her mother?"

"Shut yer gob!"

"You shoot me, who pays? You shoot her, no ransom. Checkmate, I'd say."

"Then I'll take yer daughter hostage again. But, look, can't we just settle this, 'cause everything's gettin' bollixed up now, and all I'm doin' is followin' orders—"

"Orders? Whose orders?"

"Well, he said—"

"Who said?"

"Don't ya know, ma'am?"

Laura turning to me—"Know what?"—then back to Finbar.

"Well, I suppose there's no harm in tellin' ya now. I took me orders from yer husband."

"*Mark*? What're you saying?"

"When I found out Boyne was alive, *he* told me what ta do."

"I don't believe this!"

"'Tis true."

"Come on, you mean to tell me it was *his* idea to hold Tory for ransom?"

"Right y'are, ma'am, 'to squeeze,' he said, 'bloody Boyne dry and make 'im pay.' Said he needed the funds, had some government business to take care of."

"*O Jeez*!"—and throwing up my hands in dismay—"*Poldy!*"—as the dog breaks free and leaps between us, knocking Finbar down—the gun firing wildly into the night sky—my mother losing her balance, crashing back against the battlements and toppling over, but grabbing onto Poldy's leash—"*Mother*!" "*Laura*!"—as I snatch up this Beretta (like Bond, Tory Bond!) and race to the parapet:

"*Hold on, Mother, hold on*!"

Must be a ninety-foot drop straight down! These tangled vines—

"She's *slipping*, Tory, she's *slipping*! *Poldy!*"

The dog digging four paws in on the tar and gravel and leaning back hard on his haunches.

"—I can't hold on much longer!"

"The leash is going to *break*!"

"*Pull*, Tory, *pull*!"

"You, too, Finbar!"

"And if I don't?"

"I'll blow your scuzzy *head* off!"—as I thrust out my free hand as far as I possible can—*O dear God!*—just as the leash snaps in half!

Boyne

Hustling along these stately halls of Ballyduff, home sweet home, my rambling seaside estate, and passing by works of my own and an exquisite Turner or two as I come bounding onto the stage of this vaulted banquet room in my laundered monk's attire to a chorus of laughter and applause, cameras whirring, flashbulbs popping, BBC, NBC, Telefís Éireann, and Tory, Flynn, and Poldy primly seated up here on the dais, an empty chair beside them, and Finbar briskly serving:

"Ladies and gentlemen, assorted guests, and members of the press and media," as I bend forward into the bank of mikes, "I welcome you all to this grand unveiling and bacchanalian feast, the clash of cutlery and the chime of the wineglass, to proclaim my *resurrection*!"—and stripping off this habit to reveal my green tuxedo beneath—"and featuring every food and libation I've been denied over these last desperate years!"

"And how are ya feelin' now, Mr. Boyne, after yer recent ordeal?"

"Well, I'm not as dead now as I thought I'd be. But, as you well know, I never can resist a touch of the dramatic, and the mantle of so-called genius can indeed be a crown of thorns."

"Mr. Boyne, if I may—"

"O and by the way, those eerie, keening tones you're hearing, that haunting, reedy drone arises from none other than the Irish pipes of Percy Dungannon, now high atop the ramparts and silhouetted against a silvery Wicklow sky."

"And still soundin', as usual, like the parrot house at the zoo!"

"Indeed, Flynn, 'tis true. O and, Finbar, be useful for once, would you, and bring up more wine from the cellar?"

"Right y'are, sir, right y'are."

"Mr. Boyne, please—" "Mr. Boyne—"

"But, ladies and gentlemen, no more questions now"—lifting

my Waterford crystal—"for at this time, I'd like to propose a toast. Raise your glasses, if you would, to this amazing lassie and my dear daughter, Tory—the air of Ireland's become far sweeter because of her lovely presence"—and tossing back my wine in a gulp—"though to give credit where credit is due, the fact of the matter is it was her splendid mother who taught her 'most everything she ever knew—"

"Well, *that's* nice to finally hear"—and Laura comes striding in as though on cue, buttoning up her tan tailored jacket and hugging Tory and Flynn, before taking the seat beside me—as another reporter springs to his feet.

"Could you tell us, ma'am, how *you* survived this experience?"

"'Twas the moat far below that saved her and her two-and-a-half gainer in the tuck position."

"Boyne, you're such a bloody liar!" as I burst out laughing, the whole room laughing. "Actually, it was my daughter who grabbed me by the wrist, thank God, just in the nick of time, or I would've died in Wicklow."

"And it was in Wicklow, Laura, as I'm certain you recall, where Tory was conceived."

"How could I possibly forget."

"O please," Tory raising her eyes to the ceiling, "I don't think they need to hear about this now!"

"No, no, lass, indulge your dear old resurrected da just a wee bit more. For a bewitching time it was, over seventeen summers ago, no money nor cares, while I lived on air with my Sarah Lawrence grad. And one morning atop this grassy hill in Kilcoole, after watching a herd of ponies woo one another, nuzzling about and running across a meadow with such exquisite freedom and ease, we made such passionately tender love that a month later, when your mother realized she was pregnant, she couldn't remember our lovemaking at all or precisely where you were conceived, just those ponies running along."

Laura blinking with an ironic smile as Tory leans over to whisper, "Is that true, Mother?"

"Well, I'm sure I remember something," and she keeps staring deep into my eyes a moment longer before turning back to Tory, "But, dear, I never said your father was boring."

Hagar's Dream

May 1976

One

Gulls reeling, fiercely wheeling like torn scraps of paper in this shrieking gale, everybody dying, disappearing, these nightmarish fears vaulting the sea, the immense sprawled shimmer of the Irish Sea, a green, toppling sea, dots and white smears of sailboats beneath that stormy hill of Howth, wildflowers thrashing—as I shoot straight up like a shot, gasping and panting and soaked with sweat at this ungodly hour in my king-size bed littered with books and magazines, TV still going—and *nobody* here beside me in the all-consuming dark!—then blindly groping for the remote control (*Wheel of Fortune, Odd Couple* reruns, *News at Sunrise,* phone date commercials for lonely guys?)—and blinking blurry eyes at the screen:

Who the hell is—?

My *grandma's* on Channel 2?

And my *mother's* on 4?

My *father's* on 5?

Nabokov's on 7?

And, Christ Almighty, *CIARA'S* on 9?

This's *crazy*! *Insane! I'm finally flipping out!* as I keep frantically flicking all the way back to—

And there's my Bubba *AGAIN*!

Am I *awake*? *asleep*? Losing my *mind*?

Dreaming? Right, right, I've *gotta* be dreaming! Or call a TV repairman? (No, nobody working at 4:30 in the morning!)

So pause to watch? My heart still loudly pounding—

I pause to watch:

My Bubba there in that Great Neck of my past, her face glazed by a warm blaze of Vermeer sunlight, pondering her next checker move or telling me tales of Berlin and Dvinsk, waltzes and her youth, 97th Street or her seamstress store at the end of World War II as I keep blinking and gazing hard at that aged autumn room, the leaves outdoors falling orange and russet and crackling underfoot, while we play our usual game of gin rummy throughout the late afternoon (this's REALLY *unbelievable*!), her worn Bike cards held vertically before her, knocking always with less than six, and the wondrous stories of her husband, Henry, woven into the background Yiddish of WEVD, his dark crop of hair still bold on the wall in the cracked oval frame as I twine my tousled nine-year-old self into a snug corner of that antimacassared couch, ancient stains Rorschached into patterns of soup rose and coffee bear upon its arm, and continue to listen intently, a gently glowing comfort crawling over my shoulders and nuzzling across my green flannel chest to nestle against my nape and cheekbones. (Can I ever recapture that feeling again?) And warm-shawled in our seclusion, the maid downstairs basting, my parents having just called, about to leave their Long Island City office, my Bubba beams at me, "*Oi, Eugene, mine zissa kind!*" then gazes back through Scotch-taped glasses to those tales of her past—and now, *O Christ!* there's that last nursing home scene and the frail husk of her bedridden body, oxygen mask over her face, and me beside her chanting "Bubba" again and again, tears streaming, while she rages desperately for breath—

Quickly flicking to Channel 4:

And *Jesus*, I really don't *believe* this! There's my *MOTHER* looking so young and healthy back when, and long before Lou Gehrig's disease took her last May—must be on her one day home from the office, the tail end of the termite season, snuffing out Chesterfield after Chesterfield, and glancing around the wide shadowed emptiness of her Sutton Place apartment, the organ sounds of my Bubba's early-afternoon soap opera passing her ears, gold drapes drawn closed to prevent sunlight fading the blue pile rug and white brocaded fabrics, sofa and chairs all covered with clear protective plastic, closed to the soft swoosh of tires, the coo and gargle of pigeons mincing along the tenth-floor ledge, tugboats crawling up the East River hauling barges of sand, the continuous flow of traffic on FDR Drive, and the squeal and toddle of nurse-watched children cavorting in the sand pen below (and I've *gotta* be dreaming, living alone now much too long!), till the butcher sends his meat, the grocer his vegetables, the cleaner his suits, the tailor his pants, and the elevator operator his stack of mail—another day of bills and circulars, *TV Guide* and announcements, but nothing from me on my first trip to Ireland—as my Bubba fumbles and clicks off *The Road of Life* before inserting her needle once again along a lacy hem, and my mother enters to sit and schmooze, the sun going down, and answer the eagerly awaited phone—wrong number, and switch on the TV to drowse through a *Life of Riley* rerun, awaking to the strident ring at six o'clock, and the flat, weary voice of my father announcing he will not be home for dinner, is exhausted and going to the gym, and my mother, her heart scarcely sinking anymore, answering, "All right, all right," always "All right" in the sad resignation of six o'clock as my Bubba dozes in a warm curl, before hurrying to the kitchen to remove her mother's whistling tea and await the night: the bland dinner of chicken soup, hamburgers for sensitive teeth, lumpy mashed potatoes, apricots and prunes, nibbles off Pepperidge Farm rolls, Lipton tea steaming a thin, wispy ribbon, Stella D'oros, and lemon slices, the lighting of *Yahrzeit* candles in a Sara Lee pie plate, changing to bathrobe and slippers to huddle round the Zenith as my father finally arrives with a passing kiss, glance at the paper and bills—and looking like a slope-shouldered Ralph Bellamy, with distinguished graying temples, raccoon eyes, and double chin: could be a banker, a broker, a wealthy tycoon, with his six-in-the-morning-to-seven-at-night-and-most-Saturdays' dedication to Hagar Pest

Control—then turns to the wall in sleep. And back to the den my sighing mother goes to pull out the convertible bed for my Bubba, and smile an occasional late-night smile at the humor of Jack Paar and his guests, bemused by fleeting moments, before regaining her seat in the hallway, Chesterfield puffing ceaselessly, tastelessly as she wearies herself to sleep, rises to adjust a figurine and wet her fingertip, erasing a pale ringed spot, watches her mother's high-clasped, rocking prayers by the window, and now, several minutes to one, she smiles at the thought of her "gallivanting" son on his first trip to Europe, avoiding our silence and strain, and concentrates instead on those few shining moments of tenderness and concern, certain I'll return, *Everybody goes through phases,* and take over the bug business, her hairnet arranged and stockings sorted, switches off each light of the silent apartment and pads noiselessly by my father's snore to bed.

Then flicking once more—to Channel 5:

And there's my *FATHER* and I, on a bright, windy Saturday when I was twelve, journeying up to the Stadium with me, as across those terrifying catwalks I shuffle behind his impatient, slope-shouldered stride, "Come on, come on, nothing to be scared of up here," to watch far below the groundskeepers hose down the diamond, Yankee and Red Sox pitchers slowly getting loose, kids scampering along the aisles in pursuit of batting practice homers that bounce high off the silver railings as we eagerly wait for Teddy Ballgame to appear, Mel Allen's Southern drawl on a nearby portable setting the scene, Raschi meeting with Rizzuto at the mound, the Yankee infield and outfield shifting way around to the right, and Williams, tapping the dirt from his spikes and twisting the bat in his hands, nervously digging into place with that tall, classic stance, our raccoon eyes squinting, and my father smiling and nudging me with a whisper, "This is some game, huh? Glad I took you? Huh? You've got some father. Just wait, you'll see, someday you'll really appreciate it."

And rapidly blinking now, flicking to Channel 7:

And there's *NABOKOV* at Cornell! in his dark brown and musty office with its faded, once-Turkish rug as he unwinds and removes muffler, storm coat, and earflapped cap following that theatrical, clattering entrance, and, peering over his tortoiseshell glasses, asks me, "Are you going to read Joyce on the weekend?"

"No, I think I'll do some writing."

"You want to be a writer?"

". . . Yes." Then drawing me to the window, "Come here," and pointing toward some lavender blooms, "What are those?"

"Which?"

"Those, there!"

"I don't know."

"They're lilacs! You have to know the name of every single thing if you want to write!"

Now flicking to Channel 9 and:

MY GOD, there's Ciara, my blonde poetic dream, during our first time together, with her hair of Scandinavian shine as she moves around that houseboat on the Seine in her silky purple robe—and I move, too, tumbling her waywardly onto the bed—"No, Gene, I have to wash and dress if you still want to go to the Louvre"—the firm crease of her spine as I keep widening the purple robe—"Please, leave it alone, stop playing—O all *right*!" and she flipping it open to reveal her high breasts, hips, and fleece before shutting the sight with a silent slam—

THE PHONE STRIDENTLY RINGING!

CHRIST ALMIGHTY!! Who the hell's calling NOW? On the screen? Or *really* ringing at this ungodly hour, 4:30, 5—?

No, it's quarter to *eight* already!!

Dreaming all this time? Could've sworn—as flicking off the set and licking the sweat from my upper lip, I fumble and grope across these books and tumbling pillows, "—'lo?"

"Gene, listen, sorry to wake you but I've got to talk to you—"

"Who's this?"

"Teri."

"Teri?"

"Remember, your ex-*wife,* Teri? Anyways, I really need your advice, you've got to listen to this, 'cause my class starts in twenty minutes—"

"What class?"

"Hey, wake up, will you! English 101, my English composition class at Nassau? And we had to write an obituary."

"So?"

"Well I wrote yours."

Two

Along 54th Street with the bells booming noon and quickly cutting through this midday crush *("picking up a bevy of blockers and breaking out into the clear—Hagar could go all the way!—tightroping down the sideline, the fifteen, the ten, the five, he scores, eighty-five fucking yards for a touchdown!")—This Is My Life* on TV—and by the jostling throng, Madison Avenue up ahead, still so groggy, hardly any sleep, running on sheer nervous energy, and nearing Chock Full o' Nuts, jammed as usual, this frail, white-haired lady about to push through as I hold the revolving door and let her pass—bumped twice from behind—and finally wedge inside, scouting around for an open seat, nothing—O there's one not far from the take-out counter.

And Christ, what a morning, after that crazy night of TV, then Teri *really* calling and reading me my obituary—

"Order, please?"

—and leaving the bulk of my estate to her!

"Hey, *mister*?"

"—Yes? O sorry, sorry," as still grinning, I look up at this skinny mulatto waitress scowling down—

"Watcha *want*?"—while she keeps wiping the red-topped counter.

"Want? Well I'll, uh, I'll just have a cheese-and-nut sandwich and an orange drink."

"That be all?"

"No, wait a minute, throw in a powdered doughnut, too." Need the energy for my class today.

The waitress still scowling, "That's one twenty-five," and shaking her frizzy head as she swivels away.

O fuck off! The last thing I need now is a fight in my life! And gazing around, Chock Full changing so, becoming such a madhouse, as these waitresses go gliding down the counters, filling an orange drink here, reaching for a hot dog there—and that fat momma at the back whipping up the cheese-and-nut sandwiches: spreading, slicing, wrapping—really great hands, never breaking her rhythm—probably could've used her on our old softball team, our Million Dollar Infield—and that voice up front at the take-out counter with its familiar Southern drawl: "Just an orange drink and a frank, dear."

Could it be? Or am I still back in that crazy dream? as I gaze about—

O Geez, it *is* him! Really *HIM*! Mel *Allen* in the flesh down at the take-out counter!

Calm, just stay *calm!* My heart going a mile a minute!

Big Mel looking a bit older but still trim and tanned, thinning hair—And what can I say, do? Give him the three-ring sign? Tell him how I aped his style for four years at Cornell on WVBR, "*It's going, going, it is gone! A Big Red Blast!*" Thought for a while I might even follow in his footsteps. Mel still the best play-by-play announcer of them all, including Scully, Barber, *and* Howard Cosell!

Nobody else recognizing him (how quickly they forget!) as I keep munching away like a frenzied chipmunk on this cheese-and-nut sandwich—the lunch hour crowd filing in and out—and trying to come up with a bon mot, something, anything I can say that doesn't sound too schmucky! Big Mel who's seen 'em all, the Scooter, Yankee Clipper, and Teddy Ballgame: My father and I on that raw, overcast Saturday in '66, the last time we went to the Stadium together, with Ted retired and Yaz then in left—And I've gotta talk to Mel, get his autograph—as I wipe my mouth with my napkin, stand and turn—

But he's *gone,* through the revolving door, thinning hair and tan nape lost in the crowd—

After him? No, let him go. Just knock off this pulpy orange drink, grab my doughnut, and wedge my way back into the jarring midtown bustle—my one chance in a million—Still, I saw him, just behind him, a few feet away: *How about that*?

And cantering briskly down the subway steps, dropping my token in, then sprinting headlong—*hold on, hold on, don't leave!*—and just squeezing through, the door sliding closed, stops, stutters, then closes again—and this banging, clanging, graffiti-splattered train picking up speed and insanely squealing along tunnels of flickering darkness like a silent movie screen, then screeching and swaying into the station:

"*Fourteenth Street. Watch your step. West 4th next.*"

Taking the stairs two at a time and quickly round this corner at 12:45, licking powdered sugar off my lips, the doughnut's pasty taste, as I whirl through the New School's revolving door.

"May I help you, sir?"

"Uh, yeah, I'm teaching a course here."

"O sure, sorry, go right in."

Picking up my class roster before moving alongside this bunch of long-haired teenagers and eager grandmothers lugging their chestfuls of books by the blue-tiled wall, and up the squeaky elevator to the sixth floor, then down the fluorescent hall—my door wide open, students shuffling inside.

And I take a seat behind this metal desk, pushing up the sleeves of my bulky, green crewneck sweater, and open my cluttered binder, get out my syllabus, brief smile to those glum, staring faces—more students scurrying through the door:

"Hi, I'm Gene Hagar, and this is Introduction to Creative Writing. But let me first call the roll and then I'll let you know what the course is all about—"

Two other gigglers rushing in and apologizing for being late.

"Ricardo Arreola?"

"Yo."

"Jennifer Baugh?"

"Here."

Looks just like my Bubba. Hallucinating again? This's all on TV and I'm still back in bed?

"Tammy Beckett? Tammy Beckett? *Samuel* Beckett?" No laugh. "Forget it, bad joke. Bruce Bierman?"

"Here." Wearing an old Dodger cap backward.

"Tory Boyne?"

"Yes."

Tory *Boyne*?

And I glance up into the face of a blonde, glimmering girl.

Three

"Well we're about out of time, so for next week, a chase scene, and I'll see you then. Any questions? Yes, Ricardo?"

"Could I talk to you for a second, man?"

"Sure. And I'll see the rest of you next week." Keeping one eye glued to Tory, gathering up her notebook and chatting with (my Bubba) Jennifer Baugh—cut this short if I have to—"So, Ricardo, what can I do for you?"

"Yeah, well here's the thing, see, I gotta miss the next class, got this high school reunion, y'know, in my hometown, so could I hand in this so-called chase scene like in say two weeks?"

"Absolutely." She still chatting—

"Hey, thanks, man, thanks a lot, and you run a really cool class, *ciao.*"

She leaving, nearly out the door. Hurry, hurry! "O Tory, could I speak to you a second?" And waiting for the last stragglers to finally go.

"You wouldn't, by chance, be the daughter of Seamus Boyne?"

"Why?" No lipstick or fingernail polish, her skin's silky glow, white-blonde hair bound in a loose ponytail.

"I know your father quite well."

"Is that so?"

"No, really, I do. We go back quite a ways."

"How far back?"

"Well he married my old girlfriend. . . ." She narrowing her eyes and tilting her head. "Ciara."

"You went with *Ciara*?"

"Indeed I did."

"O wow!" Her great grin. Lovely, really lovely, with wide eyes of a hyacinth blue. Nineteen? Twenty? Twenty-two? "But, you know, now that I think about it, I have heard your name, but I didn't recognize it, connect it with Ciara—"

"Well, look, are you in a rush or would you have time for a cup of coffee—though I don't drink coffee. Tea, a beer?"

"No."

"No? That was fast. How come?"

"Well I'm late for my class."

"What class're you taking?"

"No, I teach *ceili*—Irish dancing."

"Really? Where?"

"The Celtic Arts Center, down in the Village."

"Really?"

"Do you always say 'really' so much, or don't you believe me?"

"Sorry, it's a verbal tic. Well then at least, Tory, let me walk you out."

Down the elevator and through the bustling lobby behind her scuffed tennis sneakers, white turtleneck, tiny waist, and worn denim jeans snugly cupping her perky rump—

"How's your father?"—elegant and earthy at the same time.

"Fine, last I heard. He's over in Ireland."

"Carnaween—no, Ballyduff now."

"Hey, you really do know my father, don't you?"

"Really." A warm glow—she smiling back, a great smile, as she steps into the revolving door and I push her through. "Which way you going?"

"Left."

"Would you mind, Tory, if I walked you to the corner?"

"Sure, if you'd like."

Along 12th Street, her blonde strands swept by the breeze, "So what do you think of the course so far?"

"It's OK—No, you seem like a good teacher."

"Why?"

"Because you're passionate about your work. Have you been published—? O but I'm sure you have, otherwise—"

"About twenty short stories."

"Are they still in print?"

"A few, but I'll bring you one next week."

"O that'd be terrific, thank you," she stopping at the corner, cabs honking and swerving past, "Well I'm heading down Sixth, so I guess I'll see you in class."

"Right."

"And it was nice meeting you. Really."

"Really was. 'Bye, Tory."

"'Bye," she walks a few paces on, glances shyly over her shoulder, "'Bye, Gene," smiles, waves, and saunters off.

Wow!

Four

Tossing and churning with this nightmare returning and these patterned percale sheets tightly twisted about my thrashing, sweaty thighs as I abruptly awake at 5:45—and kick free my knees, my pillow tumbling violently aside, blinking and fluttering my bloodshot eyes through the dawn's early light and still feeling that suffocating fright after flicking on—no, not *This Is My Life* last night, though so wishing I might find it again—just switching back and forth from Johnny Carson to Tom Snyder to Paul Newman (my supposed look-alike, according to my folks) on *The Late Late Show,* then listening once more to Desmond's amazing solo on "Calcutta Blues," before finally falling back into that terrified sleep of my mother dying, wasting away with the unspeakable horror of ALS: the two of us coming down Central Park South, and she slowly forcing out the words with a hoarse rasp of drooling grunts and moans that I was the only one in her family ever to get a degree, that she was—stopping, unbuckling her black purse, removing her pen, twisting the gold point forward with those crepe-paper, arthritic-looking hands, and writing on a small gift card in her shaky script, "I am very proud of you," then passing it to me and smiling, a rictus smile, her eyes filmed with tears, and taking a deep breath to speak again, write again, "Your father would have been proud too. Three Ivy League degrees. Who would've believed?" And she laughed—more a frozen moment of glee, the muscles unwilling to allow laughter—as I swallowed my rage at that monstrous, absurd disease that permanently sealed her in. And I had to get out, get away, flee! As a child, running away at three, four, five—never really run away, always toward something—to find my father, who was never around, making his fortune stamping out bugs so he could move to Great Neck, stay in Great Neck. He died, and I suddenly realized I had no memories of him before the age of eight—no memories because he was never there. Out making a living, struggling to run a business, recapture the wealth he once knew. So I ran away to find him. Down to Miller's Drugstore, over a mile away, at age three, four. *Where're you going, sonny?* (To find my daddy.) But I couldn't put it in words. Found and returned. To run away again and again. A week after his funeral, sorting out his clothes and the records he kept: of Kennedy's death, Apollo probes, Yankee-Red Sox programs—and finding those piles of unopened shirts, Egyptian cottons and Sulka silks. What he'd worked for all those years to get to Great Neck, stay in Great Neck? But how many shirts can you wear at one time? Yet he had to buy more, thirty-five, forty still wrapped in cellophane. And nothing left to buy. So he died. And behind them all my birthday gifts to him, cologne and aftershave sets, odors of the sea, woods, pine, and lime, stacked in the back of the closet.

And still running? My pattern: Looking for lost loves even then? So believe in patterns we follow again and again. Running back to the moment, to the past, so that we might redo, start again—prove it false—and find what? That I was closer to her, my feelings stronger? Teri saying, "When you got mad at your mother, you really got mad." At least my father made no bones about not supporting my writing, always thought it *meshugge,* but she played at being my best friend who understood, was forever behind me, till it threatened to draw me away—then yanked the rug out from under and pulled me back beside her.

Still, no life should end with that horror, not long after my father's stroke: he falling out of bed, flailing like a beached fish on the floor of Sutton Place. And could the shock of that have triggered her disease, Lou Gehrig's disease? *Luckiest man on the face of the earth.* The Iron Horse wasting away to ninety pounds when he died. My father as a boy once shaking Gehrig's massive hand. A virus, the theory now, passed from his hand to my mother? Who knows. And she so brave at the end, wanting no pity, but shrunk to skin and bones, handwriting uncontrolled, faint speech of grunts and groans—O my mother! reaching back for you, reaching out for you—as you keep slipping away, receding from me now! And her courage alone, this scared little girl who feared everything: doctors, accidents, any kind of risk, to stay safe in her Great Neck cocoon. Safe, the operative word, so frightened since childhood, childbirth, but standing tall, chin high, in her doorway near the end and breaking into a panting, shaky Charleston just to show she wasn't dead yet—

And *Christ,* I've gotta get outta this city today!

~

Flooring my Mustang and roaring onto the Long Island Expressway, speeding by this swaying Winnebago and careening into the left-hand lane, tires squealing, bouncing over these potholes (never gonna fix this bumpy road!), and passing exits for Woodhaven Boulevard and the Van Wyck, traffic not too bad for six in the evening, after a full day of writing, and switching stations to QXR—Sibelius's Second triumphantly concluding: By Dion and the Belmonts? Try Szell and the Concertgebouw.

"*—And that was George Szell conducting the Amsterdam Concertgebouw* (hey, right again!) *in a performance of Sibelius's Second Symphony in D, Opus 43.*"

Hungry? Not really. Too revved up now to eat. Dinner last night of Stouffer's macaroni and beef and a cold bottle of Rolling Rock to wash it down, before I tossed and turned on those sweaty sheets, and this whole morning and afternoon thinking about Tory Boyne while I wrote, a soft shy slim slip of a girl, blonde and glimmering—haven't seen Seamus, her mad-ass father, since when? '67? No, '71, shared a brew at P. J. Clarke's, he wild as ever, and just before Ciara was blown to smithereens by that art gallery bomb meant for Louis Mountbatten. Learning about it after her funeral, then, two years later, he faking his own, Tory's kidnapping. And now all his fame and fortune, the Picasso of today, Kenneth Clark calling him the greatest painter of the twentieth century, and still living in Ire——

"*O fuck you, too!*" That black Caddy knifing by me and flipping me off—"Get outta your fuckin' car, farthead, and I'll ram your teeth down your fuckin' throat!" as he zooms away.

Jesus, what am I *doing*? Get shot on the LIE over some asshole tailgating?—and drying my hands on my jeans as I cut quickly into the right-hand lane—just throwing on these Levi's and sneakers—and nearing Bayside and Douglaston, Lakeville Road coming up, flicking on my signal and glancing over my shoulder as I go sweeping down the expressway ramp, close to 6:35, maybe knock off a couple of double cheeseburgers at Squire's or the old Star Diner, across Northern Boulevard and through this changing light, along Middle Neck Road toward the heart of Great Neck—still looking the same as ever, haven't been back in months—no, Christ, years! (and getting that same warm glow every time I do return)—by the train station and Gilliar's Drugstore, where the Selmix Regents used to hang out—none of them now in sight—old Otto Kregel's gone (had the finest ice cream of all time, 30 percent butterfat!), replaced by Baskin-Robbins across the street, and all these slicky boutiques!—passing between the Playhouse and Squire theaters, where at fifteen I first put my arm around a girl, "Titsy" Mitsy Weiss, and going stiff like a board before lightly cupping her sweatered breast—by the Kensington gates and Great Neck Estates—and *Jeez,* get a load of Temple Beth El (where I got bar mitzvahed), now twice its size with that modern flying wing!—as I hang a left onto Old Mill Road toward my boyhood home, and pausing at the entrance to Strathmore, where my Bubba would get off the rattling bus from Far Rockaway and wander hopelessly down into a bewildering maze of similar-looking houses, streets, and trees, till eventually I would be sent out as a search party of one to find her so lonely and forlorn and weighted down hither-thither with shopping bags full of lace,

"*Oi*, Eu-gen, Tank Got!" And entering our home with a sigh, she'd slowly mount the stairs to that aged, autumn room before soaking her aching feet in a pan of steamy water.

Turning onto Old Pond Road and up the hill toward our first Tudor home of brick and dark wood. Still standing? Yes, but now hidden away amid the manicured and groomed, ranch house boom, green, feathery trees still overlapping the road, autumn soon smoking the air with an overflow of scuffly leaves. I used to play stickball on that back lawn, with me batting left-handed as Ted Williams and belting them onto the roof.

Home . . . Yeah, once upon a time.

On through Strathmore and past the high school I graduated from in 1954 (now there are two, Great Neck North and Great Neck South), along Brokaw Lane—the route I'd take on the way to our old softball games on a lovely May day such as this, clear skies, light breeze, heading into evening, 6:50 now—McDonnell's Café on the right and Memorial Field behind, out of sight, and so many years, long gone—as I go cruising into Fairview Avenue and down to Memorial Field—

And Geez, I don't believe it! The Selmix Regents in their orange-and-blue uniforms *still* out there taking batting and fielding practice, their same Fords and Chevys, Dodge pickups and souped-up Corvairs parked one behind the other!

And Christ! (Is this part of another dream?) our team's gleaming Cadillacs and Mercedeses lined up as usual on the other side as I hop out and pass through the chain-link gate, by the wire backstop, and skinny Brian Hickey, Selmix's drill sergeant manager with his bony Irish face and huge Adam's apple (haven't seen him in what, twenty years?), tosses up his slow, floating pitches, a bucketful of balls beside him, our team now huddling together in front of their dugout and—

"Holy *shit*, guys, look who's *here*! *HAIGY BABY!*" and breaking away with an ear-to-ear grin, "Now we don't have to forfeit!"

Lou comes racing across with that same college crew cut, gold double-knit T-shirt, and bulging high school sweatpants, to squeeze me tight in a bear hug, "And it's great seein' ya, Big Guy, *great* seein' ya!"

"Easy, Lou, easy—"

"Got an extra mitt and cap in my car, don't need the shirt—"

"Yeah, well I haven't played—"

"Hey Hickey, thought ya had it made, huh?—And I'm tellin' ya, this's the year, Haig, this's the year! But here, lemme go get your mitt!" and he goes leaping over the chain-link fence toward his cardinal Eldorado just as Shelly comes striding up, flashing his toothy grin, to slap me on the back.

"Hey, how-why-ya, how-why-ya! Long time no see."

"Big Shel. Listen, I—"

"Thought you forgot about your old friends when you became a fancy writer—"

"No—"

"—cut off from your roots—"

"So how're things going?"

"Don't ask! May have to move—"

"Say, Gene," Bucky's steely handshake, "good to see you again, man."

"Yeah, you, too. What's happening?"

"O, same old same old, my father's going crazy, saying how can I possibly play softball after my son ran away."

"Your teenage son?"

"Yeah, he took off in the family car, but we caught him just as he was leaving Great Neck and brought him home. But, Gene, you can take third."

"Fine. Where's Hedon?"

"And we'll go with nine. Moved to Colorado."

"And Monte—?"

"No, ten, Buck, ten," Lou jogging and panting back with that old Rawlings mitt and a cap for me, "just spotted Shishy in the firehouse john."

Bucky shaking his head, "Jesus, what the hell's he *do* in there?"

"Piss! Whatta you think he does in there, Buckela, put out fires? Got that psychotic prostate from always worryin' about his shiksa wife fuckin' around!"

The rest of the guys now laughing and kibitzing and slapping me on the back as balding Shishy, zipping up his fly, finally arrives.

"Gene, so great to see you."

"You, too, Harry. How's your mother?"

"Still living in Great Neck."

"You're kidding! And still fighting off the water bugs?"

"Right, thirty-five years, she won't move," and he begins flipping in his high-arcing warm-up tosses, and we go trotting and wisecracking onto the field, whipping the ball around.

Big Shelly, with his ringleted Disraeli hair, gold *chai,* and sleek aquiline nose, still toe-dancing spryly off the bag at first and scooping low throws with a downward snap and flap of that black Hank Greenberg mitt; "Lookin' good this year, guys, *really* lookin' good, major league talent out there, *definite* major league talent—Million Dollar Infield doin' the *job*!" barrel-chested Lou, with his booming bartender's voice and St. Louis Cardinal cap (signed by Stan Musial), bouncing around second as usual without a jockstrap and still loudly talking it up—as he lets a routine grounder go skipping between his legs, and Shelly smirking, "Yeah, major league talent, my ass!"; freckle-faced Bucky, deep at short, with his tan crinkly hair, raking over the dirt here and there with his rubber cleats before taking off at the crack of the bat like Pee Wee Reese and gloving a high chopper over the mound, wheeling and firing in one graceful motion and the sharp, accurate, rising throw whacking into Shelly's mitt; "Wayta hum it, you Bucky baby, Wayta shoot, you Bucky *guy*—the Human Vacuum Cleaner coverin' monstro ground!" and now me, replacing Myles Hedon down at the hot corner, crouching really low and leaning forward on my toes—as I dive, backhanding a wicked smash past the bag, then gun my throw—a mile over Shelly's head: "Get 'em down, Haigy babe, get 'em down, guy!" their original Million Dollar Infield all growing up together, best friends forever (all of them having inherited, merged with, or even making a million), and the same lineup finishing last season after season to our archrivals, the Selmix Regents, who, off the diamond, would pump our gas, paint our homes, and cut our grass—as Lou keeps swatting everybody on the ass and loudly saying what he always said prior to Opening Day, "Tellin' ya *this* is the year, guys, *this* is the year, everything finally comin' *TOGETHER*!" as we all meet at the mound.

"And, guys, I gotta tell ya, I'm really feelin' *fantazmo* this season, been workin' out, cut out smokin'—best shape I been in since we *were* The Million Dollar Infield!"

Shelly smirking as he rubs up a brand-new ball, "Yeah, right, while the rest of us keep falling apart, Gene, hemorrhoids hangin', prostates achin'—look more like a Million Dollar Glue Factory!"

"Are you the oldest team in the league now?"

"Yeah, but *still* the richest!"

Bucky smiling, "You know, I forgot, who was the real Million Dollar Infield, Tinkers to Evers to Chance?" as I glance out at our hundred-dollar outfield: Elliot Cahn in left, Norm Sonnenberg in center, Yosh the short fielder—

"No way, man, no way: McInnis, Collins, Barry, and old 'Home Run' Baker!"

—and a young black guy I've never seen before.

"Bucky, who's that in right?"

"Jimmy McTee, he works for me."

"Yeah, so where's Monte?"

All of them exchanging glances.

"*Monte?* Didn't you hear?"

"Hear what?"

"Monte's dead."

"*Dead?* No way! I just saw him a few months ago in the city, this past February, and he looked terrific."

"Yeah, well he couldn't've looked that terrific, he dropped dead in March."

"O Jesus!" swallowing hard and turning aside.

"Gene, you OK?"

"He's as white as a sheet."

"Hey, relax, Haig, just relax."

"Yeah, I had the same reaction, Big Guy, hit me like a ton of bricks."

"You gonna be OK, Haig?"

"I can't believe he's dead, *everybody* dying, disappearing!"

The potbellied ump waddling out from behind home plate, "You girls innerested in playin' ball or should I send out for coffee'n cake?"

"No, no, sorry, all set to go."

And moving back to third and letting out a deep sigh—Monte and I double-dating our senior prom, now first of the guys to die—as sinewy Tony Alosia, the league's leading hitter every year, with good power and super speed, digs in, Lou chanting, "No hitta here, no hitta, guys!"—and who the hell's next? Glancing quickly around, over the Selmix bench: there's sideburned Lewicki, who once painted my parents' house years ago; Quinlan, who delivered our flowers while I was off killing bugs in the city; Colandro, who did our dry cleaning—as Shishy delivers the first high-arcing pitch of the season and—

Whack!

This hot smash heading right at me and—O Christ!—through my legs into left!

Cahn rifling the ball back in to Lou, who, rubbing up the Clincher, runs it in to Shishy, looking now like he may pee in his pants, then calling across: "Hey, get 'em next time, guy, get 'em next time! Still behind ya, Haigy *babe*!"

"Time out, ump, time out," Bucky trotting over, "Gene, you sure you're all right, wanna let McTee play third for a while till you get your head in the game?"

"No, I'll be fine."

"Great, then let's get 'em *outta* here!" and swatting me on the ass, he trots back to short as lean, mean Brian Hickey settles into his catlike crouch (in high school, he was a hot rodder with an Elvis DA)—and slashes a sizzling shot by third that I dive for and spear on a hop, so stunned I even caught it, then gun my throw and—*Damn it!* I just threw out my arm!—nail him by a step on a bang-bang play!

"Wayta go, you Haigy *baby,* wayta fire, you Haigy *guy*!"

Grimacing—what the hell am I *doing* here? Too old at thirty-nine for all this now, trying to shake off the pain.

Lou then tosses away a routine ground ball hit right at him, Shelly slams headlong into the utility pole chasing a foul pop fly, and thirteen runs later, we finally get out of the inning as I go hobbling back to the dugout, my arm so sore, I can hardly lift it.

And we end up losing 26–4—as Lou, stuffing all our bats and balls into that battered duffel bag, keeps trying to cheer us up:

"Hey, come on, we'll get 'em next time, guys, 'cause ya take away that thirteen-run first and the eight-run third and we were right with 'em, with 'em all the way!"

And grinning despite myself, I thank Bucky, Shelly, and the rest of the guys for letting me play and turn toward the street.

"Don't forget, Haig, next game's Thursday night and I *guarantee* a win, definitely—and hey, great seein' ya again, guy."

"Yeah, you, too, 'bye."

And back to my car, past Shelly's gold Eldorado with the I LOVE ♥ GREAT NECK! bumper stickers—aching all over now—still can't believe Monte dropping dead, first guy to die—as I go wheeling round the corner into Middle Neck Road—and *Christ*! suddenly burst out laughing at our game's lopsided score, *How about that?*

but even more so, at just how good a time I had tonight in my Great Neck of long ago!

Five

"OK, well that's it for today, and remember what Nabokov said—"

"Who?"

"Teddy Nabokov, left field for the Red Sox in '57."

"I thought that was Ted Williams, prof."

"Hey, good, Bruce, very good. And you know what he hit in '57?"

"Uh . . ." adjusting his Dodger cap, ".345?"

"No, that was in '56. .388 with thirty-eight home runs at age thirty-nine. Anyway, *Vladimir* Nabokov said, 'Good books should not make us think but make us shiver.' So next week on to the music of language, 'Wavewhite wedded words shimmering on the dim tide,' and a love scene to boot."

The class shuffling and scuffling out.

"O Miss Boyne?"

"Yes?" Tory stunning today in a full-length, loose-fitting lilac knit dress.

"I liked your scene." She pausing beside her desk. "You've really got a wonderful feel for words."

"Well you could've fooled me."

"Why?"

"Because of all your criticism."

"That was just to keep you on your toes."

"You're certain you don't mean my heels?"

"OK, maybe those, too."

Tory smiling, "Anyway, listen, would you, you know, still like to treat me to that cup of tea?"

"Tea? Sure, why not." What's this all about? "Though wait, don't you have your class today?"

"No, it's some kind of holiday."

"Then we're off," and on out the door, "But Tory, how 'bout lunch instead? And it's still my treat."

"Where?"

"Well what do you like? The Blue Mill for steaks? Lüchow's for schnitzel?"

"No, just something light."

"Hamburgers and beer?"

"Sounds great."

"How 'bout the White Horse?"

"Fine, that's near where I live."

And off we whirl through the Village hurly-burly and roasting coffee scent drifting under the awnings, this pink-cheeked, shining girl striding beside me with her ponytail bobbing in the breeze, soft blonde hair that I'd love to loosen and let tumble over her shoulders, the sun finding fiery strands and tawny, burnished bands, traffic rushing past—

"And you seem in good spirits today, Gene."

"Totally due to you."

"O yeah, right! But you've still got those dark circles under your eyes, like the Ghost of Christmas Past," hurrying by 8th Street's brick and shiny glass, "Having trouble sleeping?"

"A bit."

"Why—? O listen, sorry, but I do have to stop off at my class, just for a moment, it's on the way. Is that OK?"

"Fine."

"It's on MacDougal, just down there."

"No problem. And where'd *you* go to school, Tory?"

"Me? Sarah Lawrence, for two years."

"Sarah Lawrence?"

She nodding, grinning, "Yes, where the 'gals' cross their sevens and barely get along on their stipends—my mother's school."

"Somehow I don't see you at Sarah Lawrence."

"Well I've also taken a couple of courses at Barnard, another at Hunter, and now yours."

"Saving the best for last."

"Could be. O here we are, the Celtic Arts Center."

Through the fanlit door, thickly layered walls of lumpy green paint, Irish music keening the air, harps and *bodhrans*, fiddles and pipes: "And you teach Irish dancing?"

"Deed'n she does. And who might ya be?" A plump, redheaded woman with hoop earrings above a bright orange jumper.

"Gene, this is Seonard. Seonard, Gene Hagar. He's a writer."

"Ah, one of them fellas, huh?"

"And my teacher, too."

"Well don't ya be messin' with yer students, either. But, Tory, the two Scully girls have been waitin' to see ya."

"Gene, I'll be back in a minute," and spinning about, "O and don't mind Seonard, she's got a tongue on her that would clip a hedge."

And she follows her into a long, skylit room.

Photos of Yeats and O'Casey, Joyce and Synge in this dimly lit alcove—and catching a glimpse of Tory around the corner kneeling before two bespectacled little girls, hugging them and kissing their cheeks—O that that cheek were mine—"and I promise I'll see both of you next week, 'bye-bye—So, Gene, ready to go?"

"Can I come see you dance sometime?"

"Sure, if you'd like. Every Thursday night there's a *ceili* from eight-thirty to nine, so just let me know."

Along MacDougal Street, weaving a path, her tight dancer's body in that light knit dress, guiding her with my hand across Waverly and Seventh Avenue's clatter and clash.

"My flat's just a few blocks away on Bedford, and right next door to where Edna St. Vincent Millay lived in 1924."

"'My candle burns at both ends; / It will not last the night—' "

Tory beaming, "'But ah, my foes, and oh my friends— / It gives a lovely light!' "

Past Bleecker and down the length of Hudson Street into the White Horse Tavern. Where we order hamburgers and two black and tans, then move to the other room and sit under Dylan's portrait.

"Do you know his poems, Tory?"

"Somewhat."

"What's your favorite line?"

"O I have all sorts of favorites."

"Just one."

"One. OK, let's see, how about 'Over Sir John's hill, / The hawk on fire hangs still.' And yours, Gene?"

"Got two: 'Brandy and ripe in my bright, bass prime' and 'Time let me hail and climb / Golden in the heydays of his eyes.' "

"From 'Fern Hill.' "

"Right y'are! And Dylan's your favorite writer?—Ah, thank you very much."

She nodding, then chomping into her juicy burger, followed by a lusty swallow of beer and lick of her full, glistening underlip—My God!—"And yours?" as I gulp down my brew. "Vladimir Nabokov?"

"Close. James Joyce. And your favorite musician?"

"Sounds like we're playing Doctor: I'll show you mine if you show me yours. But the Chieftains, I suppose. And you?"

"Paul Desmond."

"Who?"

"Played alto sax with Brubeck."

"O right, right. I don't know much about him."

"How 'bout your favorite painter, Tory?"

She grinning, "Guess."

"Well, we both agree on that. But what's it like being the daughter of a great painter?"

"Shouldn't the question be what's it like for a painter having a great daughter like me? Sorry, just I've been asked that question about a zillion times," and she drains the last of her black and tan and brushes a blonde strand back from her brow.

"Another round?"

"Sure, why not," as I grab the waiter's eye, "And you're still writing, Gene?"

"Sort of, been trying to finish a novel." Tell her about Ciara? No. "Though at least I have the first line."

"Which is?"

"'Had she not had the zabaglione, she surely would've slid through the crevice.'"

She smiling, "And then?"

"That's the problem, can't end it."

"Writer's block or lack of sleep?"

"Probably both."

"Well can I read it sometime?"

"Uh—sure, but wait'll it's complete." My father falling out of bed, flailing like a beached fish on the floor—

Blinking hard at that TV at the far end of the bar: No, just a stupid sitcom!

"Gene, you OK?"

"—What? O yeah, fine, just thought I saw . . ."

Tory sighing as she watches her foamy collar subside, "Anyway, it's weird, really," and I catch my breath.

"What is?"

"Just that we should meet like we did, you knowing my dad and Ciara'n all. And you're the first prof I've ever, well, had a beer with. I don't usually—"

"So why did you?"

"O, 'cause I guess I wanted to learn more about Ciara, wondered what you saw in her, she saw in you."

Film of affection along the outline of her eyes. Who for? Me for. You who interlace and twine my soul in your gaze. Thump, tumblerush, piroutte in silhouettes of blue, and stunningly we are one—"I suppose she saw me jumping out of my skin, trying to break free from my parents' world, intensely physical, playing at Joyce and Nora—But what did *you* see?"

"In you? Well, I wrote a description after our first class."

"I'd like to read it, Tory."

"I'm sure you would. No, when I first saw you, that first session, you were wearing a big old, rumpled green Irish sweater that looked as if it'd seen better days, full of moth holes and stretched out at the collar, but you looked quite dashing, nonetheless."

"You know what Adlai Stevenson said about flattery, Tory?"

"No. What?"

"'Flattery's all right—if you don't inhale.' " She laughing.

"You love to quote, don't you, professor?"

Nodding as I lean even closer, "And you have lovely hyacinth eyes."

"Thank you. My dad calls them glittery. O, but talking of that, I'm flying to Ireland tomorrow—"

"You *are*?" Flash of the plane crashing!

"—so I'll say hello."

"Why?" Don't go!

"He's receiving an honorary degree from Trinity."

"What about my class?"

"O don't worry, I'll be back in time, wouldn't miss that. But anyway, Gene, listen, I have to get home and pack, haven't even started, at least get some sleep. So, here, let me—"

"No, no, I told you, my treat."

And standing, paying, and leaving the tip, then letting her pass, so wanting to hold her, stroke her, kiss her glistening lips—as we step outside to this early-evening breeze—but she just shakes my hand with a warm, firm grip, long, tapering fingers and pillowy palm smooth as silk.

"Yeah, well look, Tory, could I, you know, call you sometime, have your number?"

"O of course, sure. Here, let me find something to write on," she neatly jotting it down on a corner of a loose-leaf sheet, then ripping it off and pointing, "That's a seven, Gene, without the cross."

"Will wonders never cease? But listen, give my best to your dad."

"I shall."

"And please, have a safe trip."

"I'll try, see you next week."

And grinning, off she goes on my spinnaker of hope and tomorrow's flight to Ireland: Please don't die! So wanting to run after her, whirl her high in the twilit air, then fly off to Ireland together, Wicklow or Killybegs, Bray or Kildare. I once sang a song about Ireland, and my family fell asleep.

Words were on the lip, the tongue, stories were in the making. Thinking of a place where language is a jewel, storytelling the great delight:

One White Horse bar, windy May evening, I met a fair, pink-cheeked girl of Erin who next day was off to Dublin. We gargled three black and tans apiece, before she said it was best she was to bed. With her lilting name and lane warm in my scrawled pocket, she paused to place a sigh in my eyes. Then lifting my right hand, kissed the palm, and closed my fingers over it. "There you are," she said and so departed.

Six

"—'Lo?" blindly fumbling with the phone.

"*Big Guy!* Have I got a great piece of ass for you!"

"—Lou?"

"*Fabbo* chick, really hot to trot—just one small problem."

"What's that?"

"Ya gotta go to this funeral with me."

"Jesus Christ, what is she, *dead*?"

"No, really, Haig, believe me, she's so fuckin' alive, I got a hard-on from here to St. Louie just thinkin' about those monstro gazongas—says she's my second cousin, once removed—so I really *need* ya now!"

"What, to get laid?"

"No, no, guy, that was just to get your attention."

"Right, well who the hell died?"

"My stepmother last Friday."

"You're *kidding*?"

"No, blew out a blood vessel in her brain."

"O Geez, hey, Lou, I'm really sorry—"

"Right-right, so like I'm still on edge, ya know, pacin' all around my pad."

"How's your dad taking it?"

"Really bad, Haig, really bad, definitely a little shaky in the knees like he just got creamed by Butkus on a blitz—and lately he's been havin' these chest pains again—"

"Damn!"

"—may need a baboon heart."

"Yeah, well listen, Lou, normally I *would* go with you, but I'm really not up to it—"

"Right, right, Big Guy, I understand, understand completely, just need all the support I can get now, 'cause for me, fuckin' is the only thing that takes my mind off my grief—but hey, I'll see ya Monday night, missed ya, Haig, down at the hot corner, blew two more games without ya—"

"Monday? Yeah, well—"

"—so I gotta get goin', whip over to the funeral home and find that second cousin of mine!"

"—right, 'bye."

And rubbing the sleepflakes out of my eyes in this hazy Friday light, mild morning air, as I keep desperately rummaging through my mind, trying to hang on to that fading dream: Tory and I racing across a green Wicklow meadow hand in hand, tumbling and sinking down, kissing and clinging and fumbling over her breasts and rising thighs, her hips revolving as she kept sighing and moaning—

Or was that Ciara in my book? Can't even tell anymore! Like Fitzgerald said: "Sometimes I don't know if I'm real or a character in one of my novels." Still, what a great time we had at the Celtic Arts Center and White Horse bar—no plane crash bulletins breaking in, thank God, so she must've made it safely. 'Cause enough! One more loss, Monte, Lou's stepmother, his father's latest chest pains, and I'm going to write a story called "Half My Rolodex Is Dead"!

Yet the sun is shining, the month is May, and the only question that now remains is will I see her on Monday once more and play softball again that night? as wincing and stretching out the sinews of fatigue, I sit up blinking in my empty, cluttered bed. 'Cause the *real* question is: What the hell am I doing? *Desperately missing Tory* is what I'm doing! But I hardly know her, she's half my age, and Boyne's daughter to boot! And here I am building her into this dream girl, luminous image, the very first time we meet! What I *always* do, or overdo, fall head over heels into poetry and song—and run smack into stone-wall rejection, let down with a resounding thump! Certainly with Ciara, even with Teri, and nearly every girl I've ever been crazy about!

Tory seeing me as some rumpled old 'stiltskin in moth-eaten Irish togs. And Ciara as, what was it again? something like, *Just height and light hair, nice eyes, ears flat, large head, Roman nose.* And God only knows why Tory's so fascinated by Ciara or what Boyne'll say about his only daughter now meeting up with me—as naked I stand, staggering slightly right, balance a bit awry, and stumble woozily out to my stereo to put on Desmond's "The Way You Look Tonight." This fresh legal pad, my Ciara novel, and a cup full of pencils unused on my desk, and beside that new electric sharpener "that goes ticonderoga-ticonderoga, feeding on the yellow finish and sweet wood." *You love to quote, don't you, professor?* Not having written anything of my own in weeks, months, or maybe even longer—

The phone shrilly ringing!

Now who? Lou again? Or Tory calling from Ireland, can't stop missing me—

"'Lo?"

"Did I wake you?"

"Wake me? O no, Teri, been up for hours!"

"Somehow that seems hard to believe. Anyways, I won't keep you long."

"Yeah, and by the way," sitting down at my writing desk, "did you really call me the other night and read me my obituary?"

"Yes. Why? Don't you remember? You all right?"

"No, but that was really funny, go on."

"Well, I was just wondering if you have the time, would you like to speak to my class?"

"The one you wrote my obituary for?"

"Exactly!"

"But I'm supposedly dead."

"Come on, Gene, seriously."

"Speak about what?"

"Writing, of course! Well, think about it, give it some thought, it's still a couple of weeks off, and you can let me know."

"Teri?"

"What?"

"Are you OK?"

"O fine and dandy!"

"No, really."

"No, but nice of you to ask. The problem, as usual, is, without going into great detail now, when I get involved, I usually give up me, that's my pattern—"

"Who is he?"

"—so I'm probably healthier being alone, by myself. Anyways, let me go and I'll speak to you later, 'bye."

The phone ringing *again*!

What is with these morning calls? Was there a full moon last night or something?

" 'Lo?"

"Hagar, if you so much as lay one bloody hand on the head of my daughter, I'll feed your gonads to a piranha!"

"'Gonads'?—*Boyne?*"

"Damn straight!"

"Well it's nice to hear from you, too, old buddy."

"Don't 'old buddy' me, you horny, scheming Semite!"

"Whoa, whoa! What have I done—?"

"It's not only *what* you've done, it's what you're *planning* to do! You fucked my wife and now you're going to fuck my daughter? Well not in my life!"

"Hey, hold on—"

"'Bye!"

Christ Almighty, how's that for a wake-up call? But that means Tory might be back. Try her now? Or wait till class? Fighting my anxiety all week about her return plane crashing—Jesus, Haig, let it go, will ya! Relax! Life goes on—And where the hell's her number (and the seven without the cross)—Ah! under this unholy desktop jumble, corner of a loose-leaf sheet—

Ringing, ringing, ringing . . . No answer. Come on, come on. In the shower? Still sleeping? Nine, ten rings—*Damn!*

". . . Hello?"

"You're *home*!"

"Home? Yes, well—"

"So tell me, I want to hear it all, everything about your trip and Ireland and you—or I can pick you up at six, if that's OK, and we can grab a pizza, go to a movie—"

"Who *is* this?"

"O funny, Tory, very funny! It's your rapidly aging prof, who's been anxiously—nay, desperately—awaiting your imminent, safe return. But what did your father say about me?"

"Just one thing."

"Which was?"

"'Watch your arse.' "

"What does that mean?"

"I have no idea, but that's what he said."

"And what'd you say?"

"I just laughed."

"Right. Well, he just called here."

"Did he now? And what was on his Irish mind?"

"To watch you closely."

"Yeah, right! But Gene, six is fine. Can you meet me at the Center? You remember the address?"

"Indeed I do, and six it is. Glad you're home safely."

"Thanks."

" 'Bye."

Seven

Riddle me, riddle me, randy ro. / My father gave me seeds to sow as I go bouncing off the swaying, screeching subway at 14th Street and quickly up these grubby, dim-lit stairs to the scrubbed clean air of the rain-washed pavement, boom boxes blaring, Reeboks hippity-hopping, and this pair of Friday evening shoppers splitting asunder—sidling and striding by them, my reflection flickering past those glittering neon windows: a wild and rowdy brown bear, unruly shock of hair, navy blue raincoat with the collar raised—wayfaring Hagar holding fast to his dream, *you horny, scheming Semite*! of Boyne's lovely daughter—and she'd better be there, at five of six, heart loudly pounding, old enough to be her father—and lay off the compulsive quoting, saying "really"—cab brakes squealing—and down 8th Street jammed with Day-Glo punkers and hayseed tourists cheek by jowl, then swinging into MacDougal—

Along the brightening footpath. Runs, she runs to meet me, a glimmering *girl with gold hair on the wind.*

"O Gene, we just finished and I didn't want to miss you—"

"God, you look *fantastic*!"

Catching her breath, "Well, thank you," then smiling and glancing shyly away with her mischief-shiny eyes, "But in the immortal words of Popeye, 'I yam what I yam.' Ready to go?"

"No, I just want to look at you," clad in a dark green windbreaker, loose black sweater, and tight white jeans as I follow her back toward the corner.

"It's just been one of those days, rushed completely off my feet," the silky incandescence of her pale cheek now flushed with color, and her sunrumpus of hair tucked beneath that floppy Irish fisherman's gray tweed hat.

"So, are you hungry, Tory, or would you rather see a movie first?"

"No, let's eat, if that's all right, but just a snack, I had a monster lunch."

"Pizza OK?"

"Perfect!"

"Ray's on Sixth?"

"My favorite spot!"

"See, I knew we were in tune!"

"Except for a jarring note here and there."

"What note—?"

"I'm teasing, Gene, just teasing. Though I do think maybe 'Thou and I are too wise to woo peaceably.' "

"*Much Ado About Nothing*?"

"*Damn!* Definitely thought I'd nail you on that," and, smiling, she goes hopscotching by these puddles with their inverted reflections of trees, "So, Gene, what've you been doing since I was gone?"

"Pining."

"No, really."

"O I started a story, at least have the title."

"What's it called?"

"'The Girl Who Broke His Heart—Then Mended It.' "

"And who's that about?"

"Too soon to tell—Hey, surprise, Ray's is mobbed as usual!" teeming with people and steamy, garlic smells as we get on the end of the line, and she brushes against me, "How many slices, Tory?"

"O they're humungous—one is fine."

"Anything on it?"

"No, just cheese. And you?"

"Pepperoni."

"OK, I'll have that, too. And what movie, Gene, did you want to see?"

"Whatever you want to see. *Taxi Driver*?"

"Yuck! No way!"

"*One Flew Over the Cuckoo's Nest*?"

"I already saw it. It's OK."

"And talking about that, how *is* your father these days?"

She grinning, "Same as ever," as I glance sidelong over my shoulder, and she laughs, "still back in Ireland."

"What's your relationship with him, if I may ask?"

"O . . ." and she blinks, her hands plunged deep in her windbreaker pockets, then gazes up at me, "I guess you could say we're close."

"What would *you* say?"

"I'd say we have our moments."

"Next."

"Yeah, two pepperonis—and two Cokes, Tory?"

"Sprite for me."

"Make that two Sprites."

"And here, let me get the napkins."

And munching and hunching over as we hustle along, a lava flow of mozzarella oozing over the blistered crust, "O my God, Gene, this is *so-o-o* good!" toward *Monty Python and the Holy Grail,* and a feathery sprinkle starting to fall.

"Oyrish weather, eh?"

"'Tis indeed."

~

"Tory, you mind sitting on the side?"

"No, I like that, but not *too* far back. I'm sort of nearsighted."

"And I'm sort of farsighted. How's this, this OK?"

"I'll take the aisle."

"Still hungry?"

She shaking her head, "No," then whispering, "But we can get something after," and putting her sneakers up on the empty seat before her and scrunching low amid the chatter and bustle, popcorn's buttery reek, people sliding across or waving from their seats as the houselights dim and out of the corner of my eye, her silky cheek and—Christ! so like Ciara's—that blonde shimmer of hair.

Deep pounding drums as the credits roll, stop, the music winding down as the words on the screen keep sacking the credits and subtitles staff.

Finally:

England, 932 A.D.

A foggy plain, lone tree, hoofbeats approaching—and into the frame canters a medieval rider without a horse and followed by his heavily laden servant banging two coconut halves together.

Tory chuckling, both of us chuckling, along with the audience, and she smiling, "So silly," then taking off that fisherman's tweed hat.

Lean even closer? An arm around her? No, keeping my chuckling distance, with a silent sigh—and both of us really laughing now as the Black Knight (John Cleese) loses both arms and legs, and she edges over to whisper, "My students would just love this!"

"So would mine." She grinning. "But when can I see *you* dance?"

"How's about tomorrow night?"

"I'll be there."

And I take her hand. She squeezes back. And "The Knights Who Say Ni!" appear.

Stroking her tapering fingers now and laughing as Lancelot (Cleese again) wipes out most of a wedding party, "*Sorry. Awfully sorry,*" then on to the Bridge of Death, the keeper asking his three questions in that creepy voice: "*What is your name*? *What is your quest*? *What is your favorite color*?"

And Tory can't *stop* laughing, nudging against me, tears framing her eyes, and only after a brisk shake of her head, her hair, do two high notes spring out, followed by another rush of breathy laughter—and finally subsiding, as I keep laughing, and she whispers, "My mother—wow!—my mother has urinary incontinence, so when she laughs or sneezes or coughs, she pees in her pants—and I think maybe I—"

"Really?"

"No, only kidding, but close."

And curving toward her, I brush away her fleeting tears, then impulsively kiss over her lashes, cheeks, and tender lips.

~

"That was awesome!"

"You referring to the movie, Tory, or me?"

"Well, let's see . . . both, I'd have to say," and she jams her free hand into my back pocket as I circle her slender waist with a gentle hug, and on we stroll through the gauzy, tinseled air, "Though I might add, Professor Hagar, I love the way you are, and unlike anyone else I know."

"Not even your father?"

"No."

"How 'bout when I break into '*I'm singin' in the rain, just singin' in the rain*'?"

Tory stopping and blinking, "Gene, what're you *doing*?" as off I go skipping the light fantastic with my old soft shoe, she broadly grinning, "Though I must tell you, my father likes to do that as well."

"Do what?" as I spin round this lamppost with my invisible umbrella.

"Dance in the streets. But you are a strange and funny man, Gene Kelly-Hagar."

And I sweep her into my waiting arms, Tory so light on her feet down the pavement—where a cop, just like in the movie, gives us the fisheye as we dance politely by, and on through the Village drizzle.

"You're pretty good for an old man," she wedging closer, "maybe I should come see *you* dance," and peering up at me with that hyacinth gaze, "But who's your new story really about? Ciara?"

"*Ciara*? No. You."

"Is that so?"

And on we stroll, all my senses with their hands in their pockets, when suddenly a loud shower comes bucketing down over the pavement, and we scurry into this dark doorway, gutters gurgling, swirling off toward the river under this gray rattle of rain.

"I feel so comfortable, Gene, with you."

"Me, too."

"Did you like me when you first saw me?"

"Yes, but I was a bit reluctant."

"Why?"

"You were my best friend's daughter."

"So why did you?"

"Not friendly enough, I guess," as we kiss long and slow, her lips slightly parted, and I nose, "Mmmmmm," into the fragrant smell of her hair, whitish blonde along the brow, and she pauses to cup her wet hands around my nape, leaning back against this jamb.

"Still hungry?"

"Very."

"All right, then let's cross here," she taking my hand, "we can pop into this grocer's shop, pick up a couple of—Gene, do you like Guinness?"

"No, not for me, far too bitter."

"The Irish call it 'poetry in a glass.' Ever try Newcastle Ale?"

"Don't think so."

"Then this treat's on me. And I've got some goodies, surprises, in my fridge."

The shower now dwindling to a thinning mist as we hurry round this corner through the newly washed air, snuggling your waist, your blonde-swept hair, eyes full of wind, O girl of my dreams, halting to embrace in midstreet again, and barely make it to your place with its four stone steps and ornate railings, down a short hall, Tory tossing her fisherman's tweed deftly onto a hat tree, where it whirls twice like a top, then sags to a stop—

"You ever miss?"

"Never."

—and into a huge studio room with polished hardwood floors and whitewashed brick walls, an autumnal jumble of throw cushions, orange, russet, and tarnished gold, flung across an oatmeal couch, a couple of green sling chairs, and a large, lone painting of a young girl in a flowered hat.

"What's that?"

"My father thought she looked like me—it's called *Her Mother's Hat*."

"Who's it by?"

"Norman Hepple. He's painted the Queen and Prince Philip," she grinning, "and now me. No, no, that's his daughter, actually."

"Why don't you hang your father's work?"

"Because I'm afraid of their being stolen—O, Gene, let me take your raincoat—and 90 percent of stolen art is never found. But now for the food. You like rarebit, my own blend of mustards and spice, or would you rather—?"

"Come here."

Her mischievous smile disappearing with my gentle kiss as I press her close to nuzzle, and her hands glide under the rolled sleeves of my shirt to stroke the muscles, mine sliding down her long spinal hollow and around to these delicious, nimble breasts—as leaning back to shake loose her windbreaker, she stumbles, losing her balance, and we tumble, laughing, onto the sofa—cushions toppling off—the faint lemon tang of her tousled hair, her heat against my thighs, and her black sweater rising to a silky, concave tummy, and we're passionately kissing now, she prying open my shirt, caressing over my chest, then squirming to unbutton her jeans, arching and shimmying free to reveal bikini panties, so damp to my palm, I'm straining hard against my 505's, and she so wet as I spread her wide and bury my tongue between her thighs, "*OmyGod!*" suckling her moist lips, lightly teasing and flicking her clit, she moaning, shyly gyrating—and suddenly sitting up to ask in a trembling whisper: "Do you like doing that?"

"Mmm-hmmm," as I keep on teasing.

"Really?"

"Mmm-hmmm."

"Well, you're a very good kisser down there!" and she watches me a moment more before another feathery lick flings her back and gasping, then grasping my head, my hair, and pulling me forward as I unbuckle and unzip, and out with it at full, vertical throb, to ease deep—*O Jesus!*—inside her, our bodies perfect fit, thrusting hard and furiously kissing—wait, wait, too fast, can't—over her pale lashes, cheeks, the small cup of her shoulder, and come with a hoarse, demented cry as all these cushions go tumbling aside!

Eight

—Dreams keep reeling, everyone dying, leaving—and my raccoon-eyed father disappearing, reaching back for him, reaching out for him—as I race splashing through the rain toward that blinking neon bug sign—before breaking into song and my Gene Kelly dance, then spinning round a lamppost, wheel to a chanting chorus of "Ni's" and that creepy voice screeching, "WHAT IS YOUR NAME? *WHAT IS YOUR QUEST?"—*

—as I snap open my eyes to see—

Tory staring down at me.

"—What, what, what's going *on*?"

She warmly smiling, "Easy. Nothing, I was just watching you sleep," as lying beside me with her smooth, perky butt, she kisses me softly, lingering over my lips, in this cushiony queen-size bed with its spill of pillows, tangle of silken sheets, and blue, quilted comforter, "Were you having a bad dream, Gene?"

"Crazy, raging dream, tossing and turning!"

"So I noticed."

And this all too easy, much too fast, not ready for a relationship, no way—as she kisses me again, then broadly grins: "Though you practically shoved me off the bed, Gene, one cheek hanging over."

"I don't remember that."

"I know."

"Last thing I remember, Tory, was you taking my hands and cupping them over your breasts, then cupping your hands over mine," and sighing deeply, I glance all around, "You been up long?"

"Not too."

The sun slanting in through the white-curtained windows with their black-lacquered frames as her eyes keep roaming over my face, and she leans even closer, "But you have such great Tartar cheekbones," stroking the hair from my brow, "and such beautiful eyes."

"Thank you. You know what color they are?"

"Why, Gene, don't you?"

"I'm color-blind."

"No way!"

"But only certain shades. Did you ever take those Japanese tests, like a kaleidoscope?"

"O sure, in grade school," and squinting, she stares even more intently, "But yours, Gene, are green like a rose leaf, with gray and some flecks of blue," then squirrels her nose exuberantly into my chest, "And I love the way you smell, love caressing your body, I love how you kiss, love your hugs. And I mean I realize I'm sort of awkward at this, sure you've had a lot more experience, said she in her shy, coquettish way—no, but really, what I mean is, you know, how 'intensely physical' was I?"

"'Intensely'—O, you mean like Ciara. Well . . . very. But in a different sort of way."

"Different how?"

"Why does it matter?"

"Just tell me."

"But why—?"

"Gene, tell me!"

"Well, for one—Tory, I feel really awkward talking about this."

"Like what'd she do that I haven't done?"

"You really want to know?"

"Yes, I really want to know."

"All right then, let's see, she liked sixty-nine a lot."

"O, *soixante-neuf*, what the French do."

"Right."

"Well, we can do that, too. OK, fine, what else?"

"Tory, what's this obsession with Ciara?"

"It's not an obsession. It's just, I told you, I've always been fascinated by her and that time with my father, dreamed, I suppose, of being like her. She and my dad had this great relationship—even though their ages were, well, probably similar to ours. But he won't talk to me about her, so I figured I'd ask you. Though if you'd rather not—"

"No, it's OK. But I never really saw you as Ciara."

"You didn't?"

"O, maybe unconsciously I did, but I never thought I was comparing you to her, I swear."

"What about my hair, my—?"

"So? You're both blonde and connected to Boyne—"

"OK, OK, I won't ask anymore, Gene, I promise. Just one last question."

"What?"

"Have you fallen in love with *me* yet?"

"I already fell."

"Have you now?" Her phone stridently ringing! "Wonder who that could be?" and she reaches across, 8:23 on her GE digital, "Hello? O hi, Dad," raising her eyebrows and wryly smiling, "Fine, fine. Am I alone? Uh . . . no. Dad? *Dad!* Yes, I *hear* you, Dad—hard *not* to hear you when you're shouting, Dad. OK, OK, and I'll talk to you later, Dad, I promise, 'bye," and she hangs up.

"What'd he say?"

"He said he's on his way and woe betide."

"Woe betide, eh?"

"He's heading first to Baltimore to see my mother, should be here in another week or so."

"What's *their* relationship like?"

"I never quite know. And he's supposedly doing a Barbara Walters Special live on the nineteenth."

"You're *kidding*! Baba Wawa?"

"Right, he calls her Tweety Bird. It's his first TV appearance in two or three years, and he's laying down the ground rules, figures, Gene, he'll have some fun. Anyway, what shall we do today, my dear?"

Yawning and widely stretching, "My dear, is it now?"

"O just come here."

"Again, Tory?"

"And again!"

"Twice wasn't enough last night?"

And shaking her head no as she begins slowly kissing down my body, featherlight caresses over my chest and drawn-in stomach, then pausing to nose around my swelling erection, but not taking me in her mouth, just tender, tentative kisses and licks along the shaft and tip, before looking up with a girlish grin to ask, "Do you like that?"

"I do indeed."

"Really?"

"Really."

"Well, I'm starting to like it, too."

"I'm so glad."

"And you know what's fun?"

"What?"

"Making him stand at attention. But, Gene, be patient with me."

"Why, 'cause you're nearsighted?"

"No—O shut up, you!"

And we toss with lust, tangling comforter and sheets—till she suddenly breaks free and goes bouncing off the bed.

"All right, Tory, just leave me here throbbing with my tent-pole erection, lost in the midst of a dream!"

And smiling over her shoulder, she shakes out her hair, then shimmies that incredible butt like a go-go dancer as she moves through the room—and I move, too, ram that I am.

"No, Gene, please, I was just teasing." These kindling curves I can't stop feeling—and she pushes my hand away. "No, wait, listen, really, what do you want to do today?"

"Well . . ."

"Come on, besides that."

"Well, we've got fantastic weather. How 'bout driving out to the Island?"

"Cool! I'd really like that. And you want some breakfast, Gene?"

"No, later. We'll go get my car."

"Fine, but first let's take a shower."

And I follow her into this large, spanking clean bathroom of turquoise tile, with all its towels and washcloths, lotions and balms, as she opens the smoky glass door to turn on the taps, testing the heat with her palm, and, finally, satisfied, we hop inside under this blast of hot water, she shrieking and spinning around.

"*Hee,* I can't believe I've got *my* professor here in *my* shower!" her blonde hair plastered down, "And now, prof, I'm supposed to soap you?"

"Right—but lemme just make it hotter—" and when I turn about, she's in my arms with a childish glee.

"Give you a little rub here and here—and here, kootchie-koo?"

Water skipping, glistening off the tiles. "Hey, Tory, easy, will you, I'm ticklish—Hey, *stop* it! Don't you know more accidents are caused in the shower—Hey, come *on* now, cut it out!!"

"O let me smell you!"

"Whatta you—Hey, what the hell're you *doing*?"

"Smelling you."

"Under the arms?"

"It's clean sweat, a man's sweat. I told you, I love the smell of your skin, sniff, sniff." Shaking my head and smiling as her hands keep circling, scrubbing over my chest. "But here, let me soap you *all* over, 'cause I'm on a voyage of discovery."

"Tory?"

"What?"

"Thank you."

"Why? What for?" she still joyously scrubbing.

"Well, this's the happiest I've been in a very long time. I just hope I'm not dreaming."

"Why would you be dreaming?"

"'Cause I've had a lot of strange dreams lately."

"Don't worry, I'm really right beside you—God, so much *hair*! And on your muscled butt as well! You're such a hairy bear—who's *still* at attention!" her silky, stroking hands working up a lather, "And how about the hair on top of your head, you want it washed, your crispy mop of hair? I've got Gold Formula Breck or Herbal Essence—"

"Whatever."

Sudsy shampoo splashing all around, rinsing clean, then standing behind her with her eyes squeezed shut as she hands me the Irish Spring, shifting her face away from the spray.

"Here, now you can do me."

The slippery feel of her firm, wet flesh, and down to the sleek curve of her butt, across her belly and springy blonde fleece, delicately over her lips, ridge of sensuality, thighs, and the shadowed muscles of her calves, and up to her breasts again, tracing lightly round the nipples.

And coming closer, my hands still soaping as we kiss, gulping kisses under this hot, cascading shower, her high breasts pressed against me, and kneeling down, lifting her back to the tile, the full force of the spray hitting the side of my face, her arms round my neck, and guiding him in there—O Tory!—hugging you tight, letting your slick skin slide and still kissing, your tongue in my mouth, and now fondling, thumbing the clasp of your lips, your eyes closed, mouth parted, humping away—Amazing, three times in a day! Lately, three times in a year, two years! So stored up, forgot I had it in me, lusty old Hagar coming out of his shell and leaping all about—feverishly pumping in and out and clutching, hoisting you up, arms aching, bad angle, but loving it so—"O Tory, I'm gonna come, I'm gonna come!" she shuddering, her cries echoing mine and lemon-squeezing me now, milking me dry, then suddenly slipping, sinking to her knees—"*Christ,* Tory, you're gonna break it *off*!"—she laughing, both of us laughing and catching our breaths, as the hot water starts to fade.

Nine

"*—You make me feel so young, you make me feel so spring has sprung, and every time I see you grin, I'm such a happy individual—*"

"*Happy?* Happy's not even in the ballpark anymore!" as singing merrily along with Sinatra, I go breezing onto the expressway with Tory's hand gently squeezing mine, held between the thighs of her stonewashed jeans.

"*You and I are just like a couple of tots, runnin' across a meadow, pickin' up lots of forget-me-nots—*" bouncing over these jarring potholes and round a scattering of frayed tire treads as I flash past this Volvo, zoom by that Trans Am, then whip back into the right-hand lane, "*And even when I'm old and gray, I'm gonna feel the way I do today, 'cause you, you make me feel so young—*"

"Gene, you mind if I change the station?"

"Why, don't tell me you don't like Ol' Blue Eyes?"

"No, I do, but let me see what else's on. Is that OK?"

"Fine."

She swiveling the knob from WNEW to traffic and weather: temperature today in the low seventies—

"*—O and I'm the type of guy who will never settle down, where pretty girls are, well, you know that I'm around—*"

Tory turning to me and beaming, "Gene, you know who that is?"

"George Szell and the Concertgebouw?"

"*Who?* No, that's Dion—"

"Right, and the Belmonts."

"No, *without* the Belmonts."

"You sure, Tory?"

"Definitely." "*—I hug 'em and I squeeze 'em, they don't even know my name—They call me the Wanderer, yeah, the Wanderer, I roam around, around, around, around—*" "You like him?"

"Love 'im! Old Dion DiMucci, grew up with his music, 'The Wanderer,' 'Runaround Sue,' 'Teenager in Love.' "

"How old are you, Gene?"

"Guess," as I cut ahead of this Beetle into the center lane.

"Thirty-eight?"

"Thirty-nine, turn forty in June."

"Jeez, you *are* nearly twice my age!"

"How old are yow?"

"Twenty."

"And your birthday's when, Tory?"

"September twenty-fourth."

"Means you share a birthday with Scott Fitzgerald—or rather he shares one with you."

"And yours, Gene, is—?"

"June eighteenth."

"Gemini and Libra. Good vibes there, very good vibes. And you know who *you* share a birthday with?"

"I'll bite."

"Paul McCartney. He's bought quite a few of my father's works."

"I know," as we go speeding through Queens, past Maspeth and Rego Park, and I can't keep my hands off her, always touching, stroking, caressing, which she accepts silently, soft-smilingly, and, once or twice when I'm totally daft, with a breathy, high-pitched laugh, which glistens my eyes as she begins gently kneading my nape.

"I love this smooth part back here. Incredibly smooth, just like your—"

"My what? My thing?"

Her Texas drawl, "Your *thaang,* yeah! And you have such a big neck. What size shirt do you wear?"

"Seventeen-thirty-four."

"*Seventeen!* My God. Well, you know what they say about neck sizes, don't you?"

"Is it true?"

"I'll never tell." That two-tone van coming up fast behind. "But I think it's more the thickness than the length that matters. Anyhow, I've never gone to bed this soon with anyone before."

"How many times have you gone to bed?"

"How many lovers have I had? Three, other than you—"

"Who?"

"—I don't date all that often. My, we are nosy, aren't we?"

"Well, I told you about Ciara, didn't I?"

"Yes you did. OK, let's see, my first was an Irish boy from County Longford, Mohill, just twice, and not very good, spurt-spurt, and he was done. And then there were some one-night stands, and Max from Yale—"

"I went to Yale, graduate school," that gray-green van still tailgating me.

"—during my stay at Sarah Lawrence."

"How long did it last?"

"O, three months or so. He was very sweet, and we both fumbled around like two missionaries—our favorite position, by the way."

"Son of a bitch, get off my *ass*! And what happened? *Putz!*"

"He joined the Peace Corps."

"You still see him?"

"Occasionally. Why, you're not jealous, Gene?"

"Of course! Hey, *fuck* you, asspipe!" as he goes roaring around me, flipping me off—

"'Asspipe'?"

—then abruptly knifes in front, "Jesus *Christ,* what the hell is he *doing*?"

"Gene, relax, will you. God, you get so crazy over nothing."

"*Nothing?!* The guy's been tailgating me for miles, then cuts me off, nearly runs me into a guardrail, and that's *nothing*?"

"OK, OK, the guy's an asshole, asspipe, whatever, but that's still no reason to get a heart attack over it."

Silently driving now past Flushing and Francis Lewis Boulevard, and these staticky traffic reports on the radio of jackknifed big rigs and broken-down bobtail trucks—

"Sorry, Tory, I'm sorry, just all wound up, but I hate all vans and pickups."

"All?"

"All, every last one—and O Christ, here's another winner!" sharply swerving, slowing, "Fucking van! Go!"

"'Fucking Van Gogh'?"

Grinning, "Funny, very funny. Anyway, listen, I wanna show you Great Neck, where I grew up, but we can come back later. Is it OK with you if we head out toward the end of the Island, Suffolk County?"

"Sounds good to me."

"I'll take Cross Island into Northern State, my favorite parkway of all time."

"Why's that?"

"You'll see. But back to Max for a second, just curious, who ended it?"

"I did."

"Why?"

"O . . . I'm not really sure now. I guess some fear of abandonment. My big fear."

"How come?"

"My father, of course. Left when I was seven. Choose no-win situations."

"Me?"

"Maybe, I don't know yet. I hope not," her middle finger tapping her sunglasses back in place, before she pushes up the sleeves of her navy sweatshirt, "Or maybe I'm not supposed to win, to have a good father, a great lover."

"You deserve to lose?"

"And my mother'd hate it if I won, then I'll lose her, too. Or who knows, all psychobabble, distancing myself in small ways."

Raising her hand to my lips, I kiss her warm palm, "Well, I'll never let that happen."

Her quick grin, sidelong glance out the window, "We'll see," then back to me with those mischief-shiny eyes, "And you don't think, Gene, you're a little too old for me?"

"Maybe so, but all I know is *the moment that you speak, I wanna* go *play hide-and-seek. I wanna go and bounce the moon just like a toy balloon.*"

Under these wonderful fieldstone bridges of Northern State Parkway, dogwoods and azaleas now in bloom.

"Well, I'm certainly happy for that, Gene, because you can be sort of stiff sometimes, with your arrogant, professorial mask. I like when you let go, kick up your heels, dance, and act crazy. It turns me on."

"O it does, does it?"

"Yes it does—except when you're driving," and she continues kneading my nape.

"Yeah, right. Well, tell me this, Tory, you think there's more father in female relationships than friend, brother, or lover?"

"Are you really asking or is that a rhetorical question?"

"No, I'd like to know."

"All three, I'd say, father, lover, friend. The last being most important. I think we're all seeking comfort, support, tenderness, warmth, understanding, and joy."

"You know what I'm seeking?"

"What?"

"To recapture that feeling I had as a boy with my grandmother, that gentle, glowing comfort. I think feeling that with someone again is more important than what a person looks like, how smart or witty they are. It's like being wrapped in a warm, protective shawl. And, hey, you make me feel that way."

"Even when you're old and gray?" and she presses my palm to her silken cheek.

"Definitely. Jesus, what a day! So you getting hungry, Tory, feel like some breakfast or lunch?"

"Sure, we can stop along the road. But please, not at one of those chichi places, like the one I went to a few weeks ago that had crab and shrimp omelets with champagne caviar sauce—*Yuck!* Just plain scrambled eggs, hash browns, and a side of bacon for me, thanks."

"You're a very simple girl, eh?"

"In some ways. Are you a simple man?"

"Not bloody likely!" and off I roar toward the wilds of Suffolk County.

Ten

High, windswept, sandy bluffs overlooking these pebble-and-boulder-strewn beaches, seaweed and driftwood, periwinkles and whelks, as Tory nimbly kneels to gather seashells in her tote bag, "Reminds me of Ocean City as a girl, and paintings my dad once made of me," then slips off her scuffed Reeboks and two pair of sweat socks to skip barefoot through the foaming surf, as I follow suit, the sand lightly scalding my soles, before sprinting side by side toward that swerve of shore—faster and faster—and letting her win, jogging now, she grinning back at me—

"I love the way you run, Tory, run like a little kid."

"I know, I run with everything flying—*O Jeez!*" and she trips headlong over some driftwood and lands sprawling on her butt, "Terrific! Hell of a runner, eh, with my klutzy pigeon toes?"

"You OK?"

"Yeah, I think so."

And I start tenderly massaging her foot as she reaches over to recover her sunglasses, then gingerly rises and, fitting on her Reeboks, takes a few tentative steps on her own, "I'm fine."

"So I see."

On this brash and blazing Saturday in May, with a ruffling, shuffling breeze sifting through those scrub pine trees, I'm finally feeling, here, alone with Tory, the freedom to breathe with ease as hand in hand we stroll along the water's edge of Long Island Sound, squinting at that corrugated aquamarine sheen out there, striped spinnakers ballooning by, dots and white smears of sailboats.

And up to the top of the bluff's pine-matted path, where the wind whistles and tears through our hair, the sun flinging down hot seeds of brightness as I cuddle and muss her, fondle and buss her, O my lovely young Irish lass! Her tumble-tossed hair thrashing with a loose blonde gleam about her shoulders, and her pink lips, darker from kissing, warm within mine, before finding my ear and breathing in a hot blur as I cup and caress her braless breasts—

"Tory, there's no one around."

She backing off, "Uh, no, I don't quite think so, my insatiable woolly bear."

"Just asking."

"Hey, that's OK."

And I follow her down this sloping path, "Yeah, well it's just you look so fine from behind—"

"Do I now?"

"—that you drove me wild with desire with your great high butt, plump and sensual rump."

"You're definitely a very weird man, Gene Hagar, you really are, even accept my feet."

"Right, flawed and lovely as you are."

Then back to the car, down these narrow dirt roads, kicking up a lazy haze of dust, and west along 25A.

"So what time tonight, Tory, are you dancing?"

"O, forget it now, we can go there tomorrow. It's too nice a day to lose," her hand warm along the inside of my thigh as we pass by Rocky Point, Mount Sinai, and Port Jefferson.

"Well, when did you start Irish dancing?"

"As a little girl, actually. I took a few lessons."

"Here?"

"No, in Baltimore, and then a lot more in Ireland three years ago, when I found I sort of had a flair for it."

On through Stony Brook (where I wrote a few years back), with its white clapboard New England houses, duck pond, and charming harbor, as I kiss her cheek, "You ready for dinner yet?"

"I yam indeed."

"Well, you wanna go to a restaurant with great food but high prices?"

"Sounds good."

"Or a restaurant with great food and good prices?"

"Better."

"Or a restaurant with good food and low prices?"

"Bestest!"

"Then I've got just the place!"

And we end up at Ireland's Eye in woodsy St. James for a dinner of huge tiger shrimp with an Irish whiskey and cream sauce served over angel-hair pasta, known as Dublin lawyer, and a bracing bottle of white zinfandel to wash the lot of it down.

Tory scraping the last of her shrimp and pasta into a tidy little pile as she sticks out the tip of her kittenish tongue, "What? Why're you staring, Gene?"

"No, nothing, I just like that you're left-handed."

"You do? And why's that?"

"'Cause I always wanted to bat left-handed, like Ted Williams, though he threw—"

"My father's left-handed, too."

"That's right, he is, isn't he."

"And so were Picasso, Paul Klee, Leonardo, and me, Boyne's only lassie," and she drains her glass of wine.

Nearly quarter after ten now as we enter Northern State again under that racing moon, and Sinatra coming on the radio once more with "I Get a Kick out of You."

"Too late to go to Great Neck, Tory. Next time, I swear."

"You grew up there when?"

"'42 to '58."

"And I was *born* in '55. But why Ireland, where's that come from?"

"Ireland reminds me of my backyard in Great Neck when I was a boy. No, I'm serious, I have this theory that we all have a magical place in our childhood, a park, a treehouse, a favorite room, for me it was my backyard, that we try to recapture, recreate when we get older, only now we're responsible for it, have to pay for it, protect it"—checking the rearview mirror and flicking on my blinker—"And when I first arrived in Ireland, I had this immediate connection—not only to Joyce and Donleavy and Synge, the writers I most admired, and to all that velvety green—but the same feeling, same glow, I had in Great Neck as a boy," switching into the center lane, "Then I moved back there when I got married."

"How long were you together?"

"Seven years."

Tory wincing, "She still around?" and looking away, "Live near here?"

"Not too far, in Garden City. You OK?"

"Sort of."

"Your foot?"

"No, my kidneys," and she pulls out a bottle of Pellegrino from her tote bag—

"Have you seen a doctor?"

—and takes a couple of swallows, "I go to massage," before wiping her lips on her sleeve.

"You mean physical therapy?"

"Physical therapy, right, diathermy. But it hasn't helped very much."

"Then go see a real doctor."

"I don't like *real* doctors."

"You and my mother."

"My mother, too. But that's the way I was raised, with a healthy doubt."

"Yeah, well I'd rather you just *be* healthy."

"Yes, *Daddy,* so would I."

Eleven

Cruising slowly by Chumley's bar, down Bedford Street, looking for a place to park at twenty after eleven on this Saturday night—"There, Gene! Tight squeeze, but you might have enough room—" and I deftly swivel in. "Wow, perfect in one try!"

"The last of the red-hot parkers," and I lock my car, "O and listen, Tory, before I forget, here's a key to my apartment."

"You're kidding?" and grinning, she slips it in her hip pocket, "Me very own personal key!"

"Right, well guard it with your life."

"O I will, I will—no, thank you, Gene, really, and I do," kiss-kiss, "appreciate it," as hand in hand we head back down the empty street toward those four stone steps—

"*YEEEE-HA!*" a terrifying banshee shriek preceding a black-caped figure—robber, mugger, Caped Crusader?—who comes leaping out of the shadows, "*HAGAAAR, you treacherous BASTARD!*" and knocks me sprawling—

"What the f— *BOYNE?!*"

—then locks me in a crushing choke hold, Tory clawing and screaming, trying to break his viselike grip, "Damn it, Daddy, this's not funny, will you let, let him . . . *GO!*"—and I can't breathe, pry myself free, on the verge of blacking out—

Till he abruptly releases me, then vaults to his feet with a raging gleam to his eye, "Just lay the hell off my daughter!"—and Tory shoves him back.

"You're such a geek, dad! What is your *problem*? I thought you were best friends!"

"Friends don't betray—"

"Betray *what*? And you told me you were coming in another week—"

"Well I changed my mind."

"*Full* of surprises, aren't you? O, you can be such a pain in the ass!"

Boyne, clad in that *Phantom of the Opera* cape, staring at her, with his grizzled beard and tilted beret, "And this's the thanks I get?"

"For *what,* scaring us half to death? Leaping out of the dark like a vampire or fucking mugger?!"

"You're really angry, aren't you, lass?"

"You're damn right I'm angry! You're *impossible, certifiable*! And you must've left as soon as you hung up this morning to get here so fast. And what about Mother?"

"I'll be seeing her shortly."

"O that's nice," Tory's exasperated sigh as she raises her eyes, then turns to me, "Gene, listen, let me deal with my dad—"

"Deal with me *how*?"

"—and I'll call you later."

"Yeah, but—?"

"Gene, please."

"OK, OK."

"And my God, dad, what on earth are you *wearing*?"

"Never pays to enter Manhattoes, lass, without the proper attire!" and with a swirl of his scarlet-lined cape, he bounds into her apartment, and I'm left out here on the empty pavement.

Twelve

—Friends don't betray—What the hell's he *talking* about? *He* won Ciara!—as I toss and churn again through this scary half sleep, early-morning daze—and no calls from Tory—nor family and friends on TV anymore, though I keep on seeing Bubba, mother, and father in a tumbling haze: his raccoon eyes squinting in the sun, and saying, "I pray each night you should marry a Jewish girl." And Teri later adding, "I wonder what your folks would object to most, my being Gentile or married once before?"—Or taking that train down to Miami when I was nine in 1945, eating our dinner out of paper bags, sleeping on the seats, the roaches scurrying under our feet, to the Roney Plaza Hotel, and my father, with his salesman's smile, posing for snapshots beside Al Jolson, who sat me on his knee and sang "Sonny Boy" to the crowd, or that summer, during his visits to Camp Winaukee on Lake Winnipesaukee, asking, "Are you the best ballplayer?" his "Teddy Ballgame," and "Do you miss your father?" then dying of that stroke and my mother saying, "He was too old to work and too young to retire," everyone fading, slipping away, shadowy figures passing, brushing by: then in a dream, a sylvan beam of Irish green brings bewitching haygold hair and eyes as keen and blue as a rift in the drifting clouds—So wanting to believe in Tory, but don't get involved, 'cause if you do, you'll lose her, too! *Curious she an only child, I an only child. Think you're escaping and run into yourself. Longest way round is the shortest way home.* And wonder what Joyce would've done. What did he do on that sunny hill of Howth? Pleaded, begged, cajoled, my flower of the mountain. Believe in me. And she did, loved him whatever and the hell with guarantees as they left from Kingstown Pier—

This rustling blanket of fears, and that searing heat now feeling so near, beside me, above me, frisky tongue licking my thighs and drawn-in belly—*Dreaming?* Must be. *Soixante-neuf* on TV? Or—No, Jesus, she's *here*! with flowerpetal caresses and satiny, succulent swells, fishy, rutty smells, musk and saliva, lips and breasts and shifting hips, dewy, quivering skin, tickling blonde shower of hair—till she suddenly spins around in the pale dawn light, and moves to her knees, "Please, Gene, come inside me," as I slide shuddering within and you moan in my ear, your eyes closed tight, clutching your thrusting butt, faster and faster, my calves rising, "O Gene, I can't hold back!" arching your spine, and we come together with sighs and strangled cries—and still kissing and hugging as our spasms subside.

"—O Tory, I swear—"

"Shhhh, don't talk, just hold me, please, as close as you can," and she cuddles into my shoulder's nook while I stroke her tousled hair.

Impossible, a dream better than reality! All my life the dream's out there—When I got there, the dream was here; when I got here, the dream was there. And back and forth and over and over, and now I'm here and you're here—

"I couldn't stop thinking about you, Gene, all night . . . it was really weird, so I finally got up and left."

"What about your dad?"

"O he's still asleep, totally jet-lagged out."

"Did he tell you what this's all about?"

"No, but listen, my bladder's gonna burst unless I get to your john fast," and with a fervent kiss and flaring smile that blots out all my thoughts and makes my senses wobble and reel, she hops out of bed with that perky rump and vertebrae's ripple, scampers into the bathroom, and shuts the door partway. "Next time, Gene, I'd like you on top, so I can wrap my arms around your waist, feel all of you *over* me!" A great waterfallish clatter, "Is that *all* you want Tory?" followed by the flush. "No, I want to be sure of someone, too." She lingering in there—probably checking out my bathroom wall and those photos of Joyce, Teddy Ballgame, Nabokov, Dylan, Sibelius, George Szell, Gene Kelly, and Paul Desmond—as well as the paintings of Vermeer, Eakins, Modigliani, and two postcards from the Tate of Boyne's blazing Ciara in the nude, her hair piled high in a French twist—

Tory throwing open the door now and smirking, "Well, surprise, surprise, guess who I saw on your wall?"

"Yeah, I know but—"

CREAK!

From out in the hall.

"You sure you weren't followed?"

"What? No, I'm sure he's still asleep. But hey, if it *is* him, so? Let him come in, that's *his* problem, I'll do what *I* want and show him—"

"Wait, whoa, whoa—"

"—that it's *my* life, not his! Anyway, Gene, may I borrow a robe?"

"Sure."

And she moves nude into my writing room—

"No, not there—"

—and picks up my novel, riffling over the pages, then pausing, "Hey, wait a second, this is, this is all about *her,* about *Ciara*! And here you tell me you don't care about her, she's just an old girlfriend, never saw me as her—"

"Tory, listen—"

"God, you're *obsessed* with her!"

"I'm obsessed? Sounds more like you're the one who's obsessed."

"*Me?*"

"Trying to be like Ciara, play at Ciara, and me as your father."

"O so that's what you think this's all about? Well, fine, you go on thinking that, mister, and bringing yourself off in your work, 'cause I'm sorry I can't compete, be her for you, but you don't need me anyway, you've got Ciara on your bathroom wall!" and dashing back into the bedroom, she rapidly yanks on her tight jeans, her silky flesh disappearing with a fast slither, pulls on that white sweatshirt, and, shaking out her hair, snatches up her tote bag, and is gone in a flash—slam, bam, thank you, ma'am!

Thirteen

—And *Christ*, you talk about your panic attacks! That terrifying, suffocating, nightmarish fright, soaked in sweat, as all my losses come crushing in again and shattering this May-December fairy tale with my mother's rictus smile, father's massive stroke, falling out of bed, flailing like a beached fish on the floor, Bubba's dying breath, tears streaming—

And the phone ringing!—as I fumble round these tumbling pillows—

"'Lo?"

"*BIG GUY*!"

"O Jesus!"

"Need ya tonight, playin' the fuckin' Elks, could tie 'em for fourth place—"

"Lou, look—"

"—so be there six-thirty, quarter to seven. But, Haig, more to the point, what's your ex-wife up to?"

"My *ex-wife*? Why?"

"'Cause I've always had the hots for her, wanna ask her out, so put in a good word for the Big Fella, OK?"

"Yeah, OK," squinting now in the moted morning light, "And how was the funeral?" my head aching.

"What funeral?"

"Your stepmother's funeral?"

"O *that* funeral. Hell, I was kissin' 'bout fifty-two relatives I never even *seen* before! But that second cousin of mine was wearin' this skintight Chinky dress with a monstro slit up the thigh—whatta piece of ass, by far the best thing there! But I gotta run, guy, see ya tonight."

"Uh, yeah . . . right."

And how can I possibly go?—propping up these scattered pillows, with Excedrin headache number 39, so little sleep—and I gotta teach today as well, see Tory—Cancel the class? No, though she probably won't even show—

The phone ringing again! What is this, Grand Central Station?

"'Lo?"

"Hi, it's Teri. I didn't think you'd be up this early. You OK now?"

"No, but go on."

"What's the matter?"

"Nothing, nothing. What's happening with you?"

"O, you know, the usual same old same old. But I meant to tell you, Gene, I got an A on your obituary."

"Well that makes my day. O listen, you remember Lou Grossbard?"

"Sure, from Great Neck."

"He wants to ask you out."

"You're kidding. Why?"

"How should I know? He said he's always had the hots for you."

"For me? You're joking."

"Yeah, I'm joking. So can I give him your number?"

"Uh, well . . . what do *you* think I should do?"

"It's your call, Teri."

"OK, why not? Anyways, let me go and you can go back to sleep, 'bye."

But as soon as I hang up, the phone starts ringing once more—Now who?

"Yeah?"

"Gene, I'm sorry I overreacted—"

"Tory—"

"—and I realized a lot of it was feeling really vulnerable, but believe me—"

"I love *you,* Tory!"

"Yes, well—"

"And I'm not seeing you to get even with your father for Ciara."

"—and just because you're writing about her doesn't necessarily mean—"

"No, it doesn't."

"Though I still wonder *why* you can't finish it."

"'Cause one, we didn't go off together, live happily ever after. And two, she died, and I guess I haven't come to terms with it yet. But then it seems neither have any of us."

"Probably so. And by the way, what's with the zabaglione?"

"Ciara loved zabaglione."

"And sixty-six or sixty-seven—What's that number, Gene?"

"OK, wiseass!"

"O but I read some of your short stories last night."

"And?"

"And I really liked them. Your prose is wonderfully lyrical."

"Like my lovemaking?"

"*I've* always thought so. Anyway, I'll see you later in class."

"Right, and listen, put your father on."

"Why?"

"'Cause I want to speak to him. Is he still there?"

"Yes, he's still here, but you're not gonna fight, are you?"

"Tory, just put him on."

My headache all but gone as I hear her shouting for him—footsteps finally arriving: "*Now* what, Hagar?"

"Seamus, what're you doing around four, four-thirty today?"

"Haven't a clue, except avoiding you!"

"Then drive out to Great Neck with me."

"Well who could refuse an offer like that?"

"Look, we need to talk."

"No, Hagar, *you* need to talk! Just stop seeing Tory or—"

"Or what? Why're you so pissed off, what's *really* bugging you?"

"What's *bugging* me? Suffering *CHRIST*, and this from the man who was fucking my wife!"

"What the hell're you *talking* about? Who told you *that*?"

"She did."

Fourteen

"When?"

"When what?"

"When did Ciara tell you we were having this affair?" as we go speeding along the Expressway, bald Boyne beside me with his shaggy, grizzled beard, Tory's same eyes and pug nose, and dressed today in a dark green rugby shirt, blue seersucker shorts, knee-high white socks, and those stained black Nikes.

"I found her letter to you."

"*What* letter?" and I zoom on by this crawling Chevy with the swaying fuzzy dice.

"The letter she wrote the day before she died."

"What'd it say?"

"O I don't know! That I was choosing art over her again, spending too much time working alone, and being surrounded by hordes of adoring women."

Traffic slowing up ahead. "So why didn't she send it?"

"I have no idea, other than she died the next day and never got the chance—but I'm sure this wasn't the only letter between you."

"Seamus, I swear on my grandmother's grave, I never wrote to her, never saw her, never had an affair!"

"Then why didn't you come to her funeral? 'Cause you were so fucking guilt-ridden, right?"

"No! 'Cause I didn't hear about it till *after* her funeral. I was holed up in Stony Brook working on my novel—And I *did* write to you!"

"Yeah, and I threw it away!"

"Seamus, I swear nothing happened."

"No, of course not, Hagar, you were holed up in Stony Brook!"

"And I really do love your daughter."

"Well, sweet Jaysus, who wouldn't? Lavishly gifted with beauty and talent as she is. But do you know what Rothko once said to a collector over the price of one of his paintings?"

"No, but what does that have to do—?"

"Just answer the question."

"No I don't."

"He said, 'Look, it's *my* misery that I have to paint this kind of painting, it's *your* misery that you have to love it, and the price of this misery is thirteen hundred and fifty dollars.' " That multiple accident up ahead. "How's that for a non sequitur? But still, Hagar, of all the girls in all the world—"

"What is this, *Casablanca*?"

"—why do you choose my daughter?"

"Hey, I didn't plan it, it just happened. And I'd be in love with her even if she *weren't* your daughter," swerving around these rubberneckers and that accordioned crash, "Look, Seamus, you had what I *never* had," then cutting back into the center lane.

"But you *had* Ciara!"

"Yeah, for a fleeting moment and mostly in my mind. Tory is real."

"And don't I know it!"

"So let *her* choose."

"But why you, Hagar, of all God's endangered creatures?"

"'Cause you taught her well."

"O shut the hell up!"

And we go cruising right through Queens as I turn to him, "So tell me, when's the last time you played any softball or baseball?"

"Good *God,* boy, the last time I even had anything to *do* with softball or baseball per se was when old Rothko and I went to Ebbets Field and saw Jackie Robinson hit a triple, tearing pigeon-toed like me round the bases, hips swiveling, hands high, and hook-sliding safely into third in a cloud of dust! And bearlike old Rothko leapt to his feet and began singing 'Sleepers Awake'!"

"In German?" smiling as I weave between these campers and vans.

"Exactly! Well, Mark'd had a few jars on him," and Boyne keeps scratching his grizzled beard—as I flip on QXR—"Ah, see, how apropos!" then begins swaying to the mellow music, "Nothing like Bach to soothe the savage beast. You know this piece?"

"Sure, Suite number 3 for Cello and Orchestra."

"But who's the cellist, Gene?"

"Well, let's see. You guess first."

"Gladly, boy! You know, of course, I'm one of the world's foremost authorities on Johann Sebastian, *Gramophone* and *High Fidelity* consult me before turning to the BWV."

Grinning, "Right, right," and shaking my head.

"But as for this particular cellist, I'd have to say Casals—No, János Starker, I'll go with Starker, Gene."

"And I'll go with Rostropovich," as the suite draws to a close.

"*That was Bach's Suite number 3 for Cello and Orchestra in C major by Mstislav—*"

"Haha, told you so, Seamus!"

"*—Rostropovich.*"

"Yes, well the cries of Irish gulls are still in me ears, and once every seven years or so I've been known to be wrong. No, but seriously, very good, lad, very, *very* good, that aggressive Russki bow of Rostropovich. Though tell me now your dream of musical perfection."

"My what? What're you talking about?" Switching back into the left-hand lane, Rachmaninoff's Second Symphony, with Previn and the LSO, now playing.

"I mean if you could be present at a performance throughout time of any one composer in the perfect setting, what, where would it be?"

"Well . . . I suppose I'd probably be in Finland watching Sibelius conduct his Fifth Symphony, while outside it's freezing white winter."

"Ah, right, absolutely! But mine, Gene, would be quite different, quite different, in fact. My dream of musical perfection is to be wending my way through Weimar—Isn't that marvelous? One should always be wending one's way through Weimar—on a cold, blustery day, and I take refuge in this tiny little church with wooden pews and dusty beams of light spinning in plumes through the high windows—and no one, not a soul is there, just me at the back—and Johann Sebastian up front at the organ, testing its lungs, and playing preludes and fugues, toccatas and passacaglias just for me and me alone! O Christ, he had a mind like one of those miniature works in a drawer, all those little circuits constantly buzzing. O no, Bach really *was* insane—or rather, lucid on a well-lit plane—as were Joyce and Turner and anyone else who could see with blinding sight! And the rest of us, Gene, before we get in touch, are driven half mad by their vision. And that's what I've just *gone* through these last six months, listening to Johann Sebastian and staring at Turner, walled up in sound and melting light, and painting nonstop in my castle, all alone with my work," and glancing quickly out his window, he pianos a tune on his grizzled beard, "But where are we going again?"

"Great Neck, to play a little ball."

"Ah, Great Neck, the pearl of the Antilles, or rather of Nassau County! Haven't been there since the days of Jay Gatsby." Boyne now staring out at the sterile clutter of malls and apartment houses rushing by, "Still, so little risk to this Island landscape. The light bothering you, boy?"

"The light?"

"Yeah, the afternoon glare. You were squinting."

"O I always squint. It's a family trait."

"Your father, too? He was the bug man, right?"

". . . Yes."

"*From* Great Neck? Ah, well tell me some more about *Great* Neck, sounds like a fascinating place. Come on, just relax, Gene, and let's forget about Ciara and Tory for a while, 'cause what I'd really like to hear about is *Great* Neck, where your parents always encouraged you, didn't they, supported your writing?"

"My parents? No way!" cutting ahead of this traffic, "There were no books in my house."

"Not one?"

"None! Don't you *remember*? I wanted to become a sports announcer when I was young, another Mel Allen—"

"And Da-da wanted you to take over that Holy Vermin Empire, ha-ha! Christ, *of course* I remember! He thought he was handing you the world on a silver platter—"

"And I turned my back. 'Send him to college to become a writer? Crazy altogether!'" by the exit to the Cross Island Parkway, "Always telling me how he had to struggle for every penny till he finally moved to Great Neck."

"And he died what, ten years ago is it now?"

"Nine, right before I went back to Ireland to see you, just before retiring—the Great Neck curse: drive, drive, drive your whole life to get the Great Neck goodies, then finally retire and there's nothing left to do—all those worthless, helpless feelings as a child suddenly surfacing during sleep, and no business now to go to, to ward off the nightmares—and their wives not far behind, my mother coming down with Lou Gehrig's disease a few years later."

"Good God! That I *didn't* know! And what was *she* like?"

"Brave as hell at the end, wanting no pity, but overprotective as a mother, and always a scared little girl, afraid of any kind of risk, of change—safe in Great Neck, walled in by all the goodies—and like a lot of Great Neck women who married workaholics and stayed at home, she fell in love with her only child."

"O Jaysus, I know about *that,* Hagar, do I know about that! So this's what you've been writing about all these years?"

"Well, no, not really."

"Ah, then you should, boy, definitely, I mean it. But go on, tell me some more about *Great* Neck."

"But you said you'd been there."

"O I was, but that was some *time* ago. I haven't been there in *years.*"

"Well, it's changed a lot since I first moved there."

"How so?"

Through Bayside and Douglaston and that blinding sunburst on the windshield ahead. "Used to be woods there then."

"When was this?"

"O just after the war began, 1942."

"And now?"

"Now the trees are still there, but the woods have been removed. You know, suburbia, commuters to the city and a basketball net in each driveway, Hadassah, golf clubs, and PTA, essentially leisure living."

"Ah, right, your family and a majority of Jews. Yes, you told me that in Ireland. And what about the others?"

"O there're quite a few Catholics, too."

"But not a real balanced mixture, you would say?"

"No, not exactly, each in small doses. Basically the blacks are the maids, the Italians the gardeners, and the Chinese serve up food on Thursday nights, when the maid is finally off."

"And the Irish?"

"They put out the fires and police the streets, mostly old-time residents."

"And the Jews rush into the city to make money, and rush back at night to their plush ranch houses, where they huddle round the card table or the remote TV. O *Jaysus,* what a setup!" he grinning and emitting that sinister throaty laugh, "All those little outcast groups knuckling under the thumb of the ascendant Jew!"

"You're not too big on minorities, are you, Seamus?"

"No, I'm only teasing you, Gene. I love 'em *all,* spicks, niggers, kikes, wops—all except the Irish Jew, the Yiddish Sons of Erin. But you take these things too seriously, Hagar, all you Jews do, too sensitive on the surface, and especially your Jewish women. But hell, why not? They're from another *planet,* they're from *Jew*-piter, ha-ha!"—both of us laughing as we come sweeping down the Expressway ramp—"And my daughter, whom you adore, boy, comes, of course, from the planet Goy—Ah, entering *Great* Neck, the Gold Coast, your fabled domain! And now, Good God, you're taking me out to the ball game!"

Fifteen

"BIG GUY!"

Lou bellowing as Boyne and I stride on by these teenage girls, Elks fans, in the green slat stands, and he comes racing up, "*HAIGY BABY!*" to slap me on the back and pump my hand, then abruptly whirls about, "*Holy SHIT,* will ya look at the *TITS* on that! Whatta setta gazongas!" Lou still staring and licking his lips, before turning back to Boyne, "And who the hell're you?"

"Lou Grossbard, Seamus Boyne."

"Shaymus? Whatta you, a private eye?"

"No, no, Lou, it's an Irish name."

"Yeah, right, I knew that. Anyway, with you two, we got nine, Sonnenberg and Yosh're both workin' late—"

Bucky coming over and cordially greeting Seamus and me.

"You mind playing the outfield, guys?"

"Not at all."

"'Cause McTee's been handling third pretty well lately—"

Lou reaching out, "And, Seamus, don't mind me," to shake his hand, "good to have ya aboard. What position you usually play?"

"O anywhere I hang my hat is home."

"Uh, yeah, right. Well how 'bout right field, think ya can handle that?"

"The eternal right fielder."

"What?"

"I'll give it a try."

"Hey, Big Shame, like your style, guy!" then pulling me aside as Bucky and Boyne start talking. "So, ya speak to her, Haig?"

"Who?"

"You know, Teri, your ex."

"O yeah, she said fine."

"Wayta *go,* Big Guy! Comin' through in the clutch like Tommy Henrich, 'Old Reliable'! And sorry to bother ya 'bout this, but after my stepmother died, I was so fuckin' uptight, I was sweatin', had pains in my head, and I was workin' myself into, I wouldn't say a nervous breakdown but—*MAH-RONE!*" Lou whirling around once more toward that busty girl in the stands, "Love to muff-dive into that!" before tossing me a ball, "And right now I'm datin' this great-lookin' chick, six pounds of Maybelline and no bra, from Passaic, New Jersey, who's, ya know, boom-boom. So I been runnin' around like wild, not ready to make the commitment, still like meetin' new stuff like in the old days."

"Yeah, but you're almost forty now, Lou."

"Hey, the Big Four-O! So, Big Stan and Big Ted, your hero, both kept playin' till they were forty-two—but *hey,* here comes the Big *SHEL* in the gold Eldo*rado*!"

And Shelly comes striding by the wire backstop, his tubby little wife, Rochelle, behind him with her rhinestone glasses and wavy reddish curls, "How-why-ya, how-why-ya!" and flashes that toothy grin.

"Hey, waddiya *say,*" Lou high-fiving him, "how come you're so late?"

"Haig, good to have you back again—Had meetings all day in the city. Sell a business for three million bucks and I'm still a million in debt!" smoothing down his ringleted hair, "Ah, but what the hell, like I always say, as long as I'm living in Great Neck, there's always a way! 'Cause I'm telling you, if I move and people ask me where I'm from, what am I gonna say, Little Neck? Like this guy I met the other day who said Woodmere, but when I said Great Neck, they *all* lit up! Still the place they all try to get to! And now *me* from Woodmere or a Little Neck condo? No fucking way! 'Cause when you leave Great Neck and lose your money, you *are* a nobody. Right, Haig?"

"Well—"

"Here, Lou, toss me the ball."

And Shelly, spearing it out of the air, sidearms it back to me—just as the ump pulls up in his rusty gray Plymouth, and he, Bucky, and weazily Danny Gumpp, manager of the Elks, in his all-black uniform, begin discussing the ground rules and the height of the pitch, a maximum of ten feet—"From the *ground*!" adds Bucky, backpedaling as we go fanning out to our positions, I kick the bag at second—take it easy on my arm, still so tender—now exiled to center, Cahn in left, and Boyne, winking, the eternal right fielder—

"Play ball!"

"OK, Shishy babe, gotta team behind ya, team behind ya, *Guy*!"

Gumpp himself leading off, crowding the plate—and swinging at the first pitch: and there's a high, high pop fly drifting down the third-base line—four of our guys converging, McTee from third, Bucky from short, Cahn from left, and Baum from behind the plate, and all of them shouting, "*I got it, I got it!*" as they collide, the ball falls between them, and Shelly sneers, "I guess they don't got it."

Lou, though, still cheering them on, "Shake it off, guys, just shake it off," as Gumpp singles sharply into left on the next pitch, and comes quickly around to score as the Elks push across three in the top of the first.

We come back to tie with three of our own, and with two out, I single into center, and up steps Boyne.

Batting left-handed and looking rather awkward and stiff, he chops down on the ball and bounces a high hopper out to second—then takes off with a burst of speed for *third*!

Nobody saying a word. All of us stunned. Boyne standing on the bag, wildly grinning, as the Elks' second baseman throws him out to end the inning.

And Lou exploding, "What the fuck is *THAT*?!"

"Lou, listen—"

"Who *is* this asshole?"

"That 'asshole' just happens to be the greatest painter of the twentieth century."

"Right, and I'm Stan the fucking Man!"

"No, really, he is, hasn't played much ball lately."

Shelly joining us, "Gee, I never would've guessed," as his wife, Rochelle, comes out of the stands pointing, or rather jabbing her chubby finger at Boyne, "Wait, wait, listen a second, wasn't a picture of him on the cover of *Time* magazine a few years back? Yeah-yeah, Shelly, I saw it, I'm sure I saw it. I'm telling you, he's somebody famous, some kind of actor or painter."

Lou walking away, "Fine, them let 'im paint our fuckin' dugout!"

Moving up the third-base line, I drape my arm around Boyne, his head down.

"Figured I'd fake 'em out, boy."

"Well, you certainly did that, Ollie."

"Since speed was always my forte, a sprint man."

"I remember," and we go jogging side by side back to the outfield, where their first hitter skies one high out to him as he staggers and circles under it—O Christ!—and, closing his eyes, snags it in the webbing with a shy, self-effacing smile.

"Wayta *GO,* you Shamey *baby,* knew ya could do it, Shamey *guy*!"

Boyne's next time up, he fouls off three pitches, then over-swings at a straight pitch down the middle, practically falling, holding himself up with that "Big Daddy" bat, and lifts one in the air down the third-base line, where it's one-handed over the shoulder for the catch—but at least this time, he runs to first!

So going to the bottom of the seventh and final inning, we trail 6–4 when I come up with one out, one on, and Lou pacing along the third-base coaching box and pumping his fist in the air, "Come on, Haigy babe, you can do it, kid, you can do it, guy! Good stroke, Haig, just give it a *ride*!"

Ride, yeah! Lucky I can even keep my eyes open, so little sleep lately—but on the next pitch, I rip a hot shot by the sprawling shortstop for a hit (wish Tory could've seen it), the left fielder charging it on the run, Shishy steaming around second and giving it the Pete Rose headlong dive for third as the throw—O *Jeez!*—comes whistling all the way back to first—

"Yer *out*!" The first baseman dropping the ball—"*Safe!*"

Shelly shouting, "Jesus Christ, Haig, wake up, will ya, and keep your mind in the *game*!" and kicking the bag in disgust as Boyne steps in.

Gumpp glaring down at him, and Boyne glaring right back as the first pitch floats across for a strike.

"Atta go, Danny! Two more and he's meat!"

But the next three just miss, and on ball four, Gumpp comes charging down off the mound, "What the hell you *talkin'* about, that last pitch was perfect! Open your fuckin' *eyes,* for Chrissake!"

The ump moving out from behind the plate, "Hey, one more crack like that outta you, mister, and you're gone, you hear? So shut your mouth and just pitch!" And spinning around, he leans over, dusting off home plate, and gives Gumpp a view of his rear.

But Bucky pops out. And with two down, it's all up to Lou with the bases loaded, the stands going crazy, our winning runs aboard, as he coils into that right-handed Musial crouch, feet close together, shoulders hunched, waiting to explode, and here comes Gumpp's looping pitch: Lou swinging with all his might—and there it *goes*, a long drive soaring deep out to left field, rising into the evening sky, and caroming high off the chain-link fence three hundred feet away—Shishy and I crossing home to tie the score, but Boyne, seeing the ball bounce back into play, jams on the brakes at second base—then starts, stops again, and finally, like the fleet-footed sprinter he once was twenty years ago, throws caution to the winds and comes flying pigeon-toed around third in his seersucker shorts and, hips swiveling like Jackie Robinson, never breaking stride, just beats the tag to score standing up and win the game 7–6!

"Aw-*right,* Shamey, aw-*RIGHT*!" Lou doing a crazy boogie as he races across the diamond, thrusting his fist in the air, before backslapping and hugging Boyne, "And I'll tell ya one thing, Big Guy, you can bet your ass *Picasso* never ran that fuckin' fast!"

Sixteen

Tory's flashing feet dancing across the stage to this rollicking Chieftains' jig as off she goes in a blinding blur of rat-tat-tat-tapping heel and toe, her blonde ponytail twirling above a dark green jumper that flutters at each pivot and graceful spin of my long-muscled girl, stiff above the waist, arms down at her sides, and that sensual, rhythmic shift of her hips as she whirls to a dazzling close.

"*Bravo, encore, encore, MORE, MORE!*"

And beaming Boyne and I, and the packed Celtic Arts house, standing and raucously applauding, "Jaysus, she's *marvelous,* absolutely bloody *marvelous*!"

Seonard and her students, the two Scully girls among them,

now rushing up to kiss and embrace her, Tory's radiant grin igniting my gaze and delighting her dad. And after more cuddling and lauding, and her change of clothes, off we roar to Chumley's close to her flat.

~

All of us quaffing a foaming brew above the sawdust floor and round these scarred oak tables, with the Celtic Arts folk talking and nautically swaying, "I wonder now could I have a Red Hook porter?" "—Well, I'd heard she'd been seen in Galway playin' the violin naked wearin' a sprig of marijuana," and my pug-nosed dream snug beside me with her carefree good looks, while I drain another lager and keep quoting Millay, "We were very tired, we were very merry—"

Tipsy Tory now nibbling away at the rim of my ear, warmwet within, and whispering, "Tongue like 'a fat sleek seal,' to quote your hero, Nabokov, that flops and slides so happily—" and she curves around to kiss my nose.

Boyne still seeming so uneasy and looking off, misty-eyed.

"Dad, you OK?"

"No, I was just thinking, there was a ditty I used to sing when I was 'fighting vainly the old ennui' and right before I married Ciara."

"Sing it now, Dad."

"Ah, no."

"Come on, Seamus."

"You're certain?"

"Yes, please, I never heard it."

"O, all right," and he lowers his glass and turns to us, tears welling, "went something like this:

~

"*I'm Ciara Glasheen's lover,*
A bloody painter that's me.
I love old Bach and Turner,
But none like Ciara G!"

"*Bravo*! *Encore*! *Huzzah, huzzah*!"

"Tory's concerned about *being* Ciara."

"Gene!"

"*Ciara?* But she's *not* Ciara!"

"Dad, could we possibly not talk about this?"

"You have things, lass, she never had, would've envied."

"I do? Like what?"

"Like what? Like your *lack* of sophistication, Tory, marvelous coltish charm. Remember now, Ciara was European, Dutch-Irish, and old beyond her years, had her moods, could be brutally sardonic—and who wanted to take *care* of me. You don't want to take care of Hagar, do you?" The beer freely flowing, mugs of Red Hook porter. "No, I didn't think so. You're splendid enough in your own right!"

"Yes, well I appreciate your support, dad," her eyes growing moist as she keeps on blinking, "But I suppose, now that we're finally talking about it, getting it out in the open—OK, so what, what if I did try to be like Ciara? We've *all* been haunted by her, haven't we?"

"And now I'm haunted by *you*!"

"Well, that's because of the way you dress, Gene," she sniffling and giving me a playful nudge, "Always look like you've been in the dryer for a few days and were never folded."

Boyne's boozy glance, "Ah, not at all, lass, I think he looks more like an Irish navvy, in that bulky crewneck sweater. But how *dare* you darken the dignity of the most devastating pest control operator west of Macão! Do you have any idea, Tory, with whom you're dealing? The former Cockroach King of the Western World! Suffering Christ, Hagar is part of a dying *breed*: those who still read Joyce, recognize Rostropovich—"

"And dance like Gene Kelly!" and she gives me a vigorous, tickling hug as Seonard, with her hoop earrings, leans woozily close.

"I kissed him once."

Tory blinking, "O, you mean Gene *Kelly*! Where?"

"On the lips."

"No, here in New York?"

"Ah, no, Ireland it was. He was over on holiday. Never forget it, first time in me life I ever fell fer an older man."

Boyne slinging his arm around her plump, red-haired self and laughing, "And I hear tell, Seonard, not the last."

Seventeen

Tory tucking her knees in tight behind mine, then reaching exploring fingers round and O so teasingly down—

"Whoa! What's gotten into you this morning?"

"Nothing yet," she whispers, giggling. Giggles that pander to joyously frisky romps or woolly love-makes before a roaring blaze in the grate—and we toss with lust, tangling blankets and sheets—free now of these Jockey shorts and up again at full, vertical. Throb! The jubilation of her eyes, O sweet, sensual Tory, with your blonde, tousled hair. And off we'll soar to the Wicklow Hills, where you'll dance for me each morning or ride the white dream ponies along the seacoast of Connemara. Your hands so warm, me writing—the phone ringing.

"Don't stop! Let it ring!"

"You sure? Could be—"

"Your father? O damn it to hell!" groping for the receiver, "'Lo?"

"Haigy *BABY*!"

"*Jesus,* Lou, great timing!"

"Hadda call ya, guy, had a fantazmo night! Teri's such a fabbo chick, just wanted to thank you for the fix-up, and I'll talk to ya later."

Hanging up and sighing, my heart still wildly pounding.

"Who was that?"

"Don't ask—"

The phone ringing again—and Tory reaching over, "Yes . . . he's here," and handing it to me with a viper sneer, "A female, for you."

"(Female?) 'Lo?"

"Well I'm glad at least someone is having fun. And who was that?"

"Teri, look—"

"Sounds like somebody special."

"O she is, that she is," squeezing Tory's hand.

"Well that's nice. Anyways, Gene, what on earth were you *thinking*?"

"Why?"

"To possibly fix me up with that Neanderthal, macho dipshit! He's got the IQ of a plant! All night long he was telling old Great Neck stories and I was going, 'Please, get me out of here!' "

"Listen, I'm sorry—"

"But on a brighter note, I met someone, too."

"Really? Who?"

"Well, he's my English professor."

"At Nassau?"

"Small world, eh? And he's wonderful!"

Tory hopping off the bed, "Gene, I have to pee," and she heads into the bathroom—definitely shattered that mood!

"Yeah, and how old is he?"

"I have no idea. Well, some idea. He's younger, *much* younger, late twenties, early thirties—but who cares, he's gorgeous! And he's really interested in *me*! So I'm like—"

"Well that's great, Teri, I'm really happy for you, but—"

"And he went to Trinity College in Connecticut, isn't Jewish—"

"Thank God."

"No, but he's really sweet—reminds me a little bit of you, when I *first* knew you, likes Joyce and Dylan Thomas and Henry James."

"Well, nobody's perfect."

"I know, I told him how you hate Henry James, and he said that's OK, wait'll he gets older."

"Wait'll *I* get older?"

"OK, OK. Anyways, let me go and I'll let you get back to your lady. 'Bye."

Shouting, "Tory, sorry about that—"

"It's OK. No problem."

And suddenly so thirsty as into the kitchen I go to open my fridge for this cold plastic pitcher of OJ. Glass, need a glass—Christ! throat so parched, pouring it over the lips, the gums, watch out tum-rum, here it *comes*! "*Wah-wah!*" making huge moose-lapping noises, "—Tory, what time's your father on Baba Wawa tonight?"

"Eight. But what're you *drinking*?"

"—*Cold! Cold* is what I'm drinking! Want some?"

"No thanks."

And gulping down another glass, one long draft, the cool juice drooling over my chin.

"Feel better now?" Her nude body glistening as she steps out of the john.

"Yes," and wiping my mouth with the back of my wrist and watching her fish out her bottle of Pellegrino from her tote bag for a few short swigs, then blinking and looking straight at me.

"Gene?"

"What?"

"I'm late."

"Late?"

"Late."

"How late?"

"Three days."

"You never used anything?"

"No. But neither did you."

"How come?"

"Well, you never asked, I took a chance, and the pill made me nauseous. I took it for a while, then foam, so—"

"But how could you just jump into bed unless you wanted to—?"

"Hey, listen, mister, first of all, I didn't 'jump,' as you so charmingly put it, into bed, and second, what I need now is your support, not your slaps and quizzes, with all the stupid pressure of you and my father—"

"Tory, hey, I'm sorry, I—"

"No, forget it, just forget it. You've had a king-size bug up your butt all morning!"

"*Me?*"

"No, Teri, your ex!" and gathering her clothes, she quickly dresses.

"You're not leaving *again*?"

"Just watch me!"

"Fine, I'll call you later."

"Don't bother."

"Tory—"

And she's gone!

Jesus Christ, what'd I say *this* time? On this fucking roller coaster, not even sure what happened really happened! One of those scenes from the past sprung from recollection: a sudden glow and then gone, as the magician conjures the pearl, distracts, and presto, opens a bare, unblemished palm—and leaving me alone in this shadowy, barren room with my stupid accusations!

Tory illuminating my life, enlivening my eyes, and cutting aside these terrified feelings of loss, nightmare fears, rather than stay safe and alone, gaining comfort only upon small occasions with myself, easier to close off the world and hide away with my cast of illusions, shutting off parts of me that never bruise or care. And this precious fair-haired girl sweeping away these fears so I could take another chance on the reality of her and not a Ciara dream—as I keep on nervously pacing.

Eighteen

Down the twilit length of Bedford Street at twelve to eight with the wind fluttering the slender trees, and hoping it's just much ado, Boyne should be with Wawa at ABC—and Tory, too?

Knocking and shifting from foot to foot out here, holding on to the railing, inhaling and exhaling—as the door swings free.

Her blonde hair, green sweatshirt, blue jeans, and somber expression, "Yes?"

"Tory, listen please, granted I know—"

"I thought I said 'don't bother.' "

"You did, but wait, wait, granted I know nothing about Led Zeppelin, Moody Blues, or The Who, and you have no idea who Joe Morello, Gene Wright, and Paul Desmond are—"

"Look, I'm not in the mood now for—"

"No, no, come on, I've been rehearsing this all the way down on the subway, seventy-six blocks, and given all that, and the *huge* difference in our ages, and the fact that I sometimes put my foot in my mouth and can be totally insensitive, I still think we're incredibly connected."

". . . In some ways."

"In *most* ways!"

"So, what is your point, Gene?"

"That we're joined at the hip, which I realize causes you to be self-conscious, care what other people think of us when we're walking along, a dirty old man linked to his daughter."

"No, actually I don't, or rather I like it, like the way we look together, I really do. I mean not that you're a dirty old man, but that I *enjoy* being seen with you."

Glancing down and then back up, blinking, "Thank you. And I really am sorry."

"Well, so am I, just so edgy lately."

"Wonder why."

And we hug and kiss, a long, lingering kiss, till she guides me on inside and across the hardwood floor.

"Still, Tory, you're such a brat."

"O look who's talking! You're the stubbornest man I've ever met."

"Including your father?"

"Including my father."

"Hey, this time, miss, I came to you."

"Surprise, surprise."

"See the thanks I get. You anxious at all?"

"No—O, maybe a little, 'cause it's his first TV appearance in the States, and my mother called just before you came—which definitely helped!"

"Well we've got, what, five minutes to go?"

"No, three. Here, let me turn it on."

And I sit beside her on the oatmeal couch with its throw-cushion jumble, things still a bit tense between us, and watch the commercials conclude, before a sonorous voice announces over the logo:

"*Tonight, replacing our regularly scheduled program,* The Bionic Woman, ABC *is proud to present a Barbara Walters Special: A Live Conversation with Seamus Boyne.*"

"They sure he's alive?"

"O shut up, you!" and Tory jabs me in the ribs.

Close-up of Barbara, in a red jacket over a black blouse and gold pendant, alternately staring directly into the camera and checking her index cards.

"I'd like to start by asking my most distinguished guest if I may call you Seamus?"

Boyne, clad in an orange jailhouse jumpsuit and his green beret, grinning and sprawling back in a white wicker chair, a striped ceramic mug by his side, "Only if I can call you Baba?"

Her fast, plastic smile as she leans forward on her love seat.

("He's drunk, Gene." "How do you know?" "Trust me, I know.")

"Yes, well, the current consensus of the art world today is that you're an astounding original, who has, to quote *The New Yorker,* 'liberated contemporary art from the thrall of Picasso and European modernism.' "

"Is that so?"

"And the London *Times* called your latter Ciara portraits, 'the most important works painted by an artist in the present century.'"

"That a fact?"

"While Sir Kenneth Clark has recently said that despite all your years of obscurity, you've surpassed Degas as a draftsman and Vermeer as a—"

"Ah, Baba, Baba, Baba, what on earth were my few years of obscurity compared to Vermeer's languishing absolutely forgotten over two whole *centuries*? Were you aware, for example, that in 1870, the Louvre bought his *Lacemaker,* his *Lacemaker,* mind you! for a mere fifty-one pounds? Or that his *sublime* head of a girl, which was bought for more than a million U.S. dollars in 1959, and which is worth several *times* that sum today, was sold in Rotterdam in 1816 for three bloody florins? So *my* motto has always been, let 'em all," and he takes a long belt from his ceramic mug—

(Tory muttering, "Now he's going to say 'KMRIA.' ")

"KMRIA!"

"And what does that stand for, Seamus?"

"Stands for Kiss My Royal Irish Arse!"

Another fast, plastic Wawa smile, "Yes, well—"

"'Cause the trouble, you see, with success today is you have to keep *on* being successful. And people keep forgetting the man *behind* the work, that a man's hand held that sable brush, that a man's eye savored that saucy bosom, and that a man's lusty, pumping organs thundered at the sight of the coarse and lumpy, pulsing lovely gleam of that paint!"

("And watch, Tory, now he'll add, 'There's never art without the artist.' ")

"For there's *never* art, Baba, without the artist!"

("You really *do* know him, don't you?")

"The public always losing *sight* of the man! For every single one of us, Degas, Rothko, Rembrandt, Turner, or Vermeer has lived, loved, laughed and cried, had marvelous children, slept, ate, farted, frolicked, and touched all *sorts* of people as deeply or more so than our works, however profound they may be! Yet all most people know of Degas, say, are those dark daguerreotypes of him frowning painfully away from the camera, puffing on a Gauloise stub, or sketching backstage at the Paris ballet. Never aware of what he, or I, went through, even *denying* our struggles during our lifetime! Picasso having to paint window blinds for a few francs to stay alive, and Pollock doing hand-painted ties! And even after my beloved second wife died, I was suddenly made aware that all I was doing was wondering how I would paint the planes of her face—and it scared the bejaysus out of me!"

"Yes, but imagine if *you* were a painting, Seamus, what kind of a painting would you be?"

"Ah, well, more often than not I imagine my paintings imagining me."

Barbara broadly smiling and sorting through her index cards, "And what *keeps* you painting?"

Boyne grinning and taking another long belt of his brew.

("What *is* that, Tory?" "God only knows! Probably Tullamore Dew.")

"'Tis the joy of that first brushstroke, Baba—beginning new pictures one of the keenest pleasures mankind's ever devised, like that first warm entry into the moist sheath of a woman—and nothing, and I do mean *nothing*, rivals that!"

"Yes, Seamus, but—"

"For as long as you eat anything, trust me, that even *looks* like a sexual organ, Baba, you'll be fine! Cucumbers, Brussel sprouts, broccoli, cauliflower—and especially rutabagas!"

"Yes, well, moving on to a whole other subject, Seamus, before we go to break, you currently reside in Ireland."

"Indeed I do."

"And why is that?"

"'Cause I adore the light and the air of the ould sod! The turf smoke, the bracing winds, the racing clouds forming continents and galleons, mare's tails and feather boas—and above all, the tang of the Irish Sea!"

"And after all these years, is the work still worth it?"

"Worth it? O Suffering *Jaysus,* Baba, have you ever stared into the eyes of one of Rembrandt's self-portraits, those last, hoary ones, peered deep into that wounded gaze? But Good *God,* just look into mine! Worth it, *Christ Almighty*!"

"But they're beautiful, Seamus."

"Yes, well vouchsafe me a final word here, Baba, if you will, scapegrace that I am, before you go to break," he standing and swaying now and staring straight into the camera, "and remember only this, as my second wife liked to say, that the questions our children ask us are the same we ask ourselves till we die. And my answer this night to the most significant one of all is: I've never *stopped* loving you, Tory!"

And tears flood her eyes as he goes lurching off the set, and I rock her tight in my arms.

Nineteen

Two weeks of soaring highs and dance-away lows, those flare-up fights over my uptight outbursts while driving and, of course, Ciara once more, both of us getting edgy the closer we get to the core, but also sharing great joy and laughter, sometimes nonstop, pee-in-your-pants, hysterical laughter, orgasmic laughter, fall-down-flat-on-my-back-on-Fifth Avenue laughter, passersby tiptoeing fastidiously around me. And all our abiding and wondrous delights of sharing favorite books and music: The Dubliners' "Wild Rover," Led Zeppelin's "Fool in the Rain," and Moody Blues' "Tuesday Afternoon" for her, and Sibelius, Bach, and especially Paul Desmond's incredibly pure and mind-blowing, driving solo on "How High the Moon" for me. And Tory really appreciating my stories, wise, incisive comments, striking just the right note (my grandmother's glow): "I think it's so great, Gene, that you've finally started writing about Great Neck, what you really know." "You sound like Ciara." "O she said that, too? Well she was right. You showed her your work?" "Some of it." "I see." "Tory, I love *you,* period, end of discussion. Won't try to change you or mold you in my image." "Right, I'm sorry. It's just, well—" "Distancing yourself in small ways?" "Exactamundo." And cooking together, our homemade, off-the-wall spaghetti sauce of Italian sausage and fennel (one of Chaucer's nine holy herbs) that comes out so great as we both go farting around my apartment, she pausing, tilting her head to the side with that silly-ass grin, and announcing, "Now you know." And my class going well, Tory and Ricardo producing the best work by far, her "love scene" marvelous, half the class panting, and he asking her out once more. "Doesn't he get the hint?" "Guess he's just persistent." And shortly after a hot morning shower, she emerging to state, "My period started." Then dinner at Lüchow's to celebrate that night. And a few days later, I pull out my Trojans. No need. Why? "I'm taking a lower estrogen kind of pill. Hey, what can I say, the miracle of modern chemistry." And now much calmer, mellower lovemaking, tender and sweet and close to the bone, but a little more edgy as well, like her comment this morning, "So wild to look down and see a man's head between my thighs," and endless fondlings and strokings and patient concern—

Still, I remain unsure, a toe in the water, then a calf, now a thigh, so much easier than with Teri or even Ciara—yet those nightmare fears keep creeping in, losing her if I get too close; she, of being abandoned, since even after his stunning reassurance on national TV, Boyne left again, straight from Baba and off to Baltimore on the first flight out.

But I'm not Boyne, not even close. Nor do I want to be.

Twenty

Entering her place with these green and clinking, ice-cold bottles of Rolling Rock and tossing my Red Sox cap deftly onto that hat tree, where it teeters, totters, and hangs by the bill.

"Whatta you watching?"

"O, *All in the Family*," when the phone starts ringing. "*Kwai*'s coming on later."

"Want me to get it?"

"No, I can, Gene," and she reaches across, with her ponytail bobbing, "Is it raining out?"

"Just started. Here, let me turn this down."

"Thanks—Hello. O hi. No, nothing much, just hanging out. Yeah, I had a class tonight. Was OK. Gene helped me with my students. You are? When? Friday? Great! Mother coming, too? Well we'll be here. Sure. What time? Yes? So?" She shrugging, raising her brows and—"*WHAT?!*"—sitting upright on the couch.

"What is it?"

"What're you *talking* about? *When*? *How long?* O dear God! O Jeez!"

"Tory, what *is* it?"

"*Shhhh*! When'd you find out? Can I talk to her? No, no, don't wake her—" she sighing and pursing her lips, "O *wow*! What? Yeah, right, I'll see you Friday. No, I'm OK. Yeah, yeah, 'bye."

"What happened?"

"My mother—has lymphoma."

"O Christ!"

"Has a year to live," Tory standing now, "but my dad doesn't believe it," blinking, then staring blankly off as I move toward her—"No," she holding up her hands, "let me just think, walk around a bit—"

"You going down to see her?"

"I don't know."

"I think you should."

"Well now I'm going outside."

"But it's raining outside."

"So?"

"You want me to come with you?"

"If you'd like."

"Want your raincoat?"

"No."

Silvery sheets slanting down, puddling the Village streets, and Tory striding, splashing on, offering her my Red Sox cap—which she waves away, with me squinting, wiping my face, along Grove, into Bleecker, and by the White Horse without a word as we finally circle back toward her flat, both of us getting drenched, before I towel her off, rub her down, then run her a hot, steamy bath.

Twenty-one

"How is she?" cradling the phone on my shoulder.

"It's much worse than I thought. Nodes the size of quarters in her neck and groin."

"O Jesus, I'm sorry. And all of you are still staying at her Baltimore apartment?"

"Yes. But however weak, tired, and frail she looks, she's still as bitchy as ever."

"Well bitchy's good."

"For you maybe, not for me, you don't have to live with it. But no, actually you're right, it is a good sign."

"And the biopsy results?"

"The same. She's supposed to start radiation soon."

"For how long?"

"Three or four months. But my father won't do it here, doesn't trust U.S. doctors, nurses, or hospitals, and is taking her back to Ireland, wants me to come with."

"And?"

"I don't know, Gene. I'm going down to Ocean City for the weekend, need some time alone."

"Can I call you?"

"No, let me call you. I've gotta go, sorry—"

"Well call me, Tory, anytime you need me."

"Yeah, thanks, 'bye."

Twenty-two

A fine fume of rain still falling steadily over the city as I keep staring at my alarm clock:

6:38.

6:39.

6:40.

Call her? No! Call her! No, just fly down and see her!

No! and I fling back these twisted sheets and, staggering slightly left, go slamming—*damn*!—right into my cluttered desk, pencils and sharpener clattering over the floor as I bend my naked butt to scoop them up.

A last pencil here in the far corner. Under this dog-eared copy of *Ulysses.* My dear Joyce. Ah, Hagar. Scattered papers and bills, writing all across them, my hieroglyphic scrawl, and on the back of this, what is it? Library slip from Yale. Call numbers, some scribbled words: *Halcyon days, when Hagar whirligigged and ran his heedless ways, a fey tune piped on a holiday flute, vaulting over the sea.* Always finding a note or slip of paper later on like this in one of my shirt pockets, pants pockets, on bookmarks, in the well of a raincoat, bills to be paid. Joycean notepaper on green oval leaves.

And O Jesus, here's my mother's letter. July 28, 1967. Haven't read it in so many years:

> The tail end of a hurricane is passing thru N.Y. Raining cats & dogs. Dad's been working until 8-9 o'clock every night. Comes home pooped. You know, the height of the termite season. Should slack off by the time you get back from Ireland. You should be thankful you have such a father, all he's done for you. He's given you everything you wanted. There's nothing you don't have. He's so looking forward to your return. We're both certain you'll love the business, be a success at it, double the volume in less than 5 years. He was thrilled with your card. We think you're terrific, a born writer.

Huzzahs from my fans back home. A writer, yes. Of flashy quips and newsy tips from the flip sides of picture postcards. *The Collected Picture Postcards of E.C. Hagar.* First edition, in dark crimson morocco, gold-toothed, with a surly photo stitched to the flyleaf.

And writing the rest of the day, filling nearly three full pads as I scribble furiously away, then pause to stare at this lined yellow paper and reread what I've written. Words on the lip, the tongue, stories in the making. Thinking of a place where language is a jewel, storytelling the great delight. And producing several long descriptions of Tory, these lyrical flights. My *wavewhite wedded words* that so flutter and swerve.

I write to learn my craft, perfect a style. Nabokov's "how" above the "what," caressing details—Under the shadow of someone else. *Stand and balance yourself!* "I think it's so great, Gene, that you've finally started writing about Great Neck, what you really know." She caring, believing in me, like her father: "I heard your work and the way you handle language and, Jaysus, boy, you *have* to write!" *My* father, with his Coca-Cola smile always primed for customers, friends, and family alike, once saying, "Writing's OK, but you've still gotta earn a living. When I was your age, I had the same thoughts, the same ideas. But you'll see, you'll change. Everyone goes through stages like that. You'll look back later and see how silly your ideas were."

And language always my answer, fleeing my father's world. Joyce fleeing through flung nets to a world of his own creation. Writing of what he knew. And I had to go all the way to Dublin to write the story of Great Neck? *Yes!* The same way Joyce had to go to Paris, Zurich, and Trieste to write his own story of Dublin. Not French or Swiss stories, but father stories, Dublin stories—And not Ciara stories for me! Write about what I know, give up this novel, and let Ciara go.

And this language, lessons of Nabokov's class, my rich and lyrical sensibility? No, my rich but *limited* sensibility, the inability to wed it to life. Lyricism in the vale of tears. For what drove Keats up the wall wasn't just the nightingale's song but the *implications* of that song in his own vale of tears. And for me all these years, it's been enough to just sing the song, avoid the pain, and escape into language and poetic dreams. But you have to write about the *pain,* the *loss,* to give the lyric flight! Joyce finally confronting his pain, getting outside himself, and overcoming Stephen's smugness, arrogance, and self-pity in creating Bloom and throwing his *Hero* into the fire. And my Bloom? Father, mother, or beloved Bubba? Or that Million Dollar Infield! Lou losing his family, Shelly leaving Great Neck, Monte dying, Bucky's son trying to escape—my father and I.

And grabbing my pad and pencil again: Recalling now, after all those years of rationalizing, patronizing, correcting his slightest grammatical error, the haunting fact of two children lost in infancy, and overly healthy me with my 20/10 vision and never a broken bone, his "Teddy Ballgame," lone joy and creation, and, most of all, that daily ritual of wrestling matches when I was seventeen. My father's 220 pounds keeping me down for the frenzied opening minutes till, as he weakened, I was able to flip him over and bend his futile arm aching with bursitis into a hammerlock and make him give. Day after day I won and never felt any delight, if I expected delight, in the victory—for one never really succeeds over one's father.

* * *

Later, needing a breath of fresh air, out onto the rain-stained street toward Fifth and away from the Carlyle (where Jack Kennedy stayed), and Sotheby's (where many Boynes have sold), I stroll under those dim, featherstitched clouds drifting low over the horizon and down the dark, ferny paths of Central Park, a confetti flight of seagulls rising past my sight—

And so missing her now, her girlish joy and glow, smile that glistens my sad heart, and fine mind reasoning, perceiving, feeling as she deals with her fears—and I so wish I were there!

Twenty-three

"Hello?"

"Tory, Gene. Glad I caught you, was really getting worried. When're you leaving for Ocean City?"

"In about an hour."

"Yeah, well how you doing?"

"O, you know, about the same."

"And your mother?"

"A bit better. She's started to change her diet, cut out sweets, caffeine, her two cappuccinos a day."

"Whose idea was that?"

"My dad's. He's been in touch with these Dublin doctors, something called the Hoxsey treatment and this strict macrobiotic diet, I don't know."

"Well I hope it works. O, the class asked about you, especially Ricardo."

"And I've been doing a lot of thinking, Gene, writing in my diary."

"About what?"

"O, all sorts of stuff, always seeing Ciara as the ideal mate for my father and avoiding dealing with my mother, the friction between us. And last night, she held me and hugged me so tight, for the first time since I was eleven like that."

"And how'd it feel?"

"Fine. Sort of stiff at first, but actually it felt terrific."

"It's hard, I know."

"Gene, you know you're not the only person in the world who's suffered a loss!"

"Hey, I didn't mean—"

"No, no, I'm sorry, sorry I said that. It's just, O hell, I just don't need to be told now how to feel. Anyway, I'll speak to you later—"

"Hey, hold it, wait a second!"

"What?"

"I want to come down and see you."

"No, let me come to you. 'Bye."

~

And driving alone around Great Neck after our game, another amazing, come-from-behind win, on a roll, definitely should make the play-offs, with me patrolling center field and finally starting to hit, two ringing doubles tonight (one batting left-handed), yet still feeling numb, like I'm watching myself play—missing her so!

And those same stately homes here all of my life, slate-shingled Tudors, split-level ranches, and whitewashed Dutch Colonials. And Christ, you know what, I'm going to stop at a real estate agent before our next game and start looking for a place back here! Surrounded by all my friends, safe and secure, and write about what I know. Though houses I played in as a kid are up for sale, this rash of glitzy boutiques lining Middle Neck Road, our parents dying, all those self-made men, my father and his Great Neck friends: Shelly's dad began by sweeping floors in the garment center and worked his way to the top of the used carpet business; Bucky's came over from Russia with just a harmonica in his pocket and is now part of the royalty of Great Neck, Rockefeller's eyes and ears to the Jewish community, the richest family in town; and Lou's dad dropped out of school in the eighth grade, peddled pretzels in front of Kleins, and started the largest pharmacy on Long Island.

Then later, pacing round and round my apartment, wearing a hole in this carpet, going out of my mind, before finally calling Boyne in Baltimore and prying Tory's Ocean City number out of him, area code 410.

Busy! Again and again and again—No, now ringing eight, ten, twelve times! No answer. And no answering machine, either!

Fly down, drive down? No, honor her wishes, *let me come to you.*

~

My phone ringing at 11:42:

"'Lo?"

"Gene, my dad said you called."

"Yeah, about eight million times! Where *were* you?"

"Out . . . I went to the doctor."

"About your mother?"

"No, about me."

"I thought you don't like doctors?"

"I don't, but we—"

"Who's 'we,' your father?"

"No."

"Your mother?"

"No."

"Then who?"

"Gene!"

"*Who*?"

"Max, if you must know."

"*Max?* What's *he* doing there?"

"He lives here."

"I thought he went to Yale?"

"He did, but he comes from Ocean City. And you're pressuring me, Gene."

"Tory, listen—"

"Just give me some space. (What? O hold on.) Gene, look, I have to go. My mother needs me."

"Sure it's not Max?"

"'Bye."

~

No further word over the weekend.

But on Tuesday, her letter arrives, and on the back:

```
Ocean Crest Cottage
Ocean City, MD 21842
```

Dear Gene,

I guess the time has come for me to say goodbye. Going on for weeks now at cross-purposes, with one foot in the air, flying high along with your dreams for our future, you and I, the other planted on the shaky ground of my fears of being abandoned and the fact that maybe "thou and I are too wise to woo peaceably."

But I miss you so much, all those things that you've been to me, always and forever will be for me, lover, teacher, even better friend, showing me and guiding me, giving me the faith in me that I have yearned for, cried for, needed O so desperately, loaning me your eyes and releasing my heart to touch and stroke and dance gently over your flesh, crispy hair, vein-mapped hands, bearish bigness, and all your textures that delight me so.

And I see you, feel you, and somehow, in some way, I am you. This wonderful and talented man (and kick-up-your-heels child) trying to sort out his sadness, face his own mortality, frustrated tears filling his eyes as he strives to pull away his very own piece of sky.

Smooth and suave you are? *HA!* Wise and all-knowing? *HA!* The warm and tender underside buried deep, I believe, beneath your professor's mask that you've grown so good at using as a shield to hide behind. Amazing we saw each other's masks (my happy-go-lucky blonde or ditsy waif) and smashed them away before they ruined the chance to see each other as no one else can, does, or ever will.

But in dealing with everything that's going on now in my life, facing the loss of my mother, and fearing you'll leave, or I, ultimately, will, I feel it's enough for me to tell you that I just can't see how there can ever be a time or place where we can meet, both of us heading in the same direction, where we can be just who we are, no more, no less.

Yet I wish you all things good and warm, my sweet, sweet love.

Tory

And taking a sharp, painful breath—then rereading her letter at 4:30 in the morning over and over—and nothing on TV now but nonstop TV as I keep on flicking this remote control.

Twenty-four

Going through the motions the rest of the week, staying busy as possible, Bloomsday coming, my birthday June 18, and trying to stifle this fierce, hollow ache, my fairy tale over, act your age, old man, then, on the spur of the moment, speeding out to Beth David Cemetery early this gray, windy Saturday, amid all these granite statues and lonely mausoleums, weedy grass needing to be cut, stones and floral bouquets left behind on the chiseled tombs.

My beloved Bubba dead five years now, father nearly nine. She such a pearl of sweetness still in my mind, relaxing me so with her bemusing tales of long ago, spinning that quilted web, where I'd float below time.

And now she remains only inside, though I miss her so—and that never ends!

Dear Tory,
Your loss is unbearable.

Feel half alive floating around New York unable to breathe, gone my best friend and love of my life. For as I've told you in so many ways, I love you more than any woman I've ever met (no one's even close), as well as the bright and pretty, delightful and witty child in you, super writer, Irish dancer, and breathy, high-pitched laugher in you. I love your kindness, abundant generosity, and romping, filly-like spontaneity, hopping from pillar to post, cartwheeling through my life.

And we've grown so much together—yet keep tripping over our own and each other's feet again and again, to end up out of sync and dancing away from commitment, minor slights, or not really hearing or feeling each other.

For it's all so new to me. And scary, too, as I face my fears and the loss now of your voice, your touch, your warming laughter, and so much other soft and sweet and silly stuff, quickly picking up my drift, or cherishing the different slant your insights give, and even, believe it, your feisty, stubborn streaks—O look who's talking!—stroking my nape, caressing my hand, I your cheek, your skin, and lustrous hair.

I know this is a really stressful time for you now, but never forget I love you so, flawed and lovely as you are.

Gene

And I've *gotta* go down there! 'Cause if I don't, I'll be kicking myself for the rest of my life! Tory probably testing me, really wanting me to come down. So I *won't* abandon her, just show up at her door and hand her the letter or read it aloud and punch out fuckin' Max, whatever, but I'm on my way!

Twenty-five

And where the hell am I? My face roughly buffeted by this saltwater breeze—flight on Allegheny Air and across that long causeway bridge in my Avis Chevy, parked round the corner under those ghostly streetlamps—high school kids passing barefoot in shorts, and asking one for Ocean Crest Cottage—"Sorry, I'm from Shaker Heights." All these homes identical, quaint, two-story white clapboards out of the twenties and thirties, neat hedges and trees.

A blonde girl appearing from those shadows—"Sorry, thought you were someone else." And seeing her and an imagined Max everywhere I turn, with no idea what he looks like! What the hell do Yalies look like? William Buckley? Kingman Brewster? Johnny Lee? Eli Yale? Or me? Some geeky-looking guy clad in Brooks Brothers livery as I keep wandering hopelessly hither-thither like my Bubba by a bewildering maze of similar-looking sandy streets and swaying leaves—

This whole *idea* was ridiculous! Never gonna find her—

That ornate sign?

O Jesus, *finally*: Ocean Crest Cottage! A three-story clapboard with Victorian gables, high cement-block walls, and wrought-iron gate that opens with a squeak as I cautiously pad across the darkened lawn. No lights on. What if they're fucking? Bust in? No, just take off and shred the letter.

Deep breath. Lightly knocking on this weathered front door. . . . No answer. The breeze picking up, my heart raucously beating, squall coming up over the Atlantic. . . . Still no answer. And no lights inside that I can see. Calling "Tory!" once, twice, some half dozen times before heading back to the gate—

This old lady leaning on her cane—turns out to be a neighbor. And Tory left this morning. "When's she coming back?"

"Well, I'm not quite certain. Not for a few days, I think. May I tell her who called?"

"No, that's all right. I'm gonna leave her a letter."

And slipping it under the door, the envelope now wrinkled, smudged, and without a stamp.

~

Then later this same night, after arriving home, getting totally wasted on Newcastle Ale—swaying down 76th and into Central Park, along these dark, ferny paths, tripping, stumbling, staggering on and—*Christ! what the*—? This mounted cop before me, asking for some ID, as, sighing and rapidly blinking, I try to fumble it free, the horse twisting about to nuzzle my hand—and everything scattering over the grass, groveling on my knees to find it, the cop offering to guide me home, "Don't want you to get mugged or hit by a car," their clip-clopping echo above and beside me down the quiet length of 76th at long after midnight as I thank them both and enter my apartment alone.

Twenty-six

—Over and over, this fleeting whiff of marsala wine under my nose as I blink to clear my sleepy sight—and her hyacinth eyes swim into dreamy focus, a parfait glass filled with something sweet held gleaming in her hand:

"Beware of girls bearing zabaglione."

"... Are you the one who broke my heart?"

"Yes," and she slides smiling between the sheets, "then mended it."

Twenty-seven

In the moted morning light, Tory kittenishly licking the crumbs from the corners of my mouth, then pointing to my upper lip, "Where does this scar come from?"

"A kid kicked a tin can, playing soccer in the street, split it wide open when I was four or five, had seventeen stitches."

She leaning closer, "It's not a very large scar. I mean you can hardly see it," then kisses me tenderly again and snuggles in, "Gene, I'm sorry I got so scared, pushed you away."

"Hey, I got scared as well."

"I know. It's like you said, we're in this stupid handkerchief dance, pull in, push away, whoever gets closer, the other flees. And then it hit me I was repeating my *father's* pattern, appearing out of the blue and then taking off."

"Or vice versa."

"Yeah, right, right, and the drama and surprise making it *seem* more significant, always hoping—O Gene, but I missed you so!"

"Tell me about it!"

"And I can't go through that again, no way! And as for Max, believe me, he's only a friend—and anyway, I prefer older men—and after a few days, he was driving me up the wall!"

"Why?"

"'Cause everything I did was perfect, he'd made me into this image. God, I could hardly breathe!"

"And the Dear John?"

"My letter, you mean? O that came after I got *rid* of Max. It was one of those nights, you know, there was no one around, and I wanted to get everything off my chest, get rid of *all* men, I guess, avoid getting hurt again, so I hurt you. But it wasn't you I wanted to hurt. And I wrote *another* letter on the plane after I got yours. Want to hear it?"

"I'm all ears, Tory."

And smiling, she reaches for her purse and unfolds the letter on the sheets, "You listening?"

"I'm listening."

"*A little note to cheer you, my dearest Hagar-Bear, dashing, professorial bear, my favorite fuzzy-wuz! Do you know that I love you? Well indeed I do. Yes, most assuredly, it is true! You always make me happiest, especially when I'm blue. I don't really know what I ever did without you. It's all still so new. But when I relax and just let it flow, then I know that I've been saving up all my bestest love for you. So I hope you'll agree with my inviting how-de-do, and, my dearest Gene, now join me for a screw.*"

"You're incorrigible!"

"Look who's talking! Not too bad a letter, though, huh, for a first draft?"

"Absolutely. But tell me, Tory, what'd your doctor say?"

"O I'm fine, overstressed, just have to cut out sex."

"*Cut out s—?*"

"Gotcha!" and she squirrels her nose into my chest. "O, but you know the major difference in sex for men and for women?"

"Is this an essay question or multiple choice?"

"This's what my mother said the other night—"

"How is she?"

"Same—that for most men, sex is when the penis enters the vagina. But for most women, sex starts with the first glass of wine and ends when both nod off to sleep."

"Like our first date?"

"Right, from our first blistered piece of pizza to falling asleep in your arms," and fingernails grazing my thigh, she cuddles into the nook of my shoulder. "And now, I'm happy to note, you're getting all hot and sweaty—and so am I."

"My ex-wife hated to sweat while making love."

"O God, she's crazy! That's what I remember most about the first time we made love. It was the cleanest sweat in the world, warm and salty, light to my touch, and I rubbed it all over my body."

"O you did, did you?"

"Aye, that Oy did, darlin'. But we're *still* good in bed, fit so well together."

"'Good in bed.' I never know exactly what that means."

"Well, for me, that the man cares about my orgasms."

"Don't I?"

"Sometimes."

"'*Sometimes*'? I *always* wait for you!"

"'Always'?" her fingers still roaming, "I know, Gene, you are very considerate and giving . . . most of the time—"

"'*Most of the—*'? !"

"O shut up, I'm only teasing you. You weigh every single word."

"I'm a writer."

"O is that what you are? I thought you were a lover, a considerate, giving—"

"Just come here!"

Twenty-eight

"O dear God, that's *them*! Gene, could you please let them in? I'll be out in a jiff."

"Yeah, sure."

And sliding barefoot around the slick corner, she whips into the john as I swing wide the front door to find a gauntly attractive, middle-aged woman, with short, brassy hair, clothed in a navy blue pants suit, beige blouse, and low-heeled pumps, and Boyne broadly grinning beside her and rakishly sporting his green, tilted beret, black Burberry, and those stained black Nikes.

"Well Tory told me you were quite good-looking, had lovely eyes—"

"Mother!" her shout from the bathroom.

"And I must admit, you do sort of resemble a shaggy Paul Newman."

Boyne guiding her in, "Right, right, and frankly, most people take *me* for Pope Pius XII. You laugh, Laura? Did you ever see the two of us together?"

"No, dear, I never did. (He's been telling me jokes like this for two weeks straight!) But Gene, I'm Laura," clasping my hand warmly in hers, "Tory's mother."

"And I heard you were bitchy."

"O but I am," just as Tory comes bounding out in her flats and tan linen blazer, blonde hair swept back over her ears, hugs and kisses all around.

"Would anyone care for a drink?"

"No, not quite yet," Boyne preening, "'cause—drumroll, if you please—first we have an announcement."

"Which is?"

"*Ta-da*: we're getting married!"

Tory blinking, "To whom?" then quickly swallowing.

"Each other, of course!"

"*Again*?"

"Again and again till we finally get it right!"

"Where?"

"In Ireland again!"

"When?"

"June 26, Laura's birthday, ten days from tomorrow. And listen, lass, your mother and I were talking on the way here, why don't the two of you join us?"

"In Dublin?"

"No, in Bombay! Of course in Dublin—well, Wicklow, to be precise, my estate of Ballyduff."

"Gene, could you go?"

"Uh, well, yeah, don't see why not."

"And that leaves us two weeks to talk them out of it—No, I'm only joking, 'cause that's, *wow*! that's marvelous, fantastic!" and she girlishly hugs them both—I shake their hands—then goes pacing over the polished hardwood floor, her eyes glittery, brimming with excitement, "And we'll have to fix up your castle, Dad, you know, decorate and figure out who to invite, and not to invite, from here and Ireland, O all sorts of things, probably want just close friends, a short ceremony—and then, Gene, our ceremony could follow."

"'Our'—Wait, whoa, whoa—You and *I*?"

"Right, already discussed it with them, and they approve."

"So we're getting married, too?"

"Why, don't you want to?"

"Uh, sure, yeah, but—"

"'This is all so sudden'?"

"You read my mind. And we *have* been on a roller coaster—"

"Well it's not for nothing, lad, that she's my lassie!"

"—up and down, feast or famine—"

"You know, Tory, you'll be about the same age I married your father."

"But, Laura, I'm *twice* her age."

"Yes, and she may die *before* you."

Tory taking a deep breath, "So you don't want to do it, Gene?"

"No, no, I didn't say that. But you really *are* serious now, not gonna change your mind?"

"As I can possibly be."

"With them in Ireland?"

"Yes. I mean, hey, look, believe me, I'm just as scared as you are, but I know now I'll be more scared without you, never find someone like you—"

"That's for damn sure, lass!"

"—don't want to lose you, Gene, so—"

"OK, OK!" coming round the sofa.

"'OK' what? OK yes or OK no?"

"Well, I guess . . . OK yes."

And she leaps into my arms and kisses me full on the lips.

"Ha-ha, a fucking double wedding!" and Boyne wraps me in a tight embrace.

"Congratulations, Gene!" Laura hugging me, too, feeling rather awkward, she so brittle, as stepping back, I shake my head and keep repeating, "Unbelievable!"

Tory smiling, "Well we are a rather impulsive family, Gene."

"You could've fooled me."

~

A battered taxi rattling into view, Boyne announcing, "141 West 69th," then away we go, weaving uptown through the mad clash of the city, and he leaning forward on the jump seat, "The last cab ride I took, the driver kept staring at me in the rearview mirror and finally asked me what did I do. And I told him I was in ladies' shoes. So he said, 'Must be painful for you.'"

"O Dad, *shut* up!"

"Don't mind him, Gene, he's a painter."

"No, no, but listen, did I ever tell you the story of the Irish lad— You want to hear this?"

"We're all ears."

"I don't give a damn what you look like!"

"He's impossible. Just go on."

Tory and I exchanging a smile.

"Well there was this Irish lad—trust me, this's true—who'd never been taught anything about sex. And on his wedding night, he wouldn't go to bed 'cause his father had told him it'd probably be the most exciting night of his life. And he was afraid if he went to bed, he'd miss it."

"Just humor the man, Gene."

"Right. Well where we going?"

"To one of Laura's and my favorite haunts from our salad days, little French bistro called Fleur-de-Lis."

And pulling up on this dark, narrow street, and quickly inside behind Tory (my wife!) and the crescent outline of her panties beneath that black knit shift, a sensual parabola, to a red-checkered table in the far corner of this noisy, crowded room, coats of arms gracing the walls, and Boyne ordering a bottle of his original Irish wine, "One of the few places left that still stock it!" iced tea for Laura, then pâté, garlic sausage with potato salad, and an entrée of escalope du chef.

Some whispering at a nearby table, and Tory glancing around, "Yes, you're absolutely right. He *is* Pius XII."

And, grinning, I squeeze her hand in mine. Still can't quite believe: Gene and Tory Hagar. Take some adjusting time—though, for the moment, I've never felt any happier as Laura smiles as she watches Boyne, then turns to me.

"And Gene, as far as ordering food goes, you're in good hands, believe me, with Seamus."

"Thank you, my dear, that's most kind."

"For when we were first married, he'd never let me get near the stove."

"Well you didn't *want* to cook, my green madonna, said you needed all the cons—conveniences—I couldn't afford."

"How long were you first married, Mother?"

"Three years eight months."

"And to Mark?"

"Three, almost three and a half years."

"Whatever happened to him?"

"O he went to jail over Watergate, and last I heard was selling real estate in Appalachia."

"Perfect spot for a Jewish lawyer. But talking of that, Laura used to buy me cookbooks—Jewish cookbooks, matter of fact. Even bought me one as a wedding gift, *Tempting Kosher Dishes* it was called, and when we first arrived in Ireland and the quids were in short supply, instead of food I would read aloud to her something like—O let's see, what were some of those tempting kosher dishes: matzo-apple pudding? *Marvelous!* and we'd nibble the air with the recipe! But that was before all the cons came trundling in. Remember, dear, how I spent the entire week just opening and shutting the fridge when we finally got one, and eating those coronary tidbits we stacked it with?" Laura nodding. "Ah, here comes the wine."

The waiter returning with a green, slope-shouldered bottle, uncorking, pouring, and placing it before Boyne, who swirls it round the glass, admires the color, sniffs the bouquet, wallows it over his tongue, and sips: "Ah, still frisky, coltish, great gulping wine!"

And the appetizers arriving shortly thereafter.

"Here, Gene, have a taste of this *amazing* potato salad, very oily, highly peppered, and flavored with loads of parsley and onion."

Tory abruptly popping her eyes and breathing out, "*Jeez,* this pâté's laced with enough garlic to keep Dracula at bay!"

All of us now drinking and munching happily away.

"O, Seamus, by the way, any repercussions from your Barbara Walters show?"

"No, though she did call me, we had a bad connection, and kept asking, 'Can you hear me?' And I said, 'Of course I can hear you, Baba, I just paid twenty thousand dollars for an incredible hearing aid!' 'What kind is it?' 'It's quarter past three.' "

All of us laughing, including the nearby patrons, and Laura adding, her green eyes flashing, "You let him get you again!" as the escalope appears.

Boyne proudly explaining the contents: veal, thinly sliced and savored in butter and wine, draped with slender portions of ham and together cloaked in a thick yellow cheese sauce studded with button mushrooms. Then beaming, he raises his glass, "And soon we'll be off to tie the knot together in Ireland, breeding ground of legends and myths, chieftains and kings, where we'll be welcomed back with open arms, along with the slaying of fatted calves and free-flowing stout for the masses!"

~

And looped on each other's arms, out into the summer night we go, under the lamplight toward Lincoln Center amid a gaggle of stares, Tory grinning all the while, suddenly swings both feet high in the air, gripping tightly to our support, "O my God, I am so happy! *Wheee!!*" And Laura, at first circumspect, delighting now in her daughter's display as she watches the two of us race for the end of the block, sprinting between passersby and hydrants, Boyne at the finish line, waving his beret like a checkered flag, me straining, Tory winning—"See, I *am* faster than you, kicked your butt!"—as I slump, wine-reeling, against this corner building, while my speedy bride-to-be offers me a helping hand.

Twenty-nine

O Jesus, what am I *doing*? The jubilation of your eyes, my sweet, sensual Tory, with your blonde, tousled hair, after that Bloomsday morning "lovefest," then *this* morning, I couldn't get it up, she shrugging it off, no big deal, soon honeymooning in Ireland, and asking, "Gene, are you having second thoughts?" "What? No. Why?" "Just wondered"—as I cut across Madison Ave., narrowly missing this oncoming cab.

And tonight back to Ireland again . . . all those years ago: The plane dipping and slowly lowering over the trees, sheep and cattle scattering under the roar, skimming over the runway and suddenly down, bumping across the concrete past the tall, tufted reeds toward that white air terminal. My thick hair pelted by the breeze, raincoat flapping, as I hurried along to pick up my backpack, no one I knew among the few flagging greeters clustered together, *Hoof and Mouth Disease* and *A Hundred Thousand Welcomes*, following the priests and other passengers out of customs onto a green double-decker bus for Dublin that went careening round the airport circle—I once sang a song about Dublin and my father fell asleep, *Baile Atha Cliath!*—sunlight breaking out over the hedgerows, and down that twist of road, under the green, feathery trees, past the pubs and small shops, Afton and Gold Leaf signs hung in the windows, playing fields soon swarming with boys, goalposts looming lonely and white—and hoping Ciara's letter was waiting for me then, posted on to Dublin and reposing under the dust. Didn't really expect it, hoped, to be sure, though not much more.

But her letter *was* waiting:

Dear Gene,

If Ireland is half as lovely as you told me, please write me, and I will come.

And now Tory and I, her father and mother, poetry and song, our life together: Halcyon days? Hagar whirligigged and ran his heedless ways? Aer Lingus lifting us away from the mad clash of Manhattan tonight to dear, dirty Dublin and Boyne's castle by the sea. Landleaper me vaulting over Howth and Environs, Joyce's Dark Pool, and Ballyduff—and pausing on this car-honking corner, bus brakes squealing, caged-in feeling of marriage and commitment! 'Cause no way's Tory moving back to Great Neck with me when we return, never fit in, and I can't ruin her life, she's hardly had time to live and explore, all kinds of young guys at the door, before she's saddled with our May–December mismatch—and just making it to the curb at 76th and into my apartment, she quickly zipping up a bright yellow sundress.

"Have a good run, feel better now?"

"All right. You look very pretty in that, sets off your hair."

"Thank you. Gene, are you OK?"

"Sure. Why?"

"You're not still upset about this morning?"

"This morning?"

"Look, it happens."

"But it never happened *before*!"

"Jeez, touchy touchy."

"It's not funny!" searching for my mitt, "And where're *you* going?"

"I told you, my class's throwing me that good-bye party."

"*Today?*"

"Well you've got your softball game. And mine shouldn't take too long."

Still searching, "You speak to your folks?"

"Yes, and they're meeting me at the center."

"Listen, Tory, maybe I should just skip the game."

"No, don't be ridiculous. You're playing for the championship for the first time ever. And you'll have plenty of time, it's a six-fifty flight. Anyway, I'll see you at the airport, good luck, and Gene, *relax*, will you, 'cause your shirt's inside out," quick kiss, wry grin, "'bye."

* * *

Still rummaging wildly about for my mitt, where the hell did I—the phone shrilly ringing—

"'Lo?"

"O you're back, Gene."

"But I'm halfway out the door, Teri. What's going on?"

"I talked to your girlfriend before."

"You *did*?" About my—?

"And she's, you know, really very nice, very bright. How old is she, Gene?"

"Twenty." Too young, right?

"And blonde, of course?"

"Of course." *Ah,* here it is! My worn Rawlings jammed behind the headboard.

"But I really wanted to tell you about your friend Lou, who's been calling and calling and I kept putting him off, he wouldn't take no for an answer—"

"Teri, listen—"

"—and then his father died—"

"*What?* When?"

"Friday night. And I felt so awful, I went out with him again—and guess who ended up comforting who?"

"O Christ!"

"Well, what can I say, he's *incredible* in bed, nonstop, all night, he never gets tired! So I'm like cracking up, who knew, men your age aren't supposed to—though he kept calling me Bunny, his high school sweetheart, all night."

"Unbelievable!"

"And what about you, Gene?"

"Yeah, well, I'm, uh, getting married, flying to Dublin tonight."

"You're *kidding*? Congratulations! I assume to the girl I talked to? Well, she sounds very sweet. No, really, she does. Anyways, I'll let you go and have a safe flight. When're you coming back?"

"Not sure, but I'll let you know."

And the phone ringing again, of course!

"'Lo?"

"Big Guy, ya still got that Irish friend around, the housepainter, Picasso?"

"Yeah. Why?"

"Well we need him, Yosh can't make it."

"Look, Lou—"

"Can't forfeit now, so I'll see ya later, 'bye!"

Thirty

"—Listen, Hagar, if you think for one minute you're going to leave my daughter standing at the altar, or on the tarmac, think again, my friend!"

"Who said anything about—?"

"I'm just warning you."

"OK, fine, I've been warned," as we come wheeling into Fairview Avenue, Boyne bouncing beside me, in this blue Camaro, Thrifty Rent-a-Car, and down to Memorial Field—Tony Alosia blasting another of Hickey's BP tosses deep out to right center, Bucky, Shelly, and McTee warming up along the sideline—and jolting to a stop, my stomach so tied in knots, heart going a mile a minute, suitcases crammed in the trunk.

"Though I'm telling you, boy, there's no *need* for panic now. *Everyone* panics, including me, when that knot's about to be tied—I went off on a legendary drunken spree—but when the fog clears, you see—"

"The error of your ways?"

"Ha-ha! Well, yes, that, too, sometimes. But here you're getting a wise child, truly a gem—and why the hell she chose you, I'll never know, but she did, so I beg of you, don't screw it up, give in to your rising fears. Got it?"

"Got it, got it!"

"Good."

And we stride onto the field, bald and bearded Boyne clad once more in his green rugby shirt, blue seersucker shorts, knee-high white socks, and those stained black Nikes as Bucky hustles across, "Seamus, hey, thanks so much for helping us out, man, really appreciate it."

"My pleasure."

Shelly joining us, "How-why-ya, how-why-ya?" flipping me a ball—that I fumble and drop, "Come on, Haig, don't get me more uptight!" and Lou comes racing out of the dugout in his Cardinal cap and gold T-shirt, "Shamey Guy, great to see ya! And I hadda tell ya, I figured out why ya ran to third last time."

"And why was that?"

"'Cause in Ireland they drive on the left-hand side."

"Lou, listen, I heard about your father, really sorry—"

"What?" Lou whirling around as a busty girl passes into the stands, "Damn, just look at the *bod* on that!—O my father, yeah, right, well we lost him the other night, cardiac arrest."

"And when's the funeral?"

"*Monstro* gazongas!—Funeral? O, Tuesday, Tuesday at Riverside, so I'm like still in shock."

"Well why didn't you call me?"

"Didn't call anybody, just went out and got laid. But, Big Guy, believe me, the last thing in the world I wanna do is piss ya off, but your ex is *fantazmo,* the spittin' image of Bunny—"

"Lou, it's OK, really."

"—'cause I love ya like a brother, Haig, buddies since grade school!" and he bear-hugs me tight.

More fans, old men who wandered out of McDonnell's Café and the firehouse, schoolkids and mothers with baby carriages, Selmix groupies: a ring of high school girls, waitresses, and even some wives on this Sunday afternoon final now filling the green slat stands—as Shishy returns from the firehouse john after his psychotic pee: me now turning into Shishy, never satisfying my wife?—and Boyne pulling me aside.

"Gene, you sure you're OK?"

"I think I'm moving back here."

"Back to West Egg, eh, to your nice, warm womb—or tomb, to be precise? No, trust me, boy, I completely understand the need to go back to your past, especially after all your losses, but you can't *stay* there, bury yourself within it, however tempting it may seem. It's like coming in from the cold outdoors to a hot, steamy shower.

You don't want to leave, but if you remain, you end up with a wrinkled prune for a pecker!"

"But—"

"No, no buts, boy, you know my motto: Life is leaping, never a lying down! Just put yourself in the palm of my hand."

"But you *were* right, Tory *is* too young for me."

"Nonsense! Hell, if anything, you may be too young for *her.* She's a very wise child for her years, and always has been."

"I'm not talking about her mind!"

"Hey, guys, over here."

Bucky now gathering everybody around him, my stomach churning away—still haven't told any of *them* about Tory, or my moving back—the tension really mounting, all of us shifting from foot to foot on our sneakers and rubber cleats, patting each other on the butts, touching toes, pounding mitts—Shelly tight as a drum, Lou high as a kite, and Bucky sober and grim, "Yeah, well it took us a helluva long time to get here—and we may never get here again—so let's not *blow* it now!"

"Blow *what*?"

"Shut up, Seamus!"

"Guys, come on, get your hands in here, Big Shel, Bucker, Haig, all for one 'n' one for all!"

"*YEAHHHH!!!*"

"And win it for the Gipper!"

"Play ball!"

"The *Gipper*?"

"Yeah, Shamey, a little Knute Rockne never hurt!"

Lou still talking it up as he takes his spot in the third-base coaching box and begins his rhythmic clapping, "OK, you Bucky babe, you Bucky kid, get it started! Give us a little bingle, *guy*!"—and Bucky laces Hickey's first high-arcing pitch on a solid line into center field!

"Wayta go, you Bucky *babe,* way to start it off! Aw right, keep it goin', Haig, keep it goin', *guy*!"

Tapping the dirt from my sneakers and stepping in with a monster sigh—after that awful start, finished at .344 (Teddy Ballgame's lifetime)—the Selmix infield now chattering it up, "Let 'im hit it, Brian, let 'im hit it! Gotta team behind ya, gotta team!" as Hickey's first pitch comes spinning in on my fists: and fighting it off, I top a high Baltimore chop down to Colandro at third, who goes around the horn for one and back to first for an easy double play—*Damn,* never should've played!

All their fans on their feet chanting and hollering, Hickey grinning, and up steps harried Shelly, with his ringleted Disraeli hair, swishing his black bat back and forth and desperately trying to concentrate on not having to move out of Great Neck—the infield and outfield swinging deep and around to right for the "Levitas shift"—and Lewicki behind him, kneeling on one knee and shouting, "No hitta heah, no hitta, just a mouth!" and under his breath, "Like to lay that black bat upside your head!" "Hey, anytime, anywhere," as Hickey's first looping pitch sails across for a strike. "Atta go, you Brian babe! Keepa chuckin', kid, keepa chuckin'!" Sideburned Lewicki zipping the ball back—Hickey never flinching—as it smacks with a *whop!* in the pocket of his glove, and he quickly throws again: a surprise down-the-middle no-arcer! Shelly checking his swing and dribbling one up the third-base line, Hickey pouncing on it like a cat, whirling and slinging it sidearm to first—*hits* Shelly in the back of the head, the ball bouncing into foul territory, Shelly reeling around the bag, on his way for second—and is tagged out easily on the relay!

The Selmix fans still cheering as I trot slowly out to center field with my stomach still churning away and glance around at all these players and people in the stands whom I've known for years, grown up with, went through grade school, high school, the same doctor since I was two, same barber since I was eight—and now writing about them, Lou and Bucky stories already in my drawer—as

Alosia, who led the league as usual, with a .647 average, leads off with a wicked smash back up the middle. And shortly scores as they push across four runs in the bottom of the first.

In the third, though, McTee and Shishy both single, Boyne, unbelievably, walks on four straight pitches, and up steps Bucky with the bases loaded, nobody out—and drills a low line shot just fair down the left-field line that one-hops the foul pole as McTee scores, but Lou, coaching at third, seeing the ball carom back into play, holds Shishy and Boyne up as they jam on the brakes—then sends them—then holds them up (what is this, déjà vu all over again?) as Bucky comes thundering around second with his head down and slides into third in a cloud of dust, bowling Boyne and Shishy over!

"Christ, what the hell're you *doing* here? Get home, will ya! Just *score, score*!"

And Hickey, now windmilling his arms and screaming for the ball, finally gets the relay and goes running around tagging everyone in sight as Shishy breaks for home and is out, Bucky starts back to second and is out, and Boyne, zigzagging off into left field, with Hickey right behind him, is eventually caught and tagged out for an inning-ending triple play!

And they're all wandering about in a daze—as it takes five minutes for the umpires to restore order, with Bucky, now hot on Lou's heels, shouting, "What the hell *happened,* huh? What the fuck was *THAT?*"

Boyne and I watching and waiting in the outfield for play to begin, his hands on his knees and grinning, a thin gap along the bottom row.

"So, Gene, when you move back here, what'll you do, start killing roaches again?"

"No, write, but write about what I know."

"But Suffering Christ, you'll write about it far, far better if you're *not* living here! Didn't I first paint Ciara without ever seeing her? And that's *still* my best work, period of my greatest creativity—"

Whack! "*Haig!*"

"So—What?" This ball heading toward me—and goes whizzing past my mitt!

"Will you guys wake up and knock off the chitchat!"

"Sorry, sorry—" My relay throw coming in much too late.

The innings flying by, Boyne now silent on the bench, both of us without a hit, Shelly beside me gnawing away at his cuticles and saying he'll chain himself to the Great Neck railroad tracks before he'll ever move, Bucky's teenage son's escaped again and his father's going crazy, Lou still carrying on about his high school sweetheart, Bunny Friske—and I'm getting more uptight by the minute, this fierce sinking in my gut, knew it was all too good to be true, house of cards collapsing at my feet!

So, going to the top of the seventh and our final time at bat, it's now 5–2 Selmix—Losing her? Our dreams? What the hell else is left? Back to the single life? *No!* back to being alone, everyone dying, disappearing—as Lou keeps loudly clapping for a last-ditch, come-from-behind rally, "OK, Jimmy, get it started, get it started, Jimmy *babe*!"

But McTee and Baum both ground weakly to short, and Selmix is one out away from yet another championship and a barrel of McDonnell's beer—as Shishy flares one just over Colandro's glove and Boyne legs out an accidental swinging bunt with the "Big Daddy."

"Waya go, you Shamey *baby,* never say die! Aw right, keep it goin', Bucker, keep it *goin'*, guy!"

And he slashes a hot smash down the third-base line, off Colandro's mitt, spinning into foul territory—and Shishy slides safely into third on the throw!

This place's a madhouse now, nobody sitting, everybody standing and cheering, and it all comes down to me with the bases loaded, two out, the tying runs aboard, and hell, I'm gonna bat left-handed for my last at-bat, my stomach wound up so tight, and Lou urging me on, "Give it a *ride,* you Teddy Ballgame guy," punching his fist at the sky, "put it outta sight!"

Selmix's infield swinging around to the right, their outfield playing shallow, as Hickey, glaring in, tosses up his first floating pitch:

"Stee-rike one!"

"Atta go, you Brian, keepa chuckin', kid! No hitta heah, no hitta!" and I keep twisting this bat in my hands and viciously buggy-whipping it back and forth, back and forth. "Come on, Big Haig, you can do it, babe, you can *DO* it, guy!"

The noise steadily mounting, wives and girlfriends still shrieking and pleading or holding their breaths as Hickey sighs again and throws: and swinging from my heels, I blast a towering Williams-like drive deep out to straightaway center, Alosia turning and racing back, back, way back, his legs churning as fast as he can and leaping high like a springbok—*misses* it cleanly as the ball sails by and keeps on rolling, he finally chasing it down and firing it in to the cutoff man as Shishy, Boyne, and Bucky score and I come streaking around third and head for home, everybody screaming for me to slide, sideburned Lewicki setting himself to block the plate, the throw coming in on a low, hard bounce—"*SLIDE, HAGAR, SLIDE!*"—the ball thudding into his mitt as straining now and never breaking stride, I knock him flat—the ball squirting free, Lewicki writhing on the ground, while I keep staggering around and around, then dizzily reeling like Alec Guinness in *Bridge on the River Kwai*—Lewicki groping for the ball and swiping a moment too late—sprawl across the plate for a grand-slam home run to put us ahead 6–5!

The stands erupting, bedlam breaking loose, everyone mobbing me, Lou practically cracking my ribs. And when order's restored at last, we go to the bottom of the seventh, Lewicki muttering, "Yeah, well it ain't over till it's over!"—and I'm still trying to clear my thoughts, get a grip—and only seeing Tory's face in my mind.

"Haig?"

"—What?"

"Ya OK?"

"Why?"

"You're lookin' kinda spacy."

With one away, Alosia rips his fourth hit in a row, but Colandro pops out to Lou, so it's all up to Hickey, two down, the tying run aboard, winning run at the plate, as our players meet at the mound: Shelly still gnawing on his cuticles, Lou hyper, McTee silent, Bucky grim, and Shishy obviously trying to hold it in—

"Listen, guys, I gotta *go*!" and he tears off the field past the ump. "Where's he *goin'*?" "To the firehouse, where else!" Bucky now working out their strategy, moving me over to left center, when Shishy eventually returns, "Yeah, so?" "Just *pitch*, Shishy!" Everyone leaning forward on his toes as his high-arcer comes slowly floating down:

And Hickey, suddenly shifting his feet, drills a clothesline shot toward the gap in *right* center that has me on my horse, sprinting across, Boyne converging—we miss this, Hickey scores, we lose—the ball still hanging up there white against the sky—and that strange, dreamlike feeling as though switching into a slow-motion stride, gliding over the grass, before reaching out with a last-lunging gasp and—*whap!* reality snapping back with the smack of the ball—as I crash into Boyne, trip and fall, the ball popping high in the air and dropping—into the palm of his hand!

"*We won the fuckin' GAME! We won the fuckin' GAME! HAIG and SHAMEY BAY-BAEEEES!! We're the fuckin' CHAMPS!!!*" Lou bouncing up and down and whirling Boyne and me round and round as we head for the dugout, through the shouting, slapping, swarming crowd.

"Gene, let's go!"

"Where's he goin'? We gotta celebrate!"

"To Ireland?"

"*Ireland?*"

"He's getting married. God bless!"

And we hop in the Camaro and zoom away.

Thirty-one

Roaring along the expressway, "Get the hell off the road, you flaming asspipe!" and flashing past these dawdling cars.

"Easy, Hagar, easy, got plenty of time, at least an hour. You still hot?"

"A bit," flicking the air conditioner across to high, "still sweating from the game, I guess," and flooring this rent-a-car by bobtail trucks and pickups into the Van Wyck, he staring out the window, then back at me.

"So are you going, boy, or not?"

"I don't know," blasting my horn, "I'm not sure—Will you people *move*?"

"You're not sure of what?"

"It's just this's all so fast—"

"Well, I'll tell you what Tory said."

"What'd she say?"

"That if you're not on that plane, that's it, finished, the end, and don't even *think* about calling her or trying to get in touch with her, she's not going through that again."

"Not going through *what* again? *She* was the one who broke it off before!"

"OK, fine, fine, but the point is *now*!"

Following the signs through Kennedy's winding maze to Aer Lingus, where I swerve to a stop and he opens his door.

"So what're you going to do, Gene?"

"I—I don't know."

"Right, well I'm checking in."

"Boyne, listen—"

Slam!

And after a moment, I drive away with my head really spinning—narrowly missing that crossing porter—Christ, what the hell *am* I doing? Or *not* doing? So filled with doubts and raging fears, aging fears, my ridiculous cold, bloody feet! And where the fuck is Thrifty Rental? 175th Street—

But what if it *is* all an illusion, built her into an image out of my grieving need, and there I am *stuck* in Ireland? Or am I just fleeing from taking the risk?

157th, Thrifty should be coming up soon—'Cause you *do* love her, right? Love her more than any woman I've ever known! Love her glow, my Bubba's glow (and *she'd* truly approve)—by 159th—so no need to abandon her now, or be abandoned myself—taking another deep breath—

O NO WAY I'm letting her go! Just check in this car, they'll drive me back, then off we go to Dublin!

But whoa, where am I going *now*? *144th Street?* I just *lost* fifteen blocks? And next is 144th Terrace? Then 144th Road?! This's crazy, insane, part of totally fucked-up Queens! Streets with no rhyme or reason—And what is it now? 6:15.

Still got time as I keep driving around and around. 6:20. Gotta ask—Great! there's a cop—who tells me I'm lost! No shit, Sherlock! And then directs me down this one-way street, he'll watch, New York Boulevard to 145th Avenue, then right, left, and you'll run right into it.

Right, left—and I run right into 144th Road again! *Jesus CHRIST!* What is this, Ocean City all over again?! Now 6:30. Tory sure I'm not coming: *If you're not on that plane*—and she leaves 'cause I can't find stupid Thrifty!

Just drop the car, grab a cab, or call the airport? No, take too much time—as I go speeding by like Mario Andretti—Ask this guy: 175th Street? A hunnert seventy-fit? Never heard of it. *Terrific!* And through this red light, 6:40 now! Careening into New York Boulevard toward 145th—stop sign up ahead—Hell with it, can't wait! and weaving down the sidewalk like Popeye Doyle, people scattering in all directions—to 145th Avenue, thank God! and *unbelievably*! 175th Street and the Thrifty office!

Leaping out, drenched in sweat, and racing, raving inside, "Come on, come on, I've got five minutes to make this plane! Get in, I'll drive!" Sign here, sign there—'bye!

And wheeling back into Kennedy, through the maze, gonna die, cardiac arrest, and, grabbing my bags, "Thanks, man," sprinting flat out toward the Aer Lingus counter, "*HOLD THE PLANE! HOLD THE PLANE!! HOLD THE PLANE!!!*"

They all grinning and laughing.

"It's OK, sir, the plane's still here. There's been some commotion."

"What sort of—?"

"Ticket, please. Right up that ramp, Gate Six. Hurry, hurry, we'll get your luggage. Have a safe trip, Godspeed."

"Right, right."

And panting down this carpeted corridor and through the cabin door, into first class, where Boyne is standing and singing, drink in hand, Laura smirking, "*Now* can we finally leave?" and Tory sighing as I collapse in my seat.

"Well look who decided to show up!"

"—Listen, you deserve to be pissed off—"

"How would *you* know? And don't tell me what I deserve to be!"

"Come on, Tory—" as Boyne keeps singing and drinking.

"And what I *do* deserve is to be treated a whole lot better than this!"

"I know—"

"'Cause the whole world doesn't revolve around you, where they hold up planes and trips and weddings while you take your own stupid time to make up your own stupid mind!"

"Look, I'm sorry. What do you *want* me to do?"

"Do what you want to do, just don't do me any favors!"

"But I'm here, aren't I? And what'd you say, 'Thou and I are too wise to woo peaceably'?"

"Yeah, right!" she exchanging another glance with her mother, then cocking an eyebrow, "And you're really *sure* this time?"

"Absolutely, Tory, I can't live without you, flawed and lovely as you are! And besides, no way could I live in a place that doesn't even know who Seamus Boyne is!"

Boyne guffawing as he keeps raucously directing the other passengers in song, and I twist around to hug and kiss her—but she turns away—then quickly back with a silly grin and kisses me smack on the lips.

"You know, Tory, you're impossible!"

"Look who's talking."

"But why didn't the plane take off?"

"'Cause my father refused to sit down, then began singing 'A Nation Once Again' and 'The Rocky Road to Dublin.' "

Laura smiling, "Well, as they say, he's as mad as a hatter on a good day!" and Boyne pausing to cant his dashing beret as the pilot peers out from the cockpit.

"Ah, Captain, my Captain, 'tis time to take flight, so once round the park and away to wild Irish nights!"

Dick Wimmer is the author of *Baseball Fathers, Baseball Sons* and the highly acclaimed sequel, *The Wildly Irish Sextet.* He lives in Southern California.